This moment struck Winn with the same punch as the pig stench he'd smelled when he'd driven past the local pig farm. He was standing in a crowded Indiana coffee shop, arguing with a crazy woman over whether they'd made love in a past life.

Unbelievable.

Sydney Vaughn pulled the plug on his rationality. She made it impossible to maintain any professionalism. She pried at every belief he had firmly nailed down.

Just look at her, he thought. Frilly, little waitress uniform and clunky combat boots. Long, fairylike curls in sexy disarray. Pale skin flushed in frustration. Damn, if she didn't look like a modern-day damsel in distress.

He wanted to turn around and walk out of her life. He wanted to forget he'd ever met her. He wanted to…"Since we were lovers, I assume you won't have a problem with this, kid."

He held her face captive between his hands and kissed her, seeking an end to the sudden and mysterious hunger swirling in his gut. He caressed her lower lip with his tongue, warning her only moments before he claimed her mouth completely.

To the dreamers who still enter a dark movie theater,
eager to be touched by magic.
To the romantics who still open the pages of a love story,
eager to risk their hearts.
This adult fairy tale is for you.

Other Books by CB Scott
Scandalous Spirits
Kindred Spirits (Coming in 2003)

Knight of My Dreams

***

CB Scott

ImaJinn Books

KNIGHT OF MY DREAMS
Published by ImaJinn Books, a division of ImaJinn

ISBN: 1-893896-85-4

10 9 8 7 6 5 4 3 2 1

PUBLISHER'S NOTE:
This book is a work of fiction. Names, characters, places and incidents are products of the author's imagination or are used fictitiously. Any resemblance to actual events or locales or persons, living or dead, is entirely coincidental.

Books are available at quantity discounts when used to promote products or services. For information please write to: Marketing Division, ImaJinn Books, P.O. Box 162, Hickory Corners, MI 49060-0162, or call toll free 1-877-625-3592.

Cover design by Patricia Lazarus

ImaJinn Books, a division of ImaJinn
P.O. Box 162, Hickory Corners, MI 49060-0162
Toll Free: 1-877-625-3592
http://www.imajinnbooks.com

Prologue

"I did not mean for this to happen."

"Nor did I, m'lady. Of that you can be certain."

The maiden, clothed in scarlet fustian, looked away. "'Tis strange to hear you address me so formally when only this morn—"

"'Tis proper," the knight interrupted, his tone stiff and unyielding, like the mail draped across his chest. "Lest you forget, we are not alone." He cocked his head toward the entourage riding a short distance behind. "I suggest you guard your tongue, Lady Gillian. Voices carry."

An eerie silence settled about the dense forest, cloaking them as heavily as the swirling mist. "Pray, do not be angry with me, Baldric. 'Tis more than I can bear."

"'Tis not my anger you should be fearing." He jabbed a gloved finger toward the castle looming just beyond the forest's edge. "But his."

"He will not be angry," she reasoned, "for he will not learn the truth."

For the first time the man turned his gaze upon her. "God's teeth! Do you truly believe us able to deceive him? If so, then you underestimate your betrothed." He stared down at her, eyes burning with a warrior's strength of emotion. "Your naïveté shall be the cause of your death, woman. And most likely mine as well." He snapped his attention back to the castle.

"Do not speak as such," the maiden pleaded, following his line of vision. "Your demise is a burden I am powerless to withstand. 'Twould break my heart beyond repair."

His voice gentled. "Your heart is of utmost concern to me, m'lady. I would wish to keep it whole and beating within a breath of my own. 'Tis with this admission I beg thee one last time, utter the word and I shall steer us from this course."

"I cannot."

"Will not," he amended, his fist clenching the reins. "You mean you will not."

"'Tis not free will which guides me, sir, but duty. 'Tis a bond with which you, a sworn servant to the crown, are well acquainted. You above any should understand." Tears welled in her eyes. "I have no choice."

"There is always a choice, my love. The challenge is in choosing wisely."

"Then I have failed," she said, chin low to her chest. "For my heart has chosen you, Baldric. An unwise choice."

"Nay, not unwise," he countered. "'Tis destiny."

"It matters not." She raised her head, tears raining down her cheeks. "'Tis too late."

He turned to her, began to reach out, then dropped his hand to his armored thigh. "You are wrong, m'lady. It matters much." The jagged pain in his voice sliced the thick air between them. "We will be together. I swear."

"'Tis impossible."

"I will find a way."

The formidable walls of the castle towered before them, a beast capable of devouring their lives and then spitting out the bones.

The drawbridge lowered.

The maiden stiffened, her delicate hands trembling on the reins. "'Tis the end."

"Nay," the knight vowed, "'tis only the beginning." His eyes brimmed with strength and devotion. "You must have faith, m'lady. You must believe in us. In me." He pressed his palm against his heart. "No matter what is said within those walls, no matter what transpires, know that we will be together." His words echoed through the mist. "Trust me."

One

"Oh, my God. He's a drug dealer."

"I wish." Sydney Vaughn, good girl, country girl, had never taken anything stronger than a premenstrual pill. The way she felt right now, she might consider half a Valium. "He's a security consultant."

"A what?"

"He rigs burglar systems."

Sydney and her best friend, Ellie, watched through the screen door as the black luxury car with tinted windows pulled up the quarter-mile gravel drive. "It's about time," Ellie said. "I was beginning to think my safety lectures were in vain."

Sydney pushed her hands into the oversized pockets of her purple overalls. "It wasn't your lectures. It was my aunt. She insisted."

"Vera? The instigator of reason?" Ellie snorted. "I'm shocked."

"I know she tends to raise eyebrows—"

"Syd, your aunt's a kook."

"Eccentric maybe."

"All right," Ellie conceded, "she's an *eccentric* kook."

Sydney would purchase conservative pumps and *wear* them before admitting it aloud, but there was truth in her friend's observation. She watched the car roll to a stop. "I never should've told Vera about the crank calls." Just saying the words gave Sydney a sick feeling. She shook it off, reminding herself it was someone's bad idea of a joke. A horny teen. Five creepy calls in two weeks does not a stalker make.

Ellie cocked a thumb toward the stranger. "Considering the result, maybe you should've told her sooner. The kook took sensible action. Which is more than I can say for David."

"That's not fair, Ellie. You know David's looking into it. He's watching over me. He drops by twice a day and calls every night. He's even offered to sleep in the guestroom."

"Good God, Sydney. That's not sensible. That's selfish. David wants to get in your pants. Sleeping under the same roof narrows the odds." She rolled her eyes. "You're so naïve."

"No, I'm not. You're just overly suspicious. *And* overreacting." *You're also driving me nuts.* Sydney bit her tongue and prayed for patience. After all, Ellie was just doing what she'd done since they were kids. Looking out for Sydney. Although these days her protective tendencies were nearly suffocating. It had taken six months, but Sydney had adjusted to her mother's death, adjusted to living alone. Ellie hadn't adjusted at all. She hated the idea of Sydney living by herself, in the middle of nowhere. The *calls* only heightened her anxiety.

"You call this overreacting?" Ellie's voice jumped an octave. "I'm not overreacting, Syd. I'm concerned. There's a difference. These threatening calls—"

"Crank calls. A bored kid, a prankster." She refused to believe otherwise.

"Or a serial killer."

"In Slocum, Indiana? I don't think so." Sydney returned her attention to the security consultant, who now swung open the door of his conspicuous four-door. "And keep it down, will you? This is embarrassing enough already. An alarm system. No one in this entire county has an alarm system." She tried to look on the bright side. "Maybe he'll just install a couple of locks and be on his way."

"Maybe you should consider what he has to say."

"Maybe you shouldn't worry so much. Besides, I have my dogs."

As if on cue, two floppy-eared hounds bounded out from the backyard to lick the man's hand in shameless bids for attention.

Ellie smirked. "Oh, yeah. You got yourself a real pack of killers there."

A riot of sloppy tongues and rolling eyes, the mutts danced around him. Sydney moved to open the door to call back her beloved traitors, but then stopped and smiled. Maybe a few muddy paw prints on the man's expensive linen suit would send him packing.

She waited for him to order them down or to shout for her to call off her dogs. Instead, he scratched Lancelot and

Guinevere behind the ears and...

The hairs on the back of her neck prickled.

Something about the scene jolted her. Something about *him*. Something...

A reminiscent tightness twisted in her chest. "Does he look familiar to you, El?"

Ellie squinted. "Let's see...gold hoop earring. Tailored suit. Expensive leather loafers." She tilted her head. "Nope. Can't say I've ever seen a man in Slocum who dresses quite so...consciously. Looks like he should be on TV." She snapped her fingers. "That's it. You haven't been getting much sleep, and we all know Vera's flair for the dramatic. Maybe he's one of those infomercial guys." She affected a disembodied salesman voice. "Live alone? Bothered by crazed stalkers in the middle of the night—"

"Cut it out." Sydney chewed her lip as she examined the man's slicked-back ponytail and neatly trimmed goatee. "That's not it."

"Well, where's he from? Maybe you've met him before."

The air became too hot, too thick. "Atlantic City," she croaked, her throat suddenly dry.

"Atlantic City? New Jersey?" Ellie dropped her forehead against the doorframe. "I know your aunt lives there, but, geez! She flew him all the way to Indiana to install an alarm system?" She shook her head. "Did I mention your aunt's a kook?"

"She said he's the best." Sydney tensed as the man shooed away her dogs and headed for the house. A jittery anticipation knotted her stomach. "I feel dizzy, El."

"He's good looking, but I'm not exactly woozy."

"I'm serious. I feel nauseous."

Ellie's maternal instincts kicked in. She pressed the back of her hand to Sydney's cheek. "You don't feel warm. Though you are a little pale. And you've still got those godforsaken circles under your eyes."

"I can't help it if I can't sleep."

"I wish you'd talk to someone about that damned dream."

"I do. You."

Ellie frowned. "Listen, even though I'm anxious for this

guy to hook up his security gizmos, maybe we should tell him to come back later. When you're feeling better. I can camp out with a shotgun on your porch while you catch a nap."

"No!" The sharp command startled Sydney as much as it did Ellie. She cleared her throat and lowered her voice. "We don't want to be rude."

Ellie narrowed her eyes, forcing Sydney to squirm. The dream was getting to her. She knew it. Ellie knew it. And there was nothing Sydney could do about it. She'd been dreaming about the maiden and the knight since childhood. Every time the same dream. The same fuzzy scene in the woods. The same voices hushed and garbled as though coming through a tin can with string.

The same dream that, two weeks ago, had suddenly flashed in her mind with the clarity and sound of a big-budget film. Worse, the emotions cut through her as if they were her own. Frustration and fear so *real* that she'd awakened sobbing. Since then, the haunting vision returned nightly, unbidden, unwanted, and leaving her bereft and grieving for something which remained a mystery. If she could just get some sleep, maybe her life would return to normal.

Thankfully, Ellie's eyes lit with delight. "Ohhh, I get it. Dizzy. Nauseous. You're sick, all right. *Lovesick.*"

"Oh, please." Sydney looked through the screen. The man had paused at the edge of the sidewalk. He seemed to be sizing up the house, though she couldn't tell for sure as the late-afternoon sun glinted off his mirrored, oval sunglasses. Despite Ellie's mocking, Sydney smoothed wayward curls from her face. It wasn't like her to be concerned with her appearance, but then she hadn't exactly been herself lately. Feeling like a dandelion in a garden of roses, she asked, "How do I look?"

Ellie quirked a brow. "You look like yourself."

Sydney batted her hands. "Yes, yes. But aside from that, do I look pretty much…normal?"

Ellie hooted. "I guess that depends on your definition of normal. If it includes wearing purple overalls, purple combat boots, and a miniature sword on your necklace, then, yeah. You look normal."

"Somehow that didn't make me feel better." Self-conscious, she tugged at a long curl, then twirled it around her finger. "Do I look that...out there?"

"You look..." Being a true friend, Ellie faltered for the appropriate word. "...different. Then again, you *are* different." With a quick wave of her hand, she indicated the gargoyles and medieval swords adorning Sydney's living-room walls.

"Excuse me. *Eccentric.*"

Rickety porch steps creaked, causing the women to squeeze back into the doorframe.

"Good evening, ladies. I'm looking for Sydney Vaughn."

The deep, resonant voice shot Sydney's heart into her throat. She knew this man. But from where? *Where?*

Ellie elbowed her, then answered, "You've come to the right place."

He peered through the screen at Ellie. "I'm Baldwin D. Lacey. A friend of Vera Drake's."

Sydney could only stare as something incredible yet indiscernible tugged at her core.

"Baldwin D. Lacey," Ellie said. "Hell of a fancy name."

"So I've been told." His mouth quirked. "Call me Winn."

"Soooo, Winn," Ellie crooned, "have any trouble finding us? It's easy to get lost on these old country roads. Being from Atlantic City, you're probably used to bright lights and smooth pavement."

"I'm also used to less humidity. Mind if I come in?"

Ellie hesitated. "Got any identification?" She winked at Sydney. "For all we know, you could be a serial killer."

"I'm impressed. Vera said you trust too easily. But I assure you. You couldn't be in safer hands." He pressed the photo ID up to the screen and grinned. "Trust me."

Sydney's mind flashed white. Her thoughts drew into a violent tailspin. His words triggered remnants of the dream.

Her heart pounded.

Her breath caught. She leaned against the screen door for support.

It couldn't be.

Then Ellie flung the door open wide.

Sydney flew forward with it and slammed hard against Baldwin's chest.

He caught her, his arms around her in an instant.

His touch sparked her every nerve ending to life. She'd been here before. In his arms.

Shaken to the darkest reaches of her soul, she pleaded, "Let me go."

"She speaks."

Amused. He was amused. Sydney wanted to die. He didn't feel it. Not a flicker of recognition. No connection.

To break the bond he didn't feel, she pushed against his shoulders. Broad shoulders. An image of the knight stuck in her mind.

Impossible.

She reached up with trembling fingers and relieved Baldwin D. Lacey of his very modern sunglasses.

She met and held his curious gaze for what seemed a lifetime.

Several lifetimes.

She knew his face as well as she knew her own.

"Baldric," she whispered, then fainted dead away in the arms of the knight of her dreams.

Two

Yorkshire, England 1315

"Pray you, Father, reconsider!"

"'Tis done."

Gillian Marrick bolted to her feet. "But, Father. Nigel Redmere?"

Her sire leaned back against the bench and folded his arms as though settling in for a childhood tantrum. "You are a woman full grown, Gillian. Ten and eight, an advanced age for marriage as is. We must consider ourselves fortunate to have received the offer from the baron at all."

Gillian's legs trembled beneath her worn skirts. Afraid she might crumple into a pathetic heap, she paced the weed-infested garden. "I apologize if I do not consider myself to be fortunate."

"Why, pray tell, do you find Redmere so offensive?"

"His skin is shriveled. His pallor that of a corpse. Indeed, I marvel that his skeletal body can endure the weight of such a flamboyant wardrobe."

Lord Marrick's lips thinned. "You exaggerate, Daughter. Speak thy true mind or do not speak at all."

She shuddered to think of Nigel Redmere's lecherous hands upon her. "He frightens me. I do not relish in how he looks upon me. In that I speak the truth."

"He is taken with you, Gillian. There is naught to fear."

But fear she did. It clutched her with sharp talons, dragging her into a pit of cold despair. She sank to her knees and clutched her father's hand. "What of the rumors?"

He stiffened. "Of what rumors do you speak?"

"'Tis said that Redmere's two wives met ill-timed deaths. 'Tis said that he is obsessed with producing an heir." She lowered her voice to a desperate whisper. "Neither wife had been able to get with child."

Her father leaned forward, face mottled with outrage. She backed away. "Are you insinuating that the baron *murdered* his wives?"

Gillian cast her gaze to the ground. "'Tis so said."

"Who has supplied you with this malicious fodder?"

"I have heard talk." She refused to name faithful servants who would pay for her eavesdropping.

"Gillian, I will not have you a party to vicious gossip. I have known Redmere for years. He will not harm one hair on your precious head."

The finality of her father's words slammed into her chest. Panic rose like stinging bile. "How can you be so sure?"

"Enough!" He rose from the stone bench and drew Gillian from her knees. He held her arms and gentled his voice. "Do you honestly believe I would bid my own daughter into the hands of a murderer?"

She warmed herself for a moment under his concerned gaze. Unfortunately, 'twas not her father's integrity in question. "Nay, you would not."

He released her. "Then I will hear no more of this talk. Redmere has made a generous offer in exchange for your hand in marriage."

She clenched her jaw, imprisoning the sob burning her throat.

"Nay," he said, a telltale rumbling in his voice from somewhere deep in his chest. "Do not look upon me as though I have sold you into slavery, Daughter. My love for you is grand. This you know."

Gillian tried to swallow her pain. "I know, but—"

"He will provide for you as I no longer can." The last words were but a choked whisper as he lapsed into one of his recent coughing spells. As her father's shoulders caved forward, convulsing, and his thinning hair caught in the breeze, she worried that he had become every bit as worn as the weathered stones of their castle.

She scanned the crumbling walls of Heatherwood. Indeed, her father's spirit had crumbled along with the seasoned stones these years past. Ill luck plagued Lord Oswald Marrick as fleas plagued his mangy dogs. Were he a man of lesser morals, mayhap their fate would be less dire. Verily, it appeared that in order to prosper one must either be a noble of black heart or a calculating politician such as Baron Nigel Redmere, lord and master of the infamous Willingham Castle.

A chill rushed over her skin at the mere thought of Redmere. A man of vast properties, a man of great wealth, a man who disgusted Gillian despite her father's reassurance.

"I shan't go!" she cried. "Who will mend your clothes? Plan your meals? Monitor your cough?" Desperate tears scorched her eyes as she fought to show him reason without repeating the rumors.

"Ah, Daughter," he said with a sigh, resignation clear in his sagging tone and posture, "I had hoped you would go willingly. I had hoped to spare you."

"From what? What could be worse than marrying a man I do not love?"

"Love is not a requirement for marriage."

"You loved mother and she you. Nay. There is more to this." She clutched at her father's homespun tunic. He looked ancient. The fingers reaching for hers as thin and feeble as a seedling. "I would know the truth, Father. What forces you to do this?"

"I am dying."

He said it plainly. As though not a horrible thing. As though a simple fact of life. The sun rises and so it must set. Her mother had died unexpectedly, as had her brothers. She grieved for them to this day. Now, once again, death knocked upon the splintered portcullis of Heatherwood. Though this time, she need not raise the barrier to know what waited on the other side.

She knew not which was worse.

Gillian pressed her father's hand to her cheek. 'Twas futile to hold so tightly. Naught would keep him from leaving her. But hold on she did to fingers already cold with the inevitable. "Father."

He dried her cheeks with the tattered sleeve of his tunic. "I will know that you are settled and well provided for. I will know that Heatherwood is in capable hands and that the vassals who remain upon its battered lands are under a baron's protection. It is my dying wish, Gillian. Will you deny me?"

She bowed her head. `Twas naught to say. Fate, it seemed, had made the decision for her.

Stepping into her father's comforting embrace, she settled her cheek against his shoulder, the threadbare material scratching her skin. She cried silently in his arms. The light of youthful dreams fading to black.

He patted her back, his voice thick. "I am sorry, Gillian. `Tis for the best. For you. For our people. For Heatherwood."

Pulling away, she looked upon her beloved father. She knew of no other man who kissed his child's wounds, embellished wild tales as a bedtime treat, or stroked his daughter's hair through terrifying storms or spells of sickness. This time, `twas she who stroked the hair above his ear. She would not deny him.

"For you. I do this for you, Father."

He smiled, though it did not reach his weary eyes. "`Tis for the best."

"Aye," Gillian lied, "`tis for the best."

***

Baldric de Lacey lifted his face to the sunbeams sneaking through the treetops. The warm, spring breeze caressed his skin like a lover's gentle touch. Favorable weather never failed to lift his spirits, and this day he had much to celebrate.

Darbingshire. His birthright. Soon he would return home. It had been ten long years since his father had gambled and lost their heritage to Nigel Redmere. Baldric did not blame his neighbor for the loss. `Twas not Redmere's fault Hugh de Lacey had been poor at the game of dicing. `Twas not his fault Hugh had a weak heart and left them soon after.

Besides, Baldric owed Redmere. The man had assumed guardianship of Lisbeth, the youngest de Lacey, providing for her at Willingham while her brothers set out to carve their own lives. Now, in a further gesture of generosity, Redmere offered to return Darbingshire back to Baldric. Back into the de Lacey family.

Darbingshire. The bright, crisp colors of the day faded as he envisioned his childhood home. He knew every crevice of the magnificent tower keep, every secret spot in which he had hidden as a boy. Redmere advised he had taken diligent care of the structure, yet Baldric did not expect it to appear exactly as he remembered. Not only would the natural erosion of time have taken its toll, but no longer did he view the world through the eyes of a young man eager to travel abroad, romantically dreaming of his first taste of victory.

Nay. He would return home a warrior. A warrior who had engaged in bloody battles, seen death dance before him, then brush by, cackling...awaiting another time, another place.

Darbingshire. Anticipation made his hands twitch, eager to urge his horse faster, to be done with the assignment that would grant him his most fervent desire.

His instructions were clear.

Proceed to Heatherwood. Procure Lady Gillian Marrick and escort her in good haste and in good health to her betrothed. To the prosperous and powerful Baron Nigel Redmere.

A simple task for such a grand reward.

Baldric grinned, his elation impossible to contain.

"You are looking pleased with yourself, Brother."

Baldric turned his gaze to Simon, whose mail coif glimmered in the shafts of sunlight. "As well you should be. Smile, soon we will be home."

"To smile," Simon pointed out in his usual dry manner, "would be to suggest that one is feeling joyous."

Baldric cocked his head. "You puzzle me with your dour mood. All we need do is escort a fey girl through forest and glen to Willingham. A sennight's ride, no more. For this, and only this, we can return to our rightful home. Spill de Lacey blood protecting what is ours rather than another's."

Simon shifted his body on the back of his dark charger. "Precisely."

"This troubles you?"

"Aye." Simon knocked his fist against his armored chest. "I was not yet ready to leave the tournaments. Indeed I am not yet ready to settle down. I cannot imagine waking to the same walls, the same windows, the same view each and every morn."

"You have yet to exhaust your wandering spirit. I understand." Baldric ducked under a storm-ravaged branch of a sessile oak. "If these are your true feelings, why do you ride with me? I would have honored your decision to remain at the games."

Simon stared into the thick woods surrounding them. "'Tis uncomfortable for me to admit."

"Try."

Simon grunted. "Very well. We have traveled many years together. Fought many battles. Saved one another's lives when a blade thrust too close."

Something warm flowed through Baldric. "Are you saying that you would miss me, Simon?"

Simon avoided his brother's eyes. "Aye. But 'tis also the blood stir of battle that I shall miss."

Baldric grinned. "Think then on the thieves infesting these woods. Think on the outlaws who have been pillaging every noble on the road to Willingham these three months past. Surely Lady Gillian and her belongings will lure these curs into the open once more. 'Tis part of the reason Redmere sent us."

Simon graced his brother with a wicked grin. "You say this only to cheer me."

Baldric slapped Simon's shoulder in hearty affection. "Your love of a good fight is renowned, dear brother. In these unscrupulous times, you are easily pleased."

"Aye. I am."

Baldric sensed something remained amiss. "Simon, you are free to return to the tournament. Your loyalty is unmatched, and I would proudly stand in the way of a blade for you, as you would I. You need not accompany me if your heart beckons you elsewhere. Darbingshire awaits any time you are ready." He paused at Simon's somber features. "There is more to your troubles?"

"I am afraid I *must* accompany you this journey. I will not have your dream of Darbingshire put at risk."

"You doubt my ability to defend a mere girl with my own wits and sword?"

"You know well 'tis not what I believe. You may, however, require defense from Lady Gillian herself. 'Tis no secret women fall at your feet, begging for one touch from Baldric the

Immortal. God's teeth, they sneak into your bed at night."

"As they do yours."

Simon shook his head. "'Tis not the same. 'Tis the affection of your noble heart they seek as well."

Baldric glared at his brother. "Are you saying you fear Lady Gillian will try to seduce me?"

"You know 'tis cursed to be so fine of face and heart. Your reputation precedes you. I am sure it has not failed to reach Heatherwood."

"Think you I am powerless against the ardent charms of a virgin, when Darbingshire stands at stake? Surely that last blow you suffered minced your brains."

"Nay," Simon insisted. "They say Lady Gillian is enchanting. 'Tis rumored Redmere became obsessed with her after one holiday feast in her company. 'Tis rumored Redmere offered Lord Marrick untold amounts of gold in exchange for his daughter's hand in marriage, receiving naught in return save her person. No lands. No wealth. You know Redmere as well as I, Baldric. Does his eagerness to plunge into this fruitless alliance not puzzle you?"

Baldric sighed in dramatic jest, knowing 'twould irritate his brother. "Mayhap 'tis done for love."

"Love?" Simon spat, rising to the bait. "This is exactly of what I speak. Leave it to you to suggest such frivolous motivation. You have always been and remain still a romantic fool. I fear it shall someday be the death of you."

Baldric's mouth twitched in amusement. "Mean you, if I fall in love I shall die?"

"Mean I, steel thy lover's heart against the rumored charms of Lady Gillian. If talk is true, and she is indeed *enchanting*, I fear certain and disastrous consequences."

Baldric's hearty laugh echoed through the woods, no doubt raising the brows of the knights and squires riding a respectable distance behind. Lowering his voice, he teased, "Do strive to turn a deaf ear to your rumor-spreading lemans, Simon. Enchanting. Do you actually believe she has cast a spell over our dear neighbor, Redmere?"

Simon grunted. "'Tis easier for me to believe Redmere

has fallen under a spell rather than fallen in love. He is far too practical for that impractical emotion."

Before he could voice his counter, Baldric's squire reined in beside him, jabbing an anxious finger ahead. "Look at it, Sir Baldric," young Ivo said as they cleared the edge of the forest. "'Tis magical."

"Enchanting," Simon amended with a sideways glance at Baldric.

Taking in the breathtaking view before him, Baldric tended to agree. Heather. As far as the eye could see. The purple flowers threatened to overrun the glen as they swayed in the breeze. If fairies flew up and out of the purple sea to greet them, Baldric would be unable to feign surprise.

Sir William Giffard and Sir Robert FitzHubert, both of whom had sworn fealty to Redmere years ere, voiced their boredom.

"'Tis a field of weeds," FitzHubert said with a yawn. "Let us cross and be done with it. Ahead lies Marrick's castle."

"And within it food and drink," Giffard added.

"Aye," Baldric said. "We are all in need of rejuvenation. Let us proceed."

Redmere's men awaited no further instruction. They spurred their dark chargers forward, mindless of Baldric's watchful gaze upon their armored backs.

"There ride two of the most pitiful excuses for knights I have ever seen," Simon said with distaste. "The fact that they have been dubbed such sickens me. I would be amazed if they possess an original thought between them."

Baldric did not trust the two knights either, but Redmere had insisted on their participation, no doubt to report every movement upon arrival at Willingham. "They serve the baron well, mindlessly enforcing his will. 'Tis an important trait as far he is concerned. He surrounds himself with followers, not leaders. This you know. 'Tis the reason he refrains from pressing us to swear fealty."

"Yet he trusted not those witless mounds of muscle to escort his betrothed safely to his threshold." Simon raised his prideful chin. "For this he enlists us."

"Redmere's messenger advised me that he will pay any price to avoid mishap before the wedding. Even sacrifice Darbingshire."

Simon leveled Baldric a smug look.

"I believe your suspicious mind will stir up more trouble than my romantic heart, as you say, Brother. Redmere may be willing to sacrifice Darbingshire for a woman, but there is naught I would not sacrifice for Darbingshire." Baldric clasped his brother's shoulder. "You worry for naught, Simon. Come. The sooner we accomplish this deed, the sooner we can go home."

***

"How do I look?"

"Enchanting."

Gillian regarded her handmaiden with a doubtful frown. Faithful to the bone, Eloise would declare Gillian a goddess of beauty were she caked with straw-infested dung.

"I speak the truth," Eloise assured. "Fairies would be jealous of the radiance of your being."

Gillian blushed at Eloise's whimsical exaggeration. 'Twas a kind though false statement indeed. Gillian knew her features to be more queer than classic. Her lips too full. Her eyes, an unremarkable shade of green, stationed too widely apart. Slight of figure and height, she possessed but one visual attribute. Her hair. Dark, spiral locks that, when unbound, fell in length to the backs of her knees.

"Forgive me, m'lady," Eloise said, "but this concern over your appearance is odd. I thought you wished to discourage the baron's attentions."

"I do."

"Ahhh." Eloise did not try to hide her smirk. "Then 'tis Sir Baldric's eye you wish to catch."

Gillian studied the tippets of her gown. "I know not of what you speak."

"You tell tales, to be sure. Your eyes shone brighter than midnight stars when your father announced your escort to Willingham to be Sir Baldric."

'Twas true, though Gillian hesitated to admit it aloud. Sir

Baldric the Immortal, mayhap the noblest knight in all of England, had been chosen to act as her personal escort. According to gossip, a more chivalrous knight never lived. She could scarcely believe her good fortune. Before her father had finished raising his chalice, a far-fetched plan—a plan she would have condemned under any other circumstance— had taken root in her mind. A plan that diverted her attention from her father's impending death. A plan that relied solely on Sir Baldric's implied romantic nature.

The plan was simple and direct.

She would appeal to him as a gentleman and a knight. If he would be so kind as to impregnate her, thereby saving her life, she would be forever in his debt.

`Twas extreme but logical. Above all else, Redmere wanted a son. For her to acquire a child conventionally, through the seed of her betrothed, `twould be naught less than a miracle. Redmere's fertility had long been in whispered question. Now she was expected to succeed where two wives ere had failed.

She knew only one way to avoid their suspicious fates.

Conceive before reaching Willingham.

She dared only approach Sir Baldric. The kind, noble man who surely had sired a bastard or two in his frequent trysts. The man who loved well and loved many, according to gossip. His expertise with the ladies rivaled the legend of his swordsmanship.

Surely he would take pity on her and offer his body for her life. After all, `twould be a coupling with no marital expectations. Although, what if he found her lacking compared to the others he'd loved? What if he found her more annoying than alluring? She must consult her handmaiden in the art of seduction. The woman excelled in the craft. "Eloise, I must seek your advice—"

In the distance, anxious voices mingled with pounding hooves and barking dogs.

He had arrived.

Gillian's heart shot to her throat.

Eloise hurried to the narrow window, scattering newly placed rushes in her wake. "Be still my pounding heart!"

Gillian forced her stiff legs to carry her to the window. She stood on her toes but could see naught as Eloise's ample height and figure blocked her view. "Please to step aside so I might see as well, Eloise."

The woman edged over, enabling Gillian to fit her face into the window. Together they watched the impressive retinue approach the keep. Gillian counted four knights, each as intimidating in stature as the next, and two squires.

Her father stepped out to greet the entourage. His overly affectionate hounds ran circles about him, then trotted over to yap at the knights' heels as they dismounted.

One of the armored visitors kicked the smallest dog in annoyance, sending the mutt limping away with a whimper.

Gillian winced at his cruelty. Was she to journey in the company of such barbarians?

Another knight, easily as tall yet leaner in frame, took visible exception to the ill treatment of the dog. He approached the cowering hound, administered a kind scratch to its ear, then turned his attention to its attacker.

Tugging off his gloves one finger at a time, the compassionate knight issued a reprimand in a voice so low, Gillian could only wonder at his words.

The cruel knight stiffened, the set down ill-received, then turned to her father to grumble what she assumed to be an apology.

"'Tis him," Gillian whispered, her gaze on the gentle knight. "Sir Baldric."

"Rumor has it, there is none kinder."

Gillian prayed the rumors held true. Countless tales of the gallant knight's adventures had been told at her father's dinner table. The one recurring theme—compassion. Sir Baldric's determination to protect the lives of the innocent, mostly at his own peril and sometimes to the outrage of his fellow mercenaries.

For her plan to succeed, she needed Sir Baldric to be every bit the chivalrous paragon that daydreaming handmaidens professed him to be.

"They enter, m'lady!"

Gillian drew a deep breath, preparing herself for events to come. "Then let us greet them."

Together they left the modest bedchamber. Gillian descended the steep, circular stairs at a sedate pace, cloaking her trembling hands in the folds of her skirt. Eloise shadowed her every step, the handmaiden's presence her only comfort.

Below, hearty masculine laughter rang through the great hall.

Gillian's steps faltered. One of those voices belonged to the man she had chosen to father her child.

A stranger.

Her senses reeled. She pressed a steadying hand to the stone wall.

Again laughter chased through the hall and up the stairwell.

Gillian missed the last step completely. Her heart thundered like a war stallion's hooves as Eloise caught her by the elbow.

"Normal laughter of normal men," her handmaiden soothed.

Sir Baldric was but a man, Gillian told herself. A man who donned his breeches one leg at a time, just as any other man.

"Ah, there you are, Daughter!" Lord Marrick's voice bellowed over the din of the hall as servants hurried to ready trestle tables for the evening meal. He rushed over to meet Gillian at the bottom of the stairs, then escorted her to their waiting guests. "Good sirs," he announced, "'tis with great pleasure and pride that I introduce to you my daughter, Gillian Marrick."

The four knights, clad in mail and an intoxicating mixture of fresh air and horse sweat, bowed before her.

Gillian stared. She could help it not. They loomed larger and certainly more menacing than her father's own knights.

One by one they straightened, removing their mail-coifs in mannerly succession as Lord Marrick continued his introductions. "Sir William Giffard."

With a nose made crooked by several breaks and a scar curving from ear to chin, Sir William appeared gruesome indeed. His small, black eyes darted about like those of a scavenger animal.

"Sir Robert FitzHubert."

Gillian struggled not to recoil under the knight's lecherous perusal. Craving a hot bath and a scrubbing, she quickly shifted her attention to the right.

"Sir Simon de Lacey."

How sad, she thought, to be blessed with the fair face of an angel and blue eyes as cold as river ice. He studied her intently—searching. She saw something else in those cold eyes, something raw, and she looked away, curiously fretting whether he possessed the power to read minds.

"And—"

"Sir Baldric the Immortal," she whispered, focusing on the last man in line. She could say no more. Like an exquisite painting, the magnificent knight stole her breath. Black hair, thick as sable, brushed broad shoulders. Brown eyes, warm and inviting as a blazing hearth, glowed with vitality. A neatly trimmed beard accentuated a smile that seemed not only genuine but permanent.

Before her stood the most handsome man in all of England. Women, beautiful women, had shared his bed. Now she, a girl of unexceptional figure and face, hoped to catch his eye and regard. She stared at the extraordinary man as she pondered her collision with insanity.

Lord Marrick cleared his throat.

Sir Simon slammed the back of his hand against his brother's chest.

Gillian blinked. Hope flared in her heart as she realized Sir Baldric had also stood entranced.

"Pray, forgive me, m'lady," Baldric said. "'Twas rude of me to stare, but you bear a keen resemblance to our young sister, Lisbeth." He nudged his brother. "Does she not?"

FitzHubert grunted.

Sir Simon frowned. Encouraged by a heartier jab to his ribs, he grumbled, "Aye. Remarkable likeness to Lisbeth."

Gillian swallowed. *Sister?* How could she entice a man who considered her the image of his *sister*? She cursed herself. She had foolishly indulged in a dream, placing blind faith in a complete stranger.

Foolish. Unforgivably foolish.

Sir Baldric was not her savior. He was her executioner. He had come to deliver her into the hands of the devil himself. And beneath those gnarled hands, as had his two wives ere, she would die.

Fear, anger, hopelessness—all snaked around her like an ominous mist, obliterating rational thought.

She struck out at the unfair world.

She smacked Sir Baldric the Immortal across the face. "Murderer!"

Three

"What the hell?" Winn swept the petite woman up into his arms as his sunglasses fell from her limp fingers.

"Cripes all mighty!" The blonde woman held open the door. "Lay Sydney on the couch. I'll grab a wet cloth."

Winn followed the frantic woman into the living room. "I thought *you* were Sydney Vaughn."

"No, I'm Ellie Bane." She rushed toward what he assumed to be the kitchen. "Sydney's best friend."

"Well, damn," he grumbled, searching for space among the purple explosion of pillows on the—surprise—equally purple sofa. "It's worse than I thought."

Wishing he was the kind of guy who could dump Sydney on the purple throw rug and bolt for the car, he lowered her onto the couch. Moving at the speed of light, he plucked pillows from beneath her body, determined not to touch her. He cursed Vera Drake as he rested back on his haunches. He needed this like a hole in the head.

He observed Graveyard Girl (after years on the force, graveyard had become his code for anything bizarre), who'd gawked at him as though he'd sprouted a third eyeball…then fainted. If Ellie hadn't cleared up their identities, he'd have figured it out soon enough. '*She's obsessed with the color purple.*' Winn glanced around. "No kidding, Vera." Everything in the room was purple, including Sydney's vivid attire.

"I've known Sydney all my life," Ellie said, dashing toward the couch, then dropping to her knees. "I've never known her to faint." She draped the damp cloth across Sydney's forehead. "She was fine before you got here."

Winn grimaced. "A man dreams of a woman falling at his feet, but not because he made her sick."

Ellie's lips twitched. "I don't think that was the case."

"Has she been ill recently?"

"No."

He looked down at Graveyard Girl—GG, he decided—whose color seemed to be returning under Ellie's care. He knew how to handle one type of woman. Blonde, leggy showgirls more interested in what was in his pants—wallet and all—than anything in his head. Which suited him fine. But GG, lying on her purple couch with fresh-cut grass stuck to the cuffs of her purple overalls…he didn't know what to make of her.

"Any chance she's pregnant?"

Ellie choked. "Sydney? You've got to be kidding."

"Why? She has a boyfriend, doesn't she?"

"You don't know Syd."

"No, I don't. But accidents happen."

Ellie stood, hands on hips. "You're barking up the wrong tree, mister. Syd is *not* pregnant."

He knew when to drop a line of questioning. Instead he gestured to the grass at GG's ankles. "Maybe the heat got to her. Looks like she mowed the lawn."

"It is a big lawn," Ellie said, though she looked more concerned than convinced.

GG groaned as her head lolled toward Winn. An ebony curl fell across a face so pale that the contrast struck him. He resisted the ludicrous urge to brush the hair aside, to touch skin he knew to be as soft and smooth as a falcon's feather.

He stilled. Where the hell had that come from? Frowning, he nodded in Sydney's direction. "Looks like she's coming around."

"Thank God. She had me worried." Ellie rushed off to the kitchen again. "I'll get her something cold to drink."

Afraid GG would wake to find him staring, he stood and began to pace. A step later, he tripped over the heap of purple pillows. He counted twelve in all, and not one matched. Plaid, paisley, polka-dotted, but by God, they were all purple.

Then he spotted them. Four deadly swords. Mounted on the wall like prized possessions.

Something inside him shifted as the setting sun sparked along the edges of the long, silver blades. Fascinated, he stepped over the pillows for a closer look. The honed steel shone as though freshly polished, his reflection distorted but crisp as he tested the edge of the blade. The sharp bite made his mouth quirk. He imagined GG sharpening swords almost as tall as she while watching the evening news—*it was a crazy world out there.*

She groaned again.

He figured most people around here owned shotguns for protection. Curious as to why GG collected dangerous relics of the past—and if in fact she did own a shotgun—he found himself eager for Vera's niece to wake. He moved back to the couch, but her eyes remained closed. Her full, dark lashes cast tiny shadows across her cheeks.

He looked away, annoyed that he'd noticed.

Then the books on the coffee table caught his eye. He scanned the twenty or so titles strewn across the tapestry-covered surface. *Exploring Your Psychic Abilities, Healing Through Dreams*—oh, and his personal favorite, *Past Lives: What We Can Learn from Them.*

He shook his head. Psychic mumbo-jumbo. Pseudo self-help books that preyed on impressionable minds.

He glanced back at GG. Yup, she looked the type all right. Besides the overalls and purple combat boots, a crystal sword dangled from her necklace along with one of those jingly metal balls. He didn't believe in any of this new-age crap the public seemed to crave. Balance and harmony existed only in fleeting moments. The first drag of a cigarette after sex. The rain stopping as you step out of the restaurant. The light green when you're in a hurry. It was presumptuous to assume something like that could be harnessed. And good luck charms. It made him sick the way people clung to something hot off a Taiwanese assembly line. Worse, it instantly ID'd someone terrified of the unpredictable.

That's life, kid. Get used to it.

He shook his head. God, he grew more morose by the day. Maybe that's what Vera had meant when she'd said he needed to get out of Jersey for a while. But he didn't think Jersey was his problem, and since he didn't want to think about his problem, he concentrated on the fact that Graveyard Girl appeared innocent as an angel lying before him. He almost smiled as he noted the mud smudges on her overalls. Those overalls just did him in.

Her lashes fluttered open. Her eyes, an obscure shade of green, locked with his.

Her intense stare rattled him. "How are you feeling?"

Her lips curved into a dreamy smile.

He tried again. "Any reason you're staring?"

"I do not stare, sir. Nay, I feast upon your presence. I have long hungered for it."

Her speech pattern threw him...and the accent. She hadn't spoken much before she'd fainted, but he sure as hell hadn't detected an English accent.

Her eyes misted with tears as she waved him closer. Knowing it was a mistake, he knelt.

She laid her palm against his cheek and sighed. "Where have you been, Baldric?"

"Baldwin." That was the second time she'd mispronounced his name.

Her brows furrowed. "*Baldwin?*"

Her hand fell away, and he instantly missed the warmth of her touch. He missed it, he noted with a frown, a little too much.

Ellie returned and wedged herself on the couch next to Sydney. "Welcome back to the land of the living." She handed Sydney a ceramic goblet with one hand and checked her friend's forehead with the other. "No temperature. What happened?"

Sydney waved off the beverage. "I...I don't know."

Winn noted Ellie's look of concern. "Maybe we should call a doctor. Just to be safe."

"I don't need a doctor. I'm fine." Sydney removed the damp cloth from her forehead. "Really. Just a little lightheaded." She grinned sheepishly. "I guess I shouldn't have skipped breakfast."

Ellie gawked at her. "You never eat breakfast."

"Then the heat."

"It's been hotter."

Sydney sighed. "I haven't had a decent night's sleep in two weeks, El. I passed out from hunger, heat, and exhaustion. Now can we drop it? Please."

"But— "

Sydney maneuvered around Ellie, then stood, casually holding on to the arm of the sofa. As if no one would notice, Winn thought.

She motioned Ellie to rise as well. "Weren't you on your way to pick up Jack Jr. from baseball practice?"

Winn listened to the exchange, wondering at GG's restored midwestern twang. The cynic in him told him to write her off as a whack-job. But something inside him, something he couldn't explain, told him it wasn't that simple. He preferred to side with the cynic, knowing life would be easier, but he decided to reserve judgment. Better to be patient. The truth would reveal itself. It always did.

"Rats." Ellie glanced at her watch. "I *am* late. I have to go." She stood and extended her hand to Winn. "Nice meeting you. How long will you be staying in Slocum?"

He shook her hand. "As long as it takes to rig this house with the security of Fort Knox. Vera's words, not mine."

"Yeah, well," Ellie grabbed her purse and fished out her car keys, "Vera's a nut."

Winn wondered if it ran in the family.

"Do you need directions to the nearest motel?" she asked. "Or did Vera take care of that for you?"

"As a matter of fact, Vera did make arrangements."

"She arrange for that gangster car?"

"Who else?"

"Figures. So where are you staying?"

"Here."

"*Here*?" Ellie spun around to face her friend. "And you didn't tell me?"

"I only found out last night. I knew you wouldn't take it well."

"Take it well? Are you crazy, Syd? It's bad enough that David wanted to move in, but at least you *know* him." She jangled her keys at Winn. "*This* man's a stranger."

Narrowing her eyes, Ellie asked him, "Are you married?"

"No."

"A *single* stranger!" She jangled her keys at Sydney. "No siree, David won't like this one bit. *I* don't like this one bit." She looked to Winn. "They're practically engaged, you know."

He didn't know. No doubt Vera hadn't wanted to spoil all the surprises for him. He wondered what else she left out. Not that it mattered. He was here to rig a house, not solve a crime.

Sydney ushered Ellie toward the door. "Mr. Lacey is a friend of Aunt Vera's. He's here on business. David will understand."

"And Elvis will sing one last concert."

"Goodbye, Ellie."

"But—"

Sydney gave Ellie a friendly shove out the door then waved. "Drive safely. I'll call you later." She continued to wave as Ellie backed her pickup truck out of the long driveway.

"*Madam, we be betrayed,*" a masculine voice recited from behind her, "*yet shall my life cost these men dear.*"

Sydney's hand froze mid-air. Her guest quoted Sir Lancelot. She dropped her palm to her pounding heart. Without turning, she answered in Guinevere's words, "*Alas, there is no armour here whereby ye might withstand so many; wherefore ye will be slain, and I be burnt for the dead crime they will charge on me.*"

"*Most noble lady, I beseech ye, as I have ever been your own true knight, take courage; pray for my soul if I now be slain, and trust my faithful friends, Sir Bors and Sir Lavine, to save you from the fire.*"

Sydney closed the door on the outside world then turned and slumped against the solid wood, stunned and breathless.

"You slip into the English tongue quite easily, Miss Vaughn." Baldwin D. Lacey strolled the length of her bookshelves, leafing through the worn pages of *King Arthur and His Knights*, a collection of Arthurian legends compiled by Sir James Knowles. "Tragic passage," he said and snapped the book shut.

She swallowed the egg-sized lump in her throat. "Why

did you choose it? That particular passage, I mean."

He shrugged broad shoulders, his back to her as he returned the book to her treasured library. "I flipped to the back and skimmed a random page. Tell me, have you memorized all of these books?"

"Just portions. Can't be helped, I guess. I've read them so many times."

"What about these videos?" he asked, naming various titles in her collection. "*The Lion in Winter, Robin and Marian, Excalibur, Braveheart.* Have you memorized these as well?"

Sydney smiled. Medieval movies. A childhood obsession she'd yet to outgrow. "I've watched them countless times."

He toured his way around her living room, noting her unusual wall hangings. He stopped at her favorite gargoyle. "Gruesome looking thing."

She pushed away from the door and walked up behind him. "I don't know. I think he's kind of cute. Besides, these gargoyles protect me. They're meant to ward off evil."

He cocked a brow. "I'd use a sword for that."

She followed him over to the wall and pointed to the most impressive of the four swords. "Fourteenth-century replica. Double-edged blade with a sharp point for thrusting. Meant to shear off a limb with one powerful whack." She swung her arms like a pinch hitter. "Beautiful, isn't it?"

He looked impressed, bewildered, and amused all at the same moment. "I've never heard a woman refer to an implement of death as *beautiful.* I've also never known a woman with a fascination for medieval weaponry. Most women decorate their walls with less intimidating...art."

She knew he hadn't meant to insult her, but he'd done it just the same. Dropping her hospitable manner like last Tuesday's underwear, she folded her arms and stuck out her chin. "I'm not most women."

He gave her a slow onceover. "So I've noticed."

The sudden heat in his eyes burned away her indignation. The room became stifling.

He continued to stare, as did she. He said nothing, yet her gaze wandered to his mouth. He had a great mouth. Full and

tempting. She knew a touch of that mouth could render a
woman powerless. She also knew it could turn as hard and
cold as a fortress wall.

She wanted to taste him. His masculinity, his strength, his
virility. He embodied all of the things a man should be. She
sensed it. Knew it. As well as she knew that if she kissed him,
he'd leave nothing behind but a wild swirl of cinder dust.

Whoa. Pretty heavy notions for a man she'd just met.

She must be losing it. *Really* losing it, and it scared her.
She'd peered into his eyes for only a moment when suddenly
she knew him as well as she knew herself.

Eyes are the windows to the soul, she'd read more than
once. But never had she felt such a powerful connection.

Love at first sight?

An icy chill raced down her spine.

No. Not at first sight.

She'd seen him before. In her dreams.

She'd known him before. Loved him before. In another
life.

A past life.

Could it be?

No, no. Impossible. Stop thinking crazy. Stop…a familiar
tightness clutched her chest. She thought back to his arrival.
Watching him walk to her door, falling into his arms, looking
into his eyes. The same unsettling sensations.

Not love at first sight.

Déjà vu.

"You're not going to faint on me again, are you, kid?"

Not if I can help it. She needed distance, a minute alone to
sort through the chaos brewing inside her. "Can I get you
something to drink, Mr. Lacey? Lemonade?"

He eyed her with curiosity. Something else, too.
Trepidation? "It's cold," she added.

"Okay." He said it slowly, as though afraid she might burst
into tears if he answered otherwise.

"Okay." She turned away, afraid to look into his eyes any
longer. Afraid she might spawn another disturbing reaction.
Afraid he was assessing her mental stability. "I'll be right

back."

She made a beeline for the kitchen. As she opened the fridge and retrieved the pitcher with trembling hands, her thoughts raced faster than her heart.

Her knight in shining armor stood in her living room.

Alive.

Baldric.

Only now his name was Baldwin. And instead of a knight, he was a security consultant hired by her aunt to protect her.

As Baldric had been commissioned to protect Lady Gillian.

At least that's how the scenario played out if one believed in past lives. She'd only bought such books because they were on the shelf next to the dream books, and she needed to figure out *something*. She was desperate. She needed sleep, and despite her earlier musings, drugs were out of the question. She didn't want to cover up the problem—the dream—she wanted to get rid of it.

Was reincarnation possible? Truly possible? She'd explored the idea all week, searching through those books for possible answers. Anything to explain why the dream remained so persistent and, as of late, so *real*.

Anything was possible. And if it were true, then according to *Past Lives: What We Can Learn From Them*, history would repeat itself. Though she couldn't say how she knew, she knew that was not a good thing.

Two nights ago the dream had come through more vivid then ever. The knight had entreated, "Trust me," and she'd awoken with an alarming sense of doom.

Then the very next night—last night—she'd bolted out of a restless sleep, certain someone was in her room. Watching her. She'd switched on her bedside lamp. No one was there. But the feeling had been so strong. So *real*.

Unable to calm herself, she'd telephoned her aunt.

The result: Baldwin D. Lacey.

The phone rang, jolting Sydney back to the present. Her heart hammered as she heard the gritty, indistinct voice in her head. *You look pretty enough to eat, Sydney.* At least that's what the caller told her last night after work. She'd just stepped out of the shower, wearing nothing but a towel. *Are you wet all over?*

Exhaustion must've been the only reason she'd slept at all. She glared at the plastic offender jangling on the wall. She should just unplug the thing, but that wouldn't solve this problem either. Maybe if she just showed some force, the caller would leave her alone. In two steps, she grabbed the receiver and barked, "I have a cop here. We're tracing this call."

"Darling, never tell him you're tracing. He'll hang up."

"Vera?"

"Ex-cop," Winn said from behind her.

She spun around. Lemonade sloshed over the sides of the glass pitcher.

Winn attempted to relieve her of the pitcher, but her fingers had frozen in fear. With a look she couldn't decipher, he took the weight of the pitcher in one hand and began to pry her fingers loose with the other.

"Do I hear my Thursday night dinner date?" Vera asked. "You know, he's always prompt and always brings dessert. Me, a little old lady in a wheelchair. Imagine him on a *real* date."

The hysteria roaring inside Sydney subsided as the warmth of Winn's skin seeped up her arm. She couldn't take her eyes off the strong, tanned hand entwined with hers. A hand capable of wielding the heavy sword of a knight—or unfastening the buttons of a lady's dress. It amazed and frightened her how often she'd thought of lovemaking since she'd first set eyes on him. Then again, everything about him amazed and frightened her.

"So what do you think?" Vera asked, voice eager. "Isn't he cute?"

Winn set the lemonade on the counter and Sydney shoved her hand in her pocket. "I didn't notice," she said, her voice one long scratch.

"Syd, hon, if you're going to lie to your Aunt Vera, at least try to sound convincing."

Sydney looked over at Winn and said to her aunt, "Thursday night dinner, huh? I didn't know you two were dating."

Winn's mouth quirked as he leaned a hip against her cabinets.

"*Someone* has to screen your boyfriends."

"I don't need a—"

"Phooey. *Practically* engaged. Aren't you going a bit far with this gratitude?"

Sydney turned away from Winn. "Vera, this isn't the best time."

"Oh, sure, with me you have a backbone." She heard her aunt light a cigarette. "Did the creep call you today?"

"No."

"Good. Now after I talk to my man, I'm not calling again. Nature will just have to take its course."

"I thought you quit smoking."

"Hugs and kisses." Vera made smooching noises until Sydney handed the phone to Winn. "She's all yours."

"Vera." He listened. "She's fine." He looked Sydney up and down. Eyes intent, he said, "I didn't notice."

Sydney's face burned. She moved to the cupboard and snatched the silver chalice she'd bought at last year's Renaissance Fair. Her hand shook as she poured the lemonade.

After some "mm-hms" and an "I'll take care of it," he hung up.

She turned and found him staring at her, hands on hips. "Let's talk about the calls."

Sydney didn't want to talk about the calls. Somehow talking about the calls gave them more life. Better to ignore them. Better to ignore the fact that the prankster had known she was in the shower. *How could he have known that?* It didn't bear thinking. Besides, the kid would get bored with her soon. Wouldn't he?

"Miss Vaughn?"

Then her thoughts shifted to her past-life theory, which only intensified her gloom-and-doom mindset. She felt as though a disastrous chain of events had been set into motion. "You shouldn't have come."

"I'm glad I did. For once it appears Vera wasn't

exaggerating."

"I'm not in any real danger."

"You don't believe that."

She fixed her gaze on the chalice's etchings. A castle. A knight. A sword. As hard as she tried, she could no longer ignore the encroaching sense of doom. She just didn't know which stoked her foreboding more—the caller or the dream.

He took her chalice and set it aside. With gentle hands, he cupped her shoulders and urged her to look at him. "Listen to me. You're safe now. I won't let anything happen to you."

Instead of easing her, his assuring words generated a new wave of dizziness.

Seeking balance, she drew a quick breath and closed her eyes. His arms went instantly around her. In her mind, she saw a fleeting image of the knight and the maiden. They were standing high upon a castle. She was saying goodbye. She was frightened.

The maiden's desperation speared Sydney's heart and bled into her own fears. The sensation overwhelmed her, the experience far too vivid to endure. She opened her eyes, hoping to break the disturbing connection. Yet the knight remained before her. The same wary expression darkened his face. The same confidence sharpened his eyes. Her own eyes misted as a distant voice echoed in her head. "*I shall protect you with my life, Lady Gillian.*"

Her voice quivered as she continued to stare into the soul of her contemporary protector. "Something bad is going to happen." She knew it as sure as she knew the sun would rise in the east tomorrow.

"Nothing bad is going to happen." He leaned his face closer to hers for emphasis. "I won't let it."

The conviction in his eyes turned her already weak knees to gelatin. He brushed his lips across her forehead. Tender. Comforting. A kiss that sealed his vow and stole her very breath and soul. A kiss that filled her with such calm and peace she wondered how she'd ever lived without it. He was back. And for the first time in her life, she felt a definite purpose for being alive.

"Nothing bad is going to happen," she echoed when he drew away. "I won't let it."

He looked confused yet relieved that she'd settled down. Aunt Vera had called him an expert, and Sydney wondered if that sweet kiss was one of his professional techniques to lure women from panic. Except right now she didn't want to think of him with other women. Or sharing that sweet kiss.

The phone rang, halting Sydney's thoughts along with her heart.

Winn snatched the receiver mid-ring. "Hello?" He listened and frowned. "Winn Lacey. Who's this?" He quirked a brow, then offered Sydney the phone, with his hand over the mouthpiece. "Your *fiancé*. He doesn't sound happy."

"I'm sure he's just concerned." She took the phone with care so as not to touch Winn's hand and lose her senses. "He doesn't know you." Though she dreaded explaining Winn, she relaxed knowing it was David on the phone and not the caller. One more tug and her frayed nerves would surely snap. Turning her back to Winn, she lowered her voice. "Hi."

"Who's Winn Lacey?"

Definitely concerned. She expected no less. Ever since her mother's death and especially since the *calls* started, David had become more protective than Ellie. "A security consultant. He's here to install a few locks, then he'll be on his way. No big deal."

"Honey, I'm happy you're having new locks installed, but you don't need a security consultant. I'd be glad to—"

"I know. I didn't want to trouble you and, well, he's already here." Her cheeks burned with the burden of her half-truths. "I should go."

"I don't know a Winn Lacey, Sydney. I don't like the thought of you alone in that big house with a stranger."

"He's from out of town. Recommended by a trusted friend."

"What friend? Maybe I should swing by—"

She dropped her voice to a whisper. "Remember how I said I need to do some things on my own? This is one of those things, David. I need to feel like I have some control right now."

A long pause. "All right, Sydney, but tomorrow I'll be by to make sure this guy did a good job."

The second she hung up the phone, she felt like a heel. She'd led David to believe Winn would be gone in a couple of hours. She'd lied. And all David had ever been was kind. Overprotective, but kind.

"What's practically engaged?"

She stilled. "Excuse me?"

"Ellie said you and this David Monroe were *practically* engaged."

She stared at the phone. "It means David's proposed but I haven't accepted."

"Still waiting for Mr. Right?"

She looked up at him. A tiny smile lit his face, creasing the corners of his eyes. A shiver coursed through her even as a rush of heat warmed her skin. "Something tells me the wait is over."

Winn's brows shot up.

Her cheeks blazed. "I'm sorry. I don't know why I said that. No, that's a lie." She was full of them tonight. "I know why, it's just..." Frustrated, she grabbed the chalice of lemonade and thrust it into his hand.

He tasted his drink and eyed her over the rim. "Yes?"

"You wouldn't believe me."

"Try me."

"You'll think I'm crazy."

"Are you?"

"Crazy?" She suddenly believed with her whole heart that they'd been lovers in another life. "I'm not sure."

He made a sound in his throat that might've been a chuckle. Or a groan. "You don't own any guns, do you?"

She frowned. "No. Why?"

"Just taking stock."

She led him back into the living room, her stomach in knots. How in the world was she going to explain this to him? Past lives. It was difficult even for her to believe, and she had an incredibly open mind. He, on the other hand, seemed unfailingly rational. She paced between the couch and the front window, searching for a logical way to broach the subject.

Winn leaned against the side of her bookshelf and sipped his drink. He watched her pace.

She felt like a laboratory rat under his intense regard. "All right. I can't think of a good way to say it, so I'm just going to say it."

"That's the way I like it."

"You should probably sit down for this."

Without a word he sat on the couch.

She dropped into the chair across from him. She cleared her throat and squared her shoulders. "Do you believe in past lives?"

He cast her reincarnation literature a sideways glance. "I'm an ex-cop, Miss Vaughn. I deal in fact, not fiction."

"Please, call me Sydney." She refrained from pointing out the useless formality. He'd held her in his arms and kissed her forehead for God's sake.

No comment. He continued to sit with the studied blank face of an *ex-cop* who'd heard every cock-and-bull story known to man. Her leg began to bounce. She mentally cursed it to stop. "This isn't a fanciful notion off the top of my head. I didn't invent the concept of past lives. Reincarnation is a common belief practiced by Hindus and certain Oriental cultures. They believe we die and return in an endless cycle of death and rebirth. Some believe if we die, bogged down by some sort of guilt or sin, we return later, in another life, in another form, to be given a chance to purify our souls. To redeem ourselves." She paused as he raised one brow. "You're not buying a word of this, are you?"

He leaned forward, forearms on his knees, and fingered the etchings on the chalice. "I think life is a hell of a lot simpler than that. You're born, you make mistakes, you live with them, hopefully learn from them, then you die with them. End of story."

"No second chances?"

"If you screw it up that badly the first time, you don't deserve a second chance."

She felt his buried pain like a dagger through her own heart. "You're carrying around some heavy baggage, Winn. The question is—is it from this life or a previous one?"

He leaned in closer. "Maybe I didn't make myself clear. I don't believe in past lives. I don't want to be converted. I don't need a new religion. Got it, kid?"

Why did he keep calling her *kid?* The nickname floored her. It made her feel like a tomboy. Or worse, a bratty sister. She toyed with her necklace, cupping the harmony ball and jingling it in an attempt to remain calm. "When you walked up my sidewalk, I had this intense feeling I'd seen you before. Now I know why." She looked him dead in the eye. "You visit me every night."

"Come again?"

"In my dreams." Closing her eyes, she blurted out her theory before she lost her nerve. "I think you and I existed in medieval times. What's more, I think we were ill-fated lovers. And now, after hundreds of years, our paths have crossed again. According to my studies, we have two choices. Repeat history or rewrite it."

Silence.

She opened her eyes. Winn sat across from her with that blank expression on his handsome face.

"I know it sounds fantastic," she rambled on, knowing she sounded like a lunatic. "I have my doubts, believe me. But it would explain my recurring dream and the overwhelming sensation of *déjà vu* and—"

He held up his palm. "Hold that thought." He set the chalice on the table. "Where's your liquor cabinet? This calls for something a hell of a lot stronger than watered-down lemonade."

Four

Baldric paced the floor of the solar, absently tracing his thumbs along the etchings on his goblet. He could not sit nor could he stand still. He felt like a tiger locked in a cage— restless, anxious, waiting. As the pale moonlight filtered through the windows, he knew that surviving the interminable supper was one of his hardest-won victories.

He'd eaten the stuffed pigling, though he'd not tasted it. He'd forced himself to nibble on the cakes and wafers, hoping sweets would offset his dour mood.

He'd listened to Giffard's obnoxious boasting and suffered through FitzHubert's ill table manners. He'd endured Simon's sullen disapproval as well as their host's doomed attempt at blithe conversation.

All the while waiting. All the while battling the burning compulsion to slam his fist on the table and demand that Lord Marrick produce his daughter at once. Demand that she apologize for slapping him. For slandering him. For calling him a murderer.

Baldric clenched his jaw, the odious word ringing in his ears.

He'd killed. Aye. But not without provocation. Not without moral cause.

Murderer.

Was the woman mad?

He swallowed the last of his ale, bitter and of poor quality. He'd been pacing and drinking for hours and would surely pay for overindulgence on the morrow, but tonight he did his best to dull Gillian Marrick's stinging lash upon his honor. Not to mention the recurring vision of the full, tempting mouth from which it had sprung. Or the peculiar green eyes, first cool with a trepidation and assessment that made him ache to touch her cheek, then turning hot with an indignation and conviction that unjustly charred the edges of his conscience.

God's teeth, Simon had warned him. *Bewitched*, his brother had said. *Steel thy lover's heart against the rumored charms of Lady Gillian.*

Baldric had laughed. Laughed because he thought himself immune to Cupid's poison-tipped arrow. Laughed because he was ever the charmer and never the charmed, contrary to Simon's belief. True, he was a romantic. He loved women. Loved making love to women. He'd given his body time and again, but never his heart. Never his soul.

Never, until he set sight on Lady Gillian, when, for a moment, time ceased to pass.

God's Blood. He'd gaped at her as if he were a page stumbling upon his lady's bath. With his heart speared in his throat and his soul crying out for something he did not understand, he could only stare. Then when he'd been called upon, he'd explained his ogling by likening her to Lisbeth.

Lisbeth!

His sister was tall and fair, blue of eyes, light of heart.

Gillian was slight and dark, with features strained in a hint of torment. The loneliest hour of the night, whereas Lisbeth was the sun.

`Twas lunacy to be taken with a girl so obviously troubled, especially since they'd just met. Of course, `twas lunacy to consider any emotion whatsoever. She belonged to Nigel Redmere. His employer. His friend.

But how could he dismiss what he'd witnessed in those eyes? Flashes of desperation, hope, fear. The look of someone trapped. In countless battles he'd gritted his teeth and hardened his heart as he thrust his blade through a man with that same disturbing look in his eye. This time, however, his heart defied him. It latched on to that slight glimmer of hope he'd seen and would not loosen its grip.

He wondered what she wanted of him, and secretly feared he would offer it, whatever it may be.

Baldric shook his head. He slammed his goblet on the chipped fireplace mantle. If he cherished his life, if he cherished Darbingshire, he must immediately cease these futile musings.

He shoved his mind along another path.

Gillian was naught but a fey girl. She was comely, aye, but not beauteous. Her figure, more girlish than womanly, did not suit his taste. She was not an heiress, nor was she particularly likable. Worst of all, she had assaulted him, by all that's holy, and in the end scathed him with stricken eyes as though he were the lowest-born wretch ever to set foot in her presence.

Her father had apologized for her outburst, not once, but three times. Yet her sire could not explain her actions. *She* could explain them, however, and explain she would.

Murderer. She owed him an apology, and he was damn well going to get it. He grabbed a dish of burning reeds and stalked from his room, anticipation flickering in his belly.

He instantly tripped over the curled form sleeping just beyond his threshold.

"Ivo," he grumbled.

"Sir?" Disoriented, Ivo scrambled to his feet. He coughed, waving his hand in front of his crinkled nose to ward off the burning oil's smoke. "What is it?"

Baldric moved the lamp aside. "You possess the eyes and ears of a gossiping kitchen maid. Do you know in which room Lady Gillian sleeps?"

"Aye," the boy whispered, then grimaced. "I mean, me thinks I am insulted, sir."

"Do not be. At times like this, 'tis an admirable quality, I assure you." He passed the dish to Ivo. "Lead the way, lad."

Ivo led Baldric through the dark, unfamiliar halls of the castle, up narrow winding stairs, past snoring guards asleep at their posts. He marveled that the fortress had not fallen under siege. Undernourished and long in the tooth, Lord Marrick's knights, though loyal they may be, were an ineffectual lot.

It hit Baldric then. With the exception of Gillian and her maid, he had not set eyes on one youthful soul on the lands of Heatherwood. No children playing in the gardens. No squires training on the fields. No gaiety whatsoever. Even the court minstrel lacked zeal, playing one somber ballad after another.

Baldric envisioned the crumbling outer walls, the rotting drawbridge, the unkempt bailey. He thought of the keep with its sparse furnishings and faded tapestries.

Finally, he recalled Gillian's faint despair. He did not understand it. One would think her eager to escape the dreariness of Heatherwood for the grandeur of Willingham.

He frowned. He'd been sent to escort her to a better life. Wealth, security. Was she unaware of this?

Again he was bewildered by Gillian Marrick.

Murderer. The accusation gnawed his gut. Where had she found such reason to despise him? Had a loved one fallen under his sword? Would he not have learned of this earlier?

His body tensed. He would have his explanation.

Ivo stopped short and pointed hesitantly at an imposing door. "That one," he whispered. "I think."

"I hope you are right," Baldric said, hushed. "'Twould be unseemly to awaken the Lord of the castle at this hour."

"'Twould be unseemly to awaken the Lady."

Baldric narrowed his eyes at Ivo, who took a tentative step back. "Point taken."

At that moment, the door in question creaked open.

Baldric yanked Ivo into the shadows and doused the flame.

A small, cloaked figure slipped into the hall. Baldric recalled the sleeping guards and wondered if someone had indeed intruded…until the burning candle illuminated the pale face.

Gillian.

He spun Ivo around. "Be gone," he ordered and gave the boy a friendly shove toward the stairway. Then, with the practice of leading heavy weapons and warhorses to a midnight raid, Baldric soundlessly followed the Lady of the keep.

She moved quickly, also without sound, reminding him of a phantom as her cloak billowed about her feet. He remained a safe distance behind as she wove her way through a passage and up steep stairs. Cool wind brushed his face as he topped the last step.

The allure. A place on high where soldiers fought those trying to breach the curtain walls.

A lone knight stood watch under the heavy moon. He nodded to the girl as she swept past him. He did not stop her, nor did he follow. Most alarming of all, he did not appear surprised to see her. Baldric cursed the man's stupidity. `Twas a dangerous place for an unattended lady.

She rounded a corner and was out of sight.

Baldric backtracked, coming at her from the opposite direction. No knights blocked his path. Once again he was amazed at Heatherwood's poor defense. Were he in charge, the castle walls would be fortified, as would its men.

He stopped as he spotted Gillian. She balanced the candle on a stone parapet, then shrugged off her cloak, revealing a drab wool surcoat and a form even slighter than he remembered. She could have easily been mistaken for a squire, if not for her glorious hair. Earlier her tresses had been braided and coiled about her ears. This night it fell unbound to the backs of her knees, her ebony curls shimmering under the moon's eager caress.

Enchanting.

He shook his head again. No, he was here to dispel such thoughts, not encourage them.

Suddenly she began to climb the battlement wall.

Hell's teeth! Did she mean to jump?

He bolted toward her.

Startled by his rapid approach, the girl gasped and jerked around, teetering near the edge.

Baldric clutched her flailing wrist and yanked hard. She tumbled into his arms, smacking the air from his chest.

"Are you mad!" she exclaimed in a choked whisper.

"Nay, madam. But apparently you are."

"Set me down this instant."

"Nay."

"*Set me down.*"

He challenged her obstinate glare with one of his own. "I will have an apology first."

Her eyes darkened further. "An apology!"

"Aye. An apology."

"You nearly caused me to fall. `Tis *you* who owes *me* an apology, sir."

"`Twas I who saved you from a ruinous fall. `Twould seem

you owe me gratitude as well. But I will hear the apology first."

Defiance flashed in her eyes. "For what, pray tell, am I apologizing?"

Astounded at her audacity, he leaned his face close to hers and growled, "For declaring me murderer in front of God and kingdom."

"Oh." She blinked. "That."

"Aye. That." Baldric's ire cooled. At least she sounded somewhat contrite. He lowered her to her feet but kept a firm grip on her delicate shoulders.

She squirmed.

He held tight. "I am waiting."

She struggled to pull away.

"Madam."

"I am sorry," she mumbled, seemingly transfixed by a star in the heavens.

He cocked his head. "Again?"

She lowered her chin and glared at him. "I said, I am sorry."

Baldric frowned. "An insincere apology at best."

"I am sorry. Is that not enough?"

"Nay. I will know why you branded me murderer."

She stiffened beneath his fingers. "'Twas a momentary lapse. I apologized. Now unhand me."

Though he was nowhere near satisfied with her justification, he slid his grip to her elbow. "After I have escorted you from the allure."

She dug in her heels. "I do not wish to leave. I have business to attend."

He quirked a brow. "The business of jumping? I think not, m'lady. 'Tis my duty to see you safely to your intended husband. If you wish to throw yourself to your death, for what reason I cannot fathom, then you shall have to do it from the battlement walls of Willingham. For 'tis there that I intend to deliver you. *Alive*."

Her eyes widened, and for the first time this night, Baldric detected the same innocence that nearly brought him to his knees before she'd slapped him. "You thought I meant to kill myself?" She looked away. "An appealing thought, I must confess, Sir Baldric, but `twould do my father no good. I shall die soon enough. It need not be by my own hand."

A chill settled in his bones. "Are you ill?"

"Nay."

"Then what mean you by this talk of death?"

She yanked her arm from his grasp. "Does it matter?"

"Aye. If you are in danger, I must know. `Tis my duty to protect you."

She backed up against the stone wall. "I fear you would be unwilling to do that which would save me."

He moved forward and braced his palms on the cold stones, trapping her between his body and the wall. Her lower lip trembled, and he prayed to God that she would not cry. "I shall protect you with my life, Lady Gillian. Cease your riddles and explain yourself. I tire of your dramatics."

She squared her shoulders at his reprimand and seemed to struggle for the proper words. After a moment she said, "Baron Redmere has been married twice ere."

"Aye."

She lowered her voice. "Both wives died."

"Aye. `Tis no secret," Baldric said with regret. He'd known both women. Catherine, Redmere's first wife, had tripped and tumbled down a steep stairwell, breaking her neck. Margaret, a pale, sickly thing, had died in her sleep.

"They denied Redmere his heir," she continued in a frantic whisper. "They died by his hands."

"And you believe me to be escorting you into the hands of a murderer." He touched his finger to her chin. "Well, fear not, m`lady. Redmere did not murder his wives. One's death was accidental. The other's by the grace of God."

"There's been talk to the contrary."

"Villagers' gossip," Baldric argued. "Pay it no heed."

She grasped his forearms. "What if there is truth in the gossip? What happens when I marry Redmere and fail to conceive?"

Baldric bristled at the dubious question, but the grip of her small hands on his thin sleeve tempered his retort. "I grow impatient with your childish and misplaced fears. You are young and strong, m`lady, spirited even. I have no doubt you will bear Redmere a castle full of equally spirited sons and daughters. You will live happy and comfortable in the luxury of Willingham."

A quiet despondency settled in her moonlit eyes, stirring an unwanted ache in his chest. He wished to crush her to him, convince her that she worried for naught. That he would never let anything happen to her. Ever. But it was not his place, and it never would be. The thought cut him like a dagger as every nerve in his body seemed to pulse under her fingertips.

He pushed away from the wall. "Now let us go," he said, voice gruff.

She did not move. "I will say goodbye first."

"We are alone. To whom do you wish to bid farewell?"

Her solemn gaze drifted to the battlement wall. "Heatherwood."

He did not need further explanation. He recalled with clarity the day he had said goodbye to Darbingshire. Unlike Gillian, he had been an impassioned lad, eager to leave the trappings of home and experience the world. He had barely given his childhood home a second glance the morning he and Simon rode out. He had always regretted not savoring his last moments of home, for his memories of Darbingshire were his only comfort during the long, lonely nights spent in foreign lands.

Baldric clasped Gillian's hand. At her questioning gaze, he said, "I will hoist you up on the ledge so you might bid a proper farewell. But you must promise to hold my hand and remain still. No leaning over for a better view."

"I promise," she said, then smiled.

He had never seen her smile. It knocked the breath from his body. Her entire face brightened, like the warm, welcome glow of the sun after a violent storm. A dimple played along her left cheek, and she looked up at him as though he had just granted her the world.

If not for his honor, he would have kissed her.

Instead, he gripped her waist and lifted her onto the ledge.

As promised, she held his hand as they gazed out at the moonlit glen.

"Where is your home, Sir Baldric?"

"Darbingshire. It lies on the eastern border of Willingham. Though it has been nigh on ten years since I have seen it." He chose not to mention how Darbingshire would be his reward for delivering her safely to Redmere.

Her fingers tensed. "Then you know well Baron Redmere." It sounded more an accusation than a question. "Aye. He raised my sister, Lisbeth. He has been naught but kind and generous to her, treating her as his own flesh and blood."

"Then you will not believe me." Her eyes never moved from the fields of flowers beyond the gates.

"'Tis a better life to which I lead you. Redmere may be a hard man, but I would not entrust him with my sister's life if I thought he murdered his wives."

"Then my fate is as good as sealed." Refusing his assistance, she did not look at him as she climbed down from the wall.

He had no obligation other than her physical safety, yet he could not deny the strange compulsion to comfort her. "All will be well at Willingham, Lady Gillian. Take heart. 'Tis for the best."

She leveled her gaze upon him, her eyes deadened of emotion. "Says Redmere. Says Father. Says you, Sir Baldric the Immortal." Without another word, she spun on her heel and stalked away.

Baldric watched her retreating figure disappear into the night. He cursed under his breath as he turned and stared out over the wall.

What had she stirred up within him? She was asking him to believe the worst in someone he'd trusted for most of his life. Yet, despite his uncertainty, she appealed to his most vulnerable need—the need to protect.

Simon had foretold of such disaster. Baldric had laughed. Now he wondered if he should have paid more heed to his brother's warning.

Five

Winn woke with a start to find he'd fallen asleep on Sydney's front porch swing. Though accustomed to short naps in strange places, he sat up and shrugged off a disoriented feeling. He still clutched the whiskey bottle she'd found in the back of a kitchen cabinet. The bright orange buck-ninety-nine sticker glowed in the darkness, negating the use of a glass as well as any feeling in his throat. The harsh Kentucky blend might not have gone down as smooth as Glenlevit, but it sure took him to the same place. A place that smoothed the sharp edges of life.

What a bargain.

He rocked the swing and leaned his head back. The chains creaked in steady rhythm with the crickets, the only sounds in the heat-heavy air as he whiled away a night in the sticks. Some people needed quiet to think. Quiet drove him crazy.

He gazed up at the star-studded sky. He'd never seen so many constellations in his life. The spectrum of garish lights glaring along the Atlantic City skyline obliterated most everything but the 737s.

As he sat there, drinking a strange woman's whiskey and spending the night alone, he didn't know which was worse— the silence or the darkness.

He suddenly wished Sydney's crank caller would stroll up to the house. Whether the creep was a real threat or not, kicking the cowardly sonuvabitch's pansy ass would feel pretty good right now. It would also put an end to Winn's stay in Slocum, Indiana. Something told him the sooner he distanced himself from the purple-obsessed country bumpkin, the safer he'd be. Her big green eyes stirred a part of him he didn't want stirred— the hot urge to track down the bastard and shove fear down his throat.

He'd never bought into that love-at-first-sight bull, but God it felt like…no, he wouldn't even give the thought voice.

It was crazy. *Ludicrous.* He wondered, not for the first time, if Graveyard Girl's literary collection contained a book or two on voodoo or witchcraft. It would explain this irrational attraction he felt toward her. An attraction that went beyond simple lust. It would explain why he'd kissed her forehead. A tender, intimate, something-he'd-never-do-in-a-sane-moment gesture. She was a client. A stranger. Vera's goddamned niece! She'd cast a spell over him. At least that's what it felt like. Ridiculous to his own ears, but preferable to…the other thing.

At least she'd finally grown weary of trying to explain her past-life theory and gone to bed. Three swigs into her mind-boggling conjecture, and he'd been damn close to imagining himself in chain mail, so vivid was her tale.

Alone and half sober, or half drunk—unsure which way to call it just yet—he contemplated his own theory. After careful consideration of the day's events, he came to the only rational conclusion.

Sydney Vaughn was a new-age flake.

Fact: She was obsessed with all things medieval.

Fact: She was obsessed with reincarnation.

Fact: She was obsessed with the color purple, though how that fit into the scenario he had no clue.

Fact: She was related to Vera Cromwell. Obviously, instability *did* run in the family.

Winn downed the last of the whiskey in one scathing swallow.

Fact: She was being harassed, perhaps stalked, by a crank caller.

The only *fact* that kept his tires from spitting gravel.

It was Vera's fault he was up to his ears in gravel, dirt, and cornfields in the first place. The woman had the manipulative charm of a pump-action shotgun. Never in his wildest dreams would he have agreed to fly halfway across the country for a routine install on a broken-down farmhouse. Never would he have gone back to the business of chasing down the bad guy. Yet here he was. All because—she'd reminded him in her crotchety Vera way—he owed her for his success as Baldwin D. Lacey, Security Consultant. If not for her and the referrals to her wealthy friends, he'd still be slipping advertising flyers under windshield wipers in supermarket parking lots, which he'd never done, but that wasn't the point.

That wasn't the worst of it though.

The worst of it was this damned attraction he felt toward Sydney. An attraction that he couldn't rationalize or explain away. Even as he'd been sitting in the woman's house, tolerating her cockamamie story about past lives and wondering if he should call a therapist, something tugged at him. Something deep and impenetrable. Something stronger than his own will.

He didn't understand it. He didn't want to understand it. The idea of entangling himself with a delusional woman who was *practically* engaged was absurd. Idiotic. Yet the notion sunk its hooks in.

ID the caller, rig her house, and hop a plane back to Jersey pronto, Lacey.

Winn stood and stretched his legs. He'd start first thing in the morning. The sooner he got away from—

He took a step and tripped, catching the toe of his shoe on a loose wooden plank. He cursed under his breath. He'd fix that tomorrow, too. Rickety porch steps, creaky swings, loose boards. The whole place was falling apart.

If she couldn't afford to pay for repairs herself, why didn't she ask Vera for a loan? Oh, yeah. According to Vera, Sydney wouldn't accept money from her aunt. Nor apparently would she accept financial aid from her rich boyfriend, or rather, her rich *practically* fiancé. What had she said to the man? *I need to do some things on my own.* Pride. Now that was one thing he understood.

He wove his way toward the door, influenced by too little sleep and too much whiskey—buck-ninety-nine whiskey that left killer headaches in the morning. No extra charge.

Christ, it was dark. No safety lighting for increased visibility. No security lighting to deter intruders. Only a low-wattage porch bulb radiating a pathetic yellow fog next to the front door.

He slipped into the house as quietly as possible, shut the

door, then found himself fumbling with an ancient spring lock. "Unbelievable." She lived in the middle of nowhere. With lousy locks. Not a deadbolt in sight. Had the woman no thought for her safety?

With only pale moonlight to guide his way through the downstairs, Winn forced the rusty thumb-set window locks closed, swearing under his breath as he slid each one home. He cursed a blue streak when he discovered a flimsy latch hook on the back screen door.

"Why bother," he muttered when he saw the back porch door itself had no lock at all.

He stumbled upstairs, wondering from which corner of Sydney's bed her vicious watchdogs snored. Trudging down the hall toward the guestroom, he heard the plump down pillow calling his—

A floorboard creaked behind him. Winn spun around, reaching for the gun that hadn't been there in years.

"Miss Vaughn?"

Sydney brushed past him without a word. Her long, white nightgown glowed in the moonlight, making her appear ghostlike as she glided down the hall.

He followed her. "Sydney?"

Silence.

She stopped at the end of the hall, reached up and pulled on the thin rope dangling from the ceiling. The attic door creaked open and wooden stairs unfolded, landing at her bare feet.

She climbed up the stairs and disappeared. He squinted at his watch. Three a.m. What the hell was she doing in the attic at three a.m.? Why had she acted as if he wasn't even there?

Of course, he'd seen stranger things when he'd been on the force. Like the time a sleepwalker banged on his neighbor's front door, demanding the return of his wife and horses. Was Sydney sleepwalking? Well, hell. At this rate, Graveyard Girl couldn't surprise him.

He climbed up after her. She'd be all right so long as he didn't startle her. He'd quietly observe and make sure she returned safely to her bed. He reached the top of the steps, and the trapped heat nearly stalled his breath. He scanned the moonlit room. Where was she?

Then he saw the tall window at the end of a box-lined path. An open window.

Winn straightened and banged his head on a rafter. Rubbing his skull and biting down a curse, he crept to the window and looked out.

His heart lurched. She was standing on the roof, much too close to the edge. The stuffy night air gusted out of nowhere and whipped her nightgown against her body. Afraid she might stumble in the sudden wind, he slipped through the window and onto the roof.

Slow. Easy. One cautious step at a time—

The roof creaked.

"Pray, do not force me from my home."

A soft, pleading whisper—and definitely English.

"Baldric?" she called without turning.

She was either dreaming or delirious. When confronted with such cases, he'd learned it was best to play along. He scrambled for something medieval. "Aye?"

"I beseech thee, save me from my certain death." She swayed along the edge of the roof, gazing out over her front yard. "Baldric?"

Winn thumped his forehead with the heel of his hand. Medieval lingo. *Damn.* What had he read in that King Arthur book*? "Most noble lady, I beseech ye, as I have ever been your own true knight, take courage—"*

"You will not let him harm me?"

"I shall protect you with my life." The words tumbled out without thought, shaking something loose within him. He ignored it and inched forward. "It is I, Baldric," he lied. "Take my hand, m'lady."

She reached out.

Winn nabbed her wrist and yanked her away from the edge.

She stumbled back into his arms with a choked sob.

He closed his eyes in relief. She turned in his arms and wept against his chest. His racing heartbeat slowed to heavy, aching thuds. As a matter of fact, a disturbing familiarity slowed all of his movements. He couldn't shake the creepy feeling he'd done this before.

He shook his head. Booze and adrenaline. They had him thinking crazy. Sydney had him thinking crazy. She'd lectured him on reincarnation for close to three hours. He was tired, drunk, and stuck on the roof with a delusional sleepwalker. Wait a minute. Of course it was familiar. He'd had a similar occurrence—in *this* life. A woman, distraught over an affair gone bad, had perched herself on the sixteenth-story ledge of a prominent casino. When he'd finally talked her back in through the window, she'd collapsed in his arms and bawled as if she'd never stop.

Winn sighed, grateful to feel his world returning to normal.

Sniffling and teary-eyed, Sydney raised her head and peered out at the moonlit yard. "Aren't they beautiful?"

He followed the direction of her gaze. The birdbath-turned-swampy-science-experiment? The dandelions circling the rotting wood fence posts? Obviously, GG was still in never-never land, but instead of being annoyed, he smoothed her hair from her tear-streaked face and wondered again at the tenderness she inspired in him. The sort of tenderness reserved for close friends and lovers.

Then he pegged it. Sydney Vaughn reeked of an innocence that evoked one of man's most primitive needs. The need to protect. A long time ago he'd sworn an oath to protect, and even though he no longer served on the force, he still believed in it. Could it be as simple as that? Eager for it to be, he *willed* it to be. "What is it? What do you see?"

A wistful smile touched her lips, and his breath quickened. So much for the big, bad protector. "Heather," she whispered. "I see heather."

"Heather," Winn repeated to the stars. He closed his eyes and swallowed hard. What was he—suddenly, an image formed in his mind. Fields of purple flowers. The flowers surrounded a castle.

Shaken, he opened his eyes. The flowers and castle remained. A cold wind smacked at his skin. Unnerved, he squeezed his eyes shut and shook his head. This time when he raised his lids, he saw dandelions. His new best friend—the weed. Eager to cut the fun short, he rose to his feet with Sydney in his arms. "Come on, kid, let's get you back to bed. We've both had a long day."

He maneuvered the window opening and the cramped path without banging either of their heads. Negotiating the steep wooden steps, however, half-crocked with a sleeping girl in his arms, damn near qualified as an Olympic event.

He found her bedroom after two wrong doors and several mute curses. He gently tucked her into bed. The last thing he wanted to do was wake her. He had a lot of questions, but he wanted a clear head when he got the answers.

He headed back to the guestroom, stripped off his clothes, and stretched out on top of the sheets. No way in hell he was getting under the covers in this heat. As he yawned and tried to relax, he caught a whiff of his pillowcase. Sunshine and country air. He knew without question that the linens had dried hanging on a line in Sydney's backyard. Then again, it seemed only natural for a girl like Sydney. She didn't own a lawn edger or an air conditioner—what would she need with a dryer?

He closed his eyes and summoned sleep.

He didn't want to think just now. He didn't want to think about Sydney fainting or sleepwalking or slipping in and out of an English accent. He didn't want to think about how she'd declared them lovers in a medieval past life.

He didn't want to think about how good she felt in his arms.

So he concentrated on sleep. Instead of sheep, he counted ways to get even with his pal, Vera.

Midway to one hundred, he drifted off, and for the first time in years, he dreamed. Boyhood fantasies. Castles. Knights. Damsels in distress.

Heather.

***

Sydney woke with a dull, queasy feeling. She squinted against the sun streaming through the blinds. Sluggish and disoriented, she rolled over to check her antique clock.

"Oh, no!" She grabbed her journal from her nightstand,

scribbled a hurried entry, then shot out of bed like a launched cannonball and sailed for her closet. She should have been at work an hour ago!

She threw off her nightgown, whipped out a clean uniform, and yanked it over her head. "I can't believe this." She barreled toward her dresser and attacked the contents of her top drawer. Underwear. Pantyhose. Socks.

Back to the closet. Shoes.

"I never oversleep. *Never.*" She charged out of her room, two doors down to the bathroom, squirted paste on her toothbrush, then scrubbed her teeth. Rinse. Spit. "Never."

Deodorant. Mascara. Spritz of perfume.

She galloped down the stairs and whizzed toward the front door. Twisted the knob. Stuck. Yanked harder. Jammed.

"Unlock it. It'll make your life easier."

She gasped and spun around.

Winn.

She tried to catch her breath. "I forgot you were here."

The realization stunned her. As she stood in her front hall with toothpaste on her uniform, everything suddenly felt surreal.

"Now that's a first," he muttered.

"What?"

"Never mind."

Sydney's reeling mind slowed enough to register the reality of her houseguest. He stood midway down the stairs, one hand gripping the banister. No shirt. No socks. No shoes. He'd obviously just rolled out of bed. Thank God he'd remembered to tug on his jeans. His bare chest alone made it difficult to keep her eyes on his face. The thought of him in his briefs or, Lord have mercy, *naked* left her dizzy.

Her misery mounted as he called attention to his toned biceps by combing his hand through his hair. Bed-mussed hair that fell free of his ponytail and skimmed his muscled shoulders.

"I don't lock my doors," she blurted, trying to temper the sensual heat burning her skin from the inside out.

"You should."

The only person she needed protection from was him. She had to get out of here before she did something stupid, like beg to be kissed. "I don't have time for a lecture on crime statistics, Mr. Lacey. I'm late for work."

He came down a step. "I know. Hal's Coffee Shop called an hour ago."

"And you didn't wake me?"

He moved to the bottom of the stairs. "I didn't want to disturb you. You had a rough night."

Her stomach dropped. "Is that what you told them?"

Winn flashed a guileless smile. "*Them* being Ida Louise? Yes, that's what I told her. No need to get upset. She said she understood."

"I bet she did." Sydney tapped the toe of her paisley-printed combat boots on the hardwood floor. "A strange man answers my phone at seven in the morning and tells Ida Louise, the most notorious gossip in town, that I'm sleeping in because I had a *rough night!*" She jerked around and jiggled the lock. "I have to get to work before David gets wind of this. Do me a favor, Mr. Lacey, don't do me any more favors."

Winn ignored her request by walking up behind her and releasing the lock she continued to struggle with. "You should've told him the truth last night. About my staying over."

Sydney's cheeks burned. She felt both a liar and a fool. "I didn't have the energy."

"You said he'd understand my staying here."

She wanted to crawl back under the covers and hide. "I said that for Ellie's benefit. She thinks David's—" She stopped short. Winn wouldn't understand. He'd become suspicious of David and that was just...ridiculous.

Winn turned her around. "Go on."

Landing up close and personal with his bare chest, she closed her eyes. One minute she wanted to slug him, the next she wanted to kiss him. Somehow she resisted the urge to do either. "She thinks he's..."

"Yes?"

She fought the words but they tumbled out anyway. "Obsessed. With me."

"Is he?" His tone demanded a straight answer.

"I'll admit, David's very...attentive."

"Attentive? Sure you don't mean possessive?"

"No! No, of course not. I mean, I can't blame him for feeling a little insecure. He proposed to me at the coffee shop last month, in front of everyone, and I still haven't given him an answer."

Winn placed his fingers under her chin and tilted it up. "Look at me, Sydney."

When she did, he removed his hand, leaving her skin cold. "What about you? Are you head over heels for him?"

No, she thought, breathing in the faded scent of Winn's expensive cologne, *I'm out of my head for you.* "I don't want to hurt David. He's been extremely kind. He cared for my mother and..." *I owe him.* "Please. I have to go."

"I'd like to talk to you about last night."

She cringed. "I know my past-life theory sounded crazy. I know you don't believe me, and I don't blame you. Honestly, I'm surprised you're still here and not on a plane home. I must've rambled on about reincarnation for three hours."

His eyes narrowed with concern. "Actually, I was referring to what happened after that."

"What do you mean? I went to bed."

"You don't remember?"

"Remember what?"

"Sleepwalking."

Sydney blinked in surprise. "You sleepwalk?"

"Not me. You."

"I don't sleepwalk."

"You did last night."

She planted her hands on her hips. "You're kidding, right?"

Winn raised a skeptical brow. "You don't remember climbing out your attic window and standing on the edge of the roof? Gazing out at your yard, admiring the heather? You don't remember any of that?"

Sydney pressed her fingertips to her temples. "I remember something like that," she admitted, then realized with a rush of excitement, "I dreamed that."

"No. You did that."

"*Something* like that," she amended as she began to remember. After all these years her dream had finally opened up to reveal another scene from the lovers' lives. Her skin tingled with anticipation. "Not last night, but hundreds of years ago. And it wasn't the edge of my roof. It was the ledge of a castle. Baldric yanked Gillian from the battlement wall and saved her from a fall. I think it was when they'd first met." She paused, her eyes widening. "Did you have the same dream?" She clutched his arms. "Do you know what this means?"

Winn studied her for a long moment. "It wasn't Gillian and Baldric. It was you and me. And it happened last night, not hundreds of years ago."

She shook her head, hopes soaring. "But it *did*. Don't you see? If what you say is true, then history *is* repeating itself."

He withdrew his arms from her grasp and gestured to her bookshelves. "What I *see* is more past-life literature than a new-age bookstore. You've memorized passages from King Arthur novels and scenes from period movies. You've decorated your house like a fourteenth-century museum. Monroe may be obsessed with you, but you're obsessed with everything medieval and, quite frankly, Sydney, it troubles me."

"I told you, David's not obsessed. Neither am I." Her voice climbed an octave. "I'm not crazy."

"I didn't say you were crazy."

"You're thinking it. Deny it. Go ahead. Tell me you're not envisioning me wrapped in something white with buckles."

He jammed his hand through his hair. "I admit I'm concerned."

She crossed her arms. "Why are you concerned? Why do you care? Have you thought about that? You don't even know me. We met for the first time yesterday, or so you're certain."

"Sydney, you're asking too much of me. You said yourself, your past-life theory is difficult to believe. I don't know what you expect. Admit that I'm Baldric? Sweep you away to my imaginary castle and live happily ever after?"

His tone was gentle, cautious even, but his words still cut.

"I would've thought solving a mystery would appeal to the likes of an ex-cop. Obviously, I was wrong."

She stormed out the front door. It slammed one too many times. She spun around, glaring at Winn in a showdown on her front walk. "You don't have to follow me. I'm not going to drive off like a lunatic—oh, excuse me, bad word choice. Whatever, I'm not going to drive my car into a tree. I'm not suicidal."

"I'm not so sure," he said, hands on hips. "You climbed through a window and stood on the edge of your roof in the middle of the night."

She stalked up to within an inch of the infuriating man. "I wasn't contemplating suicide. I was saying goodbye."

He cocked his head. "To whom?"

"To Heatherwood. My home." An ache clutched her stomach. She pressed her palm against it as her thoughts muddled and blurred. "I mean...I don't know what I mean. I don't profess to have all the answers. I...I have to go. I'm late."

He grabbed her arm as she turned. "Why are you holding your stomach like that?"

She moved her hand and waved off his concern. "It's nothing. I haven't been sleeping well, that's all."

"You look like you're going to cry. Does it hurt that much?"

"I told you. I'm late for work. You know, *my job* at the coffee shop, where everyone will be whispering behind their menus, thank you very much. I'm sure Ida Louise is having a field day as we speak."

"Call in sick."

"I can't afford to." She swept her hand down her pale blue uniform and tugged at the frilly apron. "Maybe you haven't noticed, but this dress isn't exactly my style. I'm a waitress. Tips help pay the bills, and I'm not earning any standing here."

She turned her back on him and their discussion. No matter how he hedged it, he thought her crazy. Well, she wasn't. She was as sane as he. But *she* had an open mind. *She* had the ability to trust her instincts and to believe in the impossible. *He* was stubborn and too logical for his own good. He hadn't changed one bit.

"Miss Vaughn...Sydney. Wait up."

He caught her hand as she reached for the car door. As his skin connected with hers, an incredible serenity flowed through her, warming even her bones. The bright colors of the morning sharpened as she turned to face him. Longing ached in her throat. She wanted to clutch him to her, bury her face in his neck, breathe in his scent. Feel his heartbeat against her own. *She'd missed him.*

"You're upset," he said. "If you're going to be bullheaded about this, at least let me drive you."

The instant he released her hand, an inexplicable fear roared through her like howling wind. With trembling fingers, Sydney swiped at the tear sliding down her cheek. "I'll be fine."

"I insist. Wait here while I throw on a shirt and shoes."

He hurried to the house but seemed reluctant to leave her, peering over his shoulder every few steps.

I'm not crazy. I'm not.

She waited for the screen door to slam before jumping into her car and speeding away. Hot tears streamed down her face as she ran from the one man she'd been searching for all of her life.

***

"Fool." Winn slid on his mirrored sunglasses and stalked to his rental car. He'd asked her to wait. Of course she hadn't listened.

He peeled out of the long driveway, determined to catch her. The way things were going, she just might faint and crash into oncoming traffic, if there was such a thing in Slocum.

As he sped down the country lane, his city-bred eyes skimmed over the rural landscape. Fields of unidentifiable crops stretched toward the horizon on either side of the road. An occasional house or barn sprang up as if to serve as mile markers.

Out of nowhere, a foul stench slammed into him as sure as a baseball bat. Farm animals. Pigs to be precise. He spotted the pens to his left and held his breath until the odometer clocked a good half-mile. It didn't help matters that he had the mother of all hangovers. He'd give anything for an aspirin the size of a tractor tire.

By the time he caught sight of Sydney's car, his mood had turned as rank as that pig-polluted stretch of road. He parallel parked and hustled into the coffee shop hot on the heels of Sydney's psychedelic combat boots. Her shoes were as wild as her uniform was conservative. A paradox, just like the woman who wore them.

He'd handled her with the care of a suspicious package this morning, convinced she was one step from the loony bin. But when he'd looked out the window to see her racing out of the driveway without him, something inside him snapped. He'd promised Vera her niece's safety, whether the niece liked it or not. He'd never forgive himself if something happened to Sydney, and he sure as hell didn't want to fly home to explain his sudden incompetence to Vera.

He needed this worry like he needed a case of head lice.

Winn cut through the narrow aisles of the packed café, ignoring the curious glances of its patrons. Before Sydney could round the corner of the old-fashioned lunch counter, he nabbed her elbow. "I asked you to wait."

She looked nervous but not surprised. With her voice hushed and her gaze darting about the café, she replied, "I needed to be alone. I needed time to think straight. I can't seem to do that when you're around."

Winn commiserated. She was doing one helluva scramble on his own thought processes. He took off his sunglasses. "About last night…"

"We made love."

Taken aback, he lowered his own voice. "That part slips my mind, and I generally remember having sex. I didn't have *that* much to drink."

"Not last night. Centuries ago."

He shook his head. Amazing. Her eyes seemed clear, lucid. She sounded earnest, honestly believing what she was claiming. How did one argue with that? No amount of training had prepared him for this conversation. "Sydney—"

"I sorted through the puzzle while I drove. The pieces are starting to fit into place. I don't have any proof. I didn't dream about us making love…yet."

"As if that would be proof."

She ignored him. "I know it in my gut. We were lovers."

Winn held a firm grip on his patience. "You mean *they* were lovers."

"Baldric and Gillian. You and I. We're one and the same. We share the same souls. The same destiny. We'll live and die as we did centuries ago, and I fear we did not die happy."

Forks and knives clattered against plates. Breakfast chatter at the counter ceased altogether.

Winn tugged Sydney back toward the wall between the pay phone and the john. "Sydney, we met each other yesterday, not centuries ago. Past lives. Reincarnation. It's bull. Believing you lived a medieval life lands you at the same convention as Alien Abductions Anonymous. Spout these words to the wrong people, and you'll find yourself bouncing off padded walls."

She knocked his hand from her elbow. "I'm not crazy, you unenlightened cynic. Just because you don't remember our making love doesn't mean it didn't happen. The human mind has the capacity to block out damaging memories, memories too painful to deal with. Something tragic happened all those years ago. Something awful. You may not remember, you may not want to believe, but I'm telling you…*we made love!*"

The patrons sucked in a collective gasp.

Winn ignored them. Sydney's reference to memories got under his skin. He recalled the image of the castle surrounded by heather and the other bouts of déjà vu he'd experienced last night. He'd attributed them to alcohol. Now she had him wondering, and he didn't like it.

"Where?" he challenged.

"What?"

"Where did this intimate interlude, this *physical* interlude that I have no recollection of, take place? Facts, Sydney. I was a cop. I need evidence."

She faltered. "I told you. I can't prove it. It's a gut feeling."

"Information, Sydney. If you're so sure *it* happened, give

me a place."

"England, I guess."

He crossed his arms. "I've never been to England."

She frowned at him. "You know full well I'm not referring to *this* life."

An old woman cackled. "This is better than my afternoon soap."

The moment struck Winn with the same punch as the pig stench. He was standing in a crowded Indiana coffee shop, arguing with a crazy woman over whether they'd made love in a past life.

Unbelievable.

Sydney Vaughn pulled the plug on his rationality. She made it impossible to maintain any professionalism. She pried at every belief he'd firmly nailed down.

Just look at her, he thought. Frilly, little waitress uniform and clunky combat boots. Long, fairylike curls in sexy disarray. Pale skin flushed in frustration. Damn, if she didn't look like a modern-day damsel in distress.

He wanted to turn around and walk out of her life. He wanted to forget he'd ever met her. He wanted to… "Since we were lovers, I assume you won't have a problem with this, kid."

He held her face captive between his hands and kissed her, seeking an end to the sudden and mysterious hunger swirling in his gut. He caressed her lower lip with his tongue, warning her only moments before he claimed her mouth completely.

Expecting her to pull back, he groaned when she countered his assault with an urgency of her own. She plowed her fingers into his hair, pulling him closer. Her mouth was warm, silky…he'd never tasted anything sweeter.

When she moaned low in her throat, he lost any remaining control. He couldn't get enough of her. He needed to feel her heat, her softness, the rise and fall of her breath. Pressing her back against the wall with his body, she melted into him without hesitation.

His thoughts spun into a wild, unleashed funnel. The floor

seemed to drop out beneath him. Suddenly, his every tingling nerve, his pulse, his entire being connected with her, as though she were sustaining his life, supplying his very breath.

Like long-lost lovers reunited.

The sharp realization severed the surging connection.

It left him dizzy, exhausted, and scared as hell.

Sydney began to slide down the wall.

Before he could reach for her, a fist plowed into his face and knocked him cold.

Six

Simon charged into the bedchamber, nostrils flaring. "She is a brat as well as a witch. I suggest you join us in the bailey, Brother. Your diplomatic abilities are much in need." He held his capable hands a dagger's width apart. "I am *this* close to turning that girl over my knee."

Baldric motioned Ivo forth with his hauberk, then shrugged into it. "Witch. Brat. Girl. I assume you refer to Gillian?"

Simon looked as though his brother had just clubbed him from behind. "Gillian? Not Lady Marrick or even Lady Gillian, but *Gillian?*" His face burned, his warrior fire stoked. "'Tis as I feared. You have been robbed of your sensibilities. The girl slaps and insults you in front of nobles and servants alike, and you affectionately refer to her as *Gillian.*"

Baldric folded his arms over his chest, allowing Ivo to strap his scabbard and sword about his waist. "My sensibilities are intact, Brother, as is my pride. *Lady* Gillian is under the misconception that Redmere murdered Catherine and Margaret. She imagines me delivering her to the same fate, which explains if not excuses her outburst."

Simon replicated his brother's stance, though his own expression reeked of incredulity. "When, pray tell, did you learn this delicious fodder?"

"Last night." Baldric offered no further explanation. He'd foolishly betrayed his peculiar fondness for the girl by speaking familiarly of her. A mistake he vowed not to repeat. "Now, what has you in such a temper? I implore you to tread lightly, Simon. Your shouting knocks my skull like a battering ram."

"Had you not swilled ale as though your life depended on it, I dare say you would not be suffering this morn."

"Is that a reprimand?"

"Merely an observation. Were I to withstand public humiliation such as Lady Gillian bestowed upon you, I too would have sought to numb my anger. 'Tis not as if you could challenge her upon the field."

Baldric raised a brow. "Or turn her over my knee in the bailey?"

"Aye," Simon agreed, serious to the bone. "Though she could stand a good spanking."

Ivo giggled.

Baldric poked the boy with his elbow. "You have never struck a woman in your life, Simon."

Simon appeared truly disgruntled. "There is a first time for everything, I assure you."

Baldric laughed—though it hurt his head—and gave his dear brother's shoulder a good-natured rap. "Let us go and see what Lady Gillian has done to earn such a threat."

Their boots crunched over the sea of dirt and gravel as they crossed the bailey. The intermittent patches of grass struck Baldric as pitiable and sad, reminding him of Gillian, clinging to a place that could no longer support them.

Baldric halted to survey the chaotic scene before him. Servants struggled to shoulder yet another trunk onto an overloaded cart while Lord Marrick's dogs barked and ran circles around the large, wooden wheels.

Instantly, his gaze found her. She stood with her back to him but it mattered not. His memory burned with the vision of her slight frame stiff with false bravery. It burned with the knowledge that, beneath those stubborn shoulders, muscles quivered and blood ran thick with ice. God, but he wished to wrap her in his arms and assure her there was naught to fear. He wished she would turn to face him. Wished to see that his memories were naught but ale-induced dreams.

However, instead of moving forth, he remained still. Closing his eyes, he breathed in the morning mist. He would cease these futile fantasies at once. He would surrender not a fraction of his attention on the dangerous journey ahead.

"My books," he heard Gillian order. "I wish them to be packed as well."

He opened his eyes as an old man nodded and scurried back into the keep.

Simon jabbed an open palm at the scene. "Look at this

madness. She has overloaded that cart and bid another one at her disposal. I explained to her that weighted carts shall slow our travel, that we will be the fatted turkey begging to be plucked and stuffed. Would you guess that the little menace dismissed me with a scowl? Redmere will not be pleased."

"Simon, I do believe you are too easily insulted."

"*I* would not risk Darbingshire because Lady Gillian insists on packing everything but the well bucket." Without another word, Simon stalked away.

Baldric frowned. It disturbed him that Simon exhibited so little faith in him. His brother had never questioned his competence before. *Never.* Did Simon really believe Baldric would leave Gillian—or any of them—susceptible to harm by submitting to her sulking whims?

He would prove to them all, this moment, that he commanded this journey. Not Gillian.

"My spinning wheel," she said to Eloise. "That is what we have forgotten. Pray, see to it."

Eloise curtsied, then turned on her heels. When she saw him, her jaw dropped. Baldric motioned for silence, then waved her away. He stepped into her place beside Gillian. "Willingham has spinning wheels aplenty."

She did not look at him. "If I am never to see Heatherwood again, then I will take that which will keep it alive in my mind, even as my heart shrivels and dies." Her voice no longer held the quiet desperation of the eve before. Instead, a sharp edge warned him she was brewing for battle.

He tried to sidestep it. "I am sure Redmere will allow you to visit your home upon occasion."

She snorted. "I should live so long."

"Your fears are unjustified."

"Are they?" she challenged, a bitter bite in her voice.

"The spinning wheel stays."

"Goes."

"Stays."

"Goes."

Encroaching silence caught his attention. He peered up from the insolent face to find servants scrambling back to work.

Baldric grit his teeth. This childish stalemate was not easing his situation. He refused to let anyone think, even for a moment, that he could not handle one defiant woman. His reputation, any respect he would have formerly commanded, would be destroyed. 'Twould be deadly.

"'Twas suggested a good spanking might change your stubborn tune," he said loudly enough for passersby to hear. "Would you have me put that theory to the test?"

Hearing a collective gasp, he felt somewhat vindicated.

"Eloise," Gillian called, "do not trouble thyself." Then she crossed her arms and glared at him. "Happy?"

His fingers itched to complete the task Simon had recommended. "'Twould appear you are not completely ignorant of reason. In the future, however, I request that you not argue when my brother or I give you instruction. Brentwood Forest is a haven for thieves who will think naught of trying to murder us for that treasure-laden cart."

"Treasures?" she cried. "Think you if I possessed *treasures* I would not have sold them long ago for the benefit of all concerned?" She stabbed her finger at the cart. "Think you within lies a dowry? Exquisite furniture? Silk? Jewels? Think again, Sir Baldric." She swept her hand wide. "Look around. We are of humble means. My father is a noble, aye. He owns Heatherwood, aye. Yet we are rich only in our love for each other and this land."

She paused, drawing a deep breath as two hunchbacked men sidled past to hoist a crate of books onto the burdened cart. "My mother's books," she explained. "She was an educated woman. She used to read to me for hours. Memories. I have heaped them upon this cart. *Memories*. Treasures to no one but myself."

She stirred his blood with her impassioned talk of love and devotion—for her family, her home, this land, and its people. He longed to his bones for those very things himself. She possessed them, and now, this day, she was losing them.

'Twas a woman's fate to sacrifice her dreams for the benefit of a man. 'Twas rotten and despicable and he loathed it. But 'twas the way of the world, and one fool man could not take on that crusade any easier than he could take on the Scots. Nor did he wish to take it on, for in the end, 'twould do his own dreams not a bit of good. Nor was the girl his to champion.

Baldric hardened his heart and his voice. "There are other places for storing memories, Lady Gillian." With his fingertips, he tapped her forehead, "Here," then her heart, "and here. One cart. Heap on it what you can, then issue your farewells. We are leaving."

He turned and walked away.

Simon fell into step beside him. "Well said, Brother."

"Go to hell," Baldric muttered, leaving his brother behind. "Giffard! FitzHubert! Mount up. Ivo!"

The squire scrambled forth, kicking up a cloud of dust in his hurried wake. "Sir?"

"Help Maid Eloise onto the seat of the wagon, then climb up beside her. You are driving."

Ivo swelled with importance as he grinned ear to ear. "Aye, sir." He ran off to do his bidding.

Baldric wished life could be that simple again.

"She is a handful, that daughter of mine." Lord Marrick's tone held no censure or apology as he joined Baldric. He waved his gnarled hand toward the stable. "Come, let us talk in private."

Together they walked. Baldric said nothing, allowing Marrick to steer the conversation.

"Forgive me, Sir Baldric. I was detained within the keep. An argument between domestics. I did, however, notice all of the crates, trunks, and furniture being toted past me in the process of my smoothing ruffled feathers. Gillian has always been of the sentimental lot."

Baldric grunted.

"It is," Marrick continued, "perhaps the only soft thing about my daughter. She has known much sadness in her young life. It has made her…"

"Belligerent?"

Lord Marrick smiled. "Wary. Cynical, perhaps. Certainly realistic. She understands that life is sometimes—or in our case usually—disappointing. She had three brothers, you know."

Baldric furrowed his brows. "I did not."

"Oh, they loved and spoiled her so," Marrick said, with the same haunted look he'd seen in Gillian's eyes. "We lost Guy, my oldest son, to Edward I and his campaign against the Scots. My youngest boy, John, succumbed to smallpox as did his mother, God rest her soul."

They reached the weatherworn stable. He regarded the old man with restrained pity. Baldric had lost family members of his own. He'd known the pain of personal loss, though he'd never experienced the wrenching heartache of losing a son, or a wife. "What of your second son?"

"Aidan? Dead, they say…" Marrick's words trailed off into a wheeze and his chest shuddered as he tried to stay a fit of coughing.

Baldric took a step toward the flushed-faced man but was waved off. "I have refused to believe that my last son is dead," he said, breath returning, "though with each passing day it becomes more difficult. He has been missing for more than a year now. `Tis rumored he met his end on the fields of Bannockburn."

Baldric tensed, the ragged scar on his back twitching. "A humiliating defeat for the English, though I am certain your son fought bravely." He refrained from adding, *`Twas the man who led the troops who deserved the shame of the loss. No other.* Despite his heart-and-soul belief in thus, never would he speak such treason. Besides, the King's popularity already decayed like a cabbage too long on the vine. His obsession with his male lover, his idleness and frivolity, his inability to rule his kingdom with a responsible hand—all worked to turn his own people against him. Bannockburn had branded Edward II a poor soldier as well as a coward.

"Thousands suffered under the wrath of the Scots," Baldric said. "What makes you believe your son survived that which felled so many?"

"You survived."

"Barely."

"Alas, how the old mind forgets," the man sputtered

between a new bout of coughing. "You are immortal."

"So they say." Baldric frowned, concerned about Oswald Marrick. Though strong in spirit, the old man's health deteriorated seemingly by the hour. Baldric had witnessed several coughing spells since arriving yesterday, each worse than the one before. Marrick had claimed a bothersome cold. Baldric did not believe him. However, 'twas not his place to dispute.

As they stepped into the stable, Baldric surveyed the near-empty stalls. He wondered if the two horses reined to Gillian's cart had been taken from the fields. Certainly the two nags before him could not replace them, long in the tooth as they were and oblivious to their master's arrival. How would Marrick manage without his strongest laborers?

At once Baldric fully grasped the severity of Heatherwood's destitution. Surely Gillian would see that her marriage to Redmere was for the best.

"Unfortunately," Marrick said, regaining his composure and patting one of the indifferent nags on the nose, "Gilly does not share my optimistic attitude toward Aidan's fate. If he were alive, she claims, we would have heard from him by now. Thus, in her eyes, it falls to her to look after me. It angers her to be sent away. It angers her...for many reasons. She may grumble and pout along the way, but she will do as I bid. She will marry Baron Redmere. In turn, he will care for her and save our beloved Heatherwood."

Baldric did not hesitate. "I will see your daughter safely to Willingham, Lord Marrick. On this you have my word."

"The word of Sir Baldric the Immortal. There is none I trust more." He clasped the younger man on the shoulder before ambling back toward the open door of the stable to watch his daughter. "Be patient with her. Befriend her. You know Redmere. Ease her fears. They are misplaced." He looked to Baldric. "Are they not?"

"Aye," Baldric assured him, "they are misplaced."

"Good. Now, please excuse me as I must bid my daughter farewell."

Baldric lagged behind, allowing Marrick his privacy. The

man was likable enough but did not have the instincts to command a fortress. Troubles such as these at Heatherwood did not arise in one season. Nay, they resulted from years of poor choices and shortsighted planning. Baldric himself carried the weight of his father's folly, and as he witnessed the sacrifice of a daughter for the father's lacking, he vowed never to leave his children with such a dubious legacy. Once Darbingshire was his, he would dedicate his life to home and family. None of which would be possible without Redmere.

Surely in time, the distressed Lady Gillian would see past the wrinkles and the gruff to the man who'd helped Baldric at every turn in life. He had known Redmere from the time he was a boy, training as a squire upon the fields of Willingham. The baron had displayed nothing but encouragement and pride. Need Baldric even consider the kindness and generosity the baron had bestowed upon his sister, Lisbeth?

Nay, Gillian need put her fears to rest. `Twas a ridiculous notion, Redmere a cold-blooded murderer.

He strode toward his steed. He would think on the matter no more.

After tearful farewells between Gillian and those she had known and loved since birth, Baldric led the entourage through the raised gate, over the drawbridge, and out into the glen.

He rode alongside his ward but struggled to keep his eyes averted. She had a peculiar way of twisting everything inside of him. Mayhap he understood duty and the sacrifices it demanded, but loyalty could only dispel so much fear in a girl as four strange men escorted her from her only home.

She sniffled. His gaze drifted despite himself.

He watched her swipe at her tears and square her shoulders, seemingly resigning herself to her fate. Then she angled her chin as if ready to do battle with the world.

He tore away his gaze and tightened his grip on the reins.

"Steel thy heart." Simon repeated his previous warning in Baldric's ear before jerking his horse's reins and settling along the other side of the girl.

Gillian bit her lip, refusing to shed one more tear. She had to be strong. For her father. For Heatherwood.

She twisted in her saddle for one last look at her home. Her father stood just inside the weathered portcullis. He waved. She waved back. She even smiled, for his sake. He'd promised to visit her at Willingham before the winter's snow piled too high, and though he'd made the vow in earnest, she doubted she would ever see him again.

A sob scalded her throat. She swallowed hard, refusing to give it voice. Somehow she summoned the strength to turn away from all she'd ever known and loved. She would proceed. As much as it frightened her, she would proceed to Willingham. She would not deny her father his dying wish.

Sir Baldric and Sir Simon rode on either side of her. She stared straight ahead, willing the return of her composure and dignity. Just before the forest's edge, however, she faltered. Sickened with grief and pride forsaken, she slid from her mare and fell to her knees.

The two knights vaulted from their saddles.

"Please," she implored before they could haul her from the ground. "I need a moment." She turned solemn eyes to Baldric. "Only a moment."

He narrowed his eyes but nodded.

Simon signaled the entourage to hold, displeasure evident in his scowl. Baldric led his brother a few steps away, though not so far that they couldn't catch her in a breath should she decide to run.

She felt like a prisoner and knew this was only the beginning.

In a desperate, final attempt to forever embrace the essence of her home, she plucked wildly at the abundant heather, dropping the flowers into the pouch looped about her waist.

She sensed Baldric understood. Last night he had held her hand as she'd balanced on the battlement wall and bid farewell to her home. She had been grateful then, and in like, was grateful now. He did not hasten her, even though she could hear the agitated grousing of Sir Robert and Sir William as they rode forth against Simon's bidding.

She did not trust nor did she like Redmere's knights. In a short time they had shown themselves to be ignorant and cruel, and she breathed a bit easier when Baldric ordered them to fall back behind the cart.

Her pouch filled, she stood and brushed grass and dirt from her gown. Her hands stilled as a peculiar sense of calm settled over her. Were she the fanciful sort, she might have believed the heather in her pouch responsible for the tranquil sensation.

As if mere flowers could heal trampled emotions.

Impossible, she told herself.

Still, she somehow felt better armed to face whatever waited in the forest…and beyond.

A twig snapped.

Gillian jerked up her chin.

Baldric stood close, jaw hard, eyes stoic. "All is well?"

"Not well," she admitted, "but endurable."

He stared at her for a moment, eyes devoid of emotion, then wordlessly assisted her onto her horse.

She watched as he remounted his eager destier with experienced grace. Truly, he was magnificent. Mayhap there was truth in the heroic stories he inspired. Mayhap Sir Baldric the Immortal was all he'd been professed to be—good, true, kind to a fault.

Mayhap, Gillian thought, as he led the entourage under the dark green canopy of Brentwood Forest, all was not lost.

Seven

Present Day

"How much longer you think he's gonna lie there?"

Winn cracked open an eye.

The bowlegged grandpa closest to him checked his watch. "Awe, darn it. I'm out."

The sweet-faced old lady next to him shot out her hand over Winn's head. "Fork it over, Floyd. Harvey. Pete. You too, Ida Louise."

So much for sweet. Dollar bills begrudgingly appeared out of wallets and pockets and were snatched up by greedy gnarled fingers.

While the white-haired cutthroat counted her booty, Floyd leaned over at the hips and scrutinized Winn. "Two minutes, thirty-three seconds. Hope you're happy, mister. I lost my toast."

Winn closed his eyes. Great. He'd turned into a roadside attraction.

"Is he out again?"

"Not so fast with that money, Helen," said Ida Louise.

"I'm awake," Winn said and shoved himself upright. The room dipped, but he grit his teeth and focused through fuzzy eyes at the senior citizens' faces. They glared back at him.

Again that disoriented feeling. Like he expected to find himself somewhere else.

Maybe it was wishful thinking.

Oh yeah. It all came back to him now.

Chasing Sydney to the diner. Arguing. Kissing.

He pointed to his throbbing cheekbone. "Monroe?"

"You bet your home-wreckin' patooty," Floyd said.

Ida Louise, the red-headed gum-snapper and the only person in the room besides Winn under fifty, hooted. "Family friend, my foot. I've never seen friends kiss like that."

"Where's Sydney?"

Pete sniffed. "With Monroe. Where she belongs."

Helen tucked away her money, then looked at him in such disgust, he expected her to whip out a can of disinfectant. Not very appreciative since he just made her a roll of dough. "Who do you think you are kissing the sheriff's girl like that? In the very spot where he proposed?"

Sheriff? Monroe? Vera said the man had money. She never said anything about him being a cop. How the hell could she forget to tell him that? Knowing Vera, it was for the look on his face right now.

Floyd narrowed his faded blue eyes. "You're dang lucky Sydney refused to press charges."

"You're dang lucky to be breathing," Harvey added. "I ain't never seen the sheriff lose his temper like that. Never."

Winn snapped. "And you let Sydney go with him?"

Floyd stiffened and raised his chin. "Sheriff Monroe protects the people in this town. Sydney included. He's not mad at her. You're the one who attacked!"

The little crowd murmured in agreement.

Winn pressed a palm to his aching head and climbed to his feet. "Where'd he take her?"

"None of your business," said Floyd.

Helen wagged a finger at him. "Your attack made her sick to her stomach."

Winn felt like a lumbering Frankenstein about to be lynched by villagers. "I did not attack Sydney."

They stumbled over each other jumping on that one.

"Oh, and I suppose she let you kiss her?"

"You should be in handcuffs."

"Sheriff Monroe wanted you in jail for assault, but Sydney wouldn't have it." Floyd shook his head as though the world had gone to crap and he'd just stepped in it. "Don't understand her lately. Normally she's such a sensible girl."

Winn's thoughts whirled. Sydney? Sensible?

"Her mother just died," Helen scolded Floyd. "Have a little respect."

"Respect-schmect," Pete piped in. "Linda wanted Sydney to marry Monroe so bad, she probably put it in her will."

The women sucked in appalled breaths. The men tried not

to smile. Except Floyd, Monroe's pit bull.

"Dang smart of Linda if you ask me," he said. "Sydney living out there all by herself when a good man like the sheriff is crazy about her. Makes no sense." He turned on Winn, hands perched on his bony hips. "So don't think you can waltz in here, mister, and steal his woman. He won't let you. This ain't the Old West, you know."

The spinning in Winn's head slowed. "What do you mean, he won't let me?"

Helen raked her gaze over Winn. "Where you from, anyway?"

"New Jersey."

They all looked at each other. Harvey spoke their minds. "That explains it."

Floyd raised a suspicious salt-and-pepper brow. "Maybe you should clear out of here before you cause more trouble."

"You don't want to cause more trouble, young man, or Sheriff Monroe will really give you what for," Helen said. "Know what I mean?"

Winn's head cleared. No, he didn't know what she meant, but as he was about to ask, Ellie burst through the coffee shop's front door.

"Thought you were helping your boss with Sydney," Floyd said.

Ellie stalked past the old man. She had a full head of steam aimed at Winn. "She sent me back here to look after you, you...you..." She cursed and slapped his shoulder. "I don't know how things work where you're from, but around here we generally get to know a person before groping them. Even then we refrain from public groping."

"Yeah," the old folks chimed.

Winn's head throbbed. "I did not grope Sydney."

"Let's not get technical. The result's the same. You're a letch."

"You tell 'em, Ellie."

He reminded himself she was looking out for Sydney, something he was supposed to be doing. Instinct told him he wouldn't get the answers he wanted from Monroe's geriatric groupies, so he nabbed Ellie's elbow and led her from the coffee shop.

"Look at the way he manhandles these women!"

"I'm tellin' the sheriff."

Winn ignored them and let the door swing hard behind him.

"You work for Monroe?"

"So?"

The door opened and people crammed in the frame to eavesdrop. Others had their noses pressed against the front window glass.

"Where's Sydney?"

"David took her home."

Something akin to fear snaked around his heart and squeezed tight. It was a new and unsettling sensation. "Why didn't you go with her?"

"She made me stay with you. To make sure you got out of here before David came back. This is the first time he's ever lost his temper. She's scared."

He dug his keys from his pocket as he hustled to his car.

Ellie was on his heels. "She's not scared for herself. David won't hurt her. She's scared for you."

Winn spun around. "If Monroe's never lost his temper before, how can everyone be so sure he won't hurt her?"

"Because he's angry at you, not her."

"He really believes I attacked her? He doesn't blame her one little bit?"

Ellie went still a moment, then whipped out her own keys. "I know shortcuts."

He jumped into her pickup, scattering empty Happy Meal boxes and various Barbie body parts. Ellie revved the engine and ground the gears. "You've turned this town upside down, Winn Lacey. I hope you're happy."

He shoved on his sunglasses. "Why does everyone keep asking me that? Do I look goddamned happy?"

Neither of them spoke as she zoomed down Main Street, over the railroad tracks, and out of town. The stuffy air crackled with tension.

By the time they reached the road that led to Sydney's, Ellie was pushing sixty-five. She barely slowed for a curve, swerving one-handed to avoid an indecisive squirrel.

Winn clutched the dashboard. "Keep your eyes on the road, Bane, and both hands on the wheel."

"Keep your pants on, Tiger. I haven't lost a passenger yet." Against his wishes, she wagged her finger at him. "You did keep them on, didn't you? Last night. You and Sydney. You didn't—"

"No," he growled, "we didn't."

"Thank God. Not that I really thought you did. Well, you might, but Sydney wouldn't."

He raised a brow.

"That kiss steamed up every window in Slocum!"

"I didn't mean to kiss her." For the first time since he'd regained consciousness he was actually able to reflect on that kiss. He raked his hands through his hair, unsure how it had even happened. One minute he was trying to convince Sydney they'd never made love, the next he'd kissed her. Like long-lost lovers. He shivered. He was not about to explain that to the Bane woman.

"You sure looked like you meant it."

Kissing Sydney Vaughn had not been one of his smarter moves. The poor girl weaved between fact and fantasy like a New York taxi driver. Instead of putting an end to her ridiculous talk, he'd probably shoved her right over the edge.

"If you don't trust that I have Sydney's best interest at heart, trust that Vera does. She sent me."

Ellie mulled that one over.

"And about Monroe—"

She held up her hand to silence him. She shifted in her seat a couple of times and sighed.

"What?"

"I don't know why I'm telling you this. I should be mad as hell at you. I was. I am. You put Sydney in a real spot." She shifted again.

"Spit it out."

She sighed once more. "About the time David started

showing interest in Sydney, my furnace croaked and my son broke his arm. I needed work. Two incomes and all that. Anyway, David was hiring an assistant, and I thought it'd be a great way to keep an eye on him." Her shoulders sagged a little. "Have you ever had a feeling about someone? Like you don't trust him, but you don't know why?"

"Instinct is life and death to a cop." Winn didn't trust Monroe even before he met the fist.

"I knew he had a temper. I'd catch glimpses of it on his face. But before you could say boo, it'd be gone. Like it was never there. I always wondered where he hid it and if one day the lid would blow. Then you showed up."

"You're not easing my mind here, Bane."

"Sorry." Ellie floored it. "But he's never done anything wrong. I mean, the only violent thing I've seen him do is punch you. And you deserved it." She gave him a little smirk before turning serious again. "I doubt he'll even raise his voice at Sydney. He'll make her feel bad though. Guilty." Her fingers tightened on the wheel. "Now that I think of it, he'll probably use this whole episode to press her into saying yes."

Winn frowned. "Why was Sydney's mother so hot for her to marry Monroe? It's obvious she doesn't love him."

They held their breaths as the car plowed past the pig farm, then Ellie answered, "It's not about love, at least not for Sydney. It's about…gratitude. And a promise."

"The plot thickens."

"It started with Sydney's mother. David went out of his way to make Linda comfortable in the last days of her illness. Sydney wouldn't take his money, but she couldn't refuse the private nurse he supplied. He charmed Linda into helping him win Syd. On paper, he's the perfect catch, and Linda made Sydney promise that she'd give David a chance. A year, she said. You'll grow to love him." Ellie didn't bother to hide her disgust. "It was her dying wish."

Winn looked at her over the rim of his sunglasses. "You're kidding."

"Nope."

He processed this new information with the scraps of

family history provided by Vera. Not that Vera had been all that forthcoming. She'd never gotten along with her dead brother's wife. She felt bad for Linda, who'd suffered for six months before succumbing to cancer, but she also felt bad for her niece. According to Vera, Sydney was still single and living at home because her mother, before she was sick, didn't want to be left alone in the farmhouse, and Sydney, always thinking of others, was too kind for her own good.

Winn guessed, that in her final days, Linda Vaughn had been forced to look to her daughter's future. Apparently, she didn't want Sydney left alone in the farmhouse either.

Ellie slowed at a stop sign, looked both ways, then gunned through the intersection. Winn tightened his seat belt, wondering how many tickets she'd racked up for reckless driving.

"David lives in a huge house. Inherited some old family money. But he doesn't want to share it with just anybody. He wants to share it with Sydney. He says her loyal heart will make her a good mother to his children. Boy, does he want children."

"She should tell him to go to hell," Winn said, "dying wish or not." She sure didn't lack the nerve. Winn thought back on this morning's heated argument. She'd more than stood her ground with him. Then again, GG believed in past lives and karma and all that bull.

"I swear he's preying on her gratitude, but she won't listen to me."

Winn spoke Vera's sentiments aloud. "Always thinking of others ahead of herself."

"That's Syd." She sighed as the farmhouse came into view. "Maybe I'm blowing things out of proportion. Maybe David would be a good husband. I just don't want her to marry him because she's grateful."

"She won't." He wasn't sure of much these days, but as he glanced at the roof Sydney had perched upon last night, he said, "She believes she's meant for another."

Ellie frowned. "Yeah, her knight in shining armor. Like he's going to just step out of her dreams or something. I dream

about Brad Pitt, and he's yet to show up on my front porch."
Winn smirked despite his tense mood.

"Don't tell me you don't have fantasies, Tiger. Everyone
does. That's what Sydney's knight is. A remnant of her
childhood fantasies. She used to live for those King Arthur
Saturday matinees. What am I saying? She still does. No
wonder she dreams about knights. I had similar dreams when
I was little. Sydney and I used to lie on her porch swing and
tell them to each other. I outgrew my fantasies. Syd's been
holding on to hers for dear life. If you ask me, that's why she's
twenty-seven and alone. Well, that and because Linda couldn't
cut the apron strings. Not that Syd was looking to go anywhere.
It breaks my heart the way she's been waiting for her knight in
shining armor to show up on her doorstep. She—"

Ellie slammed on the brakes. The car slid over the gravel,
stopping halfway up Sydney's long driveway. Dust billowed
in through the open windows. "She thinks you're him." She
pressed splayed fingers to her open mouth. "Oh, my God. That
kiss. Sydney thinks you're her knight in shining armor."

"Something like that." He opened the car door and set off
on foot for Sydney's house. Her dogs scrambled off the porch,
tongues lolling, tails wagging. "Don't you guys ever bark?"
He brushed by them, eager to find Sydney.

Ellie charged up behind him. "Listen, I don't know what
you're up to with Sydney," she said, panting and out of breath.
"I mean, if you've got the hots for her, if you're just looking
for a roll in the hay, you'd have to be a real jerk pretending to
be who you can't possibly be."

"I'm not pretending to be anyone." He stalked toward the
porch steps, annoyed at the entire situation. What the hell had
he stumbled into? He whipped open the screen door and entered
the house. It took a moment for his eyes to adjust to the dim
interior.

Ellie followed. "David wouldn't hurt her," she insisted,
though her voice sounded a little shaky. "I admit he's upset,
but he wouldn't hurt her. Not Sydney. He—"

"Adores her. I know." And he'd caught her in the arms of
another man. Men killed over that sort of thing. Certain men,

anyway. He realized he'd heard nothing about Monroe but conflicting opinions. Vera, Ellie, Sydney, and the townsfolk— all told a different story. What kind of man *was* David Monroe? Winn tore up the stairs.

He burst open Sydney's bedroom door, nearly knocking it from the hinges. Nerves taut, he loomed on the threshold, eyes intent for Monroe. Instead of the sheriff, a suit of armor stood rigid near the window. The deadly-looking guard, as tall as he, jarred him. He shouldn't have been surprised, but he still shook off a strange feeling.

Besides the empty armor, Sydney was alone. She looked small and vulnerable, curled up in the center of her queen-sized bed, arms folded around her middle. The scene tugged at a familiar chord and filled him with an unfathomable grief.

Her green gaze locked with his. Longing. Sorrow. Pain. She said nothing, yet he heard the crying of her soul. Rooted to his spot, he wondered whom she bid. Him? Or Baldric?

Ellie pushed him aside and rushed forward. "Syd, sweetie, what is it? What's wrong?"

"Nothing."

"Don't tell me nothing. You look like death." She pressed her hand to Sydney's forehead. "No fever." She looked around the room. "Where the heck is David?"

"I told him to leave. He was fawning all over me. It made me feel worse."

Ellie's lips curved. "He actually left? You must've given it to him good."

"I think he was happy for the excuse to go. He said he had unfinished business."

They both looked at Winn.

"Let me guess," Ellie said.

Sydney shook her head. "I can't believe he hit you. He's never hit anybody."

Ellie fluttered a dismissive hand at Winn. "Oh, he'll be all right. But you...I'm calling Dr. Berkley."

"Please don't. It's just the stomach flu," Sydney said, her gaze still on Winn. "I think."

Ellie pressed on. "What can I do for you? How can

I—"

"Why don't you make her some chicken soup?" Winn suggested, hoping Bane would take the hint and leave him alone with Sydney. They needed to talk. His heart beat at a sedate pace now that she was safe. He intended to keep her that way.

Ellie frowned at him. "Why don't you?"

Sydney seemed to understand his motive and pushed herself upright, keeping an arm around her stomach. "I'm not hungry. Some tea would be nice though. Do you mind?"

"What I mind is him." Ellie brushed past Winn. "Grope her and die."

Winn heard Ellie's steps on the stairs and cleared his throat. "Sydney, I—"

She closed her eyes. "Don't you dare apologize for that kiss. Don't make me feel foolish."

"It wasn't your fault. We can just forget about it."

Her eyes sprang open. "Forget about it?"

"If it makes you uncomfortable, I mean."

"Does it make you uncomfortable?"

He shoved his hands in his pockets. "No." After a couple of body shifts, he smiled. "It was nice."

"Nice?"

What was he supposed to say? That her kiss left him shaken beyond words? That nobody, not even his ex-wife, ever made him feel so much in so little time? Hell no. Best to change the subject. "Did Monroe hurt you?"

"No. He was upset. More upset than I've ever seen him. Who can blame him?" The arm about her stomach tightened. "He's hunting you down as we speak."

She looked pale, and Winn thought it was about time he met the mysterious David Monroe. No sucker punches. Straight talk. Man to man. Find out what was going on in that thick, obtuse head. Find out if he had more to worry about than a prank caller. "You rest. I'll ask Ellie if I can borrow her truck. I need to pick up some things to start securing this house."

He turned away before his eyes betrayed him.

Sydney held her breath as she listened to Winn descend

her creaky stairs. Moments later, an engine revved and raced away.

She sagged back against the pillows. A smile crept across her lips. *Nice.* Winn thought her kiss was nice. Coming from a man like Winn, nice probably meant something pretty darn good. He was logical, and a logical man—an ex-cop—wouldn't tell a girl she was pretty darn good after knowing her one day. Especially a girl like her. Nice was good.

She rubbed her stomach. The pain had disappeared.

No more David. No more Winn. No more stomachache.

Her stomach had hurt this morning, too. It seemed lately all she had to do was mention David and then came the pain. Of course, plenty of people suffered upset stomachs when faced with unpleasant situations, but her stomach maladies seemed to coincide with David Monroe. It was downright bizarre.

Thinking back, she'd never felt completely comfortable in David's company. At first, she'd dismissed her jittery stomach to the excitement of entering into a new relationship. Later, she'd attributed the queasy feeling to his possessive tendencies.

On the surface, David Monroe was every woman's dream. Wealthy, handsome, attentive. He wore a uniform. But Sydney had learned through the grapevine that he questioned townsfolk of her comings and goings. They thought it endearing. She found it annoying. He said he loved her for her kindness, yet when she was out of his sight, it was as though he didn't trust her. He denied it, of course.

Six months to go. She wouldn't break her promise to her mother, even though she knew time would change nothing. She didn't love David Monroe.

Rolling to her side, she studied the suit of armor, lifeless and gleaming in the corner of the bedroom. A theatrical prop she'd purchased from the high school years ago. She peered into the darkness behind the visor slits.

Had Baldric really come back to her? Or was she flirting with insanity?

She recalled Winn's kiss. It was everything her dreams had promised and more. It was real, it was alive, and it had sent her soul soaring to a place she never knew existed. A place she'd wanted to remain forever.

Then she'd fainted. Again.

Sydney fell back on her pillow, draped her forearm over her eyes, and groaned. "What's happening to me?"

"You're losin' it."

Sydney let her arm fall to her side. "You think so?"

Ellie set steaming cups of herbal tea on the nightstand. "You've been under a lot of stress. You need a vacation."

Sydney sipped her tea then blurted, "It's him."

"Who?"

"Baldwin and Baldric. They're one and the same. I'm sure of it."

Ellie dragged a hand over her face. "Oh, Syd. I had a feeling you were going to say that."

"Don't look at me that way. As if I'm crazy. First Winn. Now you." Sydney set down her tea then patted the mattress. "Sit down." She pulled her dream journal from the nightstand drawer and flipped to a marked page. "Here. Read this."

Ellie took the journal and skimmed the page. Her tweezed brows shot up. "You dreamed this about Baldric and…who's Gillian?"

"The maiden."

"Ohhh. Now she has a name. Gillian. Weird. Why couldn't it be something romantic like Elizabeth or Juliet?"

"Just read."

She did. "Well, it is an awful lot like when Winn showed up yesterday, with us squeezing inside the doorframe and everything. Only you didn't slap him and call him a murderer." She shrugged. "So your mind romanticized yesterday's events and embellished them a bit. So what?"

Sydney thumbed back two pages. "Read this one."

Ellie scanned Sydney's scrawled writing. "I don't get it. It's the same as the other dream I just read, only not as detailed. Was this the first draft? Did you remember more as the day went on?"

Sydney pointed to the top of the page. "Look at the date."

Ellie gasped. "Two days before Winn showed up."

"I had the same dream the day before Winn arrived, during an afternoon nap, then again last night. Only last night there was even more to it." Sydney turned three pages.

Ellie read. "It's awfully sketchy. You jump around a lot, Syd. Your thoughts are disjointed."

"I know. I try to record my dreams as soon as I wake up. You know, while the memories are still fresh. But these, I guess I was still half asleep. It's frustrating. In the light of day, I remember only fragments instead of whole scenes. Feelings more than images."

Ellie pointed to a scribbled entry. "Oh, this part is sweet. Baldric holds her hand while she balances on the wall to say goodbye."

"According to Winn, he caught me standing on the edge of my roof last night."

"What!"

"He said I was sleepwalking."

"Since when do you sleepwalk?"

"Since last night, I guess. Why would he make up something like that?"

Ellie shook her finger at Sydney. "Fainting. Sleepwalking. Locking lips with a strange man in the middle of the coffee shop! What's happening to you?"

Sydney grinned. "I thought you said I was losing it."

Ellie glowered at her.

"I don't know for sure," Sydney finally answered with a shrug, "but my guess is I'm repeating history."

Ellie gave her best disapproving-mother glare. "You know how I feel about past lives."

"You don't believe in them."

"Right-o."

"So explain the similarities between my dreams and the events of the past two days. Not to mention the names. Baldwin D. Lacey. Baldric de Lacey."

"I can't. Not right now, not this minute. But I'm sure there's a rational explanation."

"What if there's not? What if I'm right?"

Ellie waved her hands in surrender. "Okay. Let's pretend

for a moment that you're reliving a past life. Let's pretend that you're Gillian, the damsel in distress, and Winn is Baldric, your gallant knight." She pointed to a passage. "This section is from Gillian's perspective." She flipped a page. "This section from Baldric's. If you lived Gillian's life, then you'd know Gillian's thoughts. Not Baldric's. Right?"

"I know. I don't understand that either. It's like I'm floating above them, experiencing the entire adventure."

"Kind of like watching a movie."

"Kind of."

"Uh-huh. So. Does the movie have a happy ending?"

"No."

Ellie sighed. "I was afraid of that. What happened?"

"I don't know," Sydney said with a frown. "I've never dreamed that far ahead. As hard as I try, it won't reveal itself to me. I think I need to regress."

"What?"

"Regress. Tune into the subconscious to recall memories of past experiences."

Ellie rolled her eyes. "What book did you dig that out of?"

Sydney ignored her. "Reincarnation gives us the chance to learn from our mistakes. To grow. Which is all well and good, except I don't know what I did wrong."

Ellie smacked a hand to her thigh, swept up in the moment. "Maybe it wasn't you. Maybe he screwed up."

"Whatever. The end result is the same. Tragic. Unhappy. If it's the same to you, I'd rather not go through it again."

"So regress already. Maybe you'll find out none of this really exists and you can get some sleep."

Sydney rose from the bed and began to pace. "I can't do it alone. I mean, I could try. I read a passage about self-hypnosis, but it said it's not easy. It could take several tries, several months before I even get the hang of it. I don't have months. Not if history is repeating itself. I need to regress now, soon. I need help."

"Don't look at me. I'm no expert. I'm not even a believer." She snapped her fingers. "Wait! Why don't we call one of those psychic hotlines?"

"Would you be serious?"

"I am."

"Those people aren't for real. Come on, Ellie. This is important. I need a trained professional."

"You mean a psychiatrist? You're not going to find one around here, Syd. This is Slocum, Indiana. Population 253. Max the barber is as close to a therapist as this town gets." She snapped her fingers again. "What about the Renaissance Fair this weekend? Don't they have some sort of psychic palm-reader character there?"

"Character being the operative word. I sought her out last year. Nothing but a conartist." The cutting disappointment still stung from when the psychic advised Sydney that her current husband would be the first of three losers.

"Maybe they'll have the real thing this year."

"I wouldn't hold my breath. Although…"

"What? What?" Ellie was revved up now.

"You might be on to something with the Renaissance Fair. They re-enact the period about two hundred years past the time I'm guessing Baldric and Gillian had lived. Still, it might work."

Sydney raced down the stairs and into the living room to her stack of books.

Ellie was hot on her heels. "What might work?"

Sydney located the book she was searching for and leafed through the chapters until she came to a specific page. "Here." She pointed to the third paragraph and read out loud. "If the setting is appropriate and familiar, and if the subject is open to the possibility, spontaneous regression may take place."

Ellie looked at Sydney as though the last of her marbles just rolled under the sofa. "It sounds too close to spontaneous combustion. I don't like it."

Undaunted, a plan began to unfold in Sydney's mind. "My costume. Is it almost finished?"

"Almost."

"You're making it just as I described?"

"I'm following the sketch you gave me and using the scarlet

velvet you picked out. Come by tomorrow. See for yourself. Besides, I need you for the final fitting."

Sydney sighed with relief and plopped down on her cushy sofa. "This just might work."

Ellie sank down next her, looking exhausted. "You really think he's the one?"

"Winn?" Sydney closed her eyes and answered in a subtly accented voice, "Aye. He's the one." She smiled. "He and no other."

Eight

"You cannot be serious," the maid whispered.

"But I am." Gillian huddled closer to Eloise, wanting her intentions heard by no other. "'Tis imperative I get with child before reaching Willingham. I mean to withstand the baron's touch but once, upon our wedding night. He already believes me to be uncommonly fertile, likening me to my mother of three sons and a daughter. He will not be suspicious of conception after but one coupling."

"How do you know of such things?" Eloise demanded. "You are an innocent. A maiden."

"A maiden, aye, but not oblivious. I have ears and eyes and a nimble mind. I have stumbled upon a tryst or two. Have you forgotten Guy's and Aiden's love of women? Your taste for men?"

Eloise frowned. "'Twould seem I have need to practice more discretion."

Gillian glanced nervously about. Darkness enshrouded the clearing, save for the small fire crackling before them. Baldric, Simon, and Sir William remained busy securing the cart and arranging sleeping pallets while the squires tended the horses. Sir Robert leaned against a tree not ten paces away, radiating insolence while swilling from a flask and keeping a watchful eye on the women.

Gillian fidgeted under his intense regard. As usual, his small, dark eyes followed her every move. She tried to ignore him, returning her attention to Eloise. This was the second night of the journey and the first time she'd found more than a moment alone with her maid. "Will you help me?" she pleaded.

The frown deepened. "You wish me to advise you in the art of seduction?"

"I have seen men clamor to do your bidding. I have watched you bring them to their knees with a smile and a toss of your hair. I, on the other hand, know not where to begin."

"Thank the Lord."

"I had planned to directly proposition Sir Baldric," she admitted, stealing a covert glance at the honorable knight who believed her a spoiled brat. "I now believe seduction to be the wiser course."

"Sir Baldric?" Eloise's lips twitched. "Why am I not surprised?"

"Do not tease me now. Do you wish to tend my grave?"

"Of course not."

"You have heard the rumors. `Twas you who suggested Redmere may be to blame for his childless state. If his seed is flawed, then I would appear as barren as his two wives ere. Would you have me suffer their fate, thus allowing him to snare and foul a fourth innocent wife?"

Her maid's eyes darkened. "I have been at your side for five winters, since before your mother died. I have tried to care for you as she would. I wish you nothing but happiness and a long life, dear one. You insult me to suggest otherwise."

Gillian clasped the woman's hands. "Then help me. Please."

"You realize that for Sir Baldric to give you his child, he must breech your maidenhead. Think you the baron will not be upset when you come to his bed less than pure?"

"He will not know. I will pretend."

Eloise rolled her eyes. "You have much to learn about lovemaking."

Gillian's cheeks heated with embarrassment. "`Tis why I beg of your expertise."

"No need to beg, m`lady. I would do anything you ask."

Gillian's eyes misted as she hugged her friend. She could trust only Eloise now, for Eloise would be the only person at Willingham who truly cared for her.

Sir Robert pushed away from the tree, intrigued by the women's show of affection.

Gillian elbowed Eloise. "Sir Robert."

Eloise drew away with a deep breath then winked at Gillian. "Lesson number one," she said with a grin. "Watch and learn." She tossed her flaming red curls over her shoulder with a careless hand then offered the same impish wink to the knight. "Sir Robert," she trilled, rising to her feet. "Do join us."

"He cannot."

The trio snapped their attention toward the stern voice. Baldric had somehow moved within earshot and now glared at the impudent knight. "FitzHubert is required at his post high in those branches." He pointed to a sprawling tree framed against the night sky. "'Twould be difficult to spot intruders while flirting about the fire."

Sir Robert's right eye twitched. With a curt nod, he slung the flask over his shoulder and skulked toward his post.

Gillian relaxed. To think Eloise had intended to flirt with the ignorant lecher solely for her benefit. Sentimental warmth spread through her.

"Your bed awaits, m'lady." Baldric indicated the pallet nearest to the cart. He said no more, simply stared down at her with well-honed stoicism, waiting for her to set off to where he pointed.

She wanted to snap a tart remark, anything to crack his stone countenance. She refrained. A smart retort in front of his men would be met with a swift, cutting counter, quelling any doubt of his authority. After the long, tiresome day of riding, she held no energy for a verbal skirmish.

"As you wish," she said. "Come, Eloise."

"Nay. Proceed without her." He blocked the redhead's path. "I require a moment alone with your maid."

Gillian narrowed her eyes.

"Fear not, Lady Gillian," he assured. "I have charged Simon with your safekeeping."

Gillian's jaw dropped. Her cheeks burned. Did he mean to claim the amorous attentions he'd just denied Sir Robert? She looked to her maid, whose blush rivaled her own.

Eloise shrugged helplessly and begged forgiveness with rounded eyes.

Gillian pursed her lips against the urge to curse Baldric and his randy loins. Anger simmered beneath her calm facade. Anger at Baldric, not Eloise, for the woman attracted men like bees to nectar. Of course, she knew well her anger to be unreasonable. She had no claim of him. She was betrothed to another and had no right to deny Baldric his pleasure, even if she wished he had chosen her.

She turned away from the would-be lovers and walked to her pallet with as much grace as she could summon. A forced nervous titter halted her steps.

Squinting back at the pair, Gillian watched Eloise's exaggerated gestures before Baldric escorted her farther into the woods. Her maid's nervous laughter and dramatic mannerisms told Gillian what she needed to know. Eloise had either been caught in a falsehood or backed into a corner.

Gillian bit her lip. Mayhap she'd misread Baldric's intent. Had he overheard their discussion of his seduction? She drew a nervous breath. `Twas a dishonorable scheme, aye, to beget the babe of one man and claim another as the father. An unforgivable act. Especially for a man such as Sir Baldric the Immortal. A man who lived and breathed by the knights' code. A man sworn to valor, truth, and honor. By lying with her, he would breech his very beliefs, for there was no honor in bedding another man's intended bride.

"M`lady."

Gillian jumped. She whirled around to find Simon, his eyes reflecting the cold, hard steel of his mail.

"Aye?" She threw back her shoulders, refusing to be intimidated.

"Mayhap you should retire for the evening, rather than lurking in the dark, spying on my brother like a jealous lover."

A chill shot through her. His accusation was as much an invitation to battle as if he had drawn his sword. Worse, he'd seen clear through her, as though he'd already thrust his blade and pierced the truth. She stiffened her backbone. Raised her chin. Simon was a predator on the prowl. If she displayed any sign of weakness, he would pounce and devour.

"I do not lurk, nor do I spy."

"But you *are* jealous."

"Mayhap you should retire as well, Sir Simon. Your vision appears to be deceiving you."

The bloodthirsty gleam in his eyes turned ravenous. "There is only one deception occurring here, m'lady, and I strongly recommend you cease."

It took everything she had to stand her ground. *Dear Lord, spare me the one chance to protect my life at Willingham.* Worried to her very soul that he knew her intent, Gillian drew herself up to her full, inconsequential height, and hoped for the best. "You, sir, are a study in blatant disrespect. I demand an explanation and an apology for your slanderous accusation."

He bent down to meet her defiant gaze, his chilling smile like fangs glinting in the moonlight. "You are truly gifted. An unsuspecting man could easily fall prey to your feigned innocence. You are naught but a temptress. I demand you release my brother from your spell."

"My what?"

"Your spell," he repeated, fairly growling the word. "Is it not enough that you have enchanted Baron Redmere, mayhap the most powerful, certainly the most wealthy noble in Yorkshire? Why must you torture my brother as well?" He crossed his arms over his chest and regarded her with new disdain. "Unless you feel empowered by the drama of two men fighting over you."

She shuddered at Simon's ghastly interpretations. "You are not only rude, but mad as well. I possess no mystical powers. If I did, I would not use them to entice Baron Redmere, I assure you. As for torturing your brother…" she paused, unable to decipher his cryptic charge. "I know not what you mean."

"Do you not?" His reply dripped sarcasm.

Uncertain how to defend herself, she matched his tone and bested his smirk. "Apparently your hearing has also been affected by your exhaustion." She spoke loudly and slowly, *"I know not what you mean."*

"A temptress *and* a liar." Simon grabbed Gillian's elbow and tugged her toward her pallet. "Very well. I shall cease trying to reason with you."

She snorted. "Is that what you call these vengeful accusations?"

Simon halted. His grip tightened. "Do not mock me, woman."

"Do not talk to me as if I were little better than a common wench."

"I never thought you common," he said cruelly.

Gillian swung out in blind anger.

The knight blocked her open-handed blow with a splayed palm. Flesh cracked against flesh.

The horses whinnied.

The squires' boisterous chatter died.

Gillian massaged her stinging palm. "I have done nothing to earn such disrespect," she whispered, aware that they were now the center of attention.

"I beg to differ," he grumbled through tight lips. "You have robbed my brother of his proper sense and good humor."

Though she knew not to what he referred, she savored the knowledge that he had not learned of her plan to seduce Baldric.

She heard the high-pitched sound of Eloise clearing her throat. She stepped to the side of Simon's bulky frame and found Baldric striding toward them. His agitated footsteps trampled the grass. Indeed his humor appeared less than light.

"Is something amiss?" he demanded.

Gillian and Simon quickly answered as one. "Nay."

"Then get thee some sleep," he ordered Gillian. He narrowed suspicious eyes at Simon while barking his next command to the gawking retinue. "FitzHubert and I stand first watch. The rest of you glean what sleep you can. Tomorrow we ride hard and long into the night. The sooner we get to Willingham the better."

Gillian winced as he directed his last statement at her. `Twas clear he was anxious to be rid of her. His curt tone and Eloise's flustered features confirmed Gillian's worst fear. He'd overheard her scheme of seduction.

`Twas naught to do but beg for his understanding. Simon's hostility she could endure, for it merely annoyed her. Baldric's hostility, however, knocked her heart askew. A heart already suffering on the edge of endurance. "You cannot blame me for wanting to live—"

"—life to the fullest!" Eloise interjected. "M`lady wishes not to miss a moment of this journey's adventure. She has vowed to sleep as little as possible. I, of course, shall encourage her to reconsider." She looped her arm through Gillian's and tugged her toward the pallet. "Excuse us if you will, kind sirs."

As Eloise dragged her away from the brothers, Gillian whispered, "What madness has befallen you? I wished to mend the frayed bridge between Sir Baldric and myself."

"Do not try to fix what is not broken."

Hope burst like sunshine through Gillian. "He did not overhear my plan?"

"Nay."

"Then why is he angry with me?"

"He is angry with himself."

"I do not understand."

"He has feelings for you."

The words slammed into Gillian's heart. "Do not jest with me, Eloise!"

"Shush," her maid commanded, drawing Gillian down onto the rough blankets.

"But `twas you he pulled into the shadows. You with whom he wished to dally."

Eloise chuckled, patting Gillian's hand. "Nay. He wished only to chastise me. He cautioned me against flirting with Sir Robert or any of the other men in his charge. He warned that by drawing attention to myself, I draw attention to you. This he does not want."

"What *does* he want?"

"You."

Gillian's breath deserted her.

"He knows this to be wrong. `Tis why he is angry."

Senses whirling, Gillian glanced across the clearing. Sir Baldric the Immortal appeared a mere shadow silhouetted in silvery moonlight, but it mattered not. She would recognize him anywhere. His slightest gesture, every inflection of his voice were burned indelibly in her mind.

A slow heat spread from deep within her. "He wants me? How can this be, Eloise? Sir Baldric is the noblest, most handsome knight in all of England. Surely women of great beauty beg for his attentions. Why would he want me?"

Eloise clucked her tongue. "Dear child, you know not your own worth. Beauty comes in many forms. Your beauty is rare and bewitching for it shines from within. It is everlasting, unlike that of flesh and bone. Although I do not believe you have peered at your reflection lately. You are blossoming like the heather you hold so dear."

Gillian furrowed her brows, pondering the maid's praise. "He wants me? He *said* this?"

"Actions oft times belie words."

"Actions? What has he done?"

"When he believes no one is watching, his gaze is upon you, following you."

"That proves naught. He has been charged to protect me. Besides, Sir Robert's eyes follow me as well." She shivered in disgust.

"When Sir Baldric looks upon you, he reminds me of a man who has not feasted in a fortnight and knows he may never again."

Gillian swallowed the lump in her throat. To imagine, a man such as Sir Baldric the Immortal gazing upon her as though only she could fulfill him. She shook her head. Nay, she could not afford to be swept away with such fanciful notions. She must live by her wits now, and to do so, she required clear thinking. "Then `tis possible?"

"To seduce him?" Eloise beamed. "Aye. But not with circumstances as they are. He will not weaken in front of his men. Though, if you both somehow found time alone this eve, mayhap the seeds of seduction could be planted."

"Do not suggest that I flick my hair, crook my finger, and lure him into the shadows. I would fail miserably at the game you play too well."

Eloise conceded the point with a smug grin and a toss of her fiery locks. "Indeed. `Twould be wiser to approach the matter as yourself rather than as me."

Gillian cocked a brow. "Meaning?"

"Meaning, once you are alone with Sir Baldric, simply

behave as you normally would. Be yourself. I am certain nature will take a course that will please you."

"Again, how do you propose I get him alone?"

Eloise tapped her finger on her front tooth, pondering the situation. Then her face brightened. "I have an idea, though it may be risky."

Gillian sidled closer. "Desperate people have nothing to lose. Pray, tell."

Eloise scanned the clearing.

Gillian followed her gaze. The young squires had bedded down. Sir Robert was out of sight, perched in the high branches of the tree. Sir William snored at the edge of the clearing, drunk on wine. Baldric and Simon sat side by side on a felled tree, alert and with a clear view of the women.

"Let us prepare for bed," her maid suggested. "We must not arouse their suspicions."

Gillian turned down her blanket. "Too late. Simon already accused me of casting a spell over Baldric."

Eloise sighed. "Ah. The spell of love."

"Love?" Gillian blinked in disbelief. "You fancy Baldric in love with me? Surely you are mistaken. We have known each other but three days."

"Have you never heard of love at first sight, child?"

"A whimsical notion suffered by romantics and fools," Gillian grumbled, slipping her feet beneath the blanket.

Eloise frowned. "Surely no harder rock ever tumbled down a hill. `Tis unhealthy for one so young. Have you no fantasies? No dreams?"

Aye, Gillian thought, she had dreams, but dreams they remained. For in her dreams her mother and brothers lived still, her father forever. In her dreams, `tis within Baldric's arms she slept, not Redmere's. "To dream is to know disappointment. `Tis better to approach life with open eyes, with logic. `Tis safer."

"`Tis boring." Eloise pulled the blanket to her chin and rolled close to Gillian. "Your plan to seduce Sir Baldric and to conceive his child is based on pure logic?"

"Aye. My father and all at Heatherwood will benefit from

my union with Baron Redmere. So shall it be. Redmere will believe the child his, thereby ensuring my safety within his household. More, I shall take solace in the knowledge that I have born to this world the child of a noble knight rather than of a cold-hearted murderer."

Eloise pursed her lips in disapproval. "What of the babe?"

"I shall cherish the child, of course."

"What of Sir Baldric?"

Gillian squeezed her eyes shut, unable to think of the dark, lonely nights ahead when she would lie awake, wondering if he was safe, wondering if he'd ever learn she'd denied him his own child. Wondering what a man like Baldric would do with such a painful betrayal. "What of him?" she asked, feigning indifference.

"You have given no thought to his feelings in this matter?"

"What feelings? We shall engage in coupling, as he has done with hundreds of women. An encounter driven by lust. I am sure he has been many times stroked by the fleeting wings of passion."

"I suspect his feelings run deeper than you dare to imagine. Heed my warning," Eloise said. "The good knight is besotted. Seduce him, dally with his heart, and mayhap you will regret the consequences."

"'Twill only be a physical union, Eloise. Neither heart shall suffer. This I vow." The words slid so easily from her mouth, yet each one pricked her conscience like the sharpest of thorns.

"Do not vow that which you cannot control. The heart is more powerful than the mind and about as predictable as a spring storm."

Gillian sighed. "'Tis a risk I must take. Now stop lecturing and relay to me your plan."

Eloise whispered her elaborate scheme. While Gillian concentrated, she reached for her bag of wilted heather and hugged it close to her chest. Strength. She begged of it strength...and justification. 'Twas all for the better of Heatherwood.

Despite her determination, she feared the actual act of lovemaking. 'Twas painful, she'd heard. Though 'twas preferable to endure the thrust of Baldric's masculine sword to the sting of Redmere's impotent dagger.

For all of her denial, she indeed harbored affections for the handsome knight. He was so gentle, so earnest. Surely he would be patient with her. For a moment, she considered Eloise's notion that 'twas better to love unwisely than not to love at all.

A tantalizing, romantic sentiment.

A sentiment too frightening to contemplate.

She pretended to sleep, awaiting the moment to spur the seduction plan into motion. 'Twas wiser and safer to be ruled by one's head than by one's vulnerable heart, she reminded herself.

She had loved and lost her mother.

She had loved and lost three brothers.

By all that was holy, she would not love Baldric only to lose him to duty.

'Twas his duty to deliver her to Willingham.

'Twas her duty to marry Baron Nigel Redmere.

The future held no hope for Baldric and Gillian as husband and wife. Yet she knew her heart already to be at risk.

Love at first sight. Another of Eloise's fanciful notions. A notion that rattled Gillian all the way to her sensible soul. For had that very thought not crossed her mind when she'd first set eyes upon the legendary knight three days ere? And every day since?

A perverse anticipation coursed through her body when, hours later, Eloise nudged her and whispered, "'Tis time."

Nine

Bert's Bar and Grill rivaled the sleaziest pub on Atlantic City's Pacific Avenue. It'd been a long time since Winn had seen the inside of one of these joints. An even longer time since he'd needed a drink before three in the afternoon.

He blamed Sydney Vaughn.

She was tying him up in knots. He hated knots.

Knots reminded him of Carolyn and Rick. His ex-wife and his ex-partner. Ex- plus ex- equaled a crash course in knot-proofing his life. Of course, just when he'd celebrated his third year of knot-free living—bam—Vera calls and sends him on this crazy mission. He'd known anything involving Vera and a trip to boonieland spelled certain disaster, but how could he say no?

No. N.O. Easy to say now.

Sunshine sliced through the dim interior as he walked through the door. None of the capped heads at the bar turned from the ball game.

A quick survey of the smoky room told him two things. One, no one with a crooked back sat hunched at the bar, which meant no Floyd. One less lecture for the day. Two, no one with a sidearm sat at the bar, which meant no Monroe. Winn had canvassed the town, driven to the man's home—he'd seen bigger houses—and asked questions no one would answer. The good sheriff was MIA, and Winn wondered what other 'business' could divert Monroe from playing hero for Sydney.

Next move: plant himself in the middle of town. Monroe would be looking for him sooner or later, and Winn didn't want the showdown in front of Sydney.

Christ, he nearly choked on his own hostility as he pictured Monroe laying Sydney, pale and ill, on her bed. Monroe had carried her. Winn just knew it, and it left him feeling like a snarling, jealous lover. Except he wasn't her lover. Monroe was. And Monroe had every right to be pissed.

The whole thing was nuts.

He moved toward the bar. Time to unwind some knots, maybe ask a few questions in vain, and wait.

The television blared from its mount in the corner of the bar. Bottom of the eighth. Two outs. Bases loaded. No one turned at his approach except the bartender, a beanpole with gray stubble who braced gnarled hands on the equally gnarled oak bar. "Whaddaya have?"

"Glenlivet on the rocks."

"Don't have it."

"What do you have?"

"Johnny Walker."

"Black?" he asked.

"Red."

Winn grimaced. Ordinary blended scotch, but it couldn't be worse than that backwoods swill Sydney had found. "No single-malt scotch?"

The bartender stepped back and crossed his lanky arms. "Maybe you'd be more comfortable taking your business to—"

"Never mind," Winn said. "I'll take a double shot of whatever scotch you have."

"All out."

"You just said—"

"Normally I carry Johnny Walker Red. Today I'm out."

Winn took a deep breath. *You're a stranger in this town and a public enemy to boot.* "How about a beer?"

The bartender lifted a skeptical brow. "Domestic?"

Winn nodded. At this point he'd settle for a damned wine cooler.

Seemingly appeased, the bartender set a sweating bottle in front of Winn, no glass, then offered his hand in greeting. "Bert Miller. I own the place."

"Winn Lacey." He gripped Bert's hand in a firm shake.

"Say. You one of them actors coming in with the Renaissance Fair?"

The man seated next to Winn snorted but didn't turn away

from the game.

"Pardon?" Winn asked.

"Course you are." The old man squinted at him. "The ponytail. The funny beard. You look like one of those knights."

Uh oh.

"Say, how much does one of them suits of armor weigh anyhow?"

"I'm not—"

"I mean, how do you mount a horse wearing metal pants? How do you bend your knees?"

"Hinges," the man who snorted said.

"Hinges, my scrawny ass." Bert slapped down his bar towel. "Rope, I bet. Leather straps, maybe."

"Hinges."

"Rope."

"Hinges."

"Rope."

Their arguing clanged like a fire bell to Winn's lingering hangover. "You're both right," he snapped. "The plates of metal protecting the shins and forearms are hinged at one side and held in place with rivets or straps. Satisfied?"

"That makes sense," Bert said, rubbing his scruffy beard.

"Interesting," snorting man observed.

Winn realized he'd answered the question without thought. Since when did he know about armor? He sucked back three-quarters of his beer.

Damn.

"You're kinda early, aren't ya?" Bert grabbed another frosted beer from the fridge, removed the cap, then slid the bottle down the bar to Winn. "Nothing to do in Slocum but sit around and wait." Bert narrowed his bloodshot eyes. "You *are* one of them knights, ain't you?"

Winn shook his head. "Afraid not." He started on his second beer. Knights. Renaissance Fair. What was it with the people in this town and everything medieval?

"Then whaddaya doin' in Slocum?"

"I'm—"

"He's the one who kissed Monroe's girl at the cafe." The

voice came from two stools down. The man wearing the Parker Plumbing shirt, pants sagging, crack showing. He swigged his beer and eyed Winn. "Monroe punched his lights out. Look at his face, for cryin' out loud."

Winn gripped his beer. *Go plunge a toilet, meat.*

A commercial blared, and the other men turned to glare at Winn.

Bert squinted, pulling his glasses from beneath the bar. He slipped them on and looked at Winn as though seeing him for the first time. "Oh yeah. Heard about you." He took the glasses off and returned them under the bar. "Lucky that's all you got. Kissing Monroe's girl. Why would you do such a crazy thing?"

"I—"

"Whaddaya got, a death wish?"

"I—"

"Sydney, of all people?"

"For chrissake, Bert." A man slid from the row of patrons and onto a stool to Winn's right. "You're as bad as my wife. Give the man a break." He turned to Winn. "Jack Bane. Welcome to Slocum."

Winn recalled a bad-ass blonde with the same last name. He attempted a smile, despite his ever-darkening mood. "Is that wife named Ellie?"

Jack smiled. "The same."

Winn stuck out his hand. "Winn Lacey. Sydney's *friend.* Or her aunt's friend to be exact."

Jack's smile widened. "We *all* know who you are."

Winn frowned. It was true. No matter where he'd gone in town today, everyone eyed him as if he'd taped a bomb to his chest. His personal life had become the hot topic among strangers. Worse, he had no explanation for what he'd done this morning. Not that he owed one to these people. Though he sure as hell would have liked one for himself.

"Heard that kiss was a four-alarm fire," Jack said with a laugh. "Sure sizzled up the phone lines across town."

Screw Monroe. Get off the stool, finish rigging Sydney's house, then get the hell out of Slocum.

As usual when he had that thought, he didn't move.

Bert's eyes sparked with curiosity. "Kissin' someone else's girl in the middle of folks tryin' to eat their scrambled eggs. You must be from New York."

Winn didn't know why he didn't get up and leave, but lately the simplest things seemed complicated. "Atlantic City."

"New Jersey?"

Winn saluted the bartender with his half-empty bottle. "The same," he said, then downed the last of the brew.

Bert leaned over the bar, squinty eyes conspiratorial. "Know much about blackjack?"

"Enough. Poker's my game."

Jack leaned in as well. "Are you any good?"

Winn nodded, relieved that the men had abandoned their gossip to prod him for gambling tips. They treated him to one beer after another. He wanted to ask questions about Monroe, about the Renaissance Fair Bert had mentioned, but the eager bar owner refused to let the gambling workshop veer off course.

A poker game ensued.

Winn settled into the distraction. He was exhausted. His thoughts had been consumed with Sydney for the entire twenty hours he'd known her.

Her past-life theory grated his nerves.

Bizarre brushes with déjà vu taxed his logic.

The thought of Monroe's hands on her nearly drove him wild.

He needed a break. He needed to regain his sanity.

Several pitchers and hours later, Winn had taught the men all he knew about poker. Still no Monroe.

It was time to get back to Sydney.

Half in the bag, Winn promised to return for another game. Jack offered to drive him home.

"You realize, of course," Jack said as he raced down country roads with the same breakneck speed as his wife, "your living with Sydney is high-voltage drama around here."

Winn grinned in his comfortable haze. "A small town with old-fashioned values. Where everyone knows everyone else's business. Spread the word, Jack. I'm not *living* with Sydney.

I'm *staying* with her. As a guest."

"Staying with. Living with. It's all the same in Slocum. You and Sydney are sleeping under the same roof. Alone."

"No crime in that, Bane."

"Betcha the money I won off Bert that the sheriff doesn't see it that way. Take the warning as one favor for another." Winn laughed. "Warning? What's he going to do? Lock me up and throw away the key?"

Jack shifted in his seat. "Well, he *is* the county sheriff."

"He can't toss a man in jail without cause."

"Between you and me, I've heard he's done it before. Though not since Ellie started working."

Winn's cozy world took on a chill. "Who does this guy think he is?"

"He's the man who keeps this town safe for my kids. If he sometimes has to create his own justice, so be it." Jack looked over at Winn. "Not that I think you should be arrested. I'm talking about real criminals."

"Great."

"You can't blame him for being upset. They're practically engaged."

"First of all, he was upset this morning. This morning was a long time ago. He could be feeling anything by now, but I wouldn't know because he's disappeared. Second, there's no such thing as *practically* engaged." Winn nearly shouted, releasing some of his earlier steam. "You're either engaged or you're not. He proposed. She said no. They're *not* engaged."

Jack snorted. "Strictly platonic, eh?"

"What's that supposed to mean?"

"Means you sound jealous. Which means you've got it for Sydney."

"We've only known each other for," he squinted at his watch, "twenty-eight hours."

"Ever heard of love at first sight, Lacey?"

Sweat popped out on Winn's brow. Unnerved, he rolled down the window for a blast of fresh air. Too much beer, he consoled himself. Just too much beer.

The sun dipped low in the sky, casting a burnt orange hue

across the endless horizon. It was almost nine o'clock.

He wondered if Sydney was sleeping. Wondered if she was dreaming. Or sleepwalking.

"Can you step on it, Jack?"

"I'm already pushing seventy-five. What's your hurry?"

"I don't like the idea of Sydney being alone after dark. She's been...having trouble sleeping."

"You left the poker table twice to call and check on her. Ellie told you, she's fine. When I called to tell Ellie the kids are staying at my mother's, she told me the same thing. Sydney's fine. Besides it's not that late. They're probably watching a girlie movie where they need a dozen tissues."

"You're probably right." Winn relaxed a bit against the cracked vinyl seat. "Tell me more about Monroe."

"What about him?"

"Why won't he take no for an answer?"

"No to him is an obstacle, not a destination. His words, not mine. His confidence inspires security in Slocum. Monroe can coax a cat out of a tree."

"Hasn't influenced Sydney." Winn felt a twinge of pride that his hostess hadn't cracked under the pressure of Slocum's favorite armed goon.

"True. Most folks think she's crazy for not grabbing the golden ring. Wedding ring, that is. He's wealthy and available. She's poor and available."

"What do *you* think?"

"Ellie doesn't really trust him, but no one will ever be good enough for Sydney in Ellie's eyes. God help my daughter when she starts to date." Jack shook his head. "Sydney's taking time with her decision, and I think that's smart. Of course, Monroe's toughest competition is her medieval knight obsession." He looked at Winn. "Ellie doesn't exactly whisper when she talks on the phone."

Something clicked in Winn's head. "Monroe pays for the Renaissance Fair."

"Yup. He arranged for it to come to town last year, when he started pursuing Sydney. We all grumbled when he asked us to dress in costume, but we did and it was fun. It's back again this year. This weekend to be exact."

"What a coincidence."

"Monroe figures he'll win Sydney's heart at the fair. According to Ellie, he's certain this is his winning year."

Winn suddenly felt trapped in his seat belt. "Is that so?" Jack peered at him through the dusk. "What are you thinking, Lacey?"

"I'm thinking that I've never been to a Renaissance Fair." They whizzed past the pig farm. "One more thing, Jack. Vera said Monroe is forty-something. How come he's not already married?"

"He was a while back, but his wife died in an accident. He was a mess for years. Sometimes he still comes into Bert's to toss back a few and lament how they never had kids. He's hung up on this old-fashioned legacy thing about passing on name and wealth. Personally, I just like to toss my kids over my shoulder to bounce them and hear them laugh. That's enough for me."

Winn narrowed his gaze at Jack. "Why Sydney? Why not move on and find another nice girl? A girl who loves him back. Or at least is interested in his money."

"It's not like this town—not even a dot on a map—is crammed with eligible women. Most are too young, too old, or already married with families. He was born in Slocum and he wants to settle with a local girl. He told Ellie it's important for his children to have strong roots. Beyond that, who knows what lurks in men's hearts? Or below. I'm sure you've noticed Sydney is cute. Maybe that's enough."

"From what I'm hearing, it sounds like he wants her for breeding."

Winn shook off another shiver as Jack pulled into Sydney's driveway. Eager to check on her, he thanked Jack for the lift, hopped out of the truck, then hurried for the house. The twilight must have been playing tricks on his eyes because out of nowhere he bashed his knee into Monroe's squad car. Instantly sobered, he wondered how long the man had been here. All day people had warned Winn how Monroe was going to take him to task. So why the hell hadn't he shown up?

Winn cursed. He should've been installing those damned locks instead of waiting at the bar like a lame duck. "Hoping for a jump start on that family, Monroe?"

He rushed up the porch steps. Ellie plowed through the door, almost knocking him over.

"Cripes!" she said. "You could sneak up on a ghost."

"What's Monroe doing here?"

Ellie's face glowed brighter than the sickly porch light. "Oh, great news! David—"

Jack Bane leaned on his horn.

"For crying out loud, Jack, I'm coming!"

"It's not every night we don't have the kids," he ranted from the truck. "Come on. I have a surprise for you."

"Well, hot damn! Must be my lucky night, too." Ellie hurried down the front steps. "I'll let Sydney tell you the good news."

Amidst Ellie's giggles, Jack sped away.

Winn felt a stab of fear. Had Monroe come to try for Sydney's hand again? Had it worked?

He's hung up on this old-fashioned legacy thing about passing on name and wealth. I'm sure you've noticed Sydney is cute.

He experienced a moment of horrifying helplessness before something within him, something dark and primitive, reared up and howled.

His muscles tightened.

He didn't know why, but he knew, as sure as he stood on this front porch, he could not allow Sydney Vaughn to marry David Monroe.

Winn let the screen door slam behind him.

Sydney jumped up from her purple couch. "Winn!"

"Sydney." He frowned at her chalky pallor, then glanced at the two men standing before her.

Monroe.

Winn's blood turned colder.

Tall, lanky, with salt-and-pepper hair. Standard issue brown-and-tan uniform. Badge. Sidearm. Arrogant smirk on what some women might call a handsome face. The bastard clutched a long-haired, pimple-faced teenager by the ripped collar of his Ozzy Osbourne T-shirt.

"What's going on here?" Winn felt good standing a couple of inches taller than the sheriff, until the man smiled in unsettling triumph.

"Maybe you should spend less time at the bar."

Winn clenched his fists at his sides. "Excuse me?"

"He found the crank caller!" Sydney rushed over to Winn, threw her arms out as if to hug him, but stopped short and hugged herself instead. Her eyes were a mix of anxiety and relief as she stood between him and Monroe. "I was never in real danger. Henry here made the calls. His friends put him up to it. They didn't mean any harm. It was a joke. A bad one. But the important thing is that David put an end to it." She touched Winn's sleeve. "You don't have to worry about me anymore."

"You can go home now," Monroe clarified with a smile as cold as hate. "Sydney's not in danger. She doesn't need a security consultant or whatever the hell it is you call yourself."

Winn held his temper in check. It wasn't easy. He wanted to clean the bastard's clock. But not in front of Sydney. Sydney, whose angel face seemed to draw tight at the mention of his returning home.

"Your services are no longer required, Lacey." Monroe twisted tighter on the kid's collar. "You can report to Vera that *I've* apprehended Sydney's stalker."

Winn clung to his control. "I'll leave when I'm damn ready."

The two men glared at each other for a long, tense moment.

The phone rang.

"I guess that won't be my crank caller," Sydney said with a shaky smile. She seemed hesitant to move from between them.

"It's okay, Sydney," Winn said, "you can answer it."

Monroe's face mottled. "Don't tell her what to do."

Danger brewed and Winn wanted her out of harm's way. "Please go, Sydney."

She dragged her feet and looked back the whole way to the kitchen.

Winn never took his gaze off Monroe. Now he knew the "other business." But he'd been a cop too long to accept things at face value. This resolution had come together a little too quickly and conveniently for his comfort. "How'd you make the boy? Someone tip you off?"

Monroe strained to his full height. "That's my business. Police business. A business you're not in anymore," he said with a cocked, I've-got-your-number brow. "So butt out."

"Checking up on me, Monroe?"

"A strange man is sleeping in my girl's house. Kissing her against her will. A man I've never met. You're lucky that's all I've done." He pointed to Winn's face. "Nice bruise."

Winn's left eye twitched. He'd never felt such a raw need to hurt someone. Not Carolyn, not even Rick. Winn didn't know which angered him more: the way Monroe emphasized *my girl*, the fact that he was right, or that he might know Winn's dirty laundry. Laundry Winn would gladly air out for Sydney should he feel the need to stick around and explain himself.

He took a deep breath and held fast. Despite Monroe's justification, Winn couldn't ignore the warning in his gut. Nor could he give Monroe the satisfaction.

Winn eyed the teenager.

The boy turned away, his pock-marked cheeks red with humiliation.

It disturbed Winn that the kid looked more uncomfortable than guilty. He definitely looked scared of Monroe. "So, Henry, need to get your kicks this morning over a bowl of corn flakes? Don't you think breathing over the phone at Sydney at seven a.m. is a little pathetic?"

The kid's cheeks blazed brighter. "Yeah," he croaked, his nervous gaze darting between Winn and the sheriff. "I mean, I guess so. There was nothin' to do before school. We—"

Monroe yanked up on the boy's collar, choking off his awkward confession.

Henry broke into a fit of barking coughs.

The sheriff's eyes burned a hole through Winn, who scratched his chin as if contemplating the boy's explanation. Before Winn could say anything, however, Sydney returned to the living room, her eyes wary as she entered the battlefield.

"That was Bert," she told Winn. "He wanted to make sure you got home safely."

"This isn't his home," Monroe said, hot eyes on Winn. "He's leaving." But instead of sticking around to help Winn pack his bags, he tugged the hapless kid toward the door. "Sydney, I need to get to the station to process Henry's papers."

She walked the sheriff to the door. "I honestly don't know how to thank you, David."

The gratitude in her eyes sliced through Winn. Monroe had Sydney right where he wanted her.

He moved in for the kill. "Let me escort you to the fair opening on Saturday."

Slick. Goddamned slick. Winn struggled not to boot the lawman out the door.

"Well, I was hoping…" she stammered as her gaze drifted to Winn. "I had hoped maybe…" when she turned back and saw David's frown, she faltered. Her shoulders sagged. "Sure."

Monroe beamed as though shot with a thousand volts. "You've made me a very happy man, Sydney Vaughn."

Before Sydney could change her mind, Monroe dragged his prisoner through the door. "*Adios*, Lacey. Have a safe flight home."

Sydney shut the door and slumped against it, just as she had upon Winn's arrival yesterday. She rubbed her hand against her stomach as her color began to return.

"Still feeling ill?"

"Not anymore," she mumbled as she pushed away from the door.

"Are you sure? You don't look well."

"I'm fine," she insisted. Then, without so much as a glance in his direction, she dashed up the stairs. "I'm going to bed. Good night."

Winn stood rooted for a moment, stunned by Sydney's hasty retreat. Why had she run away from him?

Maybe it was just as well, he thought. Between the heat of that kiss still burning his insides, the anger and jealousy stretching him thin, and the slight haze from the beer, he didn't think he had an ounce of control left. He wondered if she felt the same, if that's what chased her like a demon up the stairs and out of sight.

"Leave it alone, Lacey," he told himself. "You don't need this. You don't want her."

But he did.

He wanted her in the worst way.

He wanted to make love to her.

He was definitely out of control.

A breath of fresh air. That's what he needed. As he stepped out onto the porch, the dim yellow bulb burned out. "Figures." The new security lamp he'd purchased today was in Ellie's car, which was still parked in front of Bert's.

He groped his way to the porch swing and sat down with a heavy thud. He recalled the elderly proprietor of the hardware store, who'd cheerfully informed Winn, "Folks 'round here don't have much call for all this fancy security equipment. Most folks don't bother to lock their doors." Then the old man added, "We don't have a criminal element. We have Sheriff Monroe."

Winn wasn't sure if the citizens of Slocum feared or revered Monroe. On the other hand, he knew exactly how he felt about the scheming sheriff.

He didn't like him.

He didn't trust him.

He was on to Monroe's caveman tactics. Dragging that boy into Sydney's house like the big, bad hunter who'd brought down the big, bad bear. No one had called Sydney this morning. Winn knew it. Monroe knew it. The boy didn't.

David Monroe played a crooked and dangerous game, and Winn would be damned if he'd let the devious prick manipulate Sydney into an unwanted marriage. The bastard actually tried to pass off that kid as the stalker! Was Monroe so inept that he couldn't apprehend the real culprit? Was he so desperate that he needed to rely on underhanded schemes to win Sydney's hand?

Winn shook his head. Had the man no shame? Had he no clue that a moron could see through his he-man plot to show

Sydney he was the only man who could protect her?

Meanwhile the real stalker was still out there.

Deeply rooted anger simmered inside Winn.

He could honestly protect Sydney.

He would proudly defend her honor.

Chivalrous sentiments.

He froze in the swing.

A knight's sentiments.

His mind raced, rehashing the events of the past day and a half. He rose and entered the house in deep thought.

It couldn't be.

He flicked on the light in the living room and proceeded in a half-daze to the bookshelves. He skimmed the titles.

The Knights and Chivalry, the Days of Honor.

He plucked the book from the shelf and settled down on Sydney's sofa. He turned to page one and read. An odd sensation settled over him. A feeling as if he'd just ventured into a strange place but knew beyond reason that he'd been there before.

He closed his eyes.

It couldn't be.

Then he focused back on the pages and read on, needing to prove to himself that he wasn't crazy.

Ten

England, 1315

Gillian held her breath as she rolled under the cart.

Two revolutions and she lay rigid in the dirt, awaiting a cry of alarm.

None sounded.

The squires still slept.

Sir William and Sir Robert continued to wage their battle for most obnoxious snoring.

Simon, perched in the mighty oak across the small clearing, fulfilled the drunken Sir William's watch duty and seemed to have his sharp eyes trained elsewhere.

What of Baldric?

Eloise had risen moments earlier to draw him into conversation, distracting him with fears about their journey. True, Eloise could chatter the bark off a tree, but Gillian doubted Baldric would long withstand it. His mood of late was less than tolerant.

Gillian could barely discern the black shadows of tangled brush well beyond the cart.

She summoned her courage. `Twas not so far.

Crouching like a cat, she counted to three, then crawled out into the open.

Her heart hammered. Sweat beaded along her hairline. The distance to the cloaking brush seemed farther than she'd first thought.

She banged her knee on a sharp rock. Pain speared through her, but she bit her lip and crept on.

The camp's fire crackled and popped yet shed little light upon her path. It burned far enough away to neither help nor betray her progress. A mixed blessing, she supposed. Squinting, she searched for an opening in the trees through which to disappear. Finding it, she slipped into the woods and into brutal darkness.

She rose to her feet. With sore palms and a fluttering pulse, she felt her way deeper into the forest.

Neither she nor Eloise had considered navigating a path through midnight-black woods. Only intermittent shafts of moonlight penetrated the deep forest cover, and she prayed that her keen sense of direction would lead her to the stream. The place Eloise would suggest Baldric search when he discovered Gillian missing. The place located just far enough beyond the clearing that no one would overhear them.

Eloise would lie to Baldric. "M'lady oft times wakes with a need for a private moment. No need to alert the others. 'Twould be unseemly for a swarm of knights to converge upon the mistress relieving herself. 'Twould be humiliating enough to be caught as such by one knight."

Gillian stumbled.

Something scurried near her feet.

She stifled a scream as well as cold fear.

He will come for me. He will come.

To divert her fears, she concentrated on the plan at hand.

When he finds me, I shall do as Eloise suggested. I shall allow nature to take its course. Mayhap, if I am very lucky, he will make love to me tonight by the stream's edge.

'Twould be a romantic notion were she prone to such frivolous thought. As always, however, she sealed her heart like a fortress. Sir Baldric the Immortal's seed was necessary. Whispered endearments and passionate declarations were not.

She let out a sigh as she heard the gentle rush of the stream.

Then the snap of a twig.

She whipped around.

Had Baldric come so soon?

She peered into the darkness.

Nothing.

The hairs on the back of her neck prickled.

Something was amiss.

Out of the blackness, he pounced.

Her back slammed against the ground. His full weight crushed her as she fought for breath.

She opened her mouth to scream.

A rough hand clamped over it, the skin sour and putrid on

her tongue.

He hauled her up against him, squeezing her so tightly, she feared for her ribs. She could barely breathe. Within seconds, he gagged her with a cloth more foul than his skin. She nearly retched from stench and fear.

`Twas not Baldric.

Nor Simon.

Sir Robert? Sir William?

Nay.

She panicked, twisting and kicking as her unknown captor dragged her away from the stream. He was immune to her struggle.

A horse snorted.

He had the means to spirit her away!

Nay! How would Baldric find her?

She punched and flailed with renewed ferocity.

Until a sharp blow smashed into her temple.

As she descended into the depths of oblivion, she felt him toss her over his steed.

Nay! `Twas not as planned!

She battled for consciousness.

And lost.

Eleven

Present Day

Sydney screamed in terror.

She bolted upright, arms swinging. "'Twas not as planned! 'Twas not as planned!"

Something cracked, then crashed in the darkness.

Someone grabbed her shoulders. "Shhhh. It's all right." A male voice. A *gentle* male voice.

Still frightened and dazed, she struck out with a fist. "Nay! 'Twas not as planned!"

Fist cracked against bone. The man pulled her closer. "Sydney, wake up. It's me."

She struggled and thrashed against him.

He tightened his hold and leaned over her. Fear nearly split her in two. She screamed for her life.

There was a click, then light flooded her eyes. In an instant, she stopped fighting, stopped screaming. She drew a ragged breath and slumped against his chest. "Baldric."

"Easy," he whispered, smoothing her hair.

"I thought...I thought...." She hiccupped, hot tears stinging her cheeks. Winn. Not Baldric. It was Winn who held her now. She was in her bedroom. He'd switched on her lamp. "Someone else...someone grabbed me."

"There's no one here but me, sweetheart," he said against her hair. "You were dreaming. A bad dream, that's all."

Throat still tight with fear, she gripped his shirt. "Don't leave me."

"I'm not going anywhere." He stroked his hand down her back. Slow, comforting strokes.

She rested her head against his shirt and inhaled the masculine scent. She wished she could crawl inside of him. Become one with him. Become lost in sweet dreams rather than terrifying nightmares. "I thought you were him."

"Who? Monroe?"

"Monroe?" The name confused her for a moment before

the world snapped back into place. "You mean David?"

"Is there another?"

His deep voice rumbled in his chest. She ached to slip her hand inside his shirt, ached to feel his strength, his solidity, his heat. Instead, she peered up at the man who held her. "Did you break down the door?"

He looked down at her, brown eyes dark with indiscernible emotion. "Any particular reason you locked it?"

She *had* been dreaming. Or remembering. "What's happening to me?" she whispered, more than a little scared.

He continued to rub her back. "I wish I knew."

Feeling as though she teetered on the edge of a dark drop, she squeezed his shirt. "Tell me I'm not going crazy. Tell me you feel something, too. An attraction. A connection. Something. Anything."

He gently removed her fists from his shirt.

Thinking he meant to push her away, she choked on a sob and drew back.

But he pulled her close and caressed her fingers. "I feel...something."

She sagged against him. "Then you believe me. Finally. About our past lives."

"I didn't say that. I said I feel *something*. I'm having thoughts, experiencing feelings that don't make a hell of a lot of sense. That doesn't mean I'm ready to jump on the reincarnation bandwagon. There has to be a rational explanation. I'm not ready to believe otherwise."

Her throat constricted with new tears. "Can't you even try? All I'm asking is for you to trust me. To look beyond what you see. Is that so much?"

His muscles tensed beneath her trembling hands. He still held her, but she sensed his emotional withdrawal. "It's not that simple, Sydney. Not for me."

"Consider the possibility that we lived and loved once before," she pleaded softly, looking up into his face. "Consider it. Please."

Silence hung heavy in the muggy air. Silence that rang as clearly as spoken words.

He didn't believe her. He didn't believe any more tonight than he had yesterday.

Why couldn't he just go along with it, even for a minute? Funny question since *she* couldn't let it go, even for a minute.

She had no answers. The only thing she knew for sure was that every shred of life in her body strained for Winn's uncompromising trust. But it wasn't going to happen. It probably never would.

Despair the likes of which she'd only felt in her dreams dragged her down into a dark sea of emotion.

Doom. She sensed it in every tingling nerve.

For Gillian and Baldric.

For her and Winn.

She hugged him tighter, terrified of the unknown events to come. "Don't leave me," she pleaded once more, starting to shake with sobs.

He eased back on the bed, pulling her down alongside him. He held her close and stroked her hair. "Shush, baby. You're breaking my heart." He wiped her tears with the pad of his thumb. "I won't leave you."

"If you do, I'll die."

She froze. Where had *that* come from? She'd said it with conviction. She even believed it. Yet she had no idea why.

He kissed her temple and wrapped protective arms around her. "I won't let anything happen to you, Sydney. I promise. No one will hurt you, not as long as I'm here."

Spooked, she snuggled closer to him, urgent to feel the truth of his words.

She was safe now.

Resting her head on his shoulder, she drew deep breaths, hoping to slow her heart. Instead she noticed how her breath warmed the material of his shirt. Entranced, she inhaled, exhaled, over and over as she wondered if it heated his skin as well. Her limbs grew heavy with a queer lethargy. Her senses whirled in slow motion as she traced her fingers over the smooth, cool buttons of his shirt and imagined herself releasing their hold, one by one.

Her mounting need for Winn brushed against the fading memories of Gillian's mission. Another piece to the dream. Another vision of the past. "Make love to me," she whispered.

The arms about her stiffened. It took a moment for him to answer. "I can't."

Sydney buried her blazing cheeks in the crook of his shoulder. What in God's name was going on in her head? Her muffled voice asked the dreaded question. "Why not?"

"It wouldn't be right."

"Why not?" She sounded like a broken record. She felt like a complete idiot. "The way you kissed me this morning, I thought, well, I assumed you might want to make love to me."

He groaned, shifting his hips away from hers. "You have no idea."

The guttural vibe of his voice heated the cold left from her dream. "Then…why not? Why—"

He lifted her chin so she'd look at him. "Not like this. Not tonight. Your emotions are out of whack. I can't take advantage of that. No matter how much you think you want me to. No matter how much I'd really like to."

Despite the humiliation, she smiled at him. "Well, I'll be."

"What?"

"Chivalry lives. Even in the twenty-first century."

He released a deep sigh, tucked her head under his chin then wrapped his arms about her. "At least you'll respect me in the morning."

"I would have respected you either way." She closed her tired eyes. "You're an honorable soul, Winn Lacey. Be you a knight or be you a cop. Brandishing a sword or a gun. A shield or a badge. You're a good man."

She felt his smile against her hair. "You think so, huh?"

"I know so," she mumbled as she drifted into a bone-weary sleep. "I know so."

***

Sydney smiled in the haze of sleep.

Her bed hadn't exactly been a place of warmth and security lately, but waking up with Winn wrapped around her like garland about a Christmas tree, well, it was just plain heaven.

Winn.

He'd kept his promise. He hadn't left her. He'd stayed with her through the night.

And she'd slept. Really slept. For the first time in weeks, there'd been no tossing and turning, no jarring awake in a panic or a cold sweat. No dreams. Just a dark, cavernous oblivion where she'd rested peacefully.

She blinked open her eyes. The early-morning sun wedged through her curtains and sparked along the polished edges of the knight's armor. She cringed, waiting for the despair to cut through her.

It didn't come.

Nor did the wave of irrevocable loss. Or the yearning so deeply inherent she couldn't begin to fathom its source. Emotions too powerful for one person to endure. Emotions she could live without ever feeling again.

Yet despite the torment she suffered nearly every time she woke, she couldn't dispose of the armor. To dispose of it would be equal to severing her own arm. It was perverse, she knew, and sometimes it made her feel downright stupid. But the connection was there all the same, even if she couldn't explain it.

Something was different this morning.

As she watched the sun gild the imposing armor, making it appear almost magical, alive, as though it might move at any moment, new hope surged within her.

Last night she'd experienced true terror for Gillian, not to mention for herself. She'd felt the only thing left to do was curl into a tight ball and wait for the inevitable, whatever it might be. But somehow, this morning, there was a serenity whispering in her veins, a sort of calm after the storm. Her vision was crisp, her mind sharp, unencumbered by the usual morning sorrow and confusion. Somehow spending the night in Winn's arms had kept the dreams at bay. She felt refreshed and bursting with need to set things right.

It was not a coincidence.

Yesterday she'd been filled with doubt. Doubt about her beliefs, her sanity.

Today she felt nothing but courage. Conviction. Together, she and Winn could put their souls at rest.

That meant convincing Winn about past lives.

There had to be an easier way.

Maybe she'd been searching too hard in the wrong place. Maybe all of the answers weren't in the past. If their lives were recycling themselves, as she believed, then maybe she should pay more attention to the present. Like land tilled each season, who knew what might be resurfacing before their very eyes? Who knew what keys to the past Winn might be unwittingly holding?

From the crook of his arm, she glanced up at his face, relaxed in sleep. The darkening bruise on his cheek bone unsettled her. A bruise from the punch of a man he'd never met. A bruise for kissing a woman he'd known for one day. She may have driven him to that kiss, yet what really drove the cynical Baldwin D. Lacey? It stunned her to realize she knew nothing about his life. All this time she'd spent trying to convince him that they were past-life lovers, and she'd never even taken the time to learn about him. Winn. The man whose fine lines about the eyes seemed to have melted away in the night. She could almost picture how he'd have looked as a little boy, a dichotomy of lighthearted imp and dark-haired angel. But the restrained power of the body pressed to hers did not belong to a boy. Winn was every inch a man.

She sucked in a breath and twisted back to check the clock. She didn't know how much longer she could stay crushed against him before she grabbed him by the shirt and demanded he stop being a gentleman.

"Are you done squirming?"

His voice, thick with sleep, heated her even more. "I didn't mean to wake you," she whispered, not exactly disappointed.

"What time is it?"

"Six."

He frowned, his eyes still shut.

"Winn?"

"Go back to sleep, kid. The birds aren't even up yet."

"Yes, they are. Listen." The raging chirp-fest outside the

bedroom window proved worthy of any alarm clock. "Winn?"

"What?"

"Have you been with many women?"

"Hundreds," he grumbled.

Sydney poked him with her finger.

He made a noise in his throat but didn't open his eyes.

"Let me rephrase," she said.

A lazy smile broke through his grogginess. "Please do."

"Have you ever been serious with anybody?"

"Yes."

"Ever been married?"

The smile faded. "Once."

"Oh." She hadn't expected that. "What was her name?"

He slowly raised his lids. She found herself staring into a pair of dark, wary eyes. "Carolyn. Why?"

Carolyn. Sydney rolled the name around in her head like a foreign word she'd never heard. Maybe it was the jolting reality that Winn had loved someone so much that he'd married her. It hurt, and Sydney knew she was wrong, but she couldn't shake the feeling of disillusionment. She'd been building castles in the clouds, even if those clouds were dreams she couldn't control. Not wanting to look like a fool, she shrugged. "Just curious. What happened?"

He untangled his limbs from hers and climbed out of bed. Her body turned cold. "Where are you going?"

"Downstairs."

Sydney sat up, clutching the sheet to her chest. Not that she had anything to hide, clothed in a long t-shirt and oversized boxers. Not exactly the sexiest nightwear. "I didn't mean to upset you."

He jammed his loose shirttails into his jeans. "I'm not upset. I'm uncomfortable with your line of questioning."

"I just wanted to know a little more about you," she said, taken aback.

He smoothed hair out of his face then braced his hands on his hips. "How many men have *you* been with, Sydney? Have you slept with Monroe? How many times? How recently?"

She barely kicked off the sheet before jumping out of bed.

"You don't have to be so crude. That's not what I meant!"

"It's all the same." He turned on his heel and stalked from the room. Lancelot and Guinivere scrambled to their feet and followed him out as if he were the Pied Piper.

What just happened?

Did he still have feelings for his ex-wife? The thought made her ill.

She raced out the door. "Wait!"

He ignored her, descending the stairs two at a time, trying not to trip over the hungry dogs.

"Winn, please." She tagged him on the bottom stair. He whirled on her, his glare so intense, it took away her breath.

"Are you through playing amateur detective?"

"I just want to know a little about the man I slept with last night."

He looked up at the ceiling. "I'm going to finish rigging this house today if it kills me. I'm going to track down that damned stalker, put the fear of God into him, and if I'm lucky, be on a plane home by tomorrow night."

Sydney blinked at him. "What are you talking about? Henry's the stalker. Well, not a stalker. More like a prankster, and David already put the fear of God into him."

Winn sniffed. "Right."

"Henry confessed."

"So?"

"There haven't been any more calls." She knitted her brows. "Actually there haven't been any calls since you arrived."

"I've noticed."

Sydney's patience ran out. "What are you saying? That David coerced Henry into confessing to something he didn't do? That's crazy. Why would David do such a thing? He wouldn't. He cares about me. He—"

"Adores you," Winn finished with a frown. "I know. Everyone knows."

He started to turn away. She feared if she didn't stop him, he'd walk right out the door. "You can't leave," she said, cringing at the desperation in her voice. "You…you promised.

If this is about Carolyn..."

He clenched his jaw. "I promised Vera I'd secure this house and see to your safety. I'm taking care of the house today, and as for your safety, well, it seems the good sheriff has taken that job upon himself. You don't need both of us."

"No, I don't." She grasped the wooden railing. "I need you."

"Why me?" he snapped. "Because you think I'm a lover from your past come to save you from a humdrum life with Monroe?" He looked her straight in the eye. "I can't save you any more than you can save me, Sydney. So get that out of your head right now."

She didn't understand his hostility. She didn't understand how the conversation kept veering from Carolyn to David. Was he jealous? If so, that was a good thing, right? Maybe he did care. For *her*. Not for Carolyn. For *her*.

Just like that, his irrational behavior made perfect sense. She stared right back at him. "You're scared."

Winn gripped the newel post, wishing he could fast-forward his life. "I am not scared. The only thing around here to be scared of is losing my sanity." The words came out smooth, confident...just like they'd trained him at the academy. *Never let them see your fear.*

But he *was* panicking.

It was bad enough last night when he'd read *The Knights and Chivalry, the Days of Honor* and known practically every goddamned thing from cover to cover. Had someone asked him three days ago about Bannockburn, he would've thought it some exotic disease.

It was bad enough this morning waking up with his arms around Sydney and feeling content to lie there forever. It'd felt so damned natural, so perfect, that he could almost believe they'd been made for each other. Yet despite all this he'd somehow managed not to slip over the edge...somehow he'd been coping...until...until she'd asked him about the one thing in his life that left him most vulnerable. His failed marriage.

Last night he'd thought himself capable of explaining the mess should she ask. But last night he'd been half-crocked.

This morning, sober and of somewhat sounder mind, he found himself less than ready to discuss his ex-wife. What's more, he found himself dwelling on the Renaissance Fair and Sydney's acceptance of Monroe's invitation. It bothered him. A lot.

"You're scared to open up." Sydney hitched her chin, obviously determined to drag this down and beat it to death. "You're scared to trust."

"I have nothing to prove to you, Sydney. You're the one making the demands, not me. You don't even know me. Why do you blabber everything you feel to me and not to Monroe? Why don't you tell him to screw off if you don't want him? You know why? Because you have no idea how it feels to be played a fool." Working up a good head of steam, he couldn't stop now if he tried. "You want to know so much about me? Fine. You asked for it."

Sydney backed up a step, eyeing him like he might blow.

"Our marriage wasn't perfect, but I thought we were happy. That is until I looked around one day and realized we didn't talk anymore. I'd been too occupied with work, but I knew that wasn't the only reason. I felt it in my gut. I asked Carolyn if there was someone else. No, she said. *Trust me,* she said."

Sydney cringed at the bitterness in his voice. She regretted sticking her nose into his business and dredging up buried pain. On the other hand, she'd given him an excuse to vent his emotions. Something she sensed he hadn't done in a very long time, if ever. He was speaking out of anger and fear, despite his denial. Now wasn't the time to take issue with his insults.

"I did as she asked," he said, gripping the newel post with white knuckles. "I took her at her word. She swore she wasn't having an affair, and I believed her. Meanwhile I'm watching my partner's marriage fall apart. I'm listening to his heartaches during late-night stakeouts, offering him whatever support I can. He isn't just my partner, he's my best friend. It's the least I can do.

"His wife had been giving him a hard time. She wanted children, but after two years of trying, still nothing. She blamed Rick. She attacked his virility, hammered away at his male pride. A man's bound to wonder at that point. A sort of caveman need to prove his masculinity. Pursue and conquer."

Sydney's throat went dry. Remnants of her dream skidded through her mind, but she said nothing. Instead she stepped down and rested a hand on his shoulder.

He tensed beneath her touch, likely mistaking compassion for pity. He pulled away and walked into the living room.

She followed.

He stood in front of the window and stared out into the bright morning. "Suddenly Rick stopped confiding in me. Stopped asking my advice. Stopped talking to me about anything other than the case we were working on. He grew as distant as Carolyn."

He moved away from the window and toyed with a gargoyle sitting on her television. "I started to wonder. Doubting Carolyn. Suspecting Rick. It ate at me. My concentration suffered, a dangerous affliction given my occupation. So I confronted Rick. Ten years on the force together. Ten years of friendship. I figured he wouldn't lie to me, and if he did, I'd know. I asked him point-blank if he was screwing my wife."

Sydney swallowed. "He said no."

Winn winced as if slapped. "He said trust me."

"Because he was your friend, you did."

"Right up until the day, two weeks later, when I caught them in bed together." He set down the gargoyle. "I won't burden you with the ugliness that followed. I don't think it's necessary." He pinned Sydney with a look that conveyed the depth of his bitterness. "Do you?"

She shook her head, regretting she hadn't listened to him earlier and gone back to sleep in his arms. Instead she'd pushed and pried, not satisfied until she'd roused the demons he'd put to rest.

His wife and his best friend. The ultimate betrayal.

Sydney felt her own heart twist.

"I put in for a new partner but had to wrap the case with my old one first." Winn sank down on the couch and plowed a hand through his bed-mussed hair. He looked haggard.

Tortured.

She sat down beside him. She wanted to hold him, tell him everything would be all right, but she knew he'd only push her away. So she gently asked, "What happened?"

"An incident happened. An investigation happened. I was cleared of all charges, not that it mattered. Word of Rick and Carolyn's affair had leaked. Raised more than an eyebrow in the department. Raised doubts about my innocence."

"I don't understand. What incident?"

"Because of me, Rick got shot."

That knocked the breath out of Sydney. "What?"

"A drug bust. He went in first. He got shot."

"Is he," she gulped, "dead?"

"No, but he walks with one helluva limp."

She placed her hand on his. This time he didn't pull away. "Winn, you can't blame yourself for someone else's actions. It wasn't your fault Rick was shot."

"He was my partner. I was his backup. I wasn't there for him when he busted through the door."

"Where were you?"

"Dodging the bullets of a fifteen-year-old punk who got off two rounds before jumping down a fire escape." He snapped his fingers. "It happened in the blink of an eye. Kids. A bunch of doped-up kids."

"You could've been shot just as easily."

"But I wasn't."

"You were lucky. Rick wasn't. That isn't your fault. You said it yourself, you were cleared of any wrongdoing."

Winn gazed at her with eyes filled with self-condemnation. He'd been his own judge and jury. He hadn't been lenient. "He was my partner. My friend. I failed him. That's wrong, Sydney. That's as wrong as it gets."

Anger surged through her. "What about what he did to you? He betrayed you. You had no control over what happened. He did."

"Yeah, and payback's a bitch," he said. "At least that was the general consensus at the precinct. Made it hard to find a new partner. Not that I wanted one. I had to get out. For my own sanity. I walked away from Carolyn. From Rick. From the force. I declared my life a do-over.

"Four months later I was struggling to establish my own business. Protection and security. Personal and professional. That's when I met your Aunt Vera, a one-woman P.R. firm with a long line of wealthy friends. I owe much of my good fortune to her, even if she does tend to exaggerate."

Sydney frowned. "So when she asked you to drop everything and fly halfway across the country to protect her only niece from a prank caller, you could hardly refuse. I'm the debt called in."

His face softened. "I admit that's how I felt at first."

Her heart skipped a beat. "And now?"

"And now," he said as he leaned back against the pillows and stared up at the ceiling decorated with fluorescent stars, "now I worry about you, and I hardly know you. I admit it, Sydney. You scare the hell out of me. I don't want to care. Can you understand that? I don't want to get involved."

She searched the eyes of the man who'd hunted dangerous criminals, dodged deadly bullets, and essentially stared death in the face and defied it. He was a courageous man. Instinct told her he was afraid of nothing. Except for love. "I understand your reservations, but you said yourself that you need to move on. It's time to forgive Carolyn, Rick, yourself. It's time to forget. Open your heart again. Take a chance." She straddled him, grabbed two fistfuls of his rumpled shirt, and gave him a shaky smile. "On me. You said yourself you feel *something*. Something is more than nothing."

Winn looked into her soulful green eyes and could honestly admit he'd never been more confused in his life. The dark, empty place he'd once called his heart—the cold, dank hollow long abandoned of emotion—was suddenly rushed by a foreign sense of warmth. He didn't like it. "Don't do this, kid," he warned, as much to himself as to her.

She pulled him closer, her lips a breath from his own. "I have to. I need you. We are one." She leaned into him and proceeded to melt away years of icy indifference with a kiss that stoked the dying embers in his soul.

Unable to deny his feelings any longer, Winn surrendered to her touch. He captured her face in his hands, his tongue seeking hers, and she welcomed him, drew him deeper into her world. Withholding nothing. Offering everything—body, mind, and soul.

Wild with an urgency that frightened him, he buried his hands in her hair and plundered her soft mouth. He could feel her heat through her thin cotton shorts, could feel her delicate hands raking through his hair, urging him closer, begging him to devour all that she offered. Need raged through him, hot and strong.

He'd tried to hold back. Had tried to be a gentleman. Had given her every opportunity to stay away. She didn't. Couldn't. As he no longer could. The heat and the hardness pulsating throughout him nearly drove him out of his mind.

He dropped his hands to her hips, his fingers driving under her shirt, tracing the hot skin along the band of her shorts. Dragging his mouth across her jaw, her whimper deepened to a groan as he savored the sweetness pooled in the hollow of her neck, the dip of her collarbone.

Her breath became ragged, labored, and her hips began to grind against his. Like a madman, he whipped her shirt up to her shoulders and claimed one of her breasts with his mouth.

She cried out in pleasure. His blood pounded harder. As she clutched his hair in her fists, he skimmed his lips across the smooth valley to her other breast. He felt her jolt, her sharp intake of breath.

He didn't know how much more he could take. He'd never been this out of control, this driven so close to the edge. He could've sworn his ravaged mind even heard the notes of a flute.

He had to stop. For her sake. If he didn't now, there'd be no going back.

It would make leaving that much harder.

He ended the kiss and pulled down her shirt. With quick, careful maneuvering, he was on his feet. They stared at one another, barely able to breathe. He knew the hunger, hot and bright in her eyes, mirrored his own. It took every ounce of his

willpower not to grab her, lay her down, and make her his.
Forever.

He needed distance. He needed a cold shower.

He needed to get his head examined for thinking he had a chance at a normal relationship.

As he looked down at her, he was unable to tear himself away. Hair tousled, lips moist and swollen from his kiss, she looked vulnerable and sexy as hell. Why did he suddenly prefer baggy boxer shorts to a sheer black teddy?

Frantically he tried to conjure the image of Carolyn and Rick together in bed. He tried to summon the backstabbing hurt. Anything to smother the tender feelings swirling in his heart.

"Forgive and forget Carolyn," Sydney implored as though she'd read his thoughts. "It was a glitch in the grand design. The two of you weren't meant to be. *We* were meant to be."

His heart thudded in his chest. He backed away from Sydney as he would from a motion-sensitive bomb.

Sweat broke out along his brow.

That damned kiss. Sydney hadn't fainted this time, but he felt woozy as hell.

Winn knew in that mind-numbing instant that Sydney Vaughn, a woman in serious need of a reality check, had gotten to him. In that mind-numbing instant, he knew he'd never be the same.

She didn't move, watching through beseeching eyes as he backed away. "Winn, if nothing else, please promise me one thing."

Those green eyes. God, they looked right through him. He had to get the hell out of here. "What's that?"

"Don't leave."

Twelve

England, 1315

Swords clashed, shrill with the promise of death.

Baldric lunged.

Moonlight flashed off his blade before it sank deep into his attacker's shoulder.

A piteous cry bubbled in the man's throat.

Baldric withdrew the steel.

Clutching his wound, the man sank to his knees, crying for the saints to spare his miserable life.

Baldric felt no pity. As the whimpering man before him would spare no pity. But Baldric was not without charity. His enemy had proven little challenge. `Twould be naught but savagery to slay such an unworthy opponent.

With a graceful arc of his sword, Baldric relieved the man of his weapon and prodded him toward retreat. The scraggly miscreant raced toward the woods. He did not look back.

God's teeth, he knew that insufferable cart would entice trouble.

Through the chaos he found Simon holding his own against two bulky marauders. In an instant, Baldric fought at his brother's side.

Simon grinned. As usual, he brandished his sword with dramatic skill, flourishing in the element he cherished most. "For me?" he shouted to Baldric over the raging battle. "You shouldn't have."

Simon delighted in the unexpected confrontation. His devilish white smile proved as intimidating as any weapon of war. Baldric, however, savored no such thrill. Gillian Marrick remained under his protection. Until her safety was assured, there'd be no peace within him.

Fortunately, none of the attackers proved a match for the brothers' proficient swordplay. Giffard and FitzHubert, abruptly roused from their drunken sleep, offered their own brand of resistance with brute strength.

The marauding band had attacked as a dozen or more. Four remained.

Some had run off. Others lay injured or dead.

Eloise screamed. A bloodcurdling cry that knotted his gut.

Gillian.

Intent on ending the skirmish, Baldric dodged the thrust of a dagger and knocked the assailant cold with his sword hilt. Snatching the fallen man's weapon, he dashed through the fray, rolled under the cart, and handed Eloise the still clean dagger.

Then his heart stopped.

A sickening chill blew through him as he realized the second shadow beneath the cart was not Gillian, but his squire, Ivo.

The fires of hell must've burned in Baldric's eyes for Ivo scurried back against the farthest wheel, more petrified of his lord than of the raging battle.

"Dear heaven, what have I done?" Eloise cried, staring at the dagger in wide-eyed horror.

"Where is she?" The demand carried the solemn promise of retribution.

The maid shrank away from him. "The stream. I allowed her to go alone." Her mouth trembled as tears ran down her pale face. "What have I done?"

"Indeed." He sprang out from under the cart and to his feet.

Simon had felled his attacker and dallied with the last remaining. Giffard and FitzHubert surveyed the bodies—some writhing, some still—beaming with pride.

Simon looked to his brother and frowned when he saw his face.

"Gillian."

The single word registered in Simon's eyes. "Go," he ordered. "Take Giffard and FitzHubert." He deflected a blow, then slammed his boot into the gut of the pathetic creature that dared challenge him. "I am almost finished here."

Baldric sheathed his sword and waved back Redmere's knights. "Attend to the injured. I go alone." He turned back to his brother. "If I am not back…"

"I shall find you."

Baldric's heart pounded as he mounted the steed Ivo had readied. With a glare at his cowardly squire, Baldric raced headlong into the dark unknown.

Fear. An emotion that rarely plagued him. It churned inside of him, reeked in his nostrils with the heavy pungency of sweat.

He felt it not for himself. But for Gillian.

The very thought of her alone in the wild, at the mercy of man and beast, nearly drove him mad.

He urged his steed faster, barely dodging trees and brush. What had possessed her to refuse their protection?

What had possessed Eloise to allow such foolishness?

He cursed their stupidity, and mostly his own. He'd allowed himself to be distracted by that chattering magpie, Eloise.

A branch lashed his cheek. The sharp sting and the warm rush of blood brought a cynical smile to his lips. He deserved it, and worse, for his careless mistake. Should a horrific fate befall Gillian, 'twould be his fault. 'Twas his duty as a gentleman and a knight to protect her.

He'd failed.

Sweat stung his eyes, his wound. His breath heaved, rushing like the wind in his ears. *Gillian.* He prayed to God he'd find her. Prayed to God he'd find her alive.

Within moments, he rode along the stream's edge. Moonbeams slipped through the treetops, bathing the clearing in a silvery haze. He stopped his horse. The jingle of the reins echoed like a lonely cry in the night.

He was alone. He knew it before he even called her name. Once. Twice.

***

Gillian drifted along the dark edge of consciousness. She felt no fear. No discomfort. Only serenity as memories weaved through her mind like vivid threads of a tapestry. She felt sunshine warmth as she sank into the dreamy haze of one particular summer. The summer between childhood's whimsy and womanhood's duty.

Against her father's rules, she'd snuck away from the keep. She ran barefoot along the dirt path to the nearby lake, where she stripped down to her skin and dove into the cool, murky depths. Oh, the sheer freedom and daring of plowing through the silken water like an anchor, her heart in her throat as she touched the bottom of the abyss, then shooting back to the surface to rejoice in the golden sun and pure air that testified her bravery. At that moment, she'd felt invincible, as if nothing could stop her.

Agitated voices shattered her illusion. Just as when she'd shot up from the lake bottom, her mind now hurled toward the light of awareness. And pain. Burning, searing pain.

She curled stiff fingers to her wrists, feeling the rough bindings cutting her skin. Rope. Not daring any further movement, she assumed the same for her blazing ankles.

She might have screamed, but the rank cloth shoved into her mouth rendered useless any cry. Not to mention it would alert her captors of her wakeful state. Something she did not want to face.

Instead, she slightly cracked open her eyes. The pale dawn light pierced her skull despite the mist swirling through the crooked arms of the trees beneath which she lay. She did not flinch, nor did she groan. Not even when she spotted the three brutes standing a mere arm's length away.

If ever she needed to prove her bravery, it was now.

"Kill the bitch and be done with it," one spat. "She is not worth the trouble should her party discover us." He swiped a tattered sleeve across a gash in his forehead. "We've lost too many men as is."

"Nay," another argued. "She'll fetch a sack of gold in ransom. No common wench travels with such an impressive escort."

"Aye," the third man agreed. "Let us ride fast and far from here, the wench along with us. If not for ransom, then for pleasure. She's a comely one, aye. I tire of dipping my wick into pock-marked whores."

Gillian's stomach lurched.

"As long as you remember to share, Titus."

Bile stung her throat as the misbegotten curs laughed, a hoarse barking sound that echoed through the mist and straight to Hell. No matter the fate they chose for her, it would end in horror and pain. She suspected mercy had long since abandoned their wretched souls.

She must escape. Or die.

As she dug her heels into the ground, white-hot pain flashed behind her eyes. She gritted the gag between her teeth before pushing herself, ever so slowly, toward the deeper thicket of woods. The men, consumed by their heated debate, did not seem to notice.

Stones and branches bit into the soft flesh of her back. Her body screamed, but she kept moving, chased by the specter of a slow, terrible death.

Closer. Closer. Only a little farther—

"Well, well," the one called Titus drawled as he stepped over her, planting his filthy, ratty boots on either side of her hips. "The noble bitch awakens."

His dark eyes savored her like a hound would a chop. Spittle clung to his scraggly beard as he seemed to drool over his feast—yellow-brown teeth bared, ready to devour.

She'd been a fool to leave Baldric. A complete fool.

She swallowed her rising hysteria. Only her wits could protect her now, and she knew to show fear would be to slit her own throat. She remained still, without a whimper.

An odious smell arrived on Titus' heels.

Her memory stirred at the familiar stench.

Her abductor.

He grabbed her by the forearms and hauled her to her feet. Her heart nearly burst through her ribs. She twisted. Thrashed. Clawed.

"Go on," he urged, eyes bright with expectation. "Fight me. I like it rough."

He ripped the gag from her mouth and leaned in to kiss her.

His foul breath curdled the contents of her stomach. She snapped her head back and spit in his face.

"Bitch!" Features contorted in anger, he struck her temple with a meaty fist. "Whore!"

The blow sent her reeling. Ankles bound, she fell onto her

side. Hard. Her breath whooshed out in one agonizing gasp. The world began to darken as her body shut down, unable to sustain the pain or the fear.

Titus raised his fist then stopped. Something thundered toward them. The men turned—

An ebony warhorse charged out of the mist. Like an angry god, the rider's eyes blazed with vengeance. Sword drawn in attack.

Baldric.

The realization snatched her from encroaching oblivion. She sagged into the dirt.

He struck down two men as they drew their weapons. Both crumpled to the ground in silence, screams lodged in their throats

Baldric veered his mighty horse toward Titus.

The man, sword in hand, growled like a rabid canine.

Fearing for Baldric, Gillian kicked out at his adversary. She missed.

Titus did not. His kick landed swift and hard in her stomach. Crying out, she curled into a tight ball.

Baldric vaulted from his horse. In two steps, he ran his blade through Titus' heart. In an instant. Without hesitation.

The slain man dropped at her feet. The fertile brown earth ran red with his blood.

She swallowed, determined not to be sick.

"Are there more?" Baldric demanded.

His rough voice made her flinch, but she shook her head.

He sheathed his sword and dropped to his knees beside her. Wordlessly, he untied the ropes shredding her wrists and ankles. He tossed the bindings to the ground, then scooped her up and cradled her in his arms.

His tenderness undid her. She closed her eyes and wept. She hated the weak display, but there was no help for it.

"Fear not, small one." His voice softened as he stroked a calming hand along her cheek. "I am here."

The heat of his skin radiated through his mail, assuring her of his blessed presence. The scent of his sweat proved a testament to his valiant labors. Labors that had saved her own fool life.

Drawing a ragged breath, she opened her eyes, dashed her tears. That same breath caught in her throat as she spotted the nasty gash on his cheek. "You are hurt."

"A scratch," he assured. "Do not fret, m`lady. I have survived worse."

Before she could protest his disregard, he shifted, affording her a clear view of her attacker. Crimson blood gurgled from his wound.

Bile again scalded her throat. "I believe I am to be sick." She twisted in his arms, and he set her down. On her hands and knees, she retched. Her damp, matted hair hung over her face as she shivered, feverish with nausea and mortification.

He pressed a cool cloth to the back of her neck. The comforting gesture made her eyes sting with tears. The unthinkable deeds that she might have suffered this moment...

Weak, trembling, and completely empty, she allowed Baldric to sit her upright. He tipped the animal-skinned flask, soaked the cloth once more, then tended her sweating brow with sure, gentle ministrations.

Handing her the flask, he urged her to drink. "`Twill rinse the bitter taste from your mouth."

The warm compassion in his eyes wrapped around her like a thick down blanket. She mentally clutched it close, needful of his warmth and security as she drank fresh water from the flask.

Sir Baldric's legend had indeed sprouted from truth. A proud warrior, he carried himself with confidence and strength, ready for any challenge. A formidable foe, he wielded his sword with singular grace, arcing and swiping his blade in a mesmerizing dance of death. He was noble and honest, tolerating injustice as he would a snake in his bed. Most of all, he had not allowed the harsh cruelties of life to kill his heart.

She sighed. A woman could lose herself to such a man.

In that instant, morbid irony smacked her in the chest.

One should be careful for what one wishes.

She had almost lost herself to a man. The wrong man.

Not Baldric. But Titus. Or one of his wicked friends.

They'd meant to rape her.

Her pulse hammered.

What if Baldric had not discovered her in time? What if he had been slain because of her selfish endeavor?

Tears streaked hot paths down her cheeks.

Baldric smiled consolably as he smoothed away her tears with his thumb. "'Tis over, small one. Think on this no more."

He took the flask from her grip, set it on the ground, and reached for her hands. Inspecting the raw welts, he muttered a violent oath.

She flinched as he turned them over.

His dark gaze shot to her face. "Forgive me," he whispered and cautiously set her hands back onto her lap.

"'Tis my own doing," she admitted on a rasp of breath, turning away her head. 'Twas difficult to endure such kindness from the man she had plotted to deceive.

His gentle fingers nudged her to face him. "You could not have guessed at the consequences," he said, swiping at a renegade tear. "I now forbid you to wander off alone."

"I shan't leave your sight," she vowed, attempting a tremulous smile.

He smiled in turn, tucking a piece of her disheveled hair behind her ear. The smile disintegrated. His eyes burned as he glared at her throbbing temple. She assumed he found a swelling bruise.

"Bastard!" He glared with venom at Titus' corpse. "I should have left him to suffer."

Gillian watched Baldric's eyes flash with a thousand scenarios of torture. She placed her hand on his arm, ignoring what felt like a ring of fire torching her wrist. "'Tis done, Baldric," she said, abandoning formality. "You have saved my life. I am forever grateful."

He glanced at her hand, then searched her eyes for a long, aching moment. "You are most welcome, sweet lady—and most beautiful."

Her breath caught. His deep, rhythmic voice cast her heart aflutter, like a butterfly newly shed of its cocoon. "You are too kind, sir. Surely I look a dreadful sight."

"Never," he whispered.

Then, closing his eyes, he touched his lips to hers.

A threaded bolt of passion, fear, and bittersweet joy shot to her very soul. `Twas her first kiss, and she knew it had been meant for Baldric. Always Baldric.

His kiss was gentle, querying, harnessing the power to sweep her away to a secret, forbidden paradise. Guided by instinct, she answered, splaying her fingers into his silky, raven hair, drawing him deeper.

A low, animal-like growl rumbled through him as he slid his arms around her and crushed her against his hard, mailed chest.

Golden light exploded inside her as her heart forever left the darkness and found its way home. Forever it would reside with Baldric, even as her body remained locked away within the cold walls of Willingham.

"My apologies."

Gillian reared back at the voice. Breath stalled in her lungs, she half expected to find Titus looming overhead, sword drawn.

`Twas Simon.

She felt no rush of relief as he pinned her with a cold glare. Cursing her, no doubt. Branding her a witch and a whore. Indeed she did suffer shame, but not for the kiss. She regretted stealing away into the night. For endangering Baldric's life. But she did not regret the kiss. Never.

She looked to Baldric, wondering if regret chased the ardor rushing through his veins. His expression betrayed naught.

Beneath his cool facade, Baldric's heart pounded like the mighty hooves of his warhorse. God's Blood! Was he insane? Had he been touched by a mischievous wood nymph during his race through the forest?

Aye, `twas madness. `Twas unforgivable. Yet his body had moved of its own volition. When he had discovered Gillian alive, emotions he could not hope to name had overpowered him, inducing him to act without thought. To act with his heart.

A grand mistake. Twofold. Not only had he revealed his amorous feelings to her but also to his brother. `Twould be hell to pay. Simon's ominous expression promised it.

Best to diffuse the situation in haste. A light voice, a careless laugh. Simon needed to believe the kiss meant naught to Baldric. He could not guess the betrayal of his initial expression, for Gillian Marrick melted the very steel of his mail with her innocent passion.

`Twas more frightening than facing down an army of whooping, raging Scots.

He stood and carefully set her to her feet. She winced, and his heart called out to her. He wanted nothing more than to wrap her back into his arms and kiss away her pain. Instead, he turned to his stony-faced brother with a cocked brow and sly grin. "You could have announced your presence sooner, Simon."

"The brushes rustled with my approach. Twigs snapped. My steed snorted. *I cleared my throat.*" Atop his fine mount, Simon crossed his arms and watched them with imperious distaste. "Mayhap I should have blown a war horn."

"Mayhap," Baldric said with a chuckle.

Simon cocked his own brow. "Shall I have future need of one?"

"I think not," Baldric replied with a lazy stretch, hoping to soothe his brother. Never in his life had he lied to Simon, but then, was he truly lying? It had been sheer lunacy to take liberties with Redmere's betrothed. He could not imagine twice committing such a blatant act of betrayal.

Indicating the felled trio sprawled before them, Baldric said, "I rescued Lady Gillian from an unfortunate situation."

"So I see," said Simon, grudging approval in his voice.

Not daring to look at Gillian, Baldric smiled. "She was simply exhibiting her gratitude."

Simon glared at Gillian. Against his better judgment, Baldric turned to look as well.

She ignored him, her features set in granite as she returned Simon's unrelenting stare. "Were you to offer me a wit of the same consideration, mayhap I would be grateful to you as well, Sir Simon."

Smart girl. Concealing his misery, Baldric slammed his hand to his heart and sucked in a breath as though mortally wounded.

Simon smiled. A rare occurrence.

Gillian remained stoic. Baldric almost wished she would hurl scathing accusations, mayhap throw a tantrum. Anything to dispel the void deadening her lovely green eyes.

But there was naught to be done, save cooling this simmering attraction before they both got burned. Before he completely lost his mind, even if 'twas too late to save his heart.

He blamed no one but himself.

He had surrendered to his heart's desire.

He had wanted to kiss Gillian's sweet, stubborn mouth from the moment he had set eyes on her enchanting face.

Enchanting.

Simon's warning haunted him yet again.

Now, most assuredly, he would pay for this indulgence. For he wanted, more than ever, that which he could not have.

Lady Gillian.

Thirteen

"Ouch!"

"Shan shill."

"What?" Sydney dropped her distracted gaze to Ellie, causing the stool to wobble beneath her feet. "Ow!" Again the hair-prickling pinch as Ellie's pin missed the cloth and pierced her ankle.

"Shan shill!"

Her friend had surely drawn blood this time. Muttering, Sydney yanked back her assaulted foot and balanced on one leg. The stool teetered. A flamingo she was not. "I can't understand a word you're saying with those straight pins in your mouth."

"Sharry." Ellie spit the pins into her palm. "I mean *sorry.* But it's difficult to pin an even hem with you shifting around like a third-grader waiting to pee."

Sydney returned her foot to the stool. "Sharry."

Ellie cocked her head, concern in her blue eyes. "You're not yourself today."

Smoothing her hands over the folds in her skirt, Sydney sighed. "This costume is beautiful, El, just as I envisioned. It'd be a shame if the detail of the embroidered bodice goes unnoticed if I'm face down in the dirt."

"I think I heard a compliment in there somewhere." Ellie turned under an unpinned section of the velvet skirt. "I don't know why you're panicking. The Renaissance Fair won't open until tomorrow, and the dress is only four inches too long. I can whipstitch a hem in less than twenty-four hours." She looked up at Sydney and smiled. "Trust me."

Sydney shuddered. Those two innocuous words chilled her, like fingernails screeching down a chalkboard.

The stool wobbled.

"Ow!"

With a huff and the crack of a knee, Ellie stomped to her

feet. "That does it. Climb down. I'll work with what I have."
Foot tapping, she waited for Sydney to hop to the floor, then
ordered, "Turn around. Let's get you out of this contraption.
And for heaven's sake, *stand still*. I've got to undo thirty-eight
buttons."

Sydney crinkled her brows. "For all of your sewing, you
haven't heard of zippers or Velcro?"

"I was striving for authenticity, smarty-pants." Ellie's
nimble fingers made quick work of the buttons. "Just a few
more…there. That does it."

Yards of heavy velvet pooled around Sydney's ankles. She
stepped out of the gown, thankful for central air conditioning,
and reached for her lavender sundress slung over an armchair.
She dressed slowly, in no particular rush to get home. The
unspoken tension in her house was enough to strain the rafters.

Winn had given new meaning to the word aloof. Yesterday
morning she'd awoken in his arms, feeling strong, confident
that she could somehow fix their problem-plagued ties to the
past. Then her present world had been turned upside down, as
muddled and confused as her dreams.

His kiss. It was unlike anything she'd ever known, yet it
was everything she'd always imagined. She was lost to him
that first day when she'd pulled off his sunglasses and peered
into the soul behind murky brown eyes. Yet nothing prepared
her for the moment his lips touched hers. Her heart had flown
like a bird set free from its cage, spreading its wings, soaring
high, never to return to its solitary confinement. Instead her
heart perched expectantly on high hopes, waiting for Winn's
signal to swoop down and nestle alongside his own.

That gesture, however, seemed highly unlikely. She
recalled how Winn had jumped from her as though burned…or
maybe realizing he was kissing the loony woman trying to
convince him of past lives. Or maybe, dare she hope, the kiss
had convinced him, and it scared the daylights out of him.

After he'd escaped upstairs, she'd sat for a time on the
couch. Unable to move. Barely able to breathe. She could hear
him moving about, the floor creaking as he moved from dresser
to bed and back again. Then his boots rapped on the stairs. He

paused outside the arched doorway to the living room. She didn't turn. From the corner of her eye she saw him looking at her, jaw working as though wanting to say something. Finally, he said, "Two days. I'll give you two more days, Sydney, until the fair is over. Then I'm leaving." The words came out rough, as though scraping past his throat. Then he'd walked out, slamming the door.

Late last night, desolate as she'd tossed and turned in bed, alone, Bert called to let her know he would be driving Winn home. He'd thrown himself a little too heartily into a bottle of scotch and a red-eye poker game. When she hung up, she'd cried herself to sleep, wondering if he always drank so much or if she drove him to it with her constant past-life, past-lover badgering. Not to mention she'd complicated matters by digging up his long-buried wounds.

Instead of fixing things, she'd botched them worse. Instead of pulling him closer, she'd pushed him away.

Trying not to wallow in her misery, this morning she'd switched to autopilot and gone to work. She'd endured the snickers and stares from the breakfast rush. She'd ignored Ida Louise's reference to the size of Winn's shoes: *"You know what they say. Is it true?"* She'd even managed a civil lunch with David, accepting the six long-stemmed roses while dancing around his question: *"Did that security consultant leave yet?"*

She finally told him he was finishing today. She hadn't known what else to say.

Lastly she'd survived a costume fitting with Ellie, the mad pin poker.

Sydney sighed. She had two days. Two days to figure out all of the answers. Unfortunately, she felt as though she'd been dropped in the middle of nowhere, with no compass, no map, and four endless horizons that offered no clue as to which direction to take.

Ellie watched Sydney with quizzical eyes while gathering the costume in one hand and pointing to her sofa with the other. "After you finish dressing, take a seat. I'll fix us a snack."

Sydney bent down to slip on her slouch socks and boots.

"Thanks, but I'm not hungry."

Ellie frowned. "Have you been eating?"

"Yes."

"What? Granola bars and grapes? You're losing weight. I had to take your side seams in an inch, and your last fitting was two weeks ago. While we're on the subject of not taking care of yourself, why are the circles under your eyes growing darker? Wait. Let me guess. Two handsome men in your life. One's obsessed with you. You're obsessed with the other. We should all have such problems."

"Oh, Ellie, I…" Sydney bit her lip to keep it from trembling. Her fingers shook as she fumbled with the laces of her shoes. In a bid for self-control, she yanked hard, snapping off one of her shoestrings.

She burst into tears.

Ellie threw the cumbersome gown over a chair and wrapped her arms around her friend. "Syd, sweetie, what is it? What's wrong?"

"Nothing," she lied. "Oh, everything," she confessed with a choked sob. "Oh, Ellie. He…he…" She started to hiccup.

Ellie pulled Sydney's head to her shoulder and petted her in long, soothing strokes. "He who?" she asked, tone dangerous. "He, David? Or he, Winn?"

"Winn. He…he…" Her throat clogged. Tears streamed down her cheeks. She gulped, trying her best to stem her tears, but they demanded release.

She gave up, gave in, and cried in earnest on her friend's shoulder.

Ellie guided Sydney to the sofa. Together they sank down on the worn cushions. Ellie rocked Sydney in her arms, much the way she comforted her own children.

Sydney's mind reeled. Her life had turned into a roller-coaster ride. Emotional highs and lows to derail the strongest stomach. So far she'd tossed back two bottles of pink stuff and chomped down six rolls of antacid like candy. As Ellie had guessed, she had barely eaten, nor had she slept through these past few nights.

The dream. Gillian and Baldric. She had but to drift off

and they consumed her mind. True, she'd been dreaming of them intermittently for years, but since the night before Winn's arrival, the night she'd first envisioned the castle, the dream had begun to unfold in dramatic detail.

What's more, his presence seemed to trigger her ability to dream in both Baldric's and Gillian's points of view. How could that be? How could she know what they both thought and felt? Driven by the need for answers, she'd riffled through her research books and found a theory on shared dreams. Supposedly two people can experience similar or, on rare occasions, identical dreams. Could that really happen? Winn said he felt something, and though he denied it, maybe he was dreaming, too. Maybe his dreams weren't as vivid. Or maybe, he forgot upon awakening.

Sydney did her best to record her visions, immediately committing her memories to her journal before the images faded. What disturbed her most was the mounting intensity of the emotions accompanying the dream. Dread. Resignation. Hope. Fear.

What brought these ancient souls to a tragic end? Their unspoken love burned between them like a fire in the night, yet Sydney knew the real-life fairy tale in her dreams did not end happily.

Why, she wanted to cry, didn't love conquer all?

Try as she might, she couldn't dream *the dream* in its entirety. As soon as the castle appeared, she'd awaken in a panic, and when her heart finally eased out of her throat, a sense of grieving overcame her.

Death. The castle meant death.

Gillian's death.

Her death.

She couldn't shake the fear of her demise, even in the sober light of day. The only time she felt hope was with Winn. By simply walking into the room and breathing the same air, he filled a deep, nameless void within her, summoning a courage to fight for something she did not fully understand.

She wanted him. She'd asked him to make love to her. If she were completely honest with herself, she'd admit that she'd fallen in love with him. Or was she in love with Baldric? Though weren't they one and the same?

Her head ached. She felt as though she played a macabre game of pin the tail on the donkey, blindfolded, spun around, and pushed headlong into the darkness.

One day left.

She wept harder for her ineptitude.

She'd been given another chance. A chance to rectify a mistake made centuries past. A chance to solve the mystery of whatever tragedy had befallen Gillian and Baldric, she and Winn, all of those lifetimes ago.

And she'd blown it.

She'd failed to interpret the dream. Failed to make heads or tails of the clues. Twenty-three books on dream interpretation and reincarnation hadn't helped her one sorry bit. She supposed, realistically, that she was grasping at far-fetched straws. She'd always been a lousy realist. She actually believed in happily-ever-after.

Now her belief system was being sorely tested.

"I've never seen you like this." Ellie's insistent voice broke through Sydney's cloud of thoughts. "You're an emotional wreck. Swear to God, Sydney, if you don't tell me what that man did, I'm sending Jack over to beat an explanation out of Winn Lacey, ex-cop or no."

Sydney swiped her tears with trembling fingers, answering in the haze of past and present. "We made love and now he can't wait to be rid of me." She swallowed a sob. "He…he…"

Ellie shot to her feet. "That son of a bitch. That contemptible dog. To hell with Jack." She stalked to her corner closet. "I'll take care of this myself!"

Sydney choked back another sob. "Wait. You don't understand."

"I understand plenty," Ellie shouted from inside the closet. A soccer ball, basketball, and a hockey puck came flying out of the makeshift sports locker. "Don't say another word," she ordered, flinging a baseball glove over her shoulder. "You don't have to explain your actions to me. But as for that smooth-talking, seducing ex-cop…" She emerged from the closet red-faced, clutching Jack Jr.'s Little League bat. "…you stay here and pull yourself together. Leave that cad in knight's armor to me!"

Sydney bolted to her feet. "Wait!"

It was too late.

Ellie slammed the door, bat swinging at her side.

***

Winn glanced at his watch.

Five o'clock.

He glanced at the thermometer.

Ninety degrees.

Two degrees hotter than at noon.

He swiped a forearm across his sweating brow. He'd always thought Jersey summers the perfect training ground for Hell, but he'd give anything for a breeze off the Atlantic right now. Indiana felt like one giant barbecue pit, and he wasn't sure whether he owed his headache to the relentless sun driving into the top of his head or to the lingering effects of scotch, cigars, and a late-night poker game.

Cursing the day in general, he returned his attention to Sydney's back porch door, installing the last of the dead bolts he'd purchased at Hank's Hardware earlier this morning.

Key operated from the outside, hand turned from the inside, these dead bolts made damn good secondary locks to the standard door latches he'd just replaced. Next he'd install key bolts and locking pins on her double-sash windows.

If he pushed himself, he could have the old farmhouse rigged with light and motion-sensitive devices by late tonight. Except he'd agreed to give Sydney two days. Two days to…to what? To prove to him that he was her past-life lover? To save them from a certain death unless he believed? He wondered how she planned to convince him. How could one begin to prove something as *unprovable* as past lives?

But he'd agreed to stay. Agreed because of the way her moist, swollen lips had begged him to. Agreed because of the way he'd shamefully panicked and almost deserted her. Agreed because of the way something inside of him clenched at the thought of never seeing her again.

An honorable soul, she'd called him.

God, he'd tried to stay focused on doing the right thing, but nothing was clear anymore. The simple, easy life he'd created for himself lay in ruin, and, for the first time ever, he wondered where he truly belonged.

He hunkered down and concentrated on his work. It was safer and more productive than concentrating on Sydney. He could either take out his frustrations on a nine-inch nail or he could numb them with alcohol.

He'd been doing a lot of drinking lately. Too much.

Enough was enough, he decided, cursing the dull pain behind his temples. His sudden weakness for alcohol baffled him. Never had he been prone to reckless drinking—except, of course, for the roaring binge following Rick and Carolyn's surprise party. An understandable indulgence. A logical reaction.

His reaction to the ever-slightly-unstable Sydney Vaughn, however, was anything but logical.

He wanted her.

In his bed. In his life.

Totally ridiculous. Really, what did he know about this woman besides her obsession with past lives? Did she squeeze the toothpaste tube from the bottom or from the top? Did she like the beach? Did she eat crunchy or creamy peanut butter? Little details. Important details when considering a relationship with someone.

Winn jerked. The drill glanced off the screw head into the doorframe, splintering the wood.

Relationship.

Two orgasmic kisses and he was considering a *relationship*?

Stupefied, he stood at the back door while Sydney's dogs panted and watched him from beneath a tree. He stared back. Lancelot and Guinevere. Of all the names in the world, why had Sydney chosen to name her lovable mutts after a pair of traitors? The duo was medieval, of course, and superheroes to the lovelorn—probably reason enough for Sydney, a girl pumped up on romance like steroids. But these lovers were betrayers. Hardly icons to be revered. Whatever happened to loyalty and honor?

He shivered at the chivalrous sentiment.

Craving a stiff drink and a sane thought, he moved out of the sun and into the house. Hell. As if anyone could have a sane thought in this place. It seemed the more time he spent under Sydney's roof, the less in control he felt of his thoughts and actions. He needed to get out of here. So did Sydney.

With the dogs on his heels, he refilled their water bowls from the kitchen sink, then poured himself an iced tea. As he listened to their noisy slurps, he knew it was time to be honest. At least with himself.

He'd already thought about taking Sydney home to Jersey.

Of course, the instant that insanity had crept into his head, he'd made tracks away from Sydney and any ulcer-inducing inclinations. Yep, he'd managed to block out the vision of her sleeping in his king-sized bed, of making love to her every night, of waking up to her every morning. Yep, he'd handled it like any man accustomed to high-pressure situations. With plenty of scotch.

Now, out of nowhere, the desire to claim Sydney for himself was back and stronger than ever.

As was his desire to wring Vera's do-gooder neck. If not for her, he wouldn't have met Sydney Vaughn and lost his ability to think and behave like a rational human being. If not for Vera, he wouldn't have the seed of an idea growing in his head. An idea so ludicrous that anyone who knew him would rush to the phone to dial the nearest psychoanalyst.

The poker games at Bert's Bar and Grill finally paid off. The grapevine revealed Monroe was cooking up some elaborate plan to win Sydney's hand.

No one knew the details. Only that it would happen at the Renaissance Fair.

Given Sydney's obsession with everything medieval and Monroe's alleged capture of her stalker, Winn worried she might actually relent and accept Monroe's proposal. Winn didn't trust Monroe as far as he'd like to throw him. Anyone who faked an arrest to win affection deserved to be dumped.

And worse. Despite his brush with panic, Winn refused to let Sydney be duped by such a man.

Hence why he'd tailed her to work this morning. Someone had to look after her well-being, and it sure as hell wasn't going to be Monroe.

It was time to fight fire with fire.

Damn. The little idea seed was already running the show. *Goddamn.* He was a goddamned do-gooder, too, except he didn't know which fueled his fire more—his protective instinct of Sydney or his deep dislike of Monroe. Didn't matter. Either way, he meant to win. Then, even if she didn't make it to Jersey with him, he'd convince Sydney to move out of this fourteenth-century makeshift museum called home and start herself a new life.

He glanced down at the etched pewter chalice in his hand. A dragon coiled about a sword.

He shook his head. No wonder she dreamed about knights and castles and maidens in distress. He'd slept in this house for only a few nights, and *he* was having similar dreams. Similar thoughts. And worst of all, similar feelings of *déjà vu.*

Matching his experiences with her reincarnation fascination and her childlike willingness to believe in the impossible, Winn felt as though he understood her.

Almost.

There was no denying the chemistry between them, and as he gulped the last of his iced tea, her heartfelt words echoed in his head. *"We were meant to be. Trust me."*

Like cold needles of freezing rain, the old memories pricked at him, numbed him. Carolyn's and Rick's promises. "Never again," Winn mumbled, shaking his head as he placed the empty chalice in the sink. Yes, he'd give Sydney his protection, and the way things were going, perhaps even his devotion.

But never his heart.

He couldn't risk it. Something inside him wouldn't allow it. Probably old scar tissue from sharp betrayal. An obvious, rational conclusion. Nothing more deep-seated than that, as

Sydney would like him to believe.

However, as much as he tried to convince himself, something else, something equally as powerful, nagged at him. Something that hinted there was more to this story.

Winn pushed himself away from the counter and back outside, dismissing the thought with a heavy sigh. "No more investigative reading for you, Lacey." He stooped down to swipe up the drill and resume his work. "Especially when you're three sheets to the wind." Syd's new-age books had gone to his head.

"Cop or no cop, I'll beat you within a breath of your life if you ever make her cry again!"

Winn snapped his head up. Ellie Bane barreled toward him, long, agitated strides eating up the expanse of Sydney's lawn. The dogs whined and danced about her, hoping for a pat or a treat. Probably both.

"Ex-cop," he corrected as she neared, "and I'd feel a helluva lot better if you didn't punctuate each word with that baseball bat."

"I bet you would." Ellie lowered her weapon but held it firmly, eyes narrowed at him. "How could you?"

"How could I what?"

"I hope for Sydney's sake you at least used protection. Risking pregnancy is one thing, but with the things going around these days, and with you being the hound that I suspect you are...*Oh!*" Unable to finish her sentence, she jammed the tip of the bat into the grass.

Winn couldn't believe his ears. "Are you suggesting—"

"You must be one helluva charmer, Tiger. You got in four days what David Monroe's been after for a *year*! At least David is willing to marry her. All Sydney got from you was the old slam-bam, I'm-outta-here, thank-you ma'am!"

Winn tossed the drill onto the grass. "I kissed her, I admit it. I've fantasized about making love to her. Hell, I'll admit to that, too. As for literally getting her between the sheets, it hasn't happened, Bane. If Sydney led you to believe otherwise, she's lying."

Ellie waved the tip of the bat beneath his nose. "You take

that back."

He nudged the weapon aside. "Which part?"

"The part about Sydney being a liar. She'd never lie to me. Especially about something as serious as losing her virginity."

Winn cocked his head, unsure he'd heard right. "Sydney's a virgin?"

Ellie's eyes flashed as her fingers flexed on the bat. "You mean to tell me it slipped your notice? What kind of a man are you?"

Sydney? A virgin? A woman in her late twenties, in the twenty-first century, a virgin? Not that he believed her the type to sleep around. But *a virgin?*

His heart gave a sudden, primeval lurch. She'd never given herself to another man. She'd never given herself to Monroe. He'd just assumed...

A smile eased across his face. He was pleased, actually pleased.

And relieved.

Ellie scowled at him. "You're despicable."

"What exactly did Sydney say to you?"

"She said the two of you made love and now you want nothing to do with her." Ellie waved her hand. "Or something to that effect."

"Ahh," Winn said with sudden understanding. Despite himself, he chuckled at what could only be a conversation about Sydney Vaughn.

"What do you mean, *ahhh?* And what's so damned funny about stealing a woman's virginity?"

"Nothing, except she claimed the theft took place almost seven hundred years ago."

Ellie furrowed dubious brows. "What are you babbling about, Lacey?"

"Gillian and Baldric. The dream." Winn snapped his fingers in front of her puzzled face. "Get with the program, Bane. I know she talks to you about that past-life, repeating-history mumbo-jumbo."

"Oh, geez." Ellie sighed as realization dawned in her eyes.

"She tried to explain, but I was a little pumped up."

Winn indicated the bat. "Really?"

"Oh, geez," she repeated, tossing aside the weapon.

"As for wanting nothing to do with her, I confess I avoided her last night. We...there was another kiss. It left me dizzy, for chrissake." Disgruntled, he raked a hand through his hair. "That's a little scary for a man my age. I needed some distance."

Ellie's mouth twitched upward. "Dizzy, you say?"

"Repeat that to another living soul, Bane, and I'll," he eyed the bat, "deny it."

Her smile rose then fell in an instant. "Wait a minute. So you're saying, you and she...she and you...you didn't actually..."

"Not in this lifetime."

"Which means she's still a..."

"Virgin," he finished with a full-blown grin.

Ellie paled. She'd unwittingly disclosed her best friend's most guarded and personal secret. "Oh, geez," she mumbled for the third time, the wind knocked out of her.

Winn took pity on her. He looped his arm over her shoulder and guided her toward her car. "I'll make a deal with you, Bane. I won't let on to Sydney about your slip if you can hook me up with a costume by tomorrow morning."

Ellie's suspicious look matched her tone. "What sort of costume?"

"One worthy of a medieval knight, of course."

She frowned. "What are you planning to do?"

He smiled. "Let's call it an intervention."

"I was afraid you'd say that."

"Are you with me?"

Ellie raised one finely tweezed brow. "Dizzy, huh?"

He fixed his gaze on the barn's weather vane and shrugged. He couldn't stand to see Ellie gloat.

"You'll look devastating in mail. Poor David. He doesn't stand a chance."

Winn fought the sickening wave in his gut at the mention of Monroe. "I hope you're right, Bane. I hope to hell you're right."

Fourteen

England, 1315

Baldric's senses tingled at full alert.

As the sun began to sink into another world beyond Brentwood Forest, the path before them degenerated into a haven of shapes and shadows. A haven for villains and thieves. Darkness beckoned debauchery, lured a man into its cloaked embrace and seduced him to perform nefarious acts he'd dare not commit under heaven's golden light.

Baldric watched the dense brush lining the narrow path, forcing his eyes to adjust to the murky twilight.

`Twould be a winter without snow before he'd fall prey to a second attack.

No matter that two days had passed since Gillian's abduction. He'd never forget the fear in her eyes. The fear in his heart. `Twould be a far greater mercy to submit to the cold steel of his own blade than to endure the mere thought of Gillian trapped in the hands of another ruthless killer.

His blood still burned for the bastards who'd caused her pain. It had been his pleasure to deliver them all, one by one, straight into the bowels of Hell.

Yet, despite it all, the paradox of life still managed to amaze him. One moment blood and death writhed about them in a world gone mad. The next it was as though the stars had never shined brighter.

Gillian's kiss.

`Twas magical.

He'd kissed scores of women in his lifetime. Never had he imagined one kiss capable of seizing one's heart and soul. So completely. So sweetly. Not even in his dreams had he imagined a love so deep, so pure that its pulse thrummed with the very heart of Nature.

Aye, he admitted with a heavy heart, he loved Gillian Marrick in a way he did not fully comprehend. This manner of love to him was foreign. `Twas more powerful than simple lust or infatuation. This manner of love fused his heart with hers for all eternity. If he never possessed her physically, no difference would it make. She would possess his heart always.

Overwhelmed by the rushing tide of his emotions, he dared not turn his gaze from his diligent watch of the forest. One furtive glance at his beloved and his soul would be bared to all. Still, somehow, as she rode quietly beside him, he could sense her slightest movement, feel the vibration of her own taught emotions.

The group weaved its way through the woodland, a seemingly endless maze of ancient oaks and gnarled, rambling bushes. A confusing path to Gillian perhaps, but not to Baldric or to the other men. Simon and Baldric met Redmere's knights along this path only days ere, then traveled together to retain the baron's betrothed. A faceless woman to whom Baldric had not heeded much thought.

Five days ere, he'd rode along this path with a joyful heart, contemplating his good fortune, anticipating the return of his ancestral home. Five days ere, he'd dismissed Simon's talk of bewitching maidens and unrequited love, his own response a teasing smirk and a glib remark.

Five days ere, his mind had been consumed with Darbingshire. Now Gillian Marrick consumed his thoughts and, as Simon had warned, his heart.

Though she fought valiantly to hide it, Baldric suspected Gillian's heart to have suffered the same fate. She spoke not of her feelings. No need. Love shone from the depths of her beautiful, sea green eyes. Love for him.

'Twas fantastic. Fantastic and maddening. For no good could come of this insatiable wanting, no matter how mutual the need. She belonged to another. To a man he owed allegiance. To a man who'd been all but a flesh-and-blood father to Lisbeth. For that reason alone, Baldric could not, in good conscience, act upon his feelings. No matter how strong.

Unless…unless there flickered a flame of truth in Gillian's darkest fear. Unless Redmere had indeed been in some way responsible for Catherine's and Margaret's deaths. Then Baldric could, in all justifiable manner, act upon his feelings.

This did not lighten his spirits. No matter which direction the fates decided to blow, someone would suffer. Of that he was certain.

The hair on the back of his neck prickled.

He shot out his hand for all to halt.

Someone was near.

He cocked his head, straining to hear a clue that would otherwise slip by in the sounds of the living forest.

Music. A flute. Its whimsical notes danced past his ear on the evening breeze. Merry on an eve wrought with foreboding.

In tacit understanding from years of shared battle, Baldric rode ahead to investigate for friend or foe while Simon remained to guard the women. Baldric dared not leave them to the dubious protection of Redmere's knights.

Drawing upon a clearing, he was greeted by not one but six musicians, all with instruments tucked under their arms. Save for the flute player. He continued on, kicking up his heels to his own infectious melody. An olive-skinned woman draped in colorful fabrics joined in, whistling and shuffling about while she stirred a pot over a crackling fire. The pungent scent of onions and garlic wafted through the air to tempt Baldric's stomach. It growled. He and his party had yet to stop and sup.

He remained on the fringes of the woods until an old man stepped forward with a toothless but hospitable smile. He bowed low then straightened, as much as one could with a waywardly crooked back, and then waved forward the troupe. A funny-faced monkey, no bigger than a rabbit, balanced itself upon the elder's hunched shoulder. Mimicking his owner, the monkey waved its scrawny, furry arm to Baldric. An invitation to join the festivities.

Baldric's smile grew of its own volition. He cautiously urged his mount forward and surveyed the grounds. He sensed no danger. Only a collective mood of revelry. As he passed each bedraggled person, he was greeted with a welcoming smile. He found nothing in their eyes but invitation and merriment. These were people who cared not where a person was born, where he'd been, or where he intended to go. These wanderers lived for the moment, never hesitating to celebrate a warm night or a full belly.

"Join us," the old man called to him. "You look weary and we have food and good will aplenty."

"You are kind," Baldric replied with a nod before returning to the dark timber.

Tension had mounted among his party since that fateful night. Gillian and Eloise remained skittish and uneasy. Simon and he maintained their guard while Redmere's knights nurtured their aggression, eyes bright with talk of death. Good cheer, even in the whimsical form of wandering minstrels, seemed in good order.

Simon grunted his disapproval as Baldric led the group to the friendly performers. Jugglers, musicians, and a lone rosy-cheeked jester broke into simultaneous action, a comical welcome impossible to ignore, even for the mirthless Simon. His brother flattened what suspiciously resembled a grin before leaning near Baldric. "I implore you, Brother. Let us ride through the night. End this unfortunate journey before it becomes the end of you."

Baldric matched Simon's hushed tone. "For the last time... 'twas no meaning in that kiss."

Simon narrowed ice blue eyes. "*That kiss* was hot enough to singe my horse's nose hairs. I draw within four paces of you and Lady Gillian, and my skin burns from simmering passion. 'Tis as though you make love without touching! I sense it. Maid Eloise senses it. I fear Giffard and FitzHubert, half-wits that they are, will sense it, if they have not already. Think you at first opportunity they would not enlighten Redmere? God's teeth, Baldric, if you care not for your own well-being, at least consider the girl! Think of her father. Mayhap you have forgotten your love of land. She, I am most certain, has not. She carries those wilted flowers of Heatherwood in that damned pouch about her waist. A pitiful yet powerful testament to her devotion."

Baldric tightened his grip on the reins so as not to knock his brother from his horse.

"What of *your* devotion to family and home?" Simon pressed. "What of Darbingshire? What of Lisbeth?"

Baldric grit his teeth. No matter what good sense his brother spoke, he wished not to hear it. `Twas a night for them to forget who they were for a few hours and enjoy life as it was meant to be lived.

`Twas a window in time that would never be opened again.

Baldric glanced over his shoulder to Gillian. Her attention was upon neither he nor Simon, nor the elder and his monkey, but rather two jugglers across the way, tossing and catching apples in a rapid, alternating pattern.

`Twas then he noticed her smile. So tiny `twould be easily missed upon first glance, but `twas there nonetheless. A rare expression for one who moved through her days as though burdening the weight of the world upon her slight shoulders.

His heart swelled. `Twas all he needed to see.

"We accept your hospitality," he called to the old man, the apparent leader of the merrymaking band.

"Julius," the man said with his huge, cavernous grin.

Baldric dismounted. With the formalities commenced, `twas naught to do but join the excitement. They'd ridden hard this day and the day ere. On the morrow they would resume their pace. Tonight, however, they would partake in good food, wine, and company. Mayhap even enjoy a peaceful night's rest.

Baldric knew, come the morrow, he would need all of his strength.

Julius twice clapped his hands. Out of the covered carts hopped five more colorfully garbed women, giggling and waving and looking especially pleased upon seeing the knights. Giffard and FitzHubert wasted no time in dismounting and moving forth into welcoming arms.

The squires, eyes wide with delight, quickly tended the horses while Eloise, after whispering something into her lady's ear, hurried toward the brewing stew. After long hesitation, Simon dismounted and was reluctantly drawn into conversation with Julius.

Baldric and Gillian stood alone.

Their gazes locked. The longing in her soulful green eyes

pulled at him as surely as if she'd grabbed him with her two fists. He stood his ground, knowing full well that if he moved forth he risked sweeping her into his arms. Risked kissing her in front of God and immediate country. Yet he could not look away. Myriad emotions glinted in her gaze, as if the past, present, and future collided within their depths.

Longing. Sadness. Resignation.

He could stand it not.

He stepped forward.

Out of nowhere Simon's gloved hand slammed against his chest.

"Hold," he commanded softly. "Think, Brother."

At once Baldric met FitzHubert's scrutinizing gaze. Baldric stepped back. He did not look at Gillian.

For the moment.

For the moment, he allowed Simon to slide his arm over his shoulder and guide him toward their host, Julius, and to his monkey, who they soon learned to be named Skitter.

Time passed. Dusk gave way to the encroaching darkness of a starless night. Or mayhap, Gillian thought as she tipped back her head and squinted skyward, the stars did twinkle somewhere high above in the unreachable heavens.

She sighed. For now the only light radiated from the cook fire in the center of the traveling band's encampment. Beyond the glowing flames, beyond the covered carts and circle of immediate trees, darkness reigned. Evil lurked. So it seemed to Gillian as she reflected on the gruesome details of her reckless escapade.

She shivered as she glanced down at her wrists, still red and chafed from the harsh twine that had bound them so tightly. The injury seemed slight compared to the bruise marring her temple like an ugly badge of stupidity. *Served her right*, Simon had said. *How naïve she'd been to wander off alone into the forest. How incredibly dense. How selfish.* She hated nothing more than having to agree with the surly knight. However, even she would not dispute the truth.

She had risked her life as well as Baldric's.

The image of him charging forth on his warhorse, sword

drawn and mortally aimed in her defense, haunted her every moment, both awake and asleep. Her stomach still turned when envisioning the blood spilled that fateful day. Worse, she could not shake the powerful feeling that more blood would be shed in her name. Worse still, that `twould be her fault.

Death. She sensed it to her very core.

It sickened her.

True, death had visited Heatherwood enough times that mayhap she should be numb to its ever-prowling presence. Gone were her mother and her brothers, James, Guy, and Aiden. Lost were those she'd loved in her lifetime. Now her father...nay, she could not bear to think upon her father's demise. Disease and war had stormed through her family, ravaging and killing with a cold calculation that made her shiver.

This last year she had tried so very hard not to love anyone save for her father and Eloise. She had folded her emotions into tiny bits and tucked them away within the deep crevices of her heart. She'd managed to keep her distance. Until Baldric. Strong, proud, compassionate. In an instant he'd turned her world upside down and inside out.

When she had first schemed to beget his child, her thoughts had been only for her own safety. Now, days later, `twas Baldric's demise she feared most. Were she to conceive, were Redmere to discover her deception, Baldric's neck would surely be stretched in line with hers on the chopping block.

Of that she was certain.

The baron had entrusted him with his betrothed's life, her honor. Should Baldric forsake either one, `twould be hell to pay. Though `twas not her disgrace that would incite Redmere's wrath, but his own humiliation.

Nay, she already faced certain doom. She would not put the noble Sir Baldric at risk. She would not test his *Immortal* legend. She must face Nigel Redmere alone. Endure his despicable attentions and await her inevitable death.

"Alone."

"Pardon?" Baldric asked.

She started. She'd been sitting away from the roaring

celebration, picking at a full bowl of stew and feeling sorry for herself. "'Twas nothing."

He crouched beside her, his leather boots creaking softly as though muted by years of hard wear. The flickering flames of the distant fire played tricks, casting shifting shadows across his handsome features. One moment he appeared childlike, innocent of heart. The next, a warrior, hardened and impenetrable. Then finally, bone weary, as though saddened by the world that had created both.

She longed to trace her finger along each weather-etched line of his face, to erase with one deft caress his plaguing worries. She found herself longing to touch him in other places as well. Touch him as a lover might.

Intimately.

She looked away, the heat of her thoughts burning her skin.

He cupped her chin and stroked her cheek with his thumb. "What troubles you behind those beautiful eyes, m'lady?"

She swallowed, keeping her gaze diverted. If he looked deeply enough, he would discover the truth. *I want to lie with you. Become one with you, if only for a lone night.*

He studied her a moment longer, then withdrew his hand to indicate her barely touched supper. "'Tis not to your liking?"

Emptiness engulfed her at the leave of his touch. "Nay. I mean, aye. 'Tis good. I am not hungry."

Concern narrowed his eyes. "Are you in pain?"

"Nay. My wounds are swiftly healing."

"What of the music? 'Tis to your liking?"

She turned an ear to the minstrels, the complex melodies tugging at her misery. These men, though monetarily impoverished, possessed a wealth in talent. They proved much more proficient than any of Heatherwood's musicians. To think she'd deemed the lute a sad instrument. Apparently 'twas the mood of the player and not the instrument itself, for this musician strummed merry strings, instigating a hearty song that chorused with the trilling flute and bowed viele.

"Aye," she whispered, the hint of a smile on her lips. "'Tis hard not to like that which is so likable."

He stood, reached out his hand and smiled. "M'lady?"

She stared at his palm, uncomprehending.

"Would thou dance with me?" He crooked a hopeful brow.

"I know not how," she said honestly. No matter if she did. She would not dance with this man. This man who, with a simple kiss, melted her insides to run like a wild river of fire through her veins. At the mere remembrance, her breath quickened. Her heart thudded. To endure intimate contact for any duration was asking too much.

"I will teach you," he said.

Teach her? Her face reddened. Oh, aye! To dance. She should have been prepared for his generosity.

From out of the dark Skitter climbed into her lap, scaled up her arm, and perched his furry body upon her shoulder. He weighed little more than a wet kitten. She smiled at him until he started pulling at her hair. "What is he doing?"

Baldric chuckled. "'Twould appear he is searching for insects."

"Insects?" Gillian cried. She plucked Skitter from her shoulder and disentangled her curls from his padded fingers. "If anyone has insects 'tis you, my flea-ridden friend." She set him gently to the ground and gave him a small nudge forward. "Now be gone."

Skitter curled back his lips, darted out his tongue, and made a most obscene noise before scurrying toward his amused owner.

Indeed everyone seemed happy this eventide. Sir Robert and Sir William looked positively euphoric. Simple-minded men with simple wants, Gillian mused. They'd gorged themselves on the stew until their bellies stretched to near bursting, and now they feasted on wine, women, and song.

She thought them disgusting buffoons and pitied the women who would sleep beneath them this night.

Her gaze swept to Eloise, who had captured Sir Simon the Irritable's rapt attention. The redhead's gestures grew more exaggerated by the moment. No doubt she was steeped in one of her bawdy tales—tales that notoriously warmed men all the way to the tips of their ears. However, Simon's attention appeared more on Eloise's heaving bosom than on her brow-raising recital.

At the heart of it all, the musicians played on. Their melodies were growing impossible to resist. As the revelers began to sing, ringing cheer to the treetops, Gillian glanced down to find her toes tapping. She could not stop them. Nor did she want to.

Without warning, Baldric nabbed her forearms and pulled her to her feet. He maneuvered her into a round dance even as she begged him not to. Hands clasped, they danced their way in a circle for what seemed an eternity. At first she fumbled and faltered, but eventually she caught the rhythm. `Twas either that or be trampled, for the entire camp had joined in. Even Simon, much to her amazement. Mayhap he was not as rigid as he'd have her believe.

However, `twas Baldric who amazed her most. He proved swift and fancy of feet. She never imagined him capable of this sort of grace, being so muscled and inherently male.

His complexity intrigued her. She'd witnessed many sides of Sir Baldric the Immortal this sennight. The gallant knight, the merciless warrior, the seducer, the cynic, the charmer, the detached. This moment she cherished his playful side, the warmth of his smile, the impish sparkle in his eyes.

When at last the carol ended, Gillian's senses reeled. Not just from the whirlwind dance but from the realization that she was falling in love.

She'd thought it impossible. Had sworn as much to Eloise.

Foolishly she'd believed herself the ruler of her heart, guiding and bending it to her will. After all, she was a woman of logic. However, `twas as if her heart declared mutiny, severing its bounds from the rational dictates of her mind.

`Twas frightening.

She stood still, trying to catch her breath. Trying to tame her rebellious thoughts as couples broke away one by one into the night.

You are to marry another, said the voice of reason. *This man, this knight, is servant to the King. Honorable, good, and true. He fancies himself indebted to Redmere. He is not capable of betrayal.*

She seemed to glide forward, as though carried by the soft melody of the flute.

You do not love him.

You cannot love him.

You must not love him.

The melody strained higher. Louder.

Be still my heart.

Be strong my heart.

She stood before him. She did not touch him, not with her hands at least. Nay, 'twas her gaze that caressed his proud face, the throbbing pulse at his throat, his broad shoulders and muscled arms. Tears stung her eyes as she studied the callused hand that, one moment, had wielded a deadly sword, then the next, tended so gently to her wounds.

Sir Baldric the Immortal. Mayhap the noblest knight in the realm, so told the legend.

Valiant. Noble. Loyal. A knight's code. A code he will never break.

Gillian lost herself in his questioning gaze. 'Twas foolish to fall in love. Those she loved died.

Do not love him.

Do not love him.

She fought to breathe, the ache in her heart so great.

Baldric's breath lay trapped in his lungs. It took every fiber of his strength not to drop to his knees and declare his love to this woman. His skin burned where her gaze touched him with the passion of a lover's hand. Burned as she branded him hers for all eternity.

As he would be.

From very far away, he heard the faint, sweet trilling of music, the soft rustle of leaves. A horse nickered. Children giggled. Then 'twas as if all sound, save the hypnotic notes of the flute, faded away. Gillian's heated gaze seared him with divine intensity, with a need so strong only his heart could fathom its depth. She wanted him. Physically. Emotionally. Spiritually. She need not speak her desire. 'Twas simmering before him in the verdant pools of her fevered eyes.

He balled his fists at his sides so as not to grab her to him.

So as not to kiss her. And kiss her....

Then she was gone.

Or at least *he* was as Simon locked his arm over Baldric's shoulder and dragged him toward the horses.

The cool night air stabbed at him, provoking him, mocking him.

Before Baldric could gain his senses, Simon turned to him, red-faced. Then he swung Baldric around to face the group behind them. It took him but a moment to ascertain Simon's fury.

Robert FitzHubert.

Standing amidst the oblivious merrymakers, he stared at Baldric, gloating with a smile to turn a man's stomach. The dark minion possessing the deadly secret he could not wait to share with his master.

Hell's teeth!

He looked to Gillian, whose face had paled to a sickly white.

He quickly recounted their actions. They had not touched. They had not spoken. Mayhap he worried for naught.

Gillian closed the space between them.

Without a word, she slapped him across the face.

This time the woman he loved had not declared him a murderer. If her quick ruse failed, mayhap 'twould be an oath better saved for the morrow. When he delivered her unto Willingham.

Unto her betrothed.

Baron Nigel Redmere.

Fifteen

"You what?"

"I might have let it slip that you're a virgin." Ellie tossed the bat into the sports closet, then stayed hidden behind the door.

Sydney marched up behind Ellie and curled her fingers into fists so as not to curl them around her best friend's neck. "*Might* have?"

"All right!" Ellie slammed the door and spun on her sneakers to face Sydney. "I definitely let it slip! I told Winn, though not intentionally, that you're a virgin! Happy now?"

"No!" Sydney's cheeks blazed. "I'm not happy. And why are you yelling at me? I should be yelling at you!"

"You are yelling." Tears glistened in Ellie's big, round eyes. "I wish you'd stop because I'm really upset!"

Sydney threw her arms wide in disbelief then slapped them to her thighs. "*You're* upset."

"Yes." Ellie sniffled and yanked a shredded tissue from her shorts pocket. "I'm upset. I'm the one who betrayed your confidence. I'm the rotten friend. And I have no excuse, except that my big mouth tripped up my good intentions. It's just that I thought, well, you said—" She paused to blow her nose. "You intimated that Winn slept with you."

That took the wind out of Sydney's sails. "You're right. I did. I'm sorry."

"No. I'm sorry."

"We're both sorry," Sydney said with a shaky smile. "I guess it really doesn't matter. He would've found out anyway."

"Excuse me?"

"When we sleep together. It's not like he won't notice. I should thank you actually. You saved me from the 'Oh, by the way, I'm a virgin' part of the show."

Ellie glared at Sydney as though sizing her for a straitjacket. "Oh, yeah, of course. You're welcome. So glad I could help."

"Don't look at me that way, El. Winn and I made love in the past, so we'll make love in the present. Eventually. It's inevitable."

"You're having a nervous breakdown, aren't you?"

"I admit I lost it this afternoon," Sydney said, somewhat embarrassed. "I don't know what came over me except I was at the end of my rope. Winn's avoiding me. I'm avoiding David. I felt like a failure, and you got the brunt of my frustration. Anyway, I'm feeling better now."

"Zippity-do-dah," Ellie said with a frown and a sniffle.

Sydney stretched her arms above her head. "Amazing what a catnap will do for you."

"Hold the phone." Ellie pressed two fingers to her temples. "Are you saying that while I was out making a fool of myself, defending your *intact* virtue, you were sleeping snug as a bug on my couch?"

Sydney nodded, her lips curving into a satisfied grin. "And dreaming."

"Let me guess," Ellie drawled, eyes rolling. "Gillian and Baldric."

Again Sydney nodded. "When I woke I felt stronger. I can't explain it exactly, except that this afternoon I felt the true power of Gillian's and Baldric's devotion. Their selflessness. They each thought they could protect the other, save each other from themselves. It was like nothing I'd ever experienced. You could say I had an epiphany."

"What the hell's an epiphany?"

"A sudden realization. An illuminating discovery. A—"

"I get the picture, Mrs. Webster."

Sydney began to pace the worn carpet. "I've been waiting for Winn to come around," she explained, "to throw his disbeliefs to the wind and put his trust in me, a woman he considers a virtual stranger. Well, he's just not capable of it. But that's okay. I realized I've been relying on his strength when I should be relying on my own. I can do this. I can do it for both of us." She stopped in her tracks, the course before her finally clear. "It's time I took control of my life, El, my destiny."

Ellie crossed her arms. "You're not going to shave your head, are you?"

Sydney actually felt herself glowing, as though her switch had been flipped after a long stint in the darkness. "Not before I clear the air with both Winn and David." She snatched the keys to Ellie's pickup truck. "I need to do it now. Before I lose my nerve."

"Wait!" Ellie raced out the door after Sydney. "Where are you going?"

"I'll start with David."

"Start *what* with David? Wait!" Ellie caught up to Sydney as the truck door creaked open on rusty hinges. "I'll drive." Ellie plucked the baby-shoe key chain from Sydney's hand. "You're too pumped up."

Sydney slid across the vinyl bench seat, tossing action figures and an empty caramel-popcorn box to the cluttered floor. She felt ready to jump out of her skin as she surveyed the mess at her feet. She wanted this. A husband. A child. Someone with whom to share the simple pleasures of life, to share the joys and the disappointments as they discovered the surprises at the bottom of life's box, together.

This was the first step in the right direction.

Ellie gunned the gas, and they spun out of the gravel-pitted driveway like Hell's Angels on crusade. The truck bounced and rocked. As Sydney tried to fasten her seat belt, she knew her *pumped-up* driving would never compare to Ellie's everyday, turbo-charged, lead foot.

They would make it to town in fifteen minutes flat.

The sooner the better.

***

When they pulled in front of the jailhouse fourteen and a half minutes later, Sydney knew exactly what she wanted to say. She jumped out of the truck, blew through the front door like a summer storm, and rained on David's parade.

"I've had a change of heart about tomorrow, David. I hate to cancel on short notice, but I'll be attending the fair alone. You're an attractive and important man. I have no doubt you can find another date. In addition, I ask that you please stop pursuing me. I am not, nor will I ever be, interested in marrying you." She paused, then added kindly, "Have a good night."

She left him sitting open-mouthed and wide-eyed.

Breezing out of the jailhouse, she anticipated a mountain of guilt. Guilt because she'd broken her promise to her mother. Guilt because she owed David and wouldn't be issuing the expected payment.

The guilt didn't come.

She climbed into the pickup as Ellie dropped the last dime into the meter.

Ellie snapped her purse shut. "You're done already?"

"Move your butt, El," Sydney shouted through the lowered window. "I'm on a roll!" She fastened her seat belt first this time, then settled back and sighed. She felt as though she'd lost a hundred pounds of dead weight.

Dealing with David hadn't been so bad. Not that she'd given him a chance for rebuttal. He'd just sat there staring at her as though she'd suddenly gone mad. Which, in a sense, she had. She'd never been rude or lost her manners in her life, but she'd been pushed too far. Way too far—by Winn, by David, by the dream—and there was no going back. David would be angry once he recovered from his shock, and, well, it was just too bad. "He'll get over it."

"Don't be so sure," Ellie said, shifting and whizzing through the yellow of the town's only traffic light. "David's not going to take losing you lightly. Especially losing you to another man."

"This isn't a contest."

"Maybe not to you."

Sydney turned to her friend. "What's that mean?"

Ellie flexed her fingers, then gripped the chipped steering wheel. "Never mind."

"Ellie."

"What are you going to say to Winn?"

Sydney clutched the dashboard as they swung around a turn. "You're changing the subject."

"You're not going to bring up your virginity, are you?"

"Of course not. Ow!" Sydney yipped as the truck hit a pothole the size of Kentucky. "I think you need new springs in your seat. Or new shocks at least."

Ellie swiped at the sweat on her brow. "He's really not so bad."

"Who?"

"Tiger-Boy. I mean Winn. He may be bossy, overprotective, and infuriatingly linear—"

"Don't forget commitment shy."

"Right. But I have a feeling that underneath that tough bulldog exterior beats the heart of a—"

"Sensitive pussycat?"

Ellie grinned. "Exactly. So what are you going to say to him?"

Sydney stared out the window and chewed her lip a full minute before answering. "I'm not sure. I have to think of the right words."

Ten minutes later she was still thinking. No words, let alone the right words, had come to mind. She'd drawn a complete blank. Funny, it had been so easy with David. She knew exactly how she felt, knew exactly what she wanted to say, and only wondered why it had taken her so darn long to say it! Well, to say it and to mean it anyway. Winn was right. She should've told David the truth a long time ago. But she'd felt sorry for him, being a widower. She'd also felt grateful for all he'd done for her mother. Most of the time he could be charming, definitely persuasive. She'd been lonely. Other men weren't exactly beating down her door.

Then there had been the promise to her mother. She felt terrible about breaking it…although she hadn't promised to marry David. She'd only promised to consider it. For a year. Well, it had been six months. She didn't need to wait another six months to know she didn't want to walk down the aisle with David. It had never felt right. It never would.

Her heart belonged to another.

To Winn.

Ellie zipped into Sydney's gravel drive and screeched to a halt. Dust billowed into the truck's open windows. "Know what you're gonna say?"

"As a matter of fact I do." Sydney's half-second speech was suddenly and firmly in mind. She hopped out of the truck, shut the door, and peered back through the lowered window. "I forgot to ask, El. Do you mind if I spend the night at your house?"

"Must be one hell of a bomb you're about to drop." She winked, her good-humor returning. "The couch is yours."

"I'll be right back." Sydney took a steadying breath, then headed for the house in search of Winn.

Her heart tripped as she spotted him. He sat on her front porch floor, back against the house, long, denim-clad legs stretched out and crossed at the ankles. Guinevere lay curled at his side, Lancelot at his feet. A fat bumblebee hovered and buzzed about the open can of grape pop on the windowsill to his right.

She squinted against the sun as she watched her live-in security guard/handyman/past-life lover. In that moment, she saw him only as Winn. The grumbling, jaded city slicker who had come to Indiana against his will and now looked the vision of small town America. From the beginning, he had seemed incongruous with his new surroundings, almost like the proverbial bull in the china shop. His gotta-keep-moving pace running him in circles around the slow, steady amble of Slocum, Indiana. His brash, fast-talking speech leaving skid marks around the easy-does-it, Sunday-cruisin' of midwestern twangs. Yet as he sat sprawled out in the hot, lazy, country afternoon, sans air conditioning and expensive linen suit, she couldn't imagine him anywhere else.

She shivered with giddy excitement. Maybe when his job was through, he wouldn't be so eager to leave. Maybe, just maybe, he would want to stay. With her.

As she approached, her dogs raised their scraggly brows in interest but didn't budge.

Winn, on the other hand, ignored her completely. She hadn't expected that. Not after Ellie's slip. She at least expected a smug I-know-you're-most-intimate-secret grin. He didn't so much as glance at her. His chin dropped low to his chest, he appeared to concentrate awfully hard on the open book in his lap.

As she drew closer, she realized he was asleep. How could anyone, let alone a trained cop, sleep through Ellie's Dukes of Hazzard arrival? Intrigued, she crept closer, sidestepping tools, lumber, and electronic thingamajigs. Looking up, she stopped cold. Her porch. He'd rebuilt her porch. He'd pried up and replaced every rotted, splintered, and warped board. Even the front stoop was mended. And her porch swing! He'd painted it. Not brown, not gray, but purple! Purple!

He must've worked his butt off to accomplish this in one day. In ninety-degree heat. No wonder he was dead to the world. He was exhausted.

Heart racing, soul singing, Sydney leaped onto the porch, startling Winn awake.

He jumped to his feet and reached for his hip. The book thudded to the sanded two-by-fours, scattering her dogs.

Sydney glanced down at the cover. *The Knights Code, The Days of Valour.*

Winn cleared his throat, dragging a hand through his messy hair. "Sydney, I…"

She grabbed him by his paint-spattered T-shirt and kissed him. Hard. She thanked him for his thoughtfulness without a word.

Then just as quickly, she let him go. Spinning on her heels, she fled, leaving him as she'd left David, wide-eyed and speechless. Sydney hustled back to the truck and ordered Ellie, "Step on it."

"Oh, yeah," Ellie teased, peeling backward out of the drive. "You really told him off."

Sydney shrugged, unable to smother her smitten-idiot grin.

Ellie floored the pickup toward the Bane domicile. "Helluva bomb, Syd. Ten to one that kiss left Tiger-Boy with more than just lint in his pocket. Pretty ballsy leaving him in that condition. No wonder you want to spend the night with me."

Sydney blushed. "That wasn't the bomb."

"No?"

"The kiss just sort of happened. The bomb was a speech consisting of three words. I never got to that part."

"Not…"

Sydney nodded.

Ellie's brows shot to her hairline. "Wow. The big one."

"Yeah," Sydney said, suddenly gushing with confidence and joy. "The big one."

She loved Baldwin D. Lacey. Loved him with everything in her heart. It didn't matter that he was unsure of his feelings. It didn't matter that he found it difficult to trust. It certainly didn't matter that he didn't believe in reincarnation because she believed enough for the both of them. She'd regress tomorrow at the fair and learn the mistakes of their past—mistakes she would do her best to make sure they did not repeat.

As for Winn…Sydney smiled recalling the purple paint staining his stubbly cheeks and cotton shirt…he was fighting a losing battle. He loved her all right, he just didn't know it yet.

Sixteen

"Good morrow, m`lady."

Sydney followed the young squire's lead and dipped her chin in greeting. "Good morrow."

Dressed in a belted, oversized tunic, loose-fitting breeches, and knee-high boots, the rakish youth bowed low, then with a wink and a grin, waved Sydney through the vine-covered entrance of the Renaissance Faire. As she passed, he clutched his hands to his heart and sighed dramatically. "Me thinks thou art the fairest maiden in our village."

"Oh yeah, like *that's* sincere," Ellie said.

Sydney smiled at the squire, then shooed her sarcastic friend forward. "Thanks for the vote of confidence."

Ellie rolled her eyes. "You look absolutely beautiful. That costume is a stunner, if I do say so myself, and with those flowers woven through your hair, you're a dead-ringer for King Arthur's Guinevere."

Sydney shook off a sudden chill.

"You probably *are* the fairest maiden in the village. Still, I bet Lancelot-in-training back there lays that same line on the next four women who walk through that arch. He's an actor. Two-thirds of the people here are actors. You don't think they're following some kind of script?"

Sydney caught the swinging laces of Ellie's wenchlike vest and reined her to a stop. "These actors are setting a mood, putting us in the mind of another time, a mood that I desperately need to be in if I'm to regress. So do me a favor," she asked, pulling the laces of Ellie's vest so tight, her breasts nearly spilled over the plunging neckline, "play along as best you can."

Ellie cocked her head. "The point is to lose yourself in the fantasy."

"Precisely."

"To trick your mind into thinking that you're in another

century. To skew your concept of then and now in the hopes of spurring a spontaneous mind trip back in time."

"Spontaneous regression," Sydney said with a smile. At least her friend was making an effort.

"I just wanted to make sure. In that case," Ellie said, brightening, "I'll meet up with you later."

"We just got here. Where are you going?"

Ellie wiggled her brows. "To mess with your mind."

Sydney watched Ellie hurry off through the crowd. What was she up to now? But rather than follow her friend, she welcomed the time alone. Today was the last day before Winn left her. The only day she had to make this work. Somehow she knew this was her last chance.

If you leave me, I'll die.

She shivered. Were they her words or Gillian's words?

She drew a deep breath and closed her eyes. She had to stay calm. Like she'd told Ellie, she had to lose herself in the fantasy. The fair was a near-perfect setting for regression. The trick was to let go of her contemporary self, to be a participant rather than a voyeur.

Her skin tingled in anticipation.

"Here we go," she said, crossing herself even though she wasn't Catholic. She lifted her trailing hem and moved deeper into the shire.

She didn't know where to look first. Her excitement mounted as she passed the fancifully painted shops, taverns, and theatrical arenas of the sprawling fair, not to mention the impressive costumes of nearly every passerby. Slocum's citizens had gone all out this year. Dressed to the nines in assorted Medieval and Renaissance attire, they blended well with the professionals. A definite bonus.

She found her greatest delight at the shopping bazaar of Spende-Freely Lane. Peasant-garbed vendors displayed their wares in shop after cart after tent. Hand-dipped candles, forged wrought iron, Celtic jewelry, clay and bronze sculptures. Leather armor and chain mail. And the food! Various aromas— thick, sweet, pungent—all mingled in the summer breeze to tease her senses and make her stomach growl. Roasted almonds, ale, meat stewed in garlic and onions. Inviting scents. Familiar scents. Sydney smiled, feeling more at home in this pseudo-sixteenth-century village than in her own farmhouse.

Home. Where she belonged. Where she began. At least five centuries closer to it than yesterday. Her heart thudded as she stopped to admire an exquisite leather gauntlet. Yesterday she'd cried rivers, today she felt as though she could walk on one.

"He's right, you know. You are the fairest maiden. In this village and any other."

She dropped the glove. David.

She turned to face him, instantly unsettled by his choice of costume. Garbed in the flamboyant, aristocratic clothing of a high noble, David Monroe portrayed an image that repelled her beyond tangible reason. Most disturbing was the sheathed sword at his side—a reproduction of the famed Excalibur, sword of the noble King Arthur. A king betrayed by his queen. Sharp, conflicting emotions stabbed at Sydney, coiling her stomach into a knot. "Are you spying on me?"

"Admiring you," he said with a surprisingly authentic accent.

She had the insane desire to pummel him to within an inch of his life. The intensity of that desire caused her to step back. "I thought I made myself clear yesterday. I'm sorry, David, but we're through."

"Forgive me, but 'tis difficult to relinquish your heart when I have fought so hard to win it."

Sydney bristled, matching his accent. "You imagine something which has not occurred, sir."

David claimed her hand, branding her knuckles with a possessive kiss. "The day is yet young, my sweet. The possibilities endless."

***

"How do I look?"

Ellie straightened the hem of Winn's purple and gold surcoat, then stepped back to study him from head to leather boots. Mischief frolicked across her pixie face as she twirled her finger. "Turn around."

He narrowed his eyes.

She planted her hands on her hips.

Winn groaned, knowing he'd have no peace until he did as instructed. He had not missed the mace and longbow lying within her reach. Nor had he forgotten that she did not require a full moon to transform into a bat-swinging hellion.

How did Jack Bane deal with his rambunctious wife? Winn's respect for the man doubled.

She clapped her hands. "Chop-chop, Tiger-Boy. Time's a-wastin'."

Winn shook his head with a half-smile, then turned, adjusting to the feel of the weighted knee-length hauberk. When he faced front and posed, Ellie nodded and clapped with such glee that he half expected her to whip out a ten spot and tuck it into the waistband of his hose. He crossed his arms and cocked his head. "Well?"

"Lose the ponytail."

"Listen, Bane..."

"Do you want to knock her slippers off or what?"

Winn tugged off the mitten gauntlets, removed the leather tie at the base of his neck, then raked his fingers through his hair.

Ellie whistled in approval.

"I take it I'll pass?"

"No wonder Sydney fantasizes about knights. In my wildest dreams, I wouldn't have imagined you could look this devastatingly sexy."

Winn laughed despite himself. "Thanks, I guess."

Ellie peered out through the flap of the weapons tent. Mid-morning and the fair was already teeming. "Now what?"

"Now we find Sydney."

"And then?"

"I win her heart."

Ellie pulled her head back into the tent, concern replacing the mischief in her eyes. "And then?"

Winn studied the toe of his boot, the tables of weaponry, the hem of Ellie's ankle-length skirt. He struggled for an appropriate answer. It wasn't as if he hadn't given the matter due thought. He'd tossed and turned through the night, asking himself a million times what the hell he was doing, a million times why. Lying there with a headache and a wet towel from his cold shower, he knew only one thing. It was his first night without Sydney, and he didn't like it.

At four a.m., he'd surrendered his logic. Outside of pure and simple lust, there was no rationalizing his irrational attraction to Sydney.

Fact: She believes in past-lives. *I don't.*

Fact: She believes in second chances. *I don't.*

How could he fall for a crystal-wearing, reincarnation-obsessed farm girl? Somehow, he had.

"And *then?*" Ellie prodded.

"And then," Winn snapped, unleashing more frustration than he'd meant to betray, "I'll take her back to Jersey. Away from that medieval shrine she calls home. Away from the manipulating bastard she's *practically* engaged to. No doubt that'll cure her confusion between fact and fiction."

"They're not practically engaged anymore. She finally told him no yesterday."

Winn stood stunned. "From what I've heard, Monroe doesn't understand the word no."

"Unfortunately, he probably will see this as a challenge. Listen, I know how you feel about David. You don't like him. You don't trust him. I don't trust him either. But whatever your plans, promise me you won't get into a pissing match with him today. Sydney's heart deserves better than to be stuffed and mounted like some prized animal head."

Ellie's heartfelt plea quickly degenerated into a finger-wagging lecture. Her words began to warble together before fading into oblivion. Strangely, her lips still moved, but no sound reached his ears. His vision blurred for a moment, then tingled with crisp clarity as his attention shifted to the activity beyond the canvas walls. Something tugged at him to peer through the tent's opening flaps. He squinted against the sun.

"She's near."

Ellie ducked beneath his arm and poked her head out. "Where?"

He didn't answer because he didn't know...exactly. He hadn't seen her, hadn't heard her, he'd...sensed her. Confused, he struggled to slow the chaotic beating of his heart as he scanned the bustling Spende-Freely Lane. Hoards of costumed characters obscured his view. His gaze darted left then right.

"There."

Across the lane. Admiring a leathersmith's hand-tooled gauntlet. *There* stood the woman who insisted on taking pot shots at his practical mind and judicious heart. *There* stood the woman as he'd envisioned her last night after falling into a fitful sleep. Dressed in a flowing crimson gown, her dark curls falling just beyond the small of her back. *There* stood the perfect romantic image of a medieval maiden.

His maiden. His mate.

At her side, his adversary. David Monroe.

Winn's chest ached. A deep, primitive ache to snap a man's ribs. He adjusted the mail hauberk. "This isn't about winning," he said to himself as much as Ellie. "It's about revenge."

He tried to move forward but something held him back. "Let go of my shirt, Bane."

"No." She balled her fists around his surcoat and dug in her heels. With a hard yank, she tugged him back into the tent, which served as a wardrobe and weaponry storeroom.

Winn caught himself before toppling over and impaling them both on a mounted sword. "Dammit, woman. Are you nuts?"

"Nuts?" she squeaked, righting herself. "Me?" She waved her arms as though searching for words to pluck from the air.

Winn watched in wonder. Her gestures were so animated; he feared her breasts would pop out of her sixteenth-century push-up-bra contraption. He sighed in relief when she found her voice.

"*She*," she screeched, pointing beyond the tent flaps in Sydney's direction, "believes the two of you were lovers sometime around the year 1315! *You*," she jabbed an emphatic finger his way, "are claiming revenge against a man you don't even know! Revenge is a strong word, Winn. It ranks up there with hate. What did David ever do to make you *hate* him?"

"He disguised his voice and made obscene calls to Sydney. He hoped to scare her into his arms." Winn had been thinking about it for days. As sick as it was, it made sense. He'd seen it with his own eyes. Monroe was obsessed with Sydney.

Ellie snorted and sputtered three times before shouting, "That's ludicrous!"

"But his plan backfired. Instead of running to Monroe for assurance and protection, Sydney called Vera. Vera sent me."

Ellie held up her palm. "Hold on. Back up. If you recall, Henry admitted to making those calls. A teenage prank. Remember?"

"What I remember is a nervous fifteen-year-old kid choking out a rehearsed confession. A confession, I might add, that didn't jive with actual occurrences."

"Why would Henry lie? Why would he say he made those calls if he didn't?"

Winn shrugged. "Monroe told him to. Maybe he caught the kid skipping school, shoplifting, or smoking a joint. Who the hell knows? Then he bargained with the boy, 'fess up to a few prank calls and I won't tell your parents about the shoplifting, drugs, whatever.' One thing I do know, that kid was scared of Monroe. The poor sap might have confessed to a lot worse."

"You're saying David coerced him to lie about Sydney to avoid a real charge?"

"Bingo."

Ellie began to wave her arms again. "That's ludicrous! That's…hearsay. Your accusations are unsubstantiated!"

Winn rolled his eyes. "Calm down, Perry Mason."

"Did Henry confide in you? Did you overhear David in an incriminating conversation?"

"No."

"Then where's the proof? Aren't you the one who's all high and mighty on dealing with facts?"

Winn swallowed hard. He knew she meant his refusal to take Sydney at her word about their alleged medieval past-life. "I don't have hard evidence. Let's just call it cop's intuition."

She crossed her arms and smirked. "Let's call a spade a spade, Tiger-Boy. It's a *feeling*."

She stood poised, invisible rod in hand, waiting to reel him in with Sydney's favorite phrase. He didn't bite. "I observed telling gestures, expressions, and inflections of the voice. I analyzed the situation and reached my conclusion after careful thought."

"Bull crap."

"Eloquent, Bane." Winn shrugged his shoulders and sighed. "All right. It's a feeling. Christ. What's happening to me?"

Ellie grinned and fluttered her lashes. "You're in l-o-o-o-ve."

"Like hell I am." Winn moved to a prop table with hand-forged weapons. He picked up a dagger and glanced at the hilt's intricate detail. "I've been in love before and it didn't feel anything like this."

Ellie moved in front of him, studying him with intent concentration.

Winn absently tucked the dagger into his belt. "What?"

"Oh, boy."

He looked down, wondering if daisies had sprouted through his hauberk. "*What?*"

"It's worse than I thought. You're not in *I'll-die-if-I-don't-have-sex-with-you* love. You're in *Romeo-and-Juliet-til-death-do-us-part* love. Once in a lifetime love."

"Get lost."

"Deny it. It's as obvious as the goatee cropped along your stubborn chin."

Winn shook his head. "Loving someone is the same as leaving your keys in the car. You're begging to be taken for a ride. I've been that route. I don't care to go down it again."

Ellie snorted. "Strong words, Baldwin D. Lacey. But look me in the eyes. Look me in the eyes and tell me you don't care about Sydney. Tell me that you don't spend every waking moment thinking about her, every sleeping moment dreaming about her. Tell me that you don't fantasize about making love to her, about waking up next to her every morning. Swear to

me, on your honor, that your heart doesn't race like the Indy
500 every time you set eyes on her. Swear it, and I'll concede
this argument once and forever."

Winn stood rigid, prepared to slay every accusation hurled
in his direction. He longed to slice each charge into little bits
and cast them to the wind. Forgotten, like last autumn's dry,
crumbling leaves.

He stood. For that's all he could do as the truth bound him
to stillness. To silence.

"Just as I thought," Ellie gloated. Then she sighed. "This
puts a kink in things, Tiger-Boy. Up until yesterday I didn't
know what to make of you. I'm still not sure what to make of
you, but there's something between you and Sydney. Something
special. Something I can't explain. Something you're too
damned stubborn to admit aloud. I guess I'd be less than a
friend to Sydney if I didn't clue you in." She fortified her stance
as though bracing for a brisk wind. "There's something you
should know."

Winn nabbed the laces of her bodice and yanked her close.
"I'm all ears."

***

"Pickles! Steak on a Stake! Her Majesty's fruit cup!"

Sydney waved down the young vendor. "Over here, good
man!" She opened the drawstring pouch looped about her waist.
"I'm starving, El. How about you?"

Ellie frowned. "Nothing for me. Nice to know you got
your appetite back. At least one of us is having a good time. I
feel like a damned squirrel, rushing from one nut to another."
She tugged at her cinched bodice. "Whoever invented this
contraption should be shot."

Sydney passed the vendor a dollar in exchange for a large
dill. "A Steak-on-a-Stake for my sourpuss friend."

"I'm not a sourpuss," Ellie groused.

"Are too."

"Am not."

"What say you?" asked Sydney, treating the vendor to her
flawless accent.

The boy grinned. "Aye, 'tis indeed a lemon-sucking face."

Ellie waved her fist under his pointy nose. "Suck on this, fancy-pants."

The kid laughed and propped the speared meat between her curled fingers. "Enjoy the match, good ladies."

Sydney navigated Ellie through the crowd until she found a prime spot on the grassy incline. Before them stretched the life-sized chessboard, the battleground for the opposing queens' game pieces. "The Human Chess Match," Sydney said before biting into her dill, "my favorite part of the Renaissance Fair."

"I know," Ellie grumbled. "*Everyone* knows. By the way, that newfound accent of yours is creeping me out. It's too…real."

"My apologics, but 'tis yet another means of encouraging the regression."

"Feeding the fantasy. I get it," Ellie snapped.

Sydney chewed her pickle, savoring the sour juices while wondering at Ellie's prickly mood. She'd been fine an hour ago. Concerned, Sydney set the pickle aside and plucked at the wild clover in the grass. "What put the bee in your bloomers?"

Ellie twirled the stick of meat between her fingers. "Your love life."

Sydney admired a purple wild flower that looked a lot like heather. She plucked the blossom and dropped it into her pouch, a keepsake to be pressed in her journal. "'Tis somewhat of a mess," she agreed with a sigh. She'd just spent an aggravating half-hour deterring the world's most ardent suitor.

"Yeah, well I have an uneasy feeling it's about to be declared a state of disaster."

Sydney's head shot up. "You know something."

The trumpets heralded.

"Oh, look!" Ellie pointed to the game board. "The Human Chess Match is about to begin."

Sydney raised a brow at her friend. "Don't think I won't get it out of you."

"God save the Queen!" the audience chanted, kicking off the festivities.

"Very well," Sydney relented, turning her gaze to the field.

"Have it your way. For now."

She watched in fascination as costumed men and women, in lieu of inanimate game pieces, stationed themselves upon the appropriate squares. Calling the moves this day were Queen Elizabeth and her adversary, Mary, Queen of Scots.

Sydney's enthusiasm swelled as the match ensued. The game ignited a competitive spark within her. A spark that burned hotter with each confrontation. She had to restrain herself from jumping up and joining in, for she craved to participate in the mock battle as surely as she had once thrilled in participating in the games.

As *she'd* once participated?

"That's skewed," Sydney mumbled, the English accent fading and mingling with her midwestern twang. She shook her head to clear it. It didn't help.

"What's skewed?" Ellie asked, eyes riveted on the action.

Sydney set a shaky hand on Ellie's arm. "Something's wrong. I feel...strange."

Ellie patted her hand. "Maybe the pickle upset your stomach."

"I'm having weird thoughts."

"You always have weird thoughts."

Thunder clapped in the distance.

Ellie started, flipping the speared meat over her shoulder with a nervous jerk. "Geez Louise, that scared the pee out of me." She looked up and pointed to the blackening sky. "Great. A storm's brewing."

Sydney turned a suspect eye to the turbulent clouds. A perfect reflection of her sudden roiling emotions. The darkening sky rumbled as the wind kicked up, churning the clouds into a distinct, circular pattern. "Something's wrong," she insisted.

"Yeah. It's going to rain and we don't have an umbrella."

"No!" Sydney clutched Ellie's hand. "Something's going to happen. Something horrible. Someone's going to get hurt, and it'll be my fault!"

Ellie turned, concern in her eyes. "Oh, geez. I wonder...no, it couldn't. They wouldn't."

"What!" Sydney demanded over the cheering crowd. "Who

wouldn't what?"

Thunder cracked in the humid air. Lightning flashed in the distance.

The game ensued despite the worsening weather.

Sydney shivered, chilled as though pelted by a cold, hard rain. Yet a single drop had yet to fall.

The masses cheered and booed, seemingly oblivious to the violence howling in the sharp wind.

Sydney's fear mounted. She prayed for the storm to blow by, and with it, the encroaching swirl of doom.

Mary, Queen of Scots shouted her authority over the heckling crowds. "Good gentles, cheer most loudly for this game will be mine. I order to the field my most capable champion, Lord Monroe!"

Sydney watched with foreboding as David Monroe, overconfident sheriff turned ostentatious lord, strode onto the field. He bowed low to his Queen, then turned and repeated the gesture to Sydney. His smile for her and her alone.

Thunder rumbled as he pressed his fingers to his mouth and blew her a kiss.

The crowd cheered.

Sydney wrapped her arms around her stomach.

Queen Elizabeth hailed their attention. "Good gentles, hear me now. Apparently my dear cousin, Mary, thinks me witless and weak. Nay, Mary, Queen of Scots, your bold move intimidates me not." The regally attired woman peered over her shoulder before displaying a triumphant smile. "I call to my defense my most valiant—and certainly most handsome—knight, Sir Baldric the Immortal."

Ellie sucked in a sharp breath and smacked her forehead. "Too far, Tiger. Too far."

Sydney's blood froze.

Men booed and women sighed as he strode onto the field, his imposing stance a dare in itself as he straddled his spot on the board.

She felt as though the wind suddenly swirled inside her skull as she stared at the incredible man. Skintight pants accentuated his muscular thighs. Dusty leather boots rose above his knees. An intimidating glint of silver mail peeked out from beneath his purple and gold tunic. His hair, thick and black as the devil's heart, grazed freely about his shoulders.

Her love of all lifetimes.

The knight of her dreams.

Baldric.

Despite the maidens clamoring for his attention, the knight never moved his gaze from Sydney. The weight of his stare pinned her to the grass. Should the rain-soaked clouds fall from the sky, she too could not have looked away.

Lightning flashed so brightly as to almost blind her. In that instant, his challenger had moved forward and claimed the opposite block.

Sydney gripped her stomach.

Pain.

Nausea.

Her mouth went dry.

Her muscles tensed as she watched the two men square off.

"Lord Monroe," Mary, Queen of Scots entreated, "whilst thou defend my honor?"

"Aye, my Queen," he said in a crisp English accent. "With pleasure. Though might I be so bold as to request a boon?"

The Scottish Queen waved him on. "You've served me well. State your request."

"I seek Lady Sydney's hand in marriage. Should I win, would but that be my reward. Verily I am not worthy of her affection, yet I crave it as a starving man craves food. She sustains me." He leveled his possessive gaze on Sydney. "She is the inspiration for my every breath."

The day is yet young. Pain lanced Sydney's gut. *The possibilities endless.*

She knew he'd wanted her, but not this bad. She wondered if she'd sent him over some edge breaking it off like she did. Or was it inevitable? Did David play some part in her and Winn's fate? The thought never occurred to her until this moment. It never occurred to her that David might be more than some overzealous suitor.

She swallowed.

The sky rumbled.

No one moved.

If lightning sparked a ring of fire about them, she knew the spectators would remain adhered to their grassy seats.

Ellie whispered in Sydney's ear. "He'll suffer great public humiliation if you turn him down this time. Being the proud man he is, David must love you an awful lot. I'm not exactly fond of him and I know you favor Winn, but think hard before you act. Please."

Sydney felt something come over her. She did not budge her eyes from David. "This isn't about love. It's about revenge."

Ellie sucked in her breath. "That's exactly what Winn said."

"Winn?"

Ellie pointed to the knight. "Winn. You know. Baldwin D. Lacey?"

"You mean Baldric de Lacey."

"What are you talking about? Winn fed that name to the Queen. He read it in your journal or something. He's playing on your fantasies. So is David! Have you ever known him to spout romantic prose?" She snapped her fingers in front of Sydney's face. "Wake up and smell the mochaccino, girl!"

"Very well, Lord Monroe," Mary, Queen of Scots pronounced, "I shall consider your request." Looking across the field, she bellowed. "I challenge your knight, good cousin, Elizabeth Glorianna. What say you?"

Her Royal Majesty, indeed the most powerful woman in the world, addressed her ill-born cousin. "I say prepare to lose, poor dear Mary. I have the utmost confidence that Sir Baldric shall arise the victor in this most interesting of matches." She bestowed her champion with an indulgent grin. "And you, my most faithful of knights. What is your heart's desire should you, and I have no doubt you will, win?"

"I have but one desire," he said and set out across the field, his hungry gaze consuming the last feeble crumbs of Sydney's sanity.

She watched, powerless to so much as blink or draw breath as the man strode purposefully up the crowded hill. The steadfast intensity of his approach rivaled that of the invading summer storm, and she knew in that moment that neither man nor beast nor god of thunder could stop him. Her heart in her throat, she stared up at him from the grass, speechless as he bowed low and whisked her hand into his own.

He smiled, his face a captivating mix of amazement and joy, as though discovering his dime-shop painting to be a priceless Picasso. His brown eyes swirled with hopes and promises he'd yet to find courage to voice. Instead, he brushed his lips across the back of her hand, eliciting an answering sigh from the elusive depths of her soul.

"*Your desire*, Sir Baldric," Queen Elizabeth called, demanding he return his attention to the crown.

His marvelous eyes flickered with regret as he tore his gaze from Sydney and addressed the Queen, one hand splayed across his chest. "My heart's desire, my grace, is a dance with the one who colors my world with the brush of her green eyes. The one who fills the silence of my soul with the melodic strains of her laughter."

Sydney waited for the fever of his words to warm her heart.

It never came.

Instead a frigid wind blew through her, like winter's breath screaming through the dark chambers of an abandoned cave.

The Queen applauded, as did her loyal entourage. "Well spoken, Sir Baldric! We shall strive to grant your humble wish." Her smile faded as she bellowed across the field, "We accept your challenge, dear cousin Mary. Sir Baldric!" She motioned him to take his place. "Lord Monroe! Thy weapons shall be thy fists!"

Sydney watched in horror as Baldric prepared for battle. She tried to reach out to him.

Nay! He will kill you!

Her mind screamed. Her body struggled. Invisible bonds held her tongue and muscles captive.

Don't go! I shall die without you!

Baldric!

Winn narrowed his eyes and flashed his opponent a mean-spirited grin. "I'm gonna kick your ass, Monroe."

Monroe challenged Winn with his own arctic smile as he tried to push up his flowing sleeves. "You bought yourself a ticket to Hell, Lacey. You should've lit for Jersey when you had the chance."

The rivaling Queens clapped their hands twice. "Begin!"

Winn waved the man on. The mere thought of Monroe defiling Sydney's innocence made him want to tear the sheriff limb from limb. The image fueled his hostility as they circled one another, fists raised and ready. "Forgive me if I don't crumble under your threats this time, old man." In the name of Sydney's honor, he plowed Monroe in the solar plexus.

The audience gasped and groaned.

Monroe's breath hissed as he stumbled back. Glaring at Winn with pure malice, he charged forward with a well-aimed fist.

Pain exploded in Winn's jaw.

"Baldric!"

Sydney's cry cleared Winn's senses. He avoided a right hook in time to see her racing down the hill, right toward them. He took a step in her direction. He and Monroe played a dangerous game. She didn't belong anywhere near it.

The Queen's men caught her.

Monroe's fist slammed into Winn's nose.

He welcomed the pain. Beckoned it as the rage boiled up from some deep, dark fissure inside him.

He hated Monroe. Actually *hated* him.

Not because of the phone calls. Not because of his arrogant manipulation.

Because he'd hurt Sydney.

She'd never said as much, but he knew it to be true.

Somehow he knew it.

Bastard!

With a primitive cry to chill one's blood, Winn plowed his fist into his enemy's smug face. Twin red rivers flowed from the man's nose, yet sweet satisfaction remained elusive.

Monroe swiftly recovered. A feral light ignited in his dilated eyes. Without warning, he charged headfirst into Winn's gut.

Winn landed hard on the ground. His breath knocked from his lungs.

Monroe pinned him with his booted weight. "You have interfered for the last time, Lacey. She's mine!"

"Over my dead body." Winn seized the red-faced sheriff by the ankle and flipped him to the ground.

Snarling like a crazed mongrel, Monroe snatched the forgotten dagger from Winn's belt. "With pleasure."

Winn froze as the cold blade skated against his throat.

For an instant, his cop's instincts deserted him.

For an instant, time stood still.

Images flashed through his mind as clear and fleet as lightning.

A castle. A knight. A noble.

Winn stared into Monroe's turbulent eyes. Then deeper into his wicked soul.

A name echoed in his mind.

He stiffened with numbing realization.

A heart-wrenching scream rent the heavy air, jarring Winn from the cryptic waters of time like a mallard alarmed into flight.

Sydney.

Winn grabbed his enemy's wrist. "Not this time," he vowed through clenched teeth. His heart pounded and sweat stung his eyes as he struggled for the dagger. His unbridled fear for Sydney boosted his strength. As he was about to overpower the lawman, a blur of crimson velvet sailed into view and knocked Monroe to the ground.

Winn sprang to his feet. Then blood drained from his face.

That crimson velvet blur now straddled Monroe's tense body, the deadly blade straining against *his* windpipe.

Winn's heart swelled and lodged in his constricted throat. He squatted next to her and held out his hand. "Give me the dagger, Sydney."

"Nay," she spat, not sparing him a glance.

A strange silence settled about them, even as scattered leaves and littered debris whipped in the swirling, gusting wind.

Winn circled around, trying to catch Sydney's attention.

When the wind skimmed her hair from her face, the look in her eyes sent a chill down his spine.

Bloodlust.

The flame in her eyes dared Monroe to twitch, tempted him to permit his own slaying.

Monroe did not flinch. Nor did he cower. Instead he lay suspiciously still, like a hunter waiting for that perfect moment of vulnerability, the only warning the murder raging in his eyes.

In that moment, Winn knew the sheriff's mind worked somewhere beyond rational thought. Should he manage to overpower Sydney, he would steal that knife and...

"Sydney," Winn urged with more heat. "Baby, give me the knife."

"Nay," she insisted, her guttural voice foreign to his ears. "He shall pay for his sins as he had us pay for ours." A vengeful smile touched her lips as she exerted pressure on the blade. Fat droplets of blood escaped the nick in Monroe's skin, forming a grisly pool at the hollow of his throat.

Monroe winced, finally allowing a flicker of fear.

Thunder roared. Hail pelted the crowd from the sickly green sky. Chaos ensued as people stampeded for cover.

Sydney began to tremble. Silent tears rolled down her pale cheeks.

Winn saw his chance. Applying the same indulgent logic he had the night he'd found her sleepwalking, he whispered, "M'lady, 'tis I, your most humble and devoted knight."

"Baldric?" Her body shivered with the sudden and queer drop in temperature.

"Aye," he said, wrapping his arms about her. "Let me warm you, my love." He slid his hands to her wrists and eased the knife from her captive's throat. "Let me hold you."

She collapsed into his embrace and sobbed. "I have missed you."

"And I you." He lifted her into his arms. He saw Jack Bane and Bert Miller approach.

Monroe scrambled to his feet, clutching his throat and spewing obscenities. Before the two men could grab him, he bolted into the crowd.

Winn scanned the landscape for shelter.

"Sydney!" Ellie darted out from behind her husband, panting with fright. She took charge despite her frantic dismay, dragging Winn by his sleeve toward the tent they'd used that morning. Once inside, she quickly arranged a makeshift mattress out of extra costumes and blankets. "Put her down," she ordered.

Winn hesitated, not wanting to let her go.

Ellie touched his arm. "Put her down, Winn. We have to get her warm."

"'Tis not the end," Sydney said as he lowered her to the bedding. "'Tis only the beginning. You must have faith. Know that we will be together." Tears glistened in her fevered eyes as she pressed icy fingers to his cheek. Though her body was weak, her smile was sweet. "Trust me," she whispered then faded away.

Outside, the howling wind died. The beating cadence of hail ceased.

Only an eerie quiet remained in the storm's violent wake.

Seventeen

Present Day

"Sydney." Winn tapped her pale cheeks.

No response.

"Sydney," he tried again, this time gently shaking her shoulders. "Wake up, baby."

Ellie kneeled across from him and held Sydney's hand. "Come on, Syd. Stop fooling around." Choking back a sob, she glanced at Winn. "What happened? What's wrong with her?"

Winn began to feel a rare sense of panic. "I don't know."

"She didn't faint exactly. It was more like…she drifted away. Is she unconscious or just out of it?"

"I don't know," he repeated through clenched teeth. He'd never felt so helpless in his life. "Dammit! We need a doctor."

"I saw Dr. Berkley earlier," Ellie said, jumping to her feet. "All duded up like a sixteenth-century physician." She took two steps, paused, then swung around and snapped her fingers. "Wait a minute. Sydney doesn't need a doctor. She needs a psychic."

Winn used his dusty tunic hem to dab at the sweat above Sydney's lip. "What are you babbling about, Bane? Get the doctor, for chrissake!"

"No. Sydney said it herself. She said her future happiness and well-being, along with yours, were in jeopardy. She said she needed to regress to learn the mistakes of the past so as not repeat them in the present. She said the fair would provide the ultimate setting. She's been acting bizarre all day. Then when you and David launched into that no-holds-barred skirmish, she told me she was feeling funny. Said she was having weird thoughts. Then just now, the way she was carrying on in that English accent, the things she said." Ellie crouched next to Winn. "Don't you see? She's not sick. She's in a trance. She regressed!"

Winn closed his eyes and shook his head. Even though

he'd had bizarre thoughts himself these past days and even though he grudgingly agreed to consider the possibility of past lives, he could not, *would not,* put stock in a notion as fantastic as regression. Traveling back in time? Using one's mind as the way-back vehicle?

Impossible.

He clung to his logic with a desperate grip. "Get a doctor, Ellie."

Ellie hoisted up the muddy hem of her wenchlike skirt. "Merlin's Path to Enlightenment is only two village streets over. Tarot cards, palm reading. Stuff like that. I'll get a psychic. I'll—"

"Bane."

"What?"

"Shut up and move your butt!" As she scrambled for the exit, he shouted, "And get a doctor!"

She was back in three minutes flat. With a psychic.

"Madam Lavinia at your service." The veil-shrouded gypsy pressed her ringed-fingers together and bowed at Winn. "How can I help?"

Rows of silver bangle bracelets slid and jangled down her bare arms, reminding Winn that psychics were as whimsical as Santa Claus and flying reindeer. "Beats me," he snapped, overdosing on the heady scent of the exotic woman's jasmine perfume. "Unless you can track down Doctor what's-his name."

"Berkley," Ellie said as she rushed into the tent.

Winn lashed out at the defiant minx. "Are you deaf, daffy, or both, Bane? I asked for a doctor and what do I get?" He cocked an angry thumb at the pink-slippered psychic. "An *I Dream of Jeannie* wannabe." He eyed the circus-escapee in question. "No offense *Madam* Lavinia."

"None taken," the woman said, nonplussed. "Though a doctor will do her no good." She kneeled alongside Winn and rested her hand on Sydney's furrowed brow. "She's in another time, another place. She is fearful." The woman shivered, snatching back her hand as though death's icy fingers had grazed her wrist. Her otherworldly gaze traveled from Sydney to Winn. "She is in danger."

A crackpot. Winn stared back at the self-proclaimed psychic, silently branding her every synonym for charlatan. Surely she preyed upon gullible saps just like those palm-reading scam artists cluttering the Atlantic City boardwalk.

Yet something nagged him about this particular crackpot. Something told him that, if there was such a thing as an authentic psychic, Madam Lavinia was it. Maybe it was the unflinching intensity of her eyes. The way she seemed to look right through him. He didn't know.

Sydney moaned, claiming Winn's attention. He stroked her warm cheek, tacitly bidding her to open her beautiful sea-green eyes, to smile wistfully and whisper his name in that strangely endearing accented voice. Baldric, Baldwin, Bartholomew. He damn well didn't care what she called him so long as she called. "Wake up, sweetheart."

His plea fell on deaf ears. She thrashed her head from side to side and mumbled a stream of incoherent words.

All but one.

One word rang clear. It jarred Winn to the point of no return.

"Redmere."

Ellie sank to her knees across from them. "Who's Redmere?"

Winn jammed his hand through his hair and squeezed his eyes shut.

Five days. He'd rained on Sydney's past-life parade for five days, only to realize this day, this moment, that he'd been wrong. Dead wrong. A man of logic, he could explain away dreams and bouts of déjà vu till the cows came home. He could not, however, dismiss the name that had echoed in his brain when Monroe had looked into his eyes, dagger to his throat. The same name Sydney had just whispered.

He considered the impossible. "Let's suppose you're right, Madam Lavinia. Let's suppose Sydney is in another time and place. Let's suppose she regressed."

"It's about time," Ellie muttered.

"Zip it, Bane."

"Right."

Winn watched the psychic pat Sydney's hand. "How long before she comes out of it?"

The woman's smooth, rich voice did not hesitate. "Hard to say. Maybe soon. Maybe never."

"Never?" Ellie cried.

"I did not initiate this regression," Madam Lavinia said. "I am not in control of her journey. She is not in tune with my voice. Wherever she is, she is alone. Whatever she faces, she faces alone." Looking pointedly at Winn, she finished. "'Tis possible she will conquer her demons. 'Tis possible she will succumb."

Winn bolted to his feet and began to pace. Though he would never admit it, Madam Lavinia's words terrified him. The thought of Sydney alone and scared ravaged his insides until he almost doubled over in pain. He wanted to claw at the tent walls, hurl the tables as far as he could throw them, anything…anything to alleviate the helplessness and fear.

He wished life were as simple as a fairy tale. He wished he could just kneel down and kiss his princess, wait for her eyes to flutter open so they could live happily ever after. The end. *Finito*. No more spells. No more past lives. No more psychics.

Just Winn and Sydney. Two regular people living regular lives.

The weaponry table caught his eye. Rows of daggers and mounted swords. Some more ornate than others, but all of them dangerous. He fingered a blade much like the one Monroe had pressed to his throat. When he'd last seen the man, he was raving and swearing retaliation.

Winn frowned. He didn't need more trouble right now. "Ellie, where's Monroe?"

"I'm sure Jack and Bert caught him. They're probably trying to knock some sense into him. So Sydney loves you. That's no excuse to try to kill you. I'm shocked. I believe he would've sliced your handsome neck if Sydney hadn't tackled him!"

Winn envisioned Sydney defending him. *Him*, for

chrissake! A trained cop. A man twice her size. It boggled his mind and twisted his heart into an aching knot. He drew a breath, disbelieving what he was about to say. "I suspect his true motive is rooted in the past. Though it escapes my memory."

"Run that by me again, sport?"

Winn stopped and shook his head. "She loves me?"

Ellie spread her fingers into a make-believe telephone. "Earth to Tiger."

"Sydney," Winn clarified, trying not to grin. "She loves me? Actually *loves* me?"

"What are you, blind, daffy, or both?" She flung his words back in his face. "You're the man of her dreams. Her knight in shining armor, if a bit bruised and bloodied. She's waited a lifetime, heck, maybe several lifetimes for you. *She risked her life for you.* Do you need it in writing? Sheesh, for a city boy, you're pretty naïve about relationships."

He didn't argue. Couldn't argue. It was true. A midwestern farm girl, a virgin, knew more about love than he did. Christ. He shrugged out of the confining mail. "You're familiar with this regression thing, Madam Lavinia?"

She raised a haughty brow. "Of course."

"What about me?" he asked. "Can you regress me? To another time? Another place?"

"If you are a willing subject and if you truly believe. Then, yes, I can regress you."

Sydney's pleas echoed through his troubled thoughts. *Trust me. Have faith in me. Believe in me.* He glanced down at her tortured features, feeling the ultimate coward. What could it have hurt to trust her, to allow himself to believe, even for a little while? No one was more honest and true of heart than Sydney Vaughn. The woman would jump into a lake to save a drowning bug.

He knew the truth. He'd been scared. The past had taught him that trust brought nothing but pain. Baggage, as Sydney had once referred to it. He had plenty of it.

Something horrible happened all those centuries ago, she'd said. One of us died. Tragically. History is repeating itself.

Winn stood at Sydney's slippered feet. Dressed in that hauntingly familiar crimson gown, she was the epitome of a damsel in distress. Fragile. Vulnerable. Innocent.

He muttered a curse and stalked away.

If this wasn't a leap of faith, he didn't know what was.

"Where are you going?" Ellie asked.

He stopped and turned back to the woman who'd changed his life in five days and three kisses, lay down beside her, and took her cold hand. "Wherever Sydney is."

***

"Relax your chin. Relax."

One. Two. Three seconds.

"Your mind is open and willing to see and accept whatever enters into it. Relax."

One. Two. Three seconds.

"Relax the muscles in your cheeks. Relax."

Winn focused on Madam Lavinia's soothing voice. *Relax.* Drifting. He was drifting closer to wherever she was leading him. She'd started with his toes and had relaxed each portion of his body all the way up to...

"Relax your forehead. Relax."

He tried to squeeze Sydney's hand in reassurance, but his strength was ebbing. He was drifting.

"Relax. Listen to the sound of my voice. I will guide you. There are stairs ahead of you. Picture them in your mind's eye. Do you see them?"

"Yes."

"Climb them. Are you climbing, Winn?"

"Yes."

"There is a door at the top of those stairs. When you reach it, I want you to open it. When you walk through it, you will be on the other side. You will be with Sydney. Do you see the door?"

"Yes."

"Are you walking through to the other side?"

"Yes." *I'm coming Sydney*, he thought hazily. *Hang on, baby.*

"Are you there?"

Suddenly towering trees surrounded him. The scents of leather, pine, and horse mingled to fill his nostrils. Jangling reins and the soft nicker of a steed soothed his ears. Long, flowing hair, black as a winter night sky, caught his eye.

"Are you there?"

"Aye," he answered with a smile. "I am home."

Eighteen

England, 1315

"Wake up, Gillian." Baldric nudged her shoulder, careful not to frighten her.

Eyes closed, she rolled toward him. A smile touched her lips as she settled her pale cheek on his knee.

God's teeth. He wanted nothing more than to hold her in his arms again. He fought every muscle not to trace his fingers down her soft cheek, not to tuck wayward curls behind her perfect, little ear. Not to kiss her until they were both swept away to another world, where duty and convention were mere blades of grass they could pluck and flick into the wind.

He did not want to wake her. He did not want to end this blissful dream they both seemed to share.

'Twas a stolen moment in time. Nothing more.

The reality sliced Baldric's heart. If not already on his knees, he'd have surely fallen before her in that moment and begged for a miracle.

Quickly, so he could not retract the movement, he again nudged her shoulder. He experienced true mourning as her smile disintegrated and her eyes fluttered open. "Mercy, woman. You sleep like the dead." His words scraped past his throat, rough and hoarse from restrained emotion.

Her sleepy eyes struggled to comprehend. He tortured himself with the image of her waking in his arms, flushed and rumpled, with her lashes framing something other than confusion. Fear. Dread.

"Baldric, what is it? What is wrong?"

How easily his Christian name formed on her sweet lips. How easily she stoked the fires of rebellion in his belly, nearly inciting him to raise his sword and dare any to take this beautiful angel from him.

She bolted upright. "Why is everyone dashing about in chaos?"

Minstrels struggled into tunics in the weak, dawn light.

One tripped over the cook pot.

"The monkey."

"Skitter?"

"He is missing."

Gillian stood and gathered her thick robe about her. "Surely the flea-bitten rascal has simply climbed a tree."

"Julius claims the monkey is a talisman. He predicts ill luck for us all should harm befall the animal. He suspects foul play."

"Foul play?"

"The animal has never once wandered."

Gillian shook her head and noticed the heap of abandoned blankets alongside hers. "Where is Eloise?"

"With Simon. Searching. She practically dragged him into the forest."

Gillian frowned. "Indeed she is most superstitious. What of Sir Robert and Sir William?"

"Searching." He ached to smooth the lines etching her face. Even in the faint light, he saw the invading tension chase any lingering haze of serenity from her body.

"I cannot imagine those heartless warriors scouring the woods for someone's pet monkey."

Ivo tossed Baldric a flaming torch. He waved his squire and two others north. "They do it for the women warming their beds. If they thought it would benefit their illicit pursuits, they would search the muck for a slug."

Gillian stooped to tug on her slippers. "It seems futile to search for a tree-swinging creature in a vast forest."

"Julius is our host. He has begged our assistance. Now come."

"But—"

"I know you are afraid of the woods, small one, but I will not leave you. Come. I must join the search." 'Twas no matter if they located the elusive monkey. He refused to sacrifice an opportunity to speak privately with Gillian. He had slept not a wink this night. Not when his mind spun with the desire he'd seen shining in her eyes. Just before she slapped him, of course. "Have you so quickly forgotten your promise to remain at my side?"

Her green eyes sparked, and he awaited a scathing remark. Instead she turned and stalked off, leaving him behind without so much as a muttered oath.

He caught up to her in six long strides. She'd stopped short of the tangled bramble and forest bushes. Her shoulders tensed. Pride forced her this far, but not even her strong will could make her forget her last encounter in the darkened woods. He stood behind her, his breath fluttering the ebony wisps of her hair. "Never fear, sweet lady," he vowed, wishing to rest his hands on her shoulders. "I would lay down my life to protect you."

"You protect me only as far as Redmere's stronghold, good sir. Your protection is fleeting, but I shall accept it this moment as I have little choice."

In a flash of movement, he squeezed her hand and tugged her deep into the forest, using more force than he'd intended. She tripped on an exposed tree root. He righted her, then turned her to face him. "You tax my humor like no woman I've known, Gillian Marrick." He gripped her forearms and glared down to meet her obstinate gaze. "Contrary to your belief, `tis not hell to which I deliver you, but heaven on earth. Willingham's opulence is unsurpassed. You shall sup on exquisitely prepared delicacies, sleep on mattresses stuffed with not straw but feathers. Awaiting you is a wardrobe befitting a princess. No need will go unattended. God's teeth, woman, how can I ease your misplaced apprehension?"

She arched a brow. "Are you sure `tis not *your* apprehension you seek to ease, *Sir* Baldric?"

Her words struck him like a broadsword. The truth exploded like white light in his mind. Nay, he no longer wanted to deliver her unto Willingham. Unto Redmere's bed. He no longer wanted to deliver her anywhere that would take her from his sight. He, Baldric the Immortal, who had defied death time and again, felt he would surely cease to breathe the day he and Gillian Marrick forever parted.

`Twas mind-boggling. Never had his wits been so obliterated, his heart so possessed. This madness that burned between him and Gillian, this madness known as love, how did mortal men survive it? How did one survive the ravaging devastation of a bittersweet love found, only to be lost?

How did a knight survive his loss of honor? For certainly, at this moment, his honor teetered on the precarious edge of ruin.

He jammed the torch into the ground, extinguishing the flame in a mound of dark earth. Then swiftly, before she could protest, he swept Gillian into his arms and carried her farther into the timber of Brentwood.

She said nothing, did nothing, as he navigated his way through the complex maze of limbs and brush. When he considered them a safe distance from the others, he set her down. "Reveal to me your feelings, Gillian. I will know them now."

She backed up against the trunk of an ancient oak, her expression that of a trapped animal. "My feelings?"

He moved forward. "Aye. Those that exist between us."

She thrust her palm against his chest, keeping him at bay. Her gaze shifted everywhere but to his face. "There is nothing between us."

He tensed as the heat of her hand permeated his tunic, igniting a fire in his heart and shooting flames to every nerve in his body. "Trees and bushes possess no ears, small one. Let us talk plainly."

Her stubborn gaze fell to his boots. "There is nothing between us," she whispered.

His patience snapped like a winter twig. He snatched her wrist and leaned into her soft body, trapping her against the unyielding oak. "I will have the truth," he rasped, his mouth a breath from hers. "I will know your heart, Gillian." Without warning he breached her lips and possessed her mouth, a madman driven by the demons in the dark corner of his soul. He needed to hear her speak the words, just as a poor, dying wretch needed to hear his last rites.

His body burned, his mind blazed. He did not care if he scorched himself into a pile of crumbling gray ashes. He was starving, and he meant to devour her, for somewhere in the night, somewhere between duty and destiny, she had stolen his heart, his soul. Without her, he would be as dead as the leaves disintegrating beneath his feet.

Never had Gillian felt so weak, so needy. She resisted a futile moment before surrendering to Baldric's magic. She wrapped her arms about his strong neck and clung to him as though her life depended upon it. She'd spent every waking hour suppressing her desire for this man. Now unleashed, her pounding heart overruled her mind and directed her actions. Like the most brazen wanton, she arched her body to his, reveling in the madness of his hard, taut body straining against hers. She plunged her fingers deep into his hair, pulling him closer, yet knowing he could never be close enough. The world spun recklessly out of control as he tightened his arms about her waist, grinding his hips against hers in a rhythm as old as time.

He pulled back his head. "Tell me again," he demanded, breath shuddering from his chest, "that there is nothing between us."

Her senses reeled. Tears pricked her eyes. "Why do you torture me so?"

He cupped her chin and traced his thumbs across her swollen, trembling lips. "You consider my kisses torture?"

"Of the cruelest measure." She swallowed, though it did not ease the ache in her throat. "You ask that I speak plainly. I will grant your request, though most certainly I will live to regret it."

His dark eyes blazed with hunger, even as he tenderly tucked strands of hair behind her ears. Her heart fluttered, reminding her of the delicate wings of a butterfly narrowly escaping a predator. Closing her eyes, she willed her voice not to desert her. "You stir within me feelings I have never known. Wants and needs that I cannot begin to describe. They make no sense." Her voice broke. "None of this makes sense."

He smiled. "'Twould seem love defies logic, my sweet."

"'Tis not love that clouds my senses," she objected, though weakly as his body heat continued to burn her skin. "'Tis desire. I do not love you."

He pulled her into his powerful embrace. "I believe otherwise."

He sought to make her a liar, she knew, and his next assault was tempered with a tenderness she never believed possible. His kiss unhinged her so completely that she thought she might cave in on herself. Though her body succumbed to Baldric's demand, her thoughts turned to Baron Redmere. Her dismal future waved before her like a battered flag of defeat. She could stand it not.

Baldric's capable hands framed her face, holding her captive as his tongue dueled sweetly with her own. She wished to live in this moment, forever. Wished to forget everything that made it impossible to do so. For this instant, she banished her father, Heatherwood, and any dogged sense of duty from her mind. For this instant, she belonged to Baldric. Only Baldric.

"Love me," she pleaded, consumed by a fever only he could remedy.

Baldric hesitated, wondering if she knew what she asked of him. Her tentative acceptance of his tongue hinted that she possessed little knowledge of the intimacies of lovemaking. Yet, here she stood, offering herself to him, wholly, without reservation, without inhibition. His manhood swelled beneath his breeches, betraying the intensity of his want of her. Were she not a lady, were he less a gentlemen, he would lay with her this moment so crazed was his need. But more than her body, he needed to hear her words. He needed to feel her heart.

Tearing his lips from hers, he urged, "Speak thy heart, Gillian."

Her voice was breathless, weak. "I cannot."

"Speak it."

She refused, shaking her head while tears of remorse streamed down her face.

Willing great patience, he captured her chin and bade her to look into his eyes. "Then repeat now thy former declaration. Swear upon your soul that you do *not* love me. Swear it, and we will speak of this no more."

She choked back a sob. "I cannot."

A twig snapped, stilling the throbbing pulse of the moment.

Baldric swung around, sword in hand, body shielding Gillian.

She flattened herself against his back in a ludicrous attempt to become invisible. She held her breath for what felt like an eternity. Surely her drumming heart could be heard above the eerie silence of the forest.

They waited.

Baldric remained poised, ready to battle whatever phantom lurked beyond the trees.

"What is it?" she whispered, unable to withstand the strained suspense.

He raised his fingertips to his lips, bidding her silent.

Beads of sweat mingled to stream down between her breasts, dampening the chemise beneath her heavy robe. She strained her ears and eyes but heard and saw naught. A chilling fear settled in her bones. She almost wished a wild boar would charge forth from the brush, relieving them of their worst nightmare.

Her muscles ached by the time Baldric sheathed his sword. "Let us return to the camp at once."

The hard lines of his face alarmed her greater than the threat of attack. "What was it? What did you see?"

His clenched jaw worked in agitation. "I saw naught. Mayhap 'twas a squirrel."

She touched his arm, a sinking feeling in her stomach. "Or mayhap 'twas Sir Robert or Sir William."

He clutched her hand and pressed it to his heart. Though his expression softened, he could not disguise the desperation in his voice. "Come away with me."

She stared at him. 'Twas plain he meant not to the minstrel camp. "To where, Baldric? I am betrothed to your sister's guardian. To a man you call friend. Would you have him banish Lisbeth from Willingham, the only home she knows? Would you have him hunt us down like prey, intent on avenging so blatant a betrayal? Are you mad?"

Baldric frowned. His sanity was indeed in question. He'd spoken foolishly. Never had he run from a thing in his life, and it would surely solve naught now. `Twas one thing to forsake Darbingshire. `Twas quite another to put Lisbeth and Gillian at risk. "I will plead our case to the King. I am in good favor with Edward. Were he to name me as your intended, there is little Redmere could say."

"Nay," she protested, nearly dizzy at the prospect of royal intervention. "What of my father? The baron has offered to fund Heatherwood's renovation in return for my hand in marriage. I could never turn my father or my people out into the cold to indulge my selfish desires."

Baldric touched the frayed edges of her robe, then clasped her by the shoulders. "I am not a man of great wealth, Gillian, but upon my word, I would see to the needs of your father and of Heatherwood."

Her heart twisted as she shook her head. "You have your own home with which to contend. What of the needs of Darbingshire?"

"Darbingshire has not been mine for ten years. It is of no concern to me. You are of concern to me."

Tears marred her vision. "Cease! Cease tempting me with what can never be!"

"I will find a way."

"Nay!" Grief threatened to break her in two. `Twas the same heart-wrenching agony she suffered upon losing her mother and brothers. *Those she loved died.* "I do not want you to find a way. I do not want you at all."

His warrior's grip tightened about her arms. "You love me."

She raised her chin. "I never said that."

"You as good as said it."

She fought the trembling of her lip. "It matters not."

"It matters much," he vowed through clenched teeth. He nabbed her by the elbow and dragged her through the labyrinth of oaks, willows, and pines. She brooked no argument as waves of anger rolled off him, warning her he was a man strained to his limit.

Baldric stalked toward the minstrel camp with God's most infuriating creature in tow. She'd ensnared his heart, and now she dared leave it to rot in the elements. He would not have it. By her own admission, she could not deny her love for him. In his mind, there was no turning back. He would reason with Redmere. If the baron proved unresponsive, he would plead his case with the King.

Though she seemed incapable of believing, their situation was not without hope.

When they reached the camp, however, his gut warned differently. `Twould seem he and Gillian were the last to abandon the search. Somber faces greeted their return. Dread flicked its icy tongue along his spine as he strode toward Simon and Eloise. "What is it?" he asked his brother.

"'Tis Skitter," Eloise answered, her bright eyes now glum. She pointed to Julius. The old man sat, head bowed, weeping silent tears as several women tried to comfort him. The lute player stood by, strumming a sorrowful ode.

Baldric raked his hand through his hair. He'd forgotten about the monkey. Viewing the funereal scene before him, he feared the worst. He addressed Simon. "You found him?"

"With a broken neck."

Eloise made a noise in her throat. "According to Julius, ill luck shall plague us all."

"Cease your superstitious ramblings," Baldric snapped.

"Mayhap we should heed the old gypsy's warning," Simon suggested, eyeing Gillian's rumpled state before turning his censorious gaze to Baldric. "Tell me, brother, have you seen hide or hair of that miscreant Robert FitzHubert?"

Baldric remained silent as the knot in his stomach tightened. He could feel Gillian's panic, knowing her assumption mirrored his own.

"How unfortunate," Simon drawled, crossing his arms. "'Twould seem Redmere's arse-kissing vulture has flown back to the nest ahead of us."

***

Leaves of a low-hanging branch slapped Gillian's cheek as her horse sidestepped a rotting stump. The dismal fog weighted the foliage with heavy dew. She swiped at the droplets, then massaged the ache in her temple.

Too little sleep. Too much anxiety.

After a hasty investigation into the monkey's mysterious death, Baldric's dark mood turned black. He had ordered the horses saddled and the dwindling entourage ready to ride. Even now, hours later, he rode ahead of the retinue, alone and steeping in his thoughts.

She longed to reach out to him, to spur her horse forward and lay a comforting hand on his arm. To tell him that all would be well, even if she herself did not believe in fairy tales.

The fanciful notion, however, proved impossible.

From the corner of her eye, she could see Simon's stiff form at attention in his saddle. He now served as her personal guard and had yet to grant her even a sidelong glance. She imagined him for a moment in battle, aware that his broad shoulders and stoic countenance cut an intimidating figure. She almost felt sympathy for those he challenged upon the field, for his ice blue eyes proved unsettling enough, let alone finding oneself the target of his ire, his contempt. She would venture to say that he considered her an enemy, deeming her a threat to his family and everything he held dear.

Yet to whom else could she turn? Her mare would not gain three steps towards Baldric before Simon grabbed her reins and yanked her back. Nor could she very well shout the tormented questions screaming in her mind. What had they learned of the monkey's death? What had sent them racing from the minstrel camp as though the hounds of hell snarled at their heels?

Clearing her throat and flexing her fingers about her reins, she faced Simon. "What really happened to Skitter?" She cursed the quiver in her voice.

Simon stared down his nose at her, the menace in his eyes crackling like deadly lightning. "Is it not enough to know the damage you have wrought?"

She followed his glare as it settled on his brother's rigid back. Simon had effectively tossed down the gauntlet. Gillian refused to accept the contest. She needed to know what they'd learned. She needed to know if her darkest fear had hurled itself into the light. "Please," she asked, "I must know what awaits us at Willingham."

Simon crossed his gloved hands on his pommel, his every movement conveying scorn. "I see you have already guessed the truth. `Twould seem you are not as dense as I believed." She did not mistake his remark for a compliment. Fighting not to shrink under his steely gaze, she said nothing in the hope he would continue.

Simon sighed heavily, as though he too burdened the weight of the world. "FitzHubert learned of the monkey's charmed label during his toss with the doxy. Knowing the sentimental old man would incite a search, FitzHubert stole the animal." He ducked under a branch. "A crafty scheme for a thick-necked beast, I'd say. When you and Baldric entered the woods, he was waiting."

Gillian forced the next words past her tightening throat. "Why would he concoct such a ruse?"

"To learn, without a doubt, the true nature of the relationship between Redmere's betrothed and his most trusted knight."

Gillian closed her eyes, cheeks burning with the memory of what had transpired in those woods.

He sniffed with disgust. "'Tis plain to all but the blind how you feel toward one another. Alone in the misty dawn as you were, I am certain you provided FitzHurbert with the evidence he so deviously sought."

"Aye," she whispered, wishing the ground would split open to swallow her whole. She need not see Simon's face to confirm his contempt, nor could she fault him for it. From the onset of the journey, he had demanded she keep her distance from Baldric, fearing the very disaster that now lay at hand.

She had tried to stay away. Tried so very hard. But in the end, no difference did it make. `Twas as futile as trying to stop the sun from rising. Alas, `twas in this sober light of day that she realized she'd placed Baldric's life, as well as her own, in jeopardy. "I do believe, Simon, that you may soon get your wish."

He cocked a golden brow. "To what wish do you refer?"

"If my betrothed believes himself cuckolded, surely he

will seek revenge. Do you not relish the thought of me burning at the stake?"

Simon choked. "I beg your pardon?"

"You consider me a witch, do you not? I specifically recall you demanding that I release your brother from my spell."

"I never seriously thought you a witch," he said between clenched teeth. "I merely wondered at your ability to lure a fortune hunter such as Redmere into an unprofitable marriage."

"I did not *lure* him," she said with a growl. "I do not want this marriage at all. But 'tis in the best interest of my father and of Heatherwood. I will do as I must."

Simon creased his brows. "You will marry Redmere? Despite your love for my brother?"

She turned away as tears pricked her eyes. "If by some miracle Baron Redmere chooses to ignore his knight's slanderous tongue in favor of my fervent explanation, if he still wishes to marry me…so shall it be."

"What explanation? How do you mean to defend your actions, woman?"

"Deny them. 'Tis my word against Sir Robert's. I shall charge him mistaken, a liar if I must. I will say he witnessed naught but my eternal gratitude. Baldric rescued me from a murderous villain this journey. He lifted my fallen spirits by engaging me in a round dance. Redmere will appreciate his efforts, and he will believe naught occurred between Baldric and myself because he will want to believe it. Nigel Redmere considers me to be the salvation of his name, the assured mother to his heirs. He will not easily dismiss me. Certainly not upon the lone word of a drunkard." She worried her lower lip and added, "At least I hope not."

Simon remained silent for a moment. "You do know that Baldric intends to confront Redmere with the truth."

"Aye. He believes the baron a reasonable man. Alas I do not share that view." She turned her gaze to the golden knight, unable to fight the tears. Anon, she lowered the curtain of strength she raised whenever in his midst. "I fear for Baldric's well-being, Simon. You must speak to him. Convince him it is best to pretend naught exists between us. Should he fall prey to Redmere's wrath, should he suffer any harm…" With her soul naked in her eyes, she pleaded, "Speak to him. I beg you."

Simon studied her for a time before surrender passed over his chiseled features. "You put all others before yourself, Gillian Marrick. `Tis no wonder Baldric is so willing to sacrifice Darbingshire for you."

She blinked. "Baldric intimated Darbingshire belongs to another."

"Aye. Nigel Redmere."

The ache in her temple flared.

"Redmere and our father were so-called friends. Our father, rest his soul, was a gambler and a drunk. He lost Darbingshire to Redmere in a high-stakes dicing game. Redmere, politician that he is, accepted his winnings but allowed our family to remain in residence. Generous, no?" His tone held a sharp edge of resentment. "`Twas a mortal blow to our father. He'd gambled away his eldest son's inheritance. Baldric never placed blame. He was always the more forgiving of us. However, our father was unable to live with the disgrace. He drank his weak heart to death."

"How horrible." Her heart cried out to Baldric. He seemed so far away, so remote, as she burned her gaze into his back, wishing him to turn and look her way.

"Redmere invited Lisbeth to live under his protection. Baldric believes he did this hoping to ease his guilty conscience. Personally, I think it was his warped way of gaining a daughter. Barren wives have robbed him of children."

Gillian swallowed hard. "So I have heard."

"Though we set out to make our own way, Baldric's heart remained at Darbingshire. When not at war, he battled in tournaments, working to attain the wealth to reclaim his birthright. Redmere, however, refused to name his price. Until recently."

She gripped her reins. "Redmere put so great a price on my head?"

"`Tis more accurate to say he offered to return Darbingshire to Baldric as reward for your safe deliverance unto Willingham."

She watched in a daze as Simon stroked his horse's black mane. Baldric revered Darbingshire at least as much, if not more, than she did Heatherwood. That he would forsake his ancestral home for her....

The depth of Baldric's love knocked her hard in the chest. "I cannot allow this," she whispered, urging her mount ahead of her escort. She ignored his shouted reprimand, as well as Baldric's, as she drew her mare alongside his dark destier.

"I ordered you to stay back with Simon," he snapped, not looking at her. "Do you respect my wishes so little?"

She winced at the veiled suffering in his voice and looked away, ashamed. She could withstand anything...anything, save Baldric's pain.

Beside her rode a man who'd faced formidable foes, triumphed in the fiercest of battles, and survived a treacherous existence of which few lived to speak. Baldric the Immortal, he was called. Yet, in five short days, she'd managed to cut him down with her own simple kiss.

Nay, she countered, `twas not her kiss that fueled the hurt raging inside of him. `Twas the devastating blow to his warrior's pride. Her inability to believe that he could alter their fate. A wound not easily healed.

`Twas then they cleared the far side of Brentwood Forest. `Twas then she caught her first glimpse of the sprawling fortress.

Home, she thought with a sickening shudder.

Willingham.

Across the glen, atop a craggy hill, it waited imperiously, as if expecting their arrival.

Panic clawed her body like a desperate animal. "I did not mean for this to happen."

"Nor did I, m`lady. Of that you can be certain."

She stared at the tippets of her scarlet gown, not really seeing them. "`Tis strange to hear you address me so formally..." her voice broke, "when only this morn..."

"`Tis proper," he interrupted, his tone as stiff and unyielding as the mail draped across his chest. "Lest you forget, we are not alone." He cocked his head toward Sir William riding a short distance behind. "I suggest you guard your tongue more keenly than you did this morn, Lady Gillian. Voices carry."

"'Twas you who bid me to speak my feelings."

"'Twas your resistance which caused me to pry them from your lips."

Her skin heated with the memory of his kisses. Until she recalled her pleas for sanity.

I do not want you to find a way. I do not want you at all.

An eerie silence settled about the dense forest, cloaking them as heavily as the lingering mist.

"Pray do not be angry with me, Baldric. 'Tis more than I can bear."

"'Tis not my anger you should be fearing." He jabbed a gloved finger toward the castle looming just beyond the forest's edge. "But his."

"Redmere will not be angry," she reasoned, "for he will never know the truth."

For the first time, Baldric turned his gaze upon her. "God's teeth," he hissed. "Even if FitzHubert has not poisoned his mind against us, do you truly believe us capable of deceiving the baron? If so, then you are underestimating your betrothed." He stared down at her from atop his mighty horse, eyes burning with a warrior's strength of emotion. "Your naïveté shall surely be the cause of your death, woman. Most likely mine as well." He snapped his attention back to the castle.

"Do not speak as such," she pleaded, following his line of vision. "Your demise is a burden I am incapable of withstanding. 'Twould break my heart beyond repair."

His voice gentled. "Your heart is of the utmost concern to me, m'lady. I would wish to keep it whole and beating within a breath of my own. 'Tis with this admission I beg thee one last time, utter the word and I shall steer us from this course."

"I cannot."

"Will not," he amended, his fist clenching the reins. "You mean you will not."

"'Tis not free will which guides me, sir, but duty. 'Tis a bond with which you, a sworn servant to the crown, are well acquainted. You above any should understand." Tears of resignation welled in her eyes. "I have no choice."

"There is always a choice, my love. The challenge is in choosing wisely."

"Then I have failed," she said, chin low to her chest. "For my heart has chosen you, Baldric. A most unwise choice."

"Nay, not unwise," he countered. "'Tis destiny."

She lifted her head, tears raining down her cheeks. "It matters not. 'Tis too late."

He turned to her then, began to reach out his hand before dropping it to his armored thigh. "You are wrong, m'lady." The jagged pain in his voice sliced the thick air between them. "It matters much. We will be together. This I swear."

She shook her head. "'Tis impossible."

"I will find a way."

The formidable walls of the castle towered before them. A merciless beast capable of devouring their lives and then spitting out the bones.

The drawbridge lowered. From the gaping jaws of the stronghold charged a mounted retinue, the colors of their lord, Baron Nigel Remere, blazing like a beacon of dread. Even at this distance, 'twas plain to see Sir Robert FitzHubert in command.

Gillian stiffened, her trembling hands twisting the damp leather reins. "'Tis the end."

"Nay," Baldric vowed, "'tis only the beginning." His eyes brimmed with strength and devotion. "You must have faith, Gillian. You must believe in us. In me." He pressed his palm against his heart. "No matter what is said within those walls, no matter what transpires, know that we will be together." His words seemed to echo ominously across the misty glen. "Trust me."

Nineteen

Baldric clenched his gloved hand into a fist.

FitzHubert's band fast approached.

He turned back to Gillian, his urgent plea still resonating between them in the thick air. Her tears ran like hot pokers through his heart. Never in his days had he witnessed a soul wracked with such misery.

He would see himself dead before he again witnessed such a look upon her face.

She said naught, just stared into the distance.

Why can you not trust me? Trust me, Gillian. Trust me.

Sweat trickled down the back of his neck. He felt like a man kneeling before a guillotine, praying for a pardon.

As if in answer, Gillian straightened. She swiped at her tears. Chin raised, back stiff, she appeared ready for whatever FitzHubert planned to hurl in her direction.

Baldric's heart soared.

`Twould seem she no longer feared her fate.

`Twould seem she trusted him at long last.

Swelling with pride and purpose, Baldric rode forth, feeling impenetrable as a fortress wall. She trusted him. He would not let her down.

"FitzHubert," Baldric greeted as the irksome knight jerked his mount to a halt, "'tis good to see you alive and well. Your disappearance left us baffled."

FitzHubert rested his burly arm on his pommel, an insolent grin searing his face. "I trust you did not stress upon my absence, de Lacey. I rode ahead to alert my lord of our proximity so he might properly ready himself for his betrothed's arrival." His eyes glinted with malice at both Baldric and Gillian. "He so hates surprises."

Somehow Baldric refrained from ramming his fist into the bastard's dung-tipped nose. Best to keep his temper in check. Many a time had he duped an adversary utilizing brains over brawn; Robert FitzHubert posed little challenge. His implied threat reeked of a trap. Baldric prayed that Gillian sensed it as well. "Then Redmere should be in fine spirits this day, duly informed as he is."

"'Tis so." FitzHubert cast a spiteful glance at Gillian. "As we speak, your future husband is supervising the details of a welcome I am certain you will not soon forget."

Baldric bit his tongue. All bluster and brawn was FitzHubert, no more. 'Twas clear as weak broth that jealousy motivated his devious behavior. FitzHubert resented Baldric for being charged as Gillian's caretaker. Resented that Redmere had exhibited more trust in an errant knight than in he, his lord's sworn and dedicated servant. Alas, if Baldric assumed correctly, FitzHubert resented Gillian for nary sparing him a glance this past sennight when he so obviously lusted for her.

"A celebration to surpass all celebrations?" Simon eased his mount forward to flank Gillian between him and Baldric. "Sounds intriguing."

"Aye," FitzHubert gloated, sharp teeth gleaming. "Most entertaining. I for one cannot wait."

Baldric drew a breath as FitzHubert turned to his men. He yearned to wrap his hand around the cold metal of his sword, to thrust its honed point into FitzHubert's throat. He wanted nothing more than to destroy this heathen. Forever silence his malevolent taunts. Forever blind his lecherous leers.

Unfortunately, there was naught to do but wait.

FitzHubert instructed his two knights to see to the burdened cart, then bid Giffard to follow behind the entourage. He smirked and swept his palm toward the lowered drawbridge. "Shall we?"

Gillian watched Baldric stiffen, feeling the blow to his pride as he followed FitzHubert in simmering silence. She curled her fingers about her reins until they ached. She wished she could wring FitzHubert's thick neck.

The idiot's ploy was as obvious as his fat, crooked nose. He sought to torment her. Make her believe he had shared a certain naughty secret with Redmere. Cripple her with fear of her Lord's revenge. He expected her to quake and sweat, work herself into a frenzy over the details of her punishment. Undoubtedly he expected her to crumble and confess her sins, throw herself at the baron's feet, and beg for mercy he did not possess.

He could expect until forever.

She stared daggers into the knight's back. She would confess naught. *Naught.* Just as she'd informed Simon. For in truth, what tangible proof could FitzHubert offer? Nay, she would not be fooled by his cruel taunts. She would stand strong and true. She would declare herself innocent of any illicit crime. She would deny any impropriety. She would swear her heart belonged only to her intended husband.

She would lie.

'Twas her only weapon with which to protect Baldric. 'Twas her only assurance he would receive his just reward. Darbingshire.

Ironically, her biggest obstacle proved to be Baldric himself. How to convince this honorable, determined man to participate in such deceit? With a quick glance at his proud profile, she knew 'twas a deed easier hoped than accomplished.

She shifted her gaze behind her to the trailing cart, hoping for a reassuring wink from Eloise. Her maid, however, stared straight ahead, mouth agape, eyes wide. Gillian turned forward to investigate.

Willingham.

Consumed by FitzHubert's scheming, she had paid little heed to the whitewashed castle looming larger and larger at their approach. Now it filled her eyes and mind as it towered before her. Indeed Baldric had tried to relay the grandeur and size of the intimidating fortress. Awestruck, she scanned the length of the curtain wall, counting six towers and estimating at least four more. The strengthening sun cast its rays across the glittering slate rooftops, creating an illusion of warm welcome. But as her gaze drifted over the gatehouse's detestable murder holes and downward to the moat, she knew 'twas no fairy tale castle. Nay, its dark dangers became only too real as they crossed over the murky water and she swore she heard snapping jaws beneath the massive bridge.

At FitzHubert's command, knights within set to raising the portcullis. Proceeding into the outer bailey, Gillian identified the bakery, laundry, storerooms, and stables. Bread, soap, ale, and horse dung made for an intoxicating mix of odors. Aye. For all its architectural superiority, Willingham smelled much the same as Heatherwood. Were it not for the weight of the oppressive silence, her spirits might have lifted.

`Twas quiet as a mute in this bailey. All within had ceased their chores to gawk. Unsettled by their scrutiny, she whispered to Baldric, "Why do they stare at me so?"

"Mayhap because you have been named their next mistress. Or mayhap," he whispered without looking at her, "because you are breathtaking."

Her cheeks heated, though she believed herself unworthy of so great a compliment. Her fustian gown, once a brilliant scarlet, was now faded and worn. The embroidery edging the neckline and tippets had long since yellowed and frayed. Her only asset was, mayhap, her hair. In the haste to vacate the minstrel camp, she had forgone the tedious task of braiding and coiling, leaving her ebony tresses to fall in long, loose curls. `Twas not enough to think herself breathtaking, but `twas pleasing that Baldric considered her so.

As they passed into the middle bailey, her small cloud of pleasure evaporated. The stares of the higher-ranked residents proved much the same as the commoners. All, from the rugged knights in training to the delicate ladies-in-waiting, ceased their activities to study the future mistress of Willingham. Though they did not smile as she passed, they did bow respectfully.

The somber group entered the gardens, where troubadours broke into song. The cheerful melody eased the uncomfortable silence yet still somehow felt cruel. She found it impossible to savor the sweet smell of roses when she yearned for the wild beauty of her beloved heather.

When they crossed into the inner bailey, Gillian's breath stilled in her lungs. Rising like a stone marker from a cursed burial ground, Willingham's keep towered before them. Within those circular walls waited Baron Nigel Redmere. Within those circular walls lurked the man who controlled their fate like a wingless butterfly. Would he escort her and Baldric to a wedding feast in the great hall or to their last meal in the dungeon?

She trembled. The image of Baldric locked away in the cold, dank darkness, metal cuffs slicing his wrists and rats scurrying about his feet, shred the last of her frayed composure. On the verge of hysterics, she feared she might burst into laughter, tears, or mayhap both. She feared the obscenities ready to spew from her lips at first sight of her loathsome betrothed.

FitzHubert called the horses to a halt.

She sat frozen in her saddle. Unable to move. Unable to breathe.

"Fear not," Baldric bade softly, urging her to dismount. "I still believe Nigel to be a reasonable man. I am also not without a certain measure of charm." A boyish grin touched his lips as her feet touched the ground. His gentle hands lingered a precious moment about her waist. "So I have been told."

Gillian's heart fell. In that instant she knew Baldric intended to reveal his feelings. He was as fanciful as she was sensible. He honestly believed himself capable of reasoning with the manipulative noble. Or mayhap Baldric schemed to strike a bargain. *Keep Darbingshire. Forfeit your betrothed.* Or mayhap he planned to challenge Redmere's best knight upon the field. *Winner take all.* Or *mayhap*, he intended to do naught until he pleaded his case with the King.

Not one of these scenarios appealed to Gillian. For as much as she wanted to place her faith in Baldric, she could not. As much as she wanted to trust him, she could not. For it did not matter how strong Baldric was, how determined. 'Twas not his ability in question. 'Twas those more powerful than he— those with armies, those with wealth—who would decree their fate. By interference alone, Baldric beckoned a backlash she dare not consider. The moment she believed Baldric to be immortal would be the moment she left herself vulnerable to a hurt so intense, it surely 'twould cause her demise.

The singing stopped.

The hairs on the back of her neck stood as an unsettling hush fell over the bailey.

Baldric stiffened at her side.

She did not want to. Prayed she did not have to. But knowing she could not halt the sands of time, she slowly turned to face him.

Baron Nigel Redmere.

He stood at the entrance to his daunting keep, his richly embroidered robes swirling about him with an air of wickedness.

Gillian fought a wave of nausea.

He appeared as she remembered him. An ostentatious peacock that strutted and preened, expecting all to bow before him, to stroke his vanity, to concede his power. Surrounded by his usual attendant audience of visiting dignitaries, their haughty wives, and his vapid, primping advisors, 'twould appear the baron was in no risk of falling short of admirers. All stood behind their host, peering down their regal noses at his intended bride. Draped in voluminous velvet and fur, weighted down with more jewelry than the archbishop, they no doubt considered Gillian unworthy of their slightest attention. Unworthy of the highborn baron.

'Twas not their regard, however, that set her teeth to chattering.

'Twas Redmere's.

He stared down at her with a cool indifference that turned her blood to ice.

Lord. He knows. He must know.

She shivered as his faded blue gaze roved over her body in slow, deliberate inspection. Feeling like a brood mare at auction, she wanted to turn and run. Run forever, or until her lungs burned, her muscles screamed, and she could fall down into the tall grass and sob. Sob until nothing remained but a dark, empty pit where her heart once beat.

With no choice but to fight, she straightened her spine and hitched up her chin as her betrothed's assessment stretched into eternity. Two winters had passed since Redmere had last set eyes upon her. Mayhap he would be disappointed, so disappointed that he would bid Baldric to return her immediately to Heatherwood.

Her fantastical thoughts died a grueling death as Redmere's

lips curved upward. His enigmatic gaze drifted to Baldric. "`Twould seem you have altered our pact, my boy."

Her stomach churned. Did Redmere mean to confront their betrayal this moment? Condemn them before one and all? Without benefit of defense?

The baron moved forth. Gillian fought a shudder as he circled her once in keen appraisal, his garish robes brushing against her skin. He stood before her but turned his attention to Baldric. "I commissioned you to deliver Gillian Marrick to my threshold. I distinctly recall her as being a remote and unremarkable girl. In her stead, you have presented me with a proud and comely woman. A stranger. A *radiant* stranger." His right eye narrowed and twitched. "Explain this deception."

"There has been no deception, my lord," she said in a rush, hoping to thwart any claim Baldric might make. "I *am* Gillian Marrick, and I am most humbled by your generous compliment. If I am radiant, `tis because my heart swells with joy at the prospect of becoming your wife."

Redmere raised his gray brows, then nodded in approval. "Diplomatic as well as desirable. I am pleased." His repulsive gaze drifted downward and lingered on the rapid rise and fall of her breasts. "Aye, most pleased. You will serve me well, Gillian."

Fear spiraled in her stomach at the satisfaction in his eyes. She nearly crumpled as he stepped forward and kissed her cheek in greeting. "Come. I will introduce you to your new home."

Garnering more courage than she ever knew she possessed, Gillian placed her hand on Redmere's offered arm and allowed him to guide her toward the keep. She dared not look back. To witness the pain, the fury, in Baldric's eyes would be her undoing.

For she had, in all essence, forsaken him.

She had afforded him no chance to reason with Redmere. She had demonstrated no faith in him. No trust. If he hated her this moment, `twould be for the best. Hatred would keep her beloved alive.

Baldric stood powerless as he watched the woman he loved

being led into the heart of hell she feared most. The fashionable nobles herded behind them like sheep, following their shepherd into his opulent living quarters to be watered and fed. FitzHubert, the obnoxious bastard, smiled smugly at Baldric before disappearing with his knights into the dark entryway.

Eloise lingered but an instant, offering Baldric a sympathetic glance before chasing after her mistress. Ivo took hurried leave to tend the horses.

Only Simon remained, silent as he stood beside his brother.

Leaves scattered across the stones of the empty bailey. Never, not even during the most arduous of campaigns, had Baldric ever felt so close to destruction.

" Tis because my heart swells with joy at the prospect of becoming your wife."

Gillian's words plunged like daggers into his heart.

He thought he had earned her trust. He thought she had finally given it. Yet she had buckled under the first hint of pressure.

Had he not proven that she was not alone? That she need not fight this battle on her own? He thought standing by her side would give her the strength to withstand Redmere's intimidation.

He had thought wrong.

The realization frightened him more than anything else. For if she cowered under Redmere at his mere introduction, what was to happen upon their wedding night? And beyond?

My heart has chosen you, Baldric. A most unwise choice.

Too late he realized his error. That revelation, that beautiful revelation that had made his heart sing, should have warned him. For she may love him, but she believed that love a mistake. A mistake to be rectified.

Like a prisoner hoping for leniency, she had sacrificed her pride. His love.

He cursed himself a thousand times a fool for not stealing her away when he'd had the chance.

"She had her reasons," said Simon.

"She is scared." The very thought of her fear consumed him with rage so intense, his blood ran like fire in his veins, his vision burned black, nearly blinding him. Hand on his sword, he stepped forward, ready to slay any and all who stood between him and Gillian. *His* Gillian.

Simon slammed an outstretched arm across his chest. "Think, Brother. There are too many. You will be cut down before you get within twenty paces of Gillian."

Quaking with unleashed fury, Baldric slapped aside his brother's arm. "Life means naught without her. Must I torture myself with nightmares of what the bastard is doing to her? That is, if I even sleep at all? Must she endure his foul touch, fear each and every day for her life? `Tis no life at all."

"What assistance will you be to Gillian by bleeding to death on the cold stones before her? Pray, do not lose your head now. Aye, she needs you. She needs you to carefully plot your course. Otherwise you shall both fall victim to Redmere's wrath."

Baldric continued to tremble, his body prepared to wage battle to the death. Yet his brother's heed tempered his bloodlust to a roiling simmer, slowed his frenzied thoughts enough to see reason. He raked a hand through his ravaged hair. "Since when have you become her champion?"

"I am *your* champion, Brother. As I have always been. Since you are stubbornly and hopelessly in love with Gillian Marrick, then I must be, and will be from this day forth, her champion as well."

Baldric no longer attempted to deny the obvious. With a reluctant hand, he sheathed his sword.

Simon dragged his hand over his face, drawing a deep breath. "Though I do not believe charging the fortress to be our best course, indeed I do agree something must be done." He snapped the same hand toward the keep, surprising Baldric with the sudden venom in his voice. "He insulted her. He claimed her once unremarkable, then leered at her as though she were a common whore. Then, by all that's holy, he insulted you. No mention of a job well done. No mention of Darbingshire. He treated us like strangers. *Strangers*!"

A brand-new horror seized Baldric. He stared at his brother with haunted eyes. "Something is amiss."

Simon barked a short, raspy laugh. "An understatement."

"Where is Lisbeth?"

Simon stiffened. "What?"

"Lisbeth." Baldric glared at the keep and cursed Redmere to hell. "She was not amongst the welcoming party."

Simon paled, though his voice remained bold. "Mayhap she is still preparing. You know Lisbeth. She always did enjoy fussing with her hair and those damnable gowns."

"Aye. I know her well. That is what worries me. It matters not if she is in little more than her shift, she is always the first to greet us. Always."

Simon closed his eyes and cursed.

One of Redmere's fancy advisors flitted down the stone steps and genuflected before Baldric. "Sir. Baron Redmere bids you to join him and his betrothed for a celebratory feast this eve. I am to escort you and your..." he smiled coyly as his gaze danced over Simon, "...ah, brother, to your baths. Walk this way."

Simon glowered as the effeminate man flounced off ahead of them. "If I walk that way," he said to Baldric, "slit my throat." With a muttered curse, he rushed forth and grabbed the advisor by the collar. "What is your name?"

The man eyed Simon's hand and smiled. "Sedrick."

"Sedrick," Baldric said, moving in to snatch away the pest by the ruffled cuff. "Are you acquainted with Lisbeth de Lacey?"

"Is the King acquainted with the Queen?"

Simon rolled his eyes, growling like a provoked bear.

"Where is she?" Baldric demanded.

"The Queen?" Sedrick asked, batting his long lashes.

Simon clutched Sedrick by his throat. "Lisbeth."

Sedrick swatted Baldric and Simon away, then smoothed his bejeweled fingers over his disheveled clothing. "Lady de Lacey is not in residence."

"Where is she?" Baldric said through clenched teeth.

Sedrick looked bored. "I am not privy to that information. Now if you will please follow me. I do have other matters in which to attend. Such as the details of a wedding." He flicked a piece of thread from his sleeve. "Not that this union will be any more fruitful than the other two." He turned to lead them toward the keep.

Baldric raised pained eyes to the heavens.

Gillian and Lisbeth. The loves of his life. Both at the mercy of a man he had quickly come to despise.

He imagined Gillian now, this moment, her hand on Redmere's arm, smiling up at him, fear pounding in her heart.

Gillian, if your heart has truly chosen me, please endure. You must have faith.

She may not believe it, but he would get her out of here.

One way or another.

Twenty

Redmere's mind proved more twisted than Gillian had imagined.

Before there were but rumors to stoke the fear in her heart. Now, as she took her place beside him on the raised dais of the great hall, she realized the true extent of his calculating cruelty.

Redmere had insisted Baldric be seated to his left, she to his right. A seemingly innocuous request, awarding a place of honor to the knight who had safely delivered the lord's betrothed. She sat a mere arm's breadth from Baldric. It may as well have been a thousand miles. `Twas agony, and she suspected with a sickening feeling that Redmere knew it.

She longed to beg Baldric's forgiveness, ached to declare her heart, her undying love for him and only him. But she could not. Not if she cherished his life.

Sitting rigid in her chair, detesting even the touch of her betrothed's ornate possessions, she remained silent. Outwardly, she appeared calm, mayhap even aloof. Inside, she waged war with her emotions, battling them into a submission that would not come.

She wished she had never set eyes on Baldric the Immortal. This pain, this terrible, ceaseless pain, ripped her in two. `Twas too much to bear. Nay, she reconsidered, `twas not too much. For without Baldric, she would never have truly lived. No matter that the future spread before her as bleak and cold as a Northumberland winter. No matter that she would be naught but an empty shell of a woman. `Twas a woman Baldric had taught her to be. A woman she had become, in his arms, even if only for a few magical moments.

`Twas like a vice crushing her heart. She batted not an eyelash, knowing her indifference to Baldric remained his salvation.

She placed her hands on the white linen tablecloth and drew a steadying breath.

She must endure. She must.

For Baldric.

Restraining her gaze from his direction, she surveyed the chaos as the great hall prepared for the elaborate feast. Professional musicians played their various instruments with precision and zeal. Acrobats juggled and tumbled across a floor strewn with lavender, rose, and mint rushes. Servants dashed about, burdening heavy trays laden with roasted swan and exquisitely prepared peacock. The spicy aromas turned her already soured stomach. Indeed, all of her senses suffered from excess. Redmere knew naught of moderation.

Never had she seen more luxurious furnishings than those that cluttered Willingham's spacious paneled rooms. Paintings, tapestries, and ornate iron sconces adorned every wall. Her private chamber nearly came alive with the decorative tiles paving the floor, the romantic mural floating on the wall opposite her curtained bed. As for clothing, she had been dressed this eve in a breathtaking ensemble of emerald green and shimmering gold, a genteel gown befitting a princess.

As Baldric had predicted, she would want for naught at Willingham. Naught, she thought with a heavy heart, except for her true love.

"The feast is to your liking, m'lady?" Redmere dipped his fingers into his water bowl.

She bowed her head. "'Tis a glorious feast, m'lord."

He wiped his hands on the long towel spread over his knees, then reached for the herb-battered meatballs. "Yet you do not partake."

Gillian stared at her empty pewter trencher. "Forgive me. 'Tis the excitement."

He piled meatballs upon her trencher along with a thick slice of roasted swan. "Excitement or no, I insist that you eat. You are thin as is. I wish a strapping healthy boy from your womb, not a mewling runt doomed to die within days of its birth."

She sucked in a horrified breath. Quickly she turned, half expecting to find Baldric's hands around her betrothed's scrawny throat. Instead she found him paused mid-bite, glaring at Redmere with an anger that made her shiver.

Wishing to appease Redmere that he might redirect the

conversation, Gillian forced herself to eat.

Seemingly satisfied, Redmere turned his attention to Baldric. "Though she is fine of face, I find her delicate frame displeasing. Oswald had assured me his daughter had blossomed into a full-grown woman. You are well acquainted with the female anatomy, de Lacey. Tell me," he said, casting a dubious glance at Gillian, "are those narrow hips capable of bearing me the healthy son I have long desired?"

Gillian stopped chewing. It took every shred of her will not to lose the meager contents of her stomach.

"A woman's body is a miraculous vessel," Baldric said in a calm tone. "I am certain Lady Gillian will be the mother of at least one healthy and kind-hearted child."

Something in Baldric's voice caused Gillian to lean forward, to risk locking gazes. The intensity in his eyes reached down and grabbed her soul. He believed her. At long last, he believed Nigel Redmere capable of murder.

She felt absurdly euphoric.

`Twas fleeting, however, as she realized Baldric would now stop at naught to rescue her from this beast.

Naught, of course, but his own death.

She clutched her knife. She could kill Redmere now. Be done with this entire farce before the bread pudding was served.

Blood pounded in her veins. The knife grew slippery in her sweating palm. She returned the weapon to the table. `Twould seem she had no stomach for death. Not even Redmere's.

"I confess I will enjoy plowing my young bride thoroughly and often," Redmere added. "I will reap that one healthy child of which you speak, my boy. She is, as I mentioned, fine of face. I look forward to seeing it beneath me in my bed."

Nobles seated within earshot cackled in bawdy approval. Paying his simmering intended no heed, Redmere saluted the men with a raised wine goblet, then proceeded to drain it dry.

Beneath the table, Baldric twisted his metal spoon, wishing it were Redmere's neck. By all that was holy, he would give anything—Darbingshire, his life—to steal Gillian from Willingham this very moment. He had known Redmere to be a hard man but never cruel. Had the baron's mind warped in his advanced age? Or had he somehow managed to conceal his malicious side all of these years?

Knowing Lisbeth had lived under Redmere's care, knowing her to be a bright and happy girl, heightened Baldric's confusion. Though mayhap Redmere's duality was not so perplexing. For Baldric had learned, after years of battle, that a man is capable of most anything if his heart believes in the cause.

Baldric smothered his flaring temper, hoping to summon the softer side he knew of Redmere. "I wonder at my sister's absence, Nigel. I have been told she is not on the grounds."

The baron bit into his roasted swan. "I sent Lisbeth away this morn. Threw quite the tantrum, knowing you and Simon to be so close." He paused his chewing and frowned. "Her rebellion pained me. I reared Lisbeth with an indulgent hand, showered her with possessions and praise, yet she remains devoted to brothers who spend more time with their fellow mercenaries than with her."

Baldric tucked aside the old guilt for when he could beg his sister's forgiveness. Now he must focus on her immediate whereabouts, to learn if she was in danger. "My neglect of Lisbeth is inexcusable. Indeed, it has long troubled me. I intend to rectify my behavior on the morrow, if not sooner."

Redmere raised one scraggly brow. "'Twould mean you wish to see your sister."

"'Tis not so much to ask." Baldric arched the spoon beyond repair.

"Dance! Dance! Dance!" Drunken nobles and knights banged their fists upon the trestle tables, sloshing ale and clanking trenchers.

"How delightful!" Redmere exclaimed, abandoning all talk of Lisbeth. "They wish to see me dance with the future mistress of Willingham." He rose and extended a gnarled hand to Gillian. "I should hate to disappoint them."

Baldric clenched his jaw as Gillian hesitated, seeming to fight the repugnance of her betrothed's touch. She kept her gaze lowered, as though afraid to reveal the truth in her eyes.

Impatient, Redmere cleared his throat.

Seeming to stifle a shudder, she placed her hand in Redmere's and allowed him to escort her to the center of the floor. Baldric threw down the mangled spoon, its ringing clatter muffled by the clamor of the surrounding tables. As the music commenced, Gillian stole an aching glance at him. He knew her mind. Only last eve she had danced with him. Only this morn she had been in his arms.

Something inside him wrenched as he watched Redmere twirl her about like a child's puppet. The old man's strength proved deceiving. To look at his pale, skeletal frame, one would believe he struggled to climb the steps to his own bed.

His bed.

Baldric gripped his chair so as not to lunge forth and tear the baron limb from limb.

From the edge of the crowd, Simon caught Baldric's attention. His brother had forgone the feast to investigate Lisbeth's disturbing absence. Baldric quickly rose and followed Simon from the festivities. They hurried into the shadows of a private corner. "Where is she?"

"'Tis vague. After three goblets of wine, Sedrick did not wish to discuss Lisbeth." He poked Baldric in the chest. "One word and I shall flatten you where you stand."

Baldric held up his hand, the last thing on his mind a playful jest.

"Lisbeth is a pawn in whatever warped game Redmere is playing," Simon whispered, eyes wary. "He has ordered her moved about like a chess piece. Sedrick knew not her next destination though he was fairly certain where she is now." With an impatient hand, he indicated the heavy doors at the end of the hall. "If we ride now, the element of surprise is on our side."

Baldric closed his eyes, conflicting loyalties gnawing his gut. Lisbeth needed him. So did Gillian. "You go," he decided, opening his eyes. "I have absolute faith in your ability to rescue our sister. I will meet you and Lisbeth at Newcastle on the morrow."

Simon frowned. "Newcastle?"

"Dinner gossip revealed Edward and his court have arrived in Newcastle for a fortnight. A hunt in the Royal Forest. There I will plead my case with the King." Baldric held his brother's disbelieving stare. "Redmere is deranged. Indeed I fear for Gillian's life. I will contest Redmere's betrothal, his guardianship of Lisbeth, and his ownership of Darbingshire. I may not hold Edward in the highest regard, but he thinks most highly of me. I stand a fair chance that he will honor my wishes."

Simon shuddered with a burdened sigh. "Ride with me, Baldric. Pray thee, do not stay. From what I have learned, Gillian is in no immediate danger. The longer you remain at Willingham, the greater the risk." Simon cupped the back of Baldric's neck and rested their foreheads together. "I beg you, Brother, ride with me now."

Baldric choked back the lump in his throat. `Twas an uncharacteristic show of affection from Simon. "I cannot. There is something to which I must first attend." He pulled his brother into a brief hug, then ruffled his golden hair. "Go now. I will meet you and Lisbeth midday on the morrow."

His brother broke away with an oath.

"Simon."

"Aye?"

"All will be well." Baldric smiled. "Trust me."

***

Baldric surveyed the dark corridor one last time before slipping into Gillian's chamber.

His plan was in motion. Simon was en route to Lisbeth. Redmere and the majority of Willingham's occupants, drunk and exhausted from the festivities, slept soundly in their beds. Eloise, arising at the time dictated by Baldric, had enticed the guard from Gillian's threshold.

Now he stood at the foot of her bed.

The pounding of his heart seemed to echo off the thick stone walls.

He stared at the velvet curtain enshrouding her in darkness. What madness was this? Being here endangered both of their lives. Yet he could not—would not—leave without seeing her again. He would not have her think he had abandoned her. Gillian Marrick was, without a doubt, the most faithless creature he had ever known. Though she showed great strength withstanding Redmere's intimidation, he cursed her inability to believe that mayhap he, a mere mortal man, could persuade the hand of fate. One small twist to make the impossible possible. She had forgotten that `twas a man's dreams that created his reality.

Gillian had simply resigned herself to her desolate future, as though she had no power. Still Baldric loved her gentle soul more than life itself. God willing, he would spend the rest of his days teaching her that dreams did come true.

He pulled back the drawn curtains.

His breath caught in his throat. A single candle burned at her bedside, its dim glow casting a halo about the ebony tumble of her hair. She was an angel, indeed, as her slumber created an aura of vulnerability that cut straight to his heart.

The fierce need to protect swelled inside him. He longed to sweep her into his arms and carry her far, far away. Away from Willingham. Away from fear. Away from anything on God's earth that could harm her. He ached to save her from her past as well as her future. `Twas as if he had been born to defend her.

She stirred. Her eyes fluttered open, and she looked upon him as though still in dream. As the fire crackled in the hearth behind him, Baldric knew he appeared no more than a shadowed wraith.

Suddenly her eyes widened. She sucked in a breath as if to scream.

Quickly he fell upon the bed and smothered the cry with his palm. "Shhhh. `Tis I."

When she nodded in recognition, he withdrew his hand, his skin warm and moist from her captured breath. He stifled a groan as that heat surged through his body, which now lay pressed against hers. Gently, he untangled strands of her hair from her thick, dark lashes. "I had to see you."

She swallowed hard as tears pooled in her sleepy eyes. "`Tis dangerous."

"Aye," he whispered, brushing her hair from her face, "'tis why we must act quickly."

Fully awake now, she tried to push him away. "I cannot leave with you," she said, her tone edged with panic. "'Tis plain FitzHubert advised Redmere of our indiscretion. 'Tis obvious he holds Lisbeth hostage as a weapon against you. He still intends to marry me. He dangles Lisbeth's welfare before you to ensure it will happen. He will kill her if you take me. Do you not see that?"

Gillian's astuteness never failed to astound him. "I am well aware of the game Redmere plays. Though I now believe him capable of many atrocities, I cannot imagine him ordering Lisbeth dead. For all his apparent faults, I do not doubt his fatherly love for her. However, I do believe that he would arrange it so that Simon and I never lay eyes upon our sister again. Indeed, he has already set those wheels in motion."

Gillian's eyes widened. "Yet you still honor him with the benefit of the doubt, despite what you have witnessed?" She touched her hand to his cheek, her gaze softening. "You are decent beyond imagination, Baldric. But what if you are mistaken? What if he *is* capable of ordering Lisbeth dead? It need not be done by gruesome execution. Mayhap a strategic push down a stairwell? A pillow over her face as she sleeps?"

"I have considered this. Indeed, I have considered much of what you have said to me this past sennight." Capturing her hands, he laced her fingers with his own. He kissed her knuckles and felt her involuntary shiver. "That night upon the battlement wall, the day we met, you said you feared that I would not be willing to do that which will save you. Do you remember?"

Her cheeks flushed. "Aye."

"What did you mean, Gillian? Tell me now." He pressed his lips in turn to each of her fingers. "How did you fathom I could save you?"

Gillian could barely breathe. How could he expect her to think while his lips seared her skin, turning her mind into a white-hot pinpoint of light? Aye, she remembered her dream, her one and only dream, long ago on that distant, fateful night.

Though 'twas not so distant, she realized somewhere in the hazy corridors of her thoughts. 'Twas mere days since she had envisioned her bold plan, and now it seemed wont to return to haunt her.

Or mayhap to bless her. She dared not hope.

"If you had asked me that night," he uttered softly, as though privy to her muddled thoughts, "I would have refused. Despite your conclusions about men, we are not all ruled by our...that is to say, I am not accustomed to dallying with innocent virgins. I am certainly not accustomed to acting as a desperate maiden's stud."

"'Tis unforgivable, I know," she said, mortified she had ever schemed as thus.

"I am not accustomed to acting as a desperate maiden's stud," he repeated, the tenderness in his eyes glowing warm with the reflection of the candle flame, "but I am not opposed to making love to the woman who resides in my heart, in my very soul, with the second intent of providing her with a child."

Hot tears streamed down her face. "What would be your first intent?"

He did not answer by way of words. Instead he leaned down and bared his heart with a kiss so intense, so divinely intense, it surpassed far and away any verbal declaration.

She felt him tremble against her, and she wanted to cry from pure want. Wrapping her arms about his neck, she urged him closer, needing to feel him, needing to touch him. Needing to show him all that raged within her heart.

She pushed down the covers, her body craving the warmth that only his body could provide. He drew his lips from hers, and she cried in protest as his fevered eyes bore into hers. "Are you certain?"

Her love for him nearly exploded within her. She captured his handsome face between her hands. "I have never been more certain of anything in my life."

With an agonized groan, he reclaimed her mouth, branding her his for all eternity.

His gentle but frenzied hands relieved her of her thin shift, sending it billowing to the floor, forgotten. As she lay in the soft light, with naught but shadows between them, he looked upon her with such reverence that her throat ached with emotion.

"You are a goddess just floated down from heaven." His fiery gaze scorched her body wherever it touched.

"I want to see you," she said, her innocence flickering and fading on some distant horizon. Naught mattered now but Baldric. Her need for him burned from her soul, obliterating any fragment of modesty that may have lingered.

He raked his hands through her hair, kissing her thoroughly before springing from the bed to free himself of his hindering tunic and hose. His actions were swift, heated, as he tossed his clothes to the floor.

Kneeling before her on the bed, his sinuous muscles strained in the golden glow of the candlelight. She then saw the scars. Too many to count. Tears scalded her eyes as she gently traced a particularly harsh, jagged wound, muted with age but no less painful to conceive.

"My poor, beautiful, Baldric. So much pain," she whispered, rising to her own knees and pressing her lips to his chest, healing the hurts of his past. She felt his ragged breath beneath her. It only served to fuel her desire as she skimmed her hands down his sides to his taut belly, then around to feel the tight, corded muscles of his back.

His dark eyes burned through her as he reached down to cup her breast. "You are indeed bewitching, my love." His voice, thick with passion, melted over her like warm sunshine. She arched against him and moaned as his mouth closed around her eager nipple, as though it had been waiting a lifetime for his touch.

She threaded her fingers through his silken hair, urging him to take sustenance of her very being. To feel the life, the joy, the ecstasy rushing through her veins.

She wanted him now. Needed him now. For there might not be a tomorrow.

"Love me," she pleaded, her breath laboring in her lungs. "Love me now, Baldric."

He drew away from her breast, leaving her moist skin

chilled. He traced his fingertips over her face. "As you wish, my love."

Easing her back against the pillows, he lay down with her, pulling her close. She reveled in the feel of his hard, powerful body pressed to hers, making her believe for the moment that he truly could conquer the world.

She closed her eyes as he positioned himself over her, expecting him to enter her then, anticipating the pain she'd once overheard in graphic detail. Instead she felt the gentle brush of Baldric's beard as he scorched a trail of fire down her torso. She gasped as he coaxed secret, dormant crevices of her body to tingling life.

"Baldric, please," she begged, "I...I cannot bear this."

He lifted his head with a tiny grin of satisfaction. "Do you wish me to stop?"

"Nay!" She pressed her head back into the pillow. "I mean..."

"Where do you ache, my love. Show me."

Bravely, she placed her fingertips to the hilt of her thrumming womanhood. "Here."

He dipped his mouth to her fingertip, flicked his tongue beyond.

Pleasure streaked through her like summer lightning. "Baldric..."

"Hush, Gillian. Let me love you."

She could not have protested. Digging her teeth into the soft flesh of her lip, she stifled the pure animal cry that threatened to tear from her throat. He drove her beyond reason, beyond sanity, to a place that hovered at the edge of consciousness.

Fearing an impending fall, she grabbed two fistfuls of Baldric's hair and held tight. Her heart raced faster, harder...thundering in her ears as she neared the steep precipice...until at sweet last, she soared.

Throwing her head back, she coasted on a cloud of sheer bliss, murmuring Baldric's name as he entered her with an anguished moan of his own.

Baldric covered her mouth and drank in her cry as he

breached her maidenhead. God's teeth, he had wanted to prepare her, to take as much time as he could safely allow. He slowed his movements, allowing her a moment to adjust to the feel of him. Yet she undulated beneath him, clawing at his back, driving him to madness.

"Hold, Gillian," he pleaded, wiping damp strands of hair from her face. "I am hurting you."

"Nay," she countered, gripping him tightly.

"You are crying."

She smiled through her tears. "I have never known such joy. If I die tomorrow, I will die glad of heart."

Baldric framed her face in his hands. "You will not die tomorrow, my love, or the day after that or the day after that. The King is but a day's ride from here. I will plead our case with Edward. I will gain his blessing, and I will return for you before the wedding."

"But he could march me to the chancellor tomorrow..."

He smoothed the furrow from her delicate ebony brow. "Redmere revels in the pageantry of a grand and well-attended wedding. I heard stories of his first and witnessed the second. He will no doubt follow suit with the third, and that will take some time. I estimate a week. Mayhap two."

Fear flickered in her eyes. "What if you are wrong?"

Baldric sighed, cupping her chin in his hand. "Then follow through with the ceremony, but do not give your consent. Consent is a legal condition for marriage, my sweet. Do you understand me?"

"Aye. But what of Lisbeth?"

"Simon is on his way to her now. All will be well. Listen to me, Gillian. I lay with you this night to fill you with hope and mayhap a child. Submit to Redmere should he force his attentions on you. Do what you must to stay alive. Naught matters but what we feel for one another. Endure. Do you hear me? Endure. I will return. We will be together. Say that you trust me. Swear it."

Tears rained down her cheeks. "I trust you."

Her declaration filled his heart and drove him over the edge. He kissed her deeply, increasing the rhythm of his thrusts as her quaking body begged him for release.

Nearing climax, she wept openly and expressed her true heart. "I love you, Baldric."

"And I, you, Gillian."

They came as one, and somewhere deep in his heart, Baldric knew himself to be as one—body and soul—with the woman who lay trembling in his embrace.

Twenty-One

He felt the ultimate heel.

Baldric stepped into the hall, shutting Gillian's chamber door quietly behind him. He took two steps, then paused, resting his sweating palms and brow against the cool stones of the wall. The wall which now separated him from the woman to whom he had just made love. Though he could not hear it, her gentle weeping haunted him. They had professed their love for one another, and now he was leaving her. That he sought to enlist the King's aid did little to assuage his guilt. Or fear.

He wished to God there was another way. He wished he could spirit Gillian from Willingham this very night. But 'twas too dangerous for her. Unlike Heatherwood, Willingham remained a fortress, crawling with trained and skillful guards, ready to kill if necessary. They did not sleep at their posts, and though Eloise was a talented and shapely decoy, she was hardly capable of distracting an entire garrison.

Then there was Lisbeth. Until he knew her to be safe, he dared not risk Redmere's wrath. He no longer considered the baron a reasonable man. He no longer considered him a friend. If indeed he ever was one.

Baldric felt as though he had gone through his entire life with his head in the clouds, at least where Nigel Redmere was concerned. As a result, 'twould be easy to second-guess himself right now. 'Twas why he chose to rely on Simon's solid judgment. Simon deemed Gillian in no immediate danger. Baldric tended to agree. As long as Redmere considered her the future mother of his child.

Baldric smiled, remembering Gillian's tears of joy as he had spilled his seed into her womb. With any luck, he had just ensured her life.

Strengthened by the thought, he pushed off the wall, eager to set out to find the King.

Redmere blocked his path.

"I trusted you." The elder man growled the accusation, his breath fetid with onions and wine from the feast hours old.

Baldric stood steady, long weathered against the fluster of surprise. His heart, however, thundered at the thought of Gillian unprotected, her chamber mere paces away. He refrained from immediate comment, hoping Redmere would elaborate. `Twas unclear whether the baron referred to what had occurred between he and Gillian this morn in the woods or this night in her bed. Or both.

"FitzHubert warned me," Redmere began, his guttural tone singed with scorn, "but I refused to believe. Robert has always been jealous of you. His attempt to sully your irreproachable reputation came as no surprise. I easily dismissed his sordid accusation." He drew a dagger from the folds of his robe.

Baldric remained poised. Waiting.

"Do you know why?" Redmere demanded, stabbing the air with each of his words.

Baldric raised an inquiring brow while plotting his best course. The dagger complicated matters. But `twas not the dagger that kept him from knocking the old man cold, or even killing him. `Twas Gillian's life. The blood on his hands would surely be Gillian's own in the end.

The baron raked Baldric with a condemning glare. "Because I believed you incapable of so deceitful a betrayal. I believed you indebted to me, the man who took in Lisbeth, the man who provided your sister with the charmed life she deserved when you could offer her naught. At the very least, I believed in your love of Darbingshire." He grunted. "Fool was I. You sacrificed your home, your honor. For what? A woman!" Redmere shoved Baldric, knocking him hard against the wall. He pressed the blade to his throat. "Like father, like son. I cannot help but be amused by the irony."

The cryptic statement pricked the hair on Baldric's neck. "You have my attention."

Redmere's lips twitched in morbid amusement. "It amazes me still that Hugh never told you the truth of how he lost your beloved Darbingshire. Proud fool. Whether you choose to believe it or not, I was fond of your father. He saw the good in even the most despicable people. A quality inherited by you." He frowned. "Hugh de Lacey was, I think, my one and only true friend. Pity he had to ruin it by falling in love with my wife."

Baldric froze. "He admitted this to you?"

"He did not have to." Redmere snorted with disgust. "'Twas evident the night he questioned my treatment of Catherine. I confess, I was indifferent to her, mayhap spiteful. She annoyed me. I tired of plowing the damn woman with fruitless results. Your father, chivalrous bastard, demanded I alter my…what did he call it? Ah, my deplorable behavior. Never had Hugh raised his voice to me, never before had he challenged my actions. He betrayed me. My friend. My closest friend. In that moment, I wanted to destroy him. However, I had not the will to strike him down with my own sword." Redmere's eyes glittered with madness. "Knowing Hugh's weakness for gambling, I raised the stakes of our dicing game. I named Darbingshire and Catherine the spoils. Winner takes all."

Baldric swallowed the bitter bile threatening to choke him. "My father lost. Being a man of honor, he would not contest the game, not even for his children's sake. Nor would he pursue Catherine."

Redmere laughed. "It ate him alive. 'Twas the ultimate revenge. Shamed that he had gambled away your birthright, he drank himself into a despondent fog. Though 'twas Catherine's death that finally pushed him over the edge. In his eyes, he had failed to protect her."

"Did you kill her?" Baldric asked, fists at his sides.

"Aye. As I will rid myself of Gillian should she fail to provide me a son. Then again, you have done your best to ensure that blessed event."

Dread trickled icy fingers down Baldric's spine.

Redmere cocked his head. "Do not look surprised. The moment I saw you together, I knew. Love is a disgusting and obvious affliction. Whether you consummated the relationship before reaching Willingham is uncertain and, frankly, inconsequential. A sin of the heart is far more damning than a sin of the flesh." Redmere applied pressure to the dagger, nicking Baldric's throat. "You betrayed me. As your father betrayed me. I should have run you through the moment I knew FitzHubert's accusation to be true, but perversely, I could not kill the son of my best friend. So again I plotted my revenge in a way that would benefit me. I goaded you into Gillian's bed. I made sure you believed the only way to protect her was by getting her with child. And you, you pathetic lovesick fool, fell for it."

Hatred boiled within Baldric. Its dark fury destroyed any trace of humanity. With a feral cry, he flung Redmere into the opposite wall.

The dagger clattered to the floor.

Baldric ignored the blade. He did not need it.

He moved toward Redmere. Until, out of nowhere, white light exploded in his skull.

The blow knocked him to the floor, blind with pain.

A honed warrior, he rolled over despite the agony, needing to face his attacker. The world tilted as he tried to focus on the shadow looming just beyond his reach.

A familiar snicker rang from the darkness. FitzHubert.

Baldric struggled to rise, desperate to shield Gillian. Desperate to save her from what would surely come. But his body rebelled, his mind weaving in and out of some deep, black void.

Growling in frustration, he let his head fall to the floor.

"Once again, I win," Redmere said, bending down on one knee. "Once again, Darbingshire is mine. The woman is mine. And from what I viewed through a strategically placed squint this night, I venture a child is mine. Your child. Your son," he taunted in Baldric's ear. "Know this, de Lacey. There will be no accusations. There will be no confrontation. You will simply disappear, and she will be left to wonder. I will bed her often. For as long as it pleases me. I will raise your son as my own. You have failed. Like your father before you, you have failed to protect the woman that you love." He dealt a second crushing blow to Baldric's head. "She is mine."

***

Gillian endured.

She endured a sennight of surreal, prenuptial hell.

Willingham's noble guests celebrated the baron's impending marriage both day and night, delighting in the gaiety of excessive wine and song. All the while, Gillian fought to maintain her composure.

She endured Redmere's lecherous regard, his offensive remarks, and the occasional repulsive kiss he planted upon her cheek.

She endured because she had promised Baldric she would. Endured because he had promised to return. Because she trusted with all her heart that he would.

She had thought herself incapable of believing in the impossible. Now she found herself believing in miracles.

Pacing the length of her chamber, she rested her hand to the flat of her stomach, imagining herself great with her beloved's child. A miracle of miracles. The brightest light of hope she clutched nearest to her heart.

A frenzy of barking sounded from below, striking a reminiscent chord. She hurried to the window. Anticipation fluttered in her stomach as she scanned the horizon for her savior. No rider approached. She leaned forward and peered down into the courtyard. No visitors. Hounds merely vied for a bucket of scraps collected from the latest feast.

Gillian rested her elbows on the ledge and dropped her forehead into her palms. Her heart sank with the setting sun. No matter her faith in Baldric, she could not help but worry over his lengthening absence. He had claimed the King and his royal entourage a day's ride away. A favorite of the Crown, she could not imagine Baldric waiting long for an audience. Yet it had been seven days. Seven days and no word. No sight of Baldric.

Dread clutched gnarled fingers about her heart, threatening to exorcise her newly invoked optimism.

She pushed away from the window with a choked cry. If something had happened to Baldric, if she were never to see him again…

We will be together. Trust me.

She drew his words about her like a blanket, trying to warm the sudden chill in her bones. She needed all of her strength.

The wedding would take place on the morrow.

Redmere had delivered the news with eager relish this morn, going so far as to squeeze her breast and whisper all of the wicked delights he planned for her.

No matter Baldric's instruction, she feared herself incapable of walking down that aisle to hell. Becoming Redmere's wife was a sentence to death. For death she would long without Baldric de Lacey. Death she would prefer to Redmere's bed.

Daring to dream, she envisioned the ceremony coming to a dramatic halt. Baldric would return as promised, bursting through the chapel doors, sweeping her up into his arms, and carrying her off into eternal bliss.

'Twas an illogical, unrealistic dream. Yet she held onto her ridiculous faith for dear life.

Such fanciful notions. Baldric had not only tried to bless her with a child but also with the gift to dream. Indeed, *he* was the enchanted one. He had changed her life forever.

Eloise burst into the room, her normally merry eyes grim.

Heart pumping, Gillian sank into a nearby chair. She forced the words past her constricted throat. "What have you learned?"

"I cannot speak it," the handmaiden whispered.

Gillian took a deep breath and motioned Eloise into a neighboring chair. "You must. If you have news of Baldric, you must share it with me. Please, Eloise. Not knowing is infinitely worse than knowing."

Eloise paled. "Not necessarily."

Gillian clutched the arms of the chair until her nails marked the wood. "Tell me."

"Very well," Eloise grumbled, swiping a tear from her cheek. "I've done what you asked. I've eavesdropped. I've pried. No one will say a thing. Either they are ferociously loyal or incredibly ignorant. In any case, I tired of pumping a dry well. So this afternoon I went to the next logical source, FitzHubert, and pumped him instead." She smoothed her skirts, a self-satisfied grin touching her lips. "He is as stupid as he is boastful. He rewarded my ardent endeavors with a flood of information. Indeed, he rambled on throughout the entire distasteful tryst. `Twould seem to FitzHubert that bragging is as arousing as my breasts."

"Pray, stop!" Gillian's stomach turned at the thought of Eloise and FitzHubert in lurid liaison. "I am sick that you shamed yourself for me."

Eloise looked surprised. "You misunderstand my dismay, m`lady. I feel no shame for what I have done. I used FitzHubert. He did not use me. He is a pathetic wretch and easily forgotten. `Tis what I learned that breaks my heart."

Gillian swallowed, her voice lost.

"Redmere is a spider and the de Laceys flies in his web. He set a trap for Baldric and Simon, using you and their sister as bait. Simon was captured while trying to rescue Lisbeth and is now rotting in a dungeon somewhere in Yorkshire. Lisbeth has been sent to France, unaware of her brothers' fates."

Gillian's heart all but ceased to beat. "And Baldric?'

Eloise swallowed, tears brimming in her eyes. "I cannot be sure. His throat was cut. He was beaten without mercy and taken from Willingham and left God knows where. FitzHubert was not forthcoming in details, but he described Baldric as he last saw him. Unconscious and soaking in a pool of his own blood. It appears as though Baldric's wounds were," she choked on the word, "mortal."

Gillian remained still. Indeed, everything inside of her ceased to move. "He is dead?"

Eloise dropped to her knees in front of Gillian. Wringing her hands in her lady's skirts, she whispered, "I cannot be sure."

"It is what you believe."

"Given the circumstances, `tis the logical assumption." Eloise bit her lip. "I cannot believe I said that. But in this case, you must prepare yourself for the worst, m`lady. That Sir Baldric is…is…"

"Dead." The word flowed easily from Gillian's tongue. How strange. Mayhap `twas blessed denial. Or mayhap `twas because she had several times before been presented with such news. Those she loved died. How had she ever forgotten?

"You must be strong," Eloise said, "for Heatherwood. For

your father. For mayhap the child. Surely Baldric's strong seed has rooted. Honor his memory by delivering unto this world a son of his moral constitution. Tomorrow is the wedding. You have no choice but to marry Redmere. You need only lay with him once, twice at most. We will arrange it so that he believes you a virgin. There are ways. He will leave you alone once he knows you to be with child. He will worship you because you will give him what he has sought for years. A child. You are safe, Gillian. *Safe*!"

Eloise ended her desperate plea by crumpling into Gillian's lap. Gillian stared straight ahead, not really seeing as she stroked her sobbing friend's hair. She waited for her own tears to flow but none came. She was numb. Empty. Deadened of emotion.

She imagined Baldric as she had seen him last, smiling and swearing his love and devotion.

Though she had heard the words that he no longer lived, she could not fully accept them. A part of her, the hopeful part that Baldric had nurtured, wanted to believe that there was a chance, however small, that he had survived such a beating. Surely fate would not be so cruel as to bless her with the love of a lifetime only to rip him from her arms. "Nay," she uttered, "I do not believe he is dead. Baldric will come to me."

She shushed Eloise, touching the woman's damp cheek. "I know not how, but we will be together. He promised me. I trust him."

***

At the baron's request, the wedding was held not in the chapel but in the great hall. The chapel could hardly accommodate the throng of nobles and vassals who had traveled to Willingham to see the baron married.

As Baldric had predicted, Redmere proved an arrogant man who delighted in being the center of attention. Not to mention the envy of all. He had ordered the rafters and walls draped in brightly colored silks and tapestries. The floors to be covered in fresh rushes of fragrant herbs and rose petals. Candles to be lighted in every wall sconce. Flowers to be provided to every guest.

Gillian watched in horrified silence as one hundred or more visitors tossed daisies, violets, and other assorted flora ahead of her and the baron. A carpet of blossoms paving their way to wedded bliss. She knew the romantic gesture had not been to impress her but rather his guests.

Had he to pick and haul them countless miles, Baldric would have thought to use heather. He would have considered her feelings, whereas Redmere cared naught for what she did or did not like. She was merely a character, or worse, a prop in this farce he called a wedding.

Gillian had moved through the day as though floating through a bad dream. She did not want to believe it real. She could not lend it credence, for surely she would awaken any moment to find herself far from here and in Baldric's arms. For once, she preferred to exist in a fantasy rather than to confront reality. Anything to keep the pain at bay. The pain that threatened to invade and claw her to shreds.

However, 'twas becoming increasingly difficult to dodge the sharp talons of truth as they flexed, poised and ready, to gouge her heart.

Nearing the chancellor, her knees began to weaken.

Remain steady, Gillian. Steady. Baldric advised you in this matter. Walk through the motions. Withhold your verbal consent. 'Twould enable an annulment on the grounds that it had been contracted against her will. She understood this. Still, she could not help but feel she was betraying Baldric by participating in this hypocrisy. It felt wrong, terribly wrong.

As the priest launched into his oration, her heart pounded against her ribs. All too soon, she heard, "Do you take this woman…"

She'd sat awake all night, fully dressed, waiting for Baldric to steal into her room and spirit her away.

Redmere's voice permeated her hazy thoughts. "I will."

She had allowed herself this morn to be transformed into a bride of royal proportions by six ladies-in-waiting, all the while expecting Baldric to rush in and whisk her away.

"Do you take this man…"

Even now, as she stood in the midst of the actual ceremony,

she expected Baldric to lunge forth, to sweep her into his arms and out of this wretched nightmare.

The murmur of the crowd droned in the distance.

Baldric! Where are you?

"She will," Redmere said in her stead.

"If any man can show good reason…"

Gillian turned her back on the priest. She ignored Redmere's growled reprimand. Heart racing, she scanned the sea of strange, gaping faces in search of one face. The face of her one true love.

'Twas then her gaze fell upon FitzHubert…and to the sword at his side.

Baldric's sword.

She would know it anywhere. He had used it to slay Titus in her defense, the same day he had first kissed her and set her heart alight. He had drawn it in her defense while searching for the monkey, the same day he had kissed her and claimed her heart as his own. Never would he willingly part with it unless…unless he was…

"I now pronounce you man and wife."

"Dead." 'Twas the first she had spoken that day.

The pain stole her breath as it swooped down without mercy. Her mind reeled, her last hope shred beyond repair. She had tried so hard to believe, to hang on, to have faith. 'Twas for naught.

'Twas as if saying the word made it so.

She doubled over, sick with grief and sorrow. Tormented sobs erupted from deep within her, echoing like a night bird's prey throughout the great hall.

Redmere stepped away from her in shock, as did the others.

She crumpled to her knees as despair ripped her heart from her chest.

She could deny it no longer.

Baldric the Immortal, the love of her life, was dead.

Twenty-Two

"Put her down on the bed," Eloise ordered a nameless brawn of knight. "Gently, you lumbering ox! Now leave us." She hurried the man through the door, then closed it soundly. "Ignorant clods." She stomped toward Gillian with a folded cloth in hand.

The woman's voice sounded hollow, distant, as if floating to Gillian through some dark, endless tunnel. She felt the sleek coverlet beneath her. Knew she lay on her bed. Yet she could not recall how she had come to be there.

"I know not who is more thoughtless," Eloise ranted, dipping the cloth in a basin of water, "the guests who gawked at you like some freak thing, or your contemptible husband, who backed away as though you were diseased!"

It began to come back to her, like hazy fragments of a long-forgotten dream. Aye, she remembered.

Baldric was dead.

Dead.

The word echoed through her mind like the final note of a lute's sorrowful ballad.

Clutching her stomach, she curled herself into a tight ball. `Twas as if the devil's hands seized her vital organs, squeezing the breath from her lungs, the life from her heart.

She prayed for mercy. For divine intervention.

She prayed for death.

Eloise sat on the mattress edge and swabbed perspiration from Gillian's brow. "Say something, m`lady. Anything. I beg you. Your tormented sobs broke my heart, yet I prefer them to this…this horrible silence. I know not your thoughts, but truth be known, you are frightening me."

Gillian closed her eyes, unable to stand the sight of Eloise's panicked face.

Her friend sought the impossible. How could she even begin to express her grief? The extent of her loss? No words could describe the misery clutching her by the throat, demanding she end its torturous existence.

"You have accepted that Sir Baldric is dead, and you are mourning him," Eloise said. "I understand this. Others do not. As I speak, word spreads through the castle that you are touched in the head. Should you persist with this disturbing behavior, Baron Redmere may well commit you to a remote tower, away from prying ears and eyes, to do with you as he pleases." She gripped Gillian's hand, warmed it between her own. "You must rally, Gillian. If not for yourself, then for the child!"

"There is no child."

Eloise cocked her head. "Pardon?"

"I bleed. The misery is upon me now." She spoke with no emotion.

Eloise stared at her, searching. A lone tear trickled down her cheek. "I am sorry, Gillian. So very, very sorry."

Gillian drew her knees tighter to her chest. Was it possible to die of a broken heart? Mayhap if she closed her eyes, mayhap if she wished hard enough, she could make it so. Then naught would remain in this world but memories. Memories that could no longer touch her, haunt her, make her crave any sort of death to end this ceaseless torment.

"Without Baldric, without his child…" Her voice died. She abandoned any effort to explain. Pressing her hand to her heart, she willed it to slow, willed it to cease its tireless rhythm. After a long moment, she let her hand fall to the bed. 'Twas no use. She lolled onto her back and stared vacantly at the ceiling. "'Tis naught left."

Eloise bolted to her feet. Her voice trembled with outrage. "Do not say that. It sounds so…so…final!"

Gillian clutched her stomach. Grief roiled through her in sickening waves. "I cannot bear it," she cried with renewed sobs. "I cannot bear the pain."

Eloise scrambled for the door. "I will locate a physician. I will return shortly with an herbal remedy. Hold on, m'lady. Have faith."

"Faith," Gillian muttered, burying her face into the coverlet.

Faith. Hope. Trust.

Wasted sentiments.

They had died with Baldric. Died with his child that never was.

As she had. Only her body had yet to succumb.

The door opened, then slammed shut. She did not bother to turn.

"Face me, woman!"

Her fragile cocoon shattered like broken glass.

Summoning the last of her strength, she pushed herself upright and sat on the edge of the bed. Slowly she raised her gaze to Redmere.

`Twas amazing how the rage surged through her, reminding her that she still lived. That Redmere still lived. He did not deserve to. His body should be cold, rigid, rotting away in the same dank ground that would imprison her beloved for eternity.

Instead, the baron stood across her chamber, dressed in his regal wedding best, color high, eyes blazing.

Unwilling to cower like a lamb at slaughter, she stood on unsteady legs.

Redmere restrained his fury for as long as it took him to cross the room. Reaching Gillian, he slapped her hard across the face.

Her head snapped sideways, and she fell back onto the mattress.

"That is for the public humiliation I have suffered at your hand!"

She did not touch her smarting cheek. She refused to give him the satisfaction.

He expected to see fear in her eyes. She gave him hate.

His pale skin flushed crimson as he scaled the bed and straddled her hips. Grinding his rigid staff into her belly, Gillian fought the urge to claw out his eyes. Instead she glared at him as if he were naught but mud caked upon the devil's boot heel.

He slapped her harder. "*That* is to show you who is master here."

"As if I could forget."

Eyes bulging, he clutched her by the throat. "From this day forth you will sit by my side in silence. You will utter not a word unless I bid you to do so. Should you fail to meet this demand," he said, leaning his face into hers, "you shall learn how I silence the prisoners loitering in my dungeon."

She closed her eyes. The sight of Redmere's infuriated madness evoked terrible, violent images. Images of Baldric being brutalized, beaten without mercy, while the baron looked on. Mayhap 'twas FitzHubert who had mortally wounded Baldric, but 'twas Redmere who had ordered the unforgivable deed.

A tear slipped down her cheek.

She opened her eyes and stared death in the face. All she need do is shout her defiance, mayhap spit into his crazed eyes, and 'twould all be over. But mayhap death would not be the reward. Mayhap he would merely cut out her tongue and leave her to stumble through some dark tower prison, just as Eloise had said.

'Twould be a fate worse than death.

Redmere slid from the bed and hauled Gillian to her feet. "You are my wife," he said with a growl, hands clamping like manacles about her wrists. "I am immune to tears or any other feminine wile you choose to employ. My will is your own, Gillian. Accept your fate." He gave her arms a sharp tug. "*He* will not come to you. But I will, this night and any night I so desire. Bear me a son, and I will refuse you nothing. Deny me, and heaven help you."

He kissed her, his foul mouth claiming what would never be his, defiling her as surely as if he had raped her. She nearly buckled at the realization that the last kiss upon her lips would be Redmere's, not Baldric's. Was she to be left with naught of her beloved? Naught at all?

Redmere abruptly shoved her away, and she stumbled to the floor.

"You look a fright, my dear. I will order your needs directly attended. When I return, I expect to be greeted by a willing and ready wife." He turned to leave, then paused on the threshold, flashing a grin of pure evil. "Like it or not, that would be you, Gillian Redmere, and soon you will be my wife in every sense of the word."

He slammed the door behind him.

She dragged her sleeve across her mouth, desperate to rid herself of his vulgar taste.

She spat on the floor. Bastard!

He knew her heart. He knew her thoughts were of Baldric, and he made it clear her pining was for naught.

He will not come for you.

Aye, Baldric had paid for their betrayal with his life. Surely a punishment to be envied when compared to the torture planned for her by Redmere—a lifetime, no matter how long or short, in his bed.

"Never," Gillian vowed to the heavens beyond her chamber ceiling. "Not for my father. Not for Heatherwood. Not for my own life."

A sudden peace settled over her. The decision had been made.

She crawled from the floor to the head of her luxurious bed. Settling the silk-covered pillow into her lap, she procured from within the small vial of poison. She watched as the reflection of the hearth's flames licked at the clear glass. `Twas almost too easy to obtain such lethal potion. The dim-witted squire dared not question his lord's soon-to-be wife.

For a moment she pondered slipping the deadly liquid into her husband's wine chalice, serving the justice her true Lord had failed to deliver. `Twould be a fitting end to watch him sink to the floor, powerless in his knowledge that she had avenged her beloved's death.

Alas, she kept the poison for herself. She prayed that somewhere, somehow, Redmere's deceits would be met with final retribution.

She walked to the window and looked upon the world for the last time.

The sun appeared a giant fireball as it sank into fathomless darkness, painting the encroaching night sky a brilliant blood red. She breathed in the pungent scents of the living earth, longing even now for the sweet, comforting fragrance of her heather. Scanning the violent hues of the horizon, she entreated, "Hear me, my beloved Baldric. Hear me now. Never will he possess me. Never will anyone possess me. For I am yours, body and soul. Yours for all time."

Tilting the vial to her lips, she drank.

***

Baldric grabbed Eloise and yanked her into a hidden passageway.

She thrashed in his arms, her screams dying muffled and useless against his hand.

"'Tis I," he whispered. "Baldric."

She grew still, except to nod in fervid recognition. When he released his hand, she spun around and threw her arms about his neck. "Thank God!"

Baldric winced, pushing her to arm's length. "I am glad to see you as well, Eloise, but my wounds have yet to heal."

"Wounds? Who cares about a few measly wounds? We thought you to be dead!"

"I assure you that I am alive."

"Then what took you so long?"

"I was detained." FitzHubert had beaten him to within a breath of his life, then perversely left him to rot in the dungeon at Darbingshire. His childhood home. A home that meant naught to him without Gillian.

He had nursed his wounds for nearly a sennight, battling for days just to stand on his feet. The worst agony had been the thought of Gillian, trapped in the spiteful hands of Nigel Redmere. The ache in his heart, the fear in his gut, the complete and utter helplessness—all had tortured Baldric far worse than any physical injury.

It had taken six grueling days to recover strength enough to escape Darbingshire. Another full day to reach Willingham and slip unnoticed past its well-guarded walls.

He prayed he was not too late.

"Where is she?"

"In her chamber. I have spent an hour searching for a physician, a healing witch, anyone who could supply an herbal remedy. The pain is eating her alive." She waved a pungent elixir beneath his nose. "At last I found this."

Baldric pushed aside the offensive medicine. "She is ill?"

Eloise bowed her head. "She is without child."

Relief flooded Baldric. He had imagined much worse. "Stay here," he ordered. "I will return with Gillian. We will leave this place at once."

He turned but Eloise grabbed his arm. "Simon—"

"Simon and Lisbeth await us in Newcastle. Stay here." Baldric pressed her against the wall so she could not confuse his words.

"But…"

`Twas no time to indulge the garrulous maid. Holding his bruised side, he limped quickly down the passageway. By the time he reached the corridor to Gillian's chamber, sweat soaked his grimy tunic. His breath rasped in his lungs. He steadied himself against the wall as his head spun from loss of blood and lack of food. After a moment, he drew a deep breath and peered around the corner.

FitzHubert guarded her door.

Rage pumped hot and lethal through Baldric's veins. He forgot the pain. Forgot everything as the lust for vengeance smoothed his stilted movements. With the speed and silence of a jungle predator, he slid behind his unsuspecting prey and snapped his wretched neck with one swift twist.

FitzHubert crumpled to the floor, dead.

`Twas a mercy he did not deserve. Baldric dragged the knight's lifeless body into a darkened corner. Now was not the time for prolonged revenge.

He hurried to Gillain's chamber, surveying the corridor once more before slipping through her door. He retraced the steps that had brought him to Gillian's bed a sennight ago, a lifetime ago. The night they had made sweet, glorious love.

Again he found her sleeping. Her angelic face in peaceful repose. Her wild, ebony curls flung in disarray about the silk, crimson pillow.

His heart pounded in anticipation of holding her in his arms.

How he had longed for her. Her gentle touch. Her sweet smile.

She was his life.

He had been a ghost of a man without her these days past.

Unable to distinguish night from day in that black, stone coffin, he had clung to sanity with desperate fingers, begging the Lord to let him survive, to let him return to Gillian. He could not leave her this way, not with Redmere. The moment he sucked in his first breath of clear, morning air, he had vowed, no matter the sacrifice, he would never be without her again.

Skimming his fingers along the sleek coverlet, he feasted his eyes upon the beauty that was his beloved. She was the moon, the stars, a celestial light in this sordid world of darkness. Her crisp, white kirtle reflected her innocence, the purity of her soul that the same cruel world had been unable to soil. His fingers touched the elaborate silver and white surcoat tossed carelessly at her bare feet.

She had married Redmere.

She had kept the faith.

Smiling, he moved closer, eager to wake her. To hold her. To love her.

He stopped in his tracks.

His heart stumbled.

For the first time, he saw the wilted heather scattered across her body.

His panicked gaze rushed over her.

She was pale. Too pale.

Then he spotted the empty pouch discarded at her side. Along with an empty vial.

"Nay!" He threw himself across her body, his heart ripping apart. "What have you done, Gillian?" He grabbed her by the shoulders and shook her. "Wake up. Hear me, sweet lady. Wake up!" He covered her mouth with his own in a frantic attempt to breathe life into her limp body.

She would wake any moment, wrap her arms around him, cry out his name.

"I am alive. Gillian, I am alive," he sobbed. "Wake up!"

Naught.

Pressing his rough face against her smooth, cool cheek, he rocked her in his arms. And wept. "What madness is this? You promised me, Gillian. You promised you would endure."

But 'twas he who had failed her. He who had not returned

as promised.

How could he condemn his beloved when he wished for death himself?

He had failed her, and now he was doomed to life without her.

Was this his true punishment for their betrayal?

`Twas a punishment he had not the will to endure.

Redmere exploded through the door, followed by two knights and a struggling Eloise. "You!" His wild eyes turned rabid at the sight of Baldric and Gillian in bed together. Her limp form shocked him to full awareness. "You are to blame for this deed, de Lacey!"

Redmere rushed forth, sword drawn.

"Aye," Baldric agreed, opening himself up to the blade. "I am to blame."

Eloise screamed as Redmere thrust his sword through Baldric's gut.

Slumping over Gillian's body, Baldric welcomed the darkness, whispered his dying vow. "I shall know your torment, and you mine, sweet lady. My soul shall follow yours through eternity until I have proven thee my love."

***

"Until I have proven thee my love," Winn murmured. "Until I have proven thee my love."

"Come back to the present," Madam Lavinia beckoned. "Come back. Five, four, three. Come back. Two, one." She snapped her fingers.

Winn's eyes flew open. His pulse hammered as his heart burst with emotions of the past. Instinctively he rolled over to Sydney, grabbed her shoulders and shook her. "Wake up. Hear me, Gillian. Wake up!"

Ellie caught his arm. "Snap out of it! That's Sydney you're jostling like a rag doll. Not Gillian. Sydney!"

"Shut up, Bane!" Gathering Sydney into his arms, he whispered into her ear, "I have known your torment and you mine. My soul has followed yours through eternity to prove to you my love. Hear me, Sydney. Trust me. I love you."

"And I you," Sydney whispered. Her eyes fluttered open,

and though tears streamed down her cheeks, a sweet smile lit her face. She touched her hand to his stubbly cheek. "You believe me. I see it in your eyes."

"He regressed!" Ellie cried from behind them.

Sydney took Winn's hand. "One heck of a leap of faith."

"One hell of a ride. You scared me, kid." He dropped his forehead to hers. Mind still reeling, he drew a steadying breath. "How long was I under, Ellie?"

"Two hours."

"I'll be damned," he mumbled, exhausted by the experience. "I relived nine days in two hours. I need a shot of whiskey. No, make that a triple."

Madam Lavinia clucked a disapproving tongue. "Hard liquor is poison."

"Poison?" Winn's thoughts raced through the last scene of his medieval life. He pushed Sydney to arm's length. "Jesus."

Ellie screamed as David Monroe burst into the tent.

The lawman's nostrils flared as he registered their embrace. His wild eyes glittered in eerily familiar madness. Grabbing the nearest weapon, he rushed forward with a sword. "You have betrayed me for the last time!"

Winn sprang to his feet. "Not in this lifetime, you bastard."

"No!" Sydney leaped from the bed of blankets and threw herself between Winn and the blade.

Winn shoved her aside.

Steel penetrated his left shoulder.

Ellie swiped a helmet from the ground, then hurled it at David.

The helmet struck his temple, knocking him cold.

"That's been a long time in coming," she muttered, not entirely sure why. Shaking her head, she pried the bloodied sword from David's hand and held the point to his throat. Madam Lavinia whipped scarves from her costume and tied them tightly about his wrists and ankles.

Sydney crouched over Winn, desperately trying to stem his bleeding. "What have you done?" she sobbed. "Weren't you paying attention back there?"

"Back where?" Winn teased, using his right hand to brush

disheveled hair from her tear-streaked face.

"In the past! This was my chance to change history and you, you chivalrous fool, ruined it! You took David's blade as you took it before and now you're going to die!"

"I'm not going to die."

She sniffled. "What?"

"I'm not going to die." He grinned at her. "Believe me, I've suffered worse."

Ellie bent down and eyed the wound through his ripped tunic. "He's right, Syd. Maybe some peroxide and a few stitches." She handed Sydney a folded cloth. "Keep the pressure on. Madam Lavinia and I will find Dr. Berkley."

"Call the county sheriff while you're at it," Winn said.

Sydney glanced at David and shivered. "What's going to happen to him?"

Winn squeezed her hand. "That's for the law to decide."

"I'm on it," Ellie said. She prodded David's bound body with her toe and got no response. "Harmless."

Winn winked at Ellie. "Thanks to you."

"My pleasure, Tiger." With the help of Madam Lavinia, she dragged David from the tent. "Just in case," she said, then disappeared.

Sunlight streamed through the open flap in the aftermath of the storm. "Ten to one there's a rainbow out there," Winn said, touching Sydney's cheek and thinking her the most beautiful of God's creations. "Hope. Faith. You've taught me to trust again. To believe in the impossible. In happily-ever-afters. A rare gift and I thank you for it, Sydney."

Yes, he believed in all of these things now, especially as the road to the future lay paved and sparkling before them. He also knew that if he lost her again, there would be no more second chances. No more light. No more love. No more life. He smiled then, realizing his stint in the past had left him waxing poetic. Just like Baldric. Or Gillian.

Winn clutched Sydney's hand. He would never let her go. Never. She was the one who insisted on opening this can of worms, and now she was stuck with him. Forever.

His heart swelled with ancient and renewed love.

She was his beloved. His beloved for all time.

"I'm a changed man," he announced, lips quirking at his understatement.

Her brows furrowed. "Your sentiments sound like Gillian's."

Winn laughed, wincing slightly as pain shot through his shoulder. "Now who wasn't paying attention back there? Or to her own reincarnation research?" He tweaked her nose. "You'd make a lousy detective, kid."

She stared at him a moment, confused. Then realization dawned in her eyes. "Souls know no race, no religion...no *gender*." She sucked in her breath. "My God, Winn. All this time I assumed I was Gillian, when in truth *you* were Gillian. *I* was Baldric. A soul switch!"

He stroked her hand. "More like a merging of the souls. Baldric's dying vow acted as a spell, a curse, a blessing, whatever. *I shall know your torment and you mine.* The reason you and I experienced the thoughts and feelings of *both* Gillian and Baldric."

"A merging of the souls. Radical thinking for a realist," she said, lowering her face to within a breath of his own.

He caught one of her spiral locks between his fingers and winked. "That was the old me."

"I was rather fond of the old you." With a grin, she amended, "That is, the *old* old you."

"I assure you, no matter who I was, my feelings for you this moment are entirely those of a hot-blooded male." He buried his hand in her hair and pulled her into a tender kiss.

Sydney's heart sang as their lips touched. She and her beloved were together at last. At long, long last. As he weaved a veil of passion about her, centuries of unrest died a sweet, everlasting death, and a bright, new future was born.

Drawing back from the kiss, she whispered breathlessly, "I love you, Winn. I have always loved you."

He smiled, contentment in his misty eyes. "And I you, sweet Sydney. In this life and into the next. Forever as one."

ABOUT THE AUTHOR

Think Thelma and Louise.

Think Laverne and Shirley.

Somewhere in between you'll find Cyndi and Beth. A lively combination of adventure and comedy. Chemistry and magic. Grit and fun.Cyndi and Beth attended their first New Jersey Romance Writers meeting on the same day. Finding they had much in common—the pure love of storytelling, escapades, and anything funny, not to mention never having the same hair color for more than three months—they became instant friends and critique partners. Later, both won Honorable Mentions for their solo projects in NJRW's 'Put Your Heart In A Book' contest.Intrigued by their similar styles and opposing strengths, Cyndi and Beth made an enthusiastic decision to write as a team. Hence, CB Scott was born. Their writing worlds meshed into an anythinggoes playground and they eagerly invite readers to come along for the ride.

Quick tour of partnership adventures:

2000 RWA Golden Heart finalists for their paranormal romance Scandalous Spirits

Cowriting and directing the 2000 and 2001 Mr. Romance Competition for Romantic Times Magazine's Booklovers ConventionTouring Italy with their RT friends and Lady Barrow herself, Kathryn Falk

Teaching the conference workshop 'Writing As Partners'Serving on the NJRW boardWriting articles published in romance newsletters and Romantic Times Magazine

Rebels without a cure, Cyndi and Beth continue to write the stories of their hearts—Paranormal, Romantic Comedy, Romantic Suspense—and enjoy barreling along the creative detours of their latest CB Scott adventure. Their goal? To entertain. (Though Cyndi draws the line at tap dancing, telling Beth, "I'll learn to tap when you learn to kickbox.") For now, they're sticking to romantic fiction and screenplays.

Don't Miss
CB Scott's
Scandalous Spirits

ISBN 1-893896-23-4

Marcus Van Buren's ghostly family has been a thorn in his backside since the day he was born. Now he's paying someone to get rid of them.

Inexperienced ghostbuster Daisy Malone should be ecstatic that ultra-wealthy, tabloid darling Marcus Van Buren is paying her big bucks to conduct a sham of an investigation. The windfall will bail her family out of financial ruin. According to Marcus, all she has to do is tell the truth. Sign a document swearing the old family home, Laguna Vista, is 100% ghost-free.

Unfortunately, Daisy knows otherwise.

Brought together by their quirky relatives (three of them dead), Marcus and Daisy learn the power of forgiveness, the beauty of love, and the true meaning of "*all for one and one for all.*"

Available Now from
ImaJinn Books
www.imajinnbooks.com